Sailing Free

PREVIOUS BOOKS BY GABRIEL STEIN:
An English Revenge
An English King
An English Succession
Omnibus version An English Varangian
King Oscar's Gamble – Sweden's Secret Plan to Attack Russia in 1856

PREVIOUS BOOKS BY JOHN NUGÉE:
Reminiscences of a Private Secretary
Confessions of a Business Traveller
The Gulf Region – a new hub of Global Financial Power (ed)
Reflections on Global Finance
The Wisdom of Markets and the Madness of Crowds
A Psalm a Day

Gabriel Stein and John Nugée

SAILING FREE

The saga of Kári the Icelander

Published in 2021
by Rhomphaia Books in association with Laburnum Publishing

Copyright © Gabriel Stein and John Nugée, 2021

The rights of Gabriel Stein and John Nugée to be identified as the authors of this work have been asserted in accordance with the Copyright, Designs and Patents Act 1988

All rights reserved. No part of this publication may be reproduced or used in any manner without the prior written permission of the copyright owner, except for the use of brief quotations in a book review.

Publishing services provided by Self Publishing House

The photograph used on the front cover shows the knarr *Vidfamne*, built by Sällskapet Vikingatida Skepp (The Viking Age Ships Society) in Gothenburg, and is used courtesy of the Society and the photographer, Emma Helgesson

"Með lögum skal land byggja"
With laws shall the land be built

– Njáls saga

Contents

Preface		ix
Introduction		xi
Chapter 1	Winter – Summer 1055	1
Chapter 2	Spring 1060	23
Chapter 3	Spring 1060	39
Chapter 4	Summer 1060	55
Chapter 5	Summer 1060	79
Chapter 6	Autumn 1060 – Autumn 1064	97
Chapter 7	Winter – Summer 1066	125
Chapter 8	Spring 1066 – Spring 1067	149
Chapter 9	Autumn 1066	165
Chapter 10	Autumn 1066 – Winter 1067	193
Chapter 11	Winter – Spring 1067	213
Chapter 12	Winter – Summer 1067	245
Chapter 13	Spring – Summer 1067	267
Chapter 14	Summer 1067	281
Chapter 15	Summer 1067	299

Preface

The inspiration for this book was a suggestion by Michel Kelly-Gagnon, Director of the Institut économique de Montréal (Montreal Economic Institute, IEDM/MEI). The IEDM/MEI's interest in the concepts of liberty and freedom, and how different societies interpret and incorporate personal freedom in their laws and customs, is long-standing. Following a conference of the Mont Pelerin Society in Iceland on the subject of 'Liberty and Property in the 21st Century', which despite its title drew heavily for its inspiration on Icelandic history and the period of the Icelandic Commonwealth, Michel wondered if it would be possible to write a novel that would take place in Iceland in the Commonwealth era and through it highlight the fascinating society, with its most unusual social structure and belief in personal liberty, that developed there around the turn of the first millennium.

We gladly accepted his challenge; Iceland is a country that between us we have visited many times and whose people we both much admire. Viewed from the 21st century and with the eyes of social historians, the Icelandic Commonwealth, which flourished from 930 to 1262, stands out as very different from other societies of the period; to contemporaries, it was extraordinary and unnatural in its alternative way of structuring a society.

Michel and his colleagues remained a source of advice and encouragement throughout the writing of the book, and we are very grateful for both; without them, the book would not have been completed.

We also want to thank Father Ulf Jonsson SJ for help with the Latin; and May Ben Khadra and Maryam al-Farsi for help with the Arabic. We owe substantial thanks to our wives, Fiona and Vicky, for their careful reading of the text and for suggesting many improvements.

But above all, we want to thank the freedom-loving people of Iceland, whose amazing story and example inspired this book, and to whom it is gratefully dedicated.

Introduction

Sailing Free: The Saga of Kári the Icelander is a novel. Apart from a few leading figures, such as Harald Hardrada, King of Norway from 1046 to 1066, all the characters are fictional.

The novel is set in the Icelandic Commonwealth or Free State in the middle years of the 11th century. At this time, Iceland was unusual in not having a king or central government, or many of the other attributes of a nation state. Even so, its independence was accepted by rulers elsewhere, most notably by the King of Norway, from whose realm most Icelanders had originally come.

Instead, Iceland was governed by its law. In modern terms, there was no executive branch of government, and the legislative and judicial branches were combined into assemblies known as Things (Icelandic *Þingi*). There were regional Things for local justice and the first hearing of court cases, and an annual national assembly known as the Althing (Icelandic *Alþingi*) which met at *Thingvellir* or 'Parliament Plains', where appeals might be heard and national laws were debated.

The central role in maintaining these laws and keeping order fell to a group of chieftains, known as *Goði*, plural *Goðar*. They had both a legislative role, sitting in law-creating assemblies, and a judicial role in determining court cases. Below the goðar were a class of farm-owning Icelanders known as *Bóndi*, plural *Bændr*. The bændr were the core of society, made up of farmers and craftsmen; they were free men and were entitled to carry weapons and attend the local Things.

Goðar were not, however, territorial chieftains: bændr could choose which goði they gave their allegiance to and would expect their support in return for this freely-given allegiance. They could also change goði if they were unhappy. The goði was the proprietor of the *Goðorð*, a term which strictly speaking denotes the authority of the goði. Later on, in the 12th and 13th centuries, these could be combined so that one goði could hold or control more than one goðorð.

Iceland was largely self-sufficient, but traded for goods not readily available at home. This trade was carried out in ships known as *knarr*. A knarr was wider and deeper-hulled than the more familiar Norse longship and was typically up to 16 metres long, with a capacity of about 20 tonnes of cargo. They had both oars and a square-set sail and could easily be managed by a crew of no more than ten to twelve men, including the steersman.

*

Icelandic has a few letters that do not exist in modern English.

- Ð, ð   pronounced as *th* in *the*
- Þ, þ   pronounced as *th* in *thin*
- Æ, æ   pronounced as *i* in *fine*

In this text, we follow the usual modern convention of writing Þ, þ as Th, th; Ð, ð and Æ, æ are written as in Icelandic.

Place names of countries and larger geographical features are given in their modern form; those of smaller geographical features, cities, towns and other settlements are in general given in their 11th-century form, the modern versions of which are shown below:

Dyflin	Dublin
Færeyjar	the Faroe Islands
Heiðabyr	Hedeby, a Danish trading town, now in Germany (no longer inhabited)
Hjaltland	the Shetland Islands
Jórvik	York
Kirkjuvágr	(or 'Church Bay') Kirkwall, in Orkney
Lishbuna	Lisbon
Niðaros	Trondheim
Nörvasund	the Strait of Gibraltar
Suðreyjar	(or 'the southern isles') the Hebrides
Syllingar	the Scilly Isles
Særkland	a generic term for Muslim lands, here used for North Africa
Vínland	North America, discovered by Icelanders around the year 1000

Snæströnd, or 'Snowy Coast', the home farm of Kári and his family, is fictional and is located on the north side of the Snæfellsnes peninsula in west Iceland.

Map 1: Iceland in the Commonwealth Age

Map 2: Kári's travels

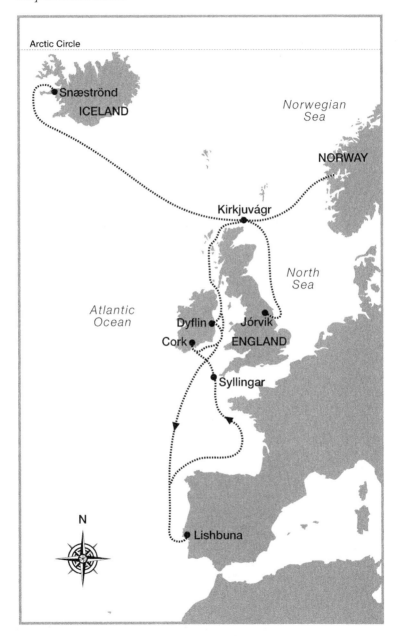

Chapter 1

Winter – Summer 1055

"Careful, Kári, the eyes are the most difficult to carve, and you are going too deep!"

The thirteen-year-old gave no sign of listening, although a tightening of his shoulders showed that he had heard. Inwardly he seethed. He knew perfectly well what he was doing. After all, it was not the first time he had carved walrus ivory. His father could just never stop nagging him. It was unfair. All he was trying to do was to get rid of a small uneven part at the end of the eye. This would be the best chessman he had ever carved. Now, if only his father would leave him alone.

From the other side of the room, Guðmundr looked at his younger brother and smiled. Their father was right, he thought, Kári was too fussy with details but at the same time not careful enough. But Kári would never acknowledge it; he was a good carver and telling him to be careful would only make him more stubborn.

Kári looked at the chessman again in the flickering light from the fire. He felt along the eye. It was still a little uneven, but all he would need to do was carve slightly deeper and then sand it down and the face would be perfect. He took up the knife again and began to whittle down the uneven point. As he carved, he felt a resistance in the ivory and pushed the point of the knife in just a little bit deeper. As he did, he suddenly felt, rather than heard, a crack, and watched in horror how the face of the chessman suddenly seemed to split in two. With an annoyed cry he flung the chessman and the knife into a corner of the farmhouse's long hall.

The noise made the others look up. Guðmundr was not surprised and remained seated. But Kári's father stood up and approached the boy, lifting his hand. As Kári cowered, waiting for a strike, a woman spoke up.

"Wait, Ragnar."

Ragnar turned towards the speaker. "Why?" he asked. "I told him what would happen, and it did. You know we need the chess set and we need it *now*. He needs to learn discipline."

"You don't need it just yet. We are still months before the next meeting of the Thórsnesthing. There is plenty of time for the boy to carve another chessman, and it's not as if we don't have more than enough ivory in store."

"That is as may be, Hallgerður. But we don't have so much ivory that the boy can spoil it at will."

"Then teach him that instead. That is a much better lesson for him and will make him more careful later in life."

Ragnar looked at his wife and considered her words. Maybe she was right. And he didn't like to hit his son. Punishment should come for disobedience, or if he broke a clearly set rule that he was old enough to understand, not for accidents or even carelessness. Above all, it should not be arbitrary. But the loss of the chessman still rankled.

He turned back towards Kári. The boy had straightened up again, as if ready to take his punishment, and tried to look unafraid.

Ragnar chewed his lip for a moment, then said, "You were told that you were digging too deeply and risked cracking the ivory. You didn't listen and it happened. This is my judgement: the time lost in carving was your own. You will now have to spend time starting on a new chessman." The boy relaxed. "But", he continued, "the ivory was mine and was difficult enough to get hold of. It is not to be wasted. When the walrus return and are close enough to hunt, you will come with me. It is your responsibility to kill one and bring me the tusks."

Kári's face suddenly changed, from apprehension to joy. "Thank you, Father", he said. "I'll get you the biggest walrus tusks we have ever had."

Guðmundr snorted. He agreed with Kári. This was reward, not punishment. Once again, his younger brother seemed to have escaped proper retribution.

"Just get me the tusks and worry about the size later", Ragnar replied gruffly. "In the meantime, we'd better get you a new piece of ivory so that you can start from the beginning. And be more careful this time."

He went out and shortly afterwards returned with a seasoned piece of ivory, twice the size of a man's thumb, which he handed over to Kári.

As he sat down again, Hallgerður asked, "Are you really going to let him hunt a walrus on his own?"

"He has to learn. But I will be there, of course. And so will Guðmundr."

"And what about the chess set? Will it be ready in time?"

"Yes, I am not worried about that. But it sticks in my throat that I have to do this."

Hallgerður looked fondly at her husband. It had taken her some time to convince him to marry her, but eventually he had given in to the fate spun by the Norns. She didn't think he regretted it – she certainly never did. He was of course older than when she had first set eyes on the stocky fair-haired man with the piercing green eyes and fallen headlong in love with him. His beard had then been a few scraggly wisps, struggling to show that he was an adult. Now it was long and thick, and beginning to grey. But the eyes were still as piercing and still lit up when he became animated. He had railed then against injustice and oppression. He still did, occasionally. But it seemed that he brooded more over them and felt less able to change things than he had once thought.

He must have been thinking about the same thing, because he suddenly sighed and said, "You don't have to tell me. I know. I need the support of our goði in order to win my case. And in order to get Gunnar's support, I need to present him with a suitable gift. He likes to think he can play chess, so a beautiful chess set it is."

"Are you giving my chess set away? Why?" Kári had been

listening and now spoke up, but first putting both knife and ivory down – carefully, Ragnar noted with some pleasure.

"Yes I am. I have to."

"But why? It is mine! I'm carving it. You can't just give it away."

"I don't want to. Once I would not have had to either. Once, our laws were fair and applied equally to all. If you brought a case to the Thing, men would judge your case on its merits and deliver a just verdict, and all would obey. But this is no longer the case. Now, whatever the case, there is no justice. The verdict is in favour of he who brings the greatest force to the Thing. Or is supported by someone else with the greatest force."

"I know, my love. But this is part of what the goðar do", Hallgerður said.

Suddenly Ragnar exploded. "Of course they do! And who are they to do this? All they have is that they came here first. They tell us that their ancestors did not want to live as thralls under a king in Norway. So when Harald defeated them at Hafrsfjord, they all set sail and came to Iceland and parcelled out the land between themselves. Isn't it amazing? They were not going to live under a king in Norway, so they came here and set themselves up as petty kings instead. And I, who have fared widely and am wealthier by far than many of them, just because my ancestors came here later, I have to bow to someone like Gunnar to ensure that I get my rights at the Thing, and I am forced to listen as he talks about how wonderful it is to be a free man with no king."

"And what can you do about it? Life is what it is. Right now, you need Gunnar's support. And he will not give it unless you give him something greater in return. Is a chess set really worth losing a case?"

"That is not the point, Hallgerður. I have the right and the law on my side. I should not have to grovel to a goði or to any other man to get that recognised. I am giving him something valuable, but he is giving me nothing except what is already mine by right." Ragnar was red in the face as he shouted, even though he recognised that Hallgerður was only trying to calm him down.

Both Kári and Guðmundr watched their father raging. They had heard this before, but, at least for Kári, it suddenly felt much more serious when he realised that this was why his chess set would be given to Gunnar. And Gunnar didn't even know how to play chess properly! Kári could defeat him any day if he wanted to. This was unfair. Life was unfair!

*

Over the next few months, as winter turned slowly to spring and the sun rose slightly further above the horizon each day, Kári and Ragnar continued to carve the chessmen. Although Kári's pleasure in the carving had disappeared once he knew that the set was to be given away, he knew better than to challenge his father. But the thought of creating something for someone else without receiving something in return rankled with him. At least the prospect of the walrus hunt remained.

And so he forgot all his frustration when his father suddenly said one evening, "It is getting warmer. I think it will snow tomorrow. The ice is thinning and the wind is right. Tomorrow, we go walrus hunting. Time for Kári to make good on his promise."

The next morning, Ragnar and his two sons set off well before sunrise, pulling a sled laden with harpoons and spears for the hunt, knives and hatchets to cut up their prey, and food for the two or three days they were likely to be away. Hallgerður watched them go, their breath clearly visible in the early morning cold as they breasted the rise. The boys had been so excited the previous evening, it had been difficult to get them to sleep at all, and now she could hear them chattering away happily to Ragnar as they went out of sight.

The ground had frozen overnight, though there were a few places where there was only a thin skin of ice over a puddle of meltwater, and Kári, naturally, was the one to put his foot through. In recoiling, he stumbled and fell backwards into a snowdrift, but he soon joined his father's and brother's laughter.

As the sun rose, Ragnar sniffed deeply of the cold air and began to reminisce about other such mornings, telling his sons about previous walrus hunts. Encouraged by the boys' eager attention, he went on to talk about other episodes of his life – travels to faraway places like Norway, Orkney, England and Scotland. He noticed how Guðmundr preferred listening to stories of the land, while Kári always wanted to hear about foreign places.

"Why don't you go there anymore?" Kári asked.

"It is true I have not gone for some years", Ragnar replied. "My ship goes and Odd goes with it to trade for me. But there has been so much to do at home, lately …" His voice trailed off; the truth was that he really wasn't too keen on travelling again. Oh, short trips, like to Orkney, were fine. But further afield, to England or Norway or Scotland or even Ireland, took much longer. And everywhere there were royal servants, puffed-up little men who felt that, just because they had a king somewhere behind them, they could order honest traders around and levy whatever taxes they pleased on them.

As long as Knut had been alive and ruled England, Denmark and Norway, a trader could travel in peace and security in all his realms and trade freely. But after his death, the kings and their men seemed to compete as to who could best steal or defraud the merchants. They would impose one fee when you arrived, telling you that there was nothing more to pay; but when you left, suddenly there was another. Not to mention payments to be allowed to buy and to sell. He was tired of pretending to be grateful each time they invented a new reason to take his money or his goods for free, behaving as if they were doing him a favour at the same time. Far better to send Odd in his stead. Odd had worked for him for many years and could be trusted. He was much calmer and did not risk quarrelling with some petty trade overseer.

Ragnar and his sons' goal was a small island well offshore where, in the past, walrus had been known to gather. They cautiously crossed the vast white expanse of sea ice, listening to its creaking underfoot. It was a nice judgement, catching the ice at the right moment when it was strong enough to bear their weight but thin enough for the walrus to break through to breathe. So, although the distance was not far, they did not arrive at their hunting ground until well after noon.

Once they arrived, they unloaded the sled, took out their spears and harpoons, and sought out a good vantage point where they could wait, from which they could see all around but be unseen themselves. For the first time, Kári was going to use a harpoon. On previous hunts, he had only been allowed a spear and then only to approach the walrus when it was already badly wounded and dying – even a wounded walrus could be dangerous. That his father now gave him one of his valuable harpoons was a sign that he was really a man. Or almost a man, anyway.

Ragnar looked at the other harpoon. He probably ought to keep it for himself. But then he looked at Guðmundr. The boy was busying himself with arranging their supplies on the sled and had his back turned, but Ragnar could imagine his thoughts. If Kári were given a harpoon and Guðmundr only a spear, how would the older boy feel? He made up his mind quickly. "Guðmundr, you take the other harpoon. But remember, the first blow is for Kári to strike. And, both of you – keep as quiet as possible; walrus have very good ears!" Guðmundr said nothing, but his broad smile was like the sun rising, and Ragnar knew he had made the right decision. He set aside two heavy spears for himself and settled down to watch and wait.

Although this had frequently been a good place to hunt walrus, there was no certainty that one would appear today, only the hope. Kári gazed out over the frozen sea. The morning's early promise had not been fulfilled and the sky was grey; as the first few flurries of the snow that Ragnar had predicted began to fall, Kári tucked his hands firmly under his armpits to try to keep some warmth in them. He gazed and gazed, squeezing his eyes almost shut in the hope of spotting a walrus, as the sun sank lower in the sky. Yet it was Guðmundr who suddenly called out, "There! There!" and pointed.

Ragnar sighed; had he not told the boys several times that walrus have keen hearing and that they must not frighten them away? But he also shared their excitement, and although the sun was already low in the sky, when he and Kári followed the direction of Guðmundr's outstretched arm, they could see the ice breaking up and a dark form appearing and humping itself up on the ice.

"Mine, mine!" Kári shouted, snatching up his harpoon and starting to run towards the beast.

"Wait!" Ragnar suddenly bellowed so loudly that Kári scudded to a halt. "If you run out like that then, first, he may notice you and escape. And second, the ice will be thinner there. You risk falling through. Move slowly and carefully, and he will still be there when you are close enough."

"Yes, Father", Kári replied, blushing. As ever, it was clear that he did not like to be told off, but he listened and took greater care in his movements.

Fortunately, the walrus seemed not to have heard them and was still on the ice. Guðmundr and Ragnar also seized their weapons, and all three began to edge slowly towards it. Moving carefully and quietly, testing the bearing of the ice and trying to avoid alarming the walrus.

It seemed an eternity to Kári, but eventually they came within range of their quarry, which was still unaware of their approach. Ragnar told the boys to spread out more so that they would approach the walrus from different sides.

As they drew nearer, he could see that this was a large beast, and old too, judging by the length of its tusks. When he judged that they were close enough, he signalled the boys. Kári could barely see his father in the rapidly waning light but spotted the move. Carefully, he stood up, hefted his harpoon, pulled back his arm and then let fly in one smooth movement. The harpoon flew straight and true towards the walrus and the sharp point pierced the animal's skin and pushed deeply into its flesh. The shocked animal started and bellowed in pain.

Kári didn't wait for his father and brother to strike. With a shout of "I got him!" he stood up and began rushing towards the thrashing beast. It was not clear what he was trying to do, but before Ragnar could shout at him to stand back, the walrus' frantic movement began to break the ice around him. As Ragnar watched horrified, the cracks in the ice rapidly spread towards Kári. He did not even have time to call out a warning, before he heard his son scream in shock and fear as the ice around Kari opened and he slid into the cold waters.

Ragnar felt a cold hand grip his heart. He was on the wrong side of the walrus, with no hope of reaching the boy in time to save him. Without knowing what he was trying to do, he hurled his spear at the walrus, partly to release his anger and partly in the hope that pinning and killing the animal would enable him to rush past it and rescue his son.

When the ice broke up around him, Kári didn't at first realise what was happening. But a strange feeling of flying through the air was suddenly replaced by an icy shock as he plummeted into the water. For a brief moment his warm clothes protected him from the cold, but suddenly there was such an intense chill that it felt as if his chest contracted, and he could not even breathe. He opened his mouth to scream again but only managed to fill it with water. Briefly he sank under the water, before resurfacing.

Then he heard a shout. It was Guðmundr. As soon as he realised what had happened, the elder boy knew that there was only one hope of saving Kári. He flung himself flat on the ice in Kári's direction, hoping that spreading his weight would stop the ice from breaking beneath him. When he stopped gliding, he flung the harpoon towards Kári, yelling, "Grab it!" He hoped his brother would hear, understand and act.

Kári could not hear what Guðmundr had shouted, but he could see something coming towards him on the ice. Without recognising the harpoon, he grabbed for it, missed, and grabbed again, desperately trying to crawl up onto the ice which kept breaking beneath him. He managed to get one hand round the harpoon and then the other, clinging on for dear life.

When Guðmundr felt his brother's grip on the harpoon, he started pulling the rope, slowly dragging Kári out of the water and up onto the ice. He wasn't sure if he would manage – the boy was being weighed down by his waterlogged clothes – but suddenly he felt a strong grip on his legs and found himself being pulled backwards, towards the shore. Ragnar had seen what his son was doing and had come to help him.

Together, the two managed to get Kári back on the island. While Ragnar stripped the boy of his icy, wet clothes, Guðmundr was striking tinder and steel to light a fire, cursing all the gods when the fire was slow to catch.

Although it seemed like an eternity, the fire did eventually begin to burn more warmly. Ragnar had managed to get Kári naked and wrapped him in a fur from the sleigh, almost pushing him into the fire in his haste to get the boy warmer. Meanwhile, Guðmundr got more furs to cover the boy.

Once this was done, Ragnar brought out some of the food they had taken along. The dried fish wasn't going to help, but they had brought a flask of broth and also some beer, and this he heated and tried to get the boy to drink. Kári was not able to swallow much, but Ragnar continued to try to force something down him in order to warm him from the inside as well.

When there was nothing else they could do, Ragnar stood back and watched Kári. The boy's teeth were still chattering, but, remarkably, he seemed little the worse for wear in spite of his bath.

"What now?" Guðmundr asked.

"We cannot go home. He has no warm clothes and would freeze to death. In any case, it is too late. We have to stay here tonight. See if there is any wood around to feed the fire."

"There isn't much wood on this island. The fire won't last, Father."

"I fear you may be right. But we have to make as much use of it as we can. He will have to sleep between us so that we can keep him warm. And let's hope that his clothes will be dry by tomorrow. Start digging down into the snow for a shelter." This was something that the boys had been trained in from an early age: if caught outdoors overnight in the winter, the way to survive is to dig a snow hole and hunker down in its shelter. Guðmundr took the shovel from their supplies on the sled and began to dig.

Years later, Kári would remember this night – how his father and his brother had kept him warm with their own bodies, but how he still seemed to be freezing all night. But he was never sure whether he really remembered it, or whether this was what he felt he should remember because he had been told what had happened.

Certainly, on the night itself, he barely knew what was going on around him.

The next morning, Ragnar woke startled. He hadn't even realised that he had gone to sleep, he had been so worried about Kári's life. But he must have slept a bit at least, otherwise he could not have woken up.

When he touched Kári's head, the boy was warm, and he seemed to be sleeping normally. Ragnar crawled out from beneath the furs and stood up. The fire had indeed died down, but not too long ago – some embers were still glowing. He vaguely remembered Guðmundr feeding it sparingly through the night.

He went off to relieve himself. When he came back, he felt Kári's clothes. They were dry, or at least dry enough for the boy to wear them. Now Kári would live to come home, although his survival beyond that was still, Ragnar feared, in doubt.

Meanwhile, Guðmundr was also getting up. He stood up, looked at his father and smiled. Then he looked out over the sea and suddenly pointed. "Look", he said. "The walrus."

Ragnar turned around and was surprised to see that the walrus was lying on the beach, completely still.

"He must have tried to get away and beached himself and died", Guðmundr said. "Trust Kári to be so lucky – surviving and getting his walrus too." But he grinned as he said it, showing that, far from being jealous of his younger brother, he was happy for him.

There was not much fuel left for the fire, but Guðmundr managed to get something going. Then father and son left Kári, who was still asleep, and went down to dismember the dead walrus. When they cut out the tusks, Ragnar marvelled at their size. Kári had promised him the biggest tusks he had ever had, and it really looked as if the promise had been kept.

At least the journey back to Snæströnd was uneventful, though it was painfully slow, with Kári sharing the sleigh with as much of the walrus as they had been able to fit and carry. Close to home they passed some of their neighbours and Guðmundr could not refrain from telling them about their adventure and showing off the huge tusks.

When they finally came home, Ragnar braced himself for Hallgerður's comments. But after she had bedded the younger boy down, she only praised Guðmundr for saving Kári's life.

The next day Kári was showing signs of a fever. But this only lasted for a few days, and five or six days later he was up and moving again. During his fever he had often asked about 'his' walrus tusks. But when the fever broke, the first thing he asked for was Guðmundr.

"Big brother, you saved my life", he said.

Guðmundr looked embarrassed and tousled Kári's dark hair. "That's what big brothers are for, isn't it? Saving your life, beating you up when you do silly things, and making fun of you."

"No, I really mean it. You saved my life, and I will never forget it. One day, I will save your life in return – I swear it."

Guðmundr felt even more embarrassed and began to laugh, but his younger brother's face was so serious that he stopped. "I hope you never have to", he mumbled and went outside.

*

Weeks passed, the days grew longer and the thaw continued. Kári showed no long-term effects from his narrow escape and was clearly fully recovered. Meadows began to look green again and shy flowers turned their faces towards the sun. People found more energy with the longer daylight hours and set to repairing the winter's damage on the farm. Old folk found relief from stiff joints, and young folk were keen to be out and about again and to see what promises the summer held. All this meant that it was soon time for the spring Thing. Ragnar and his household, including Hallgerður and the two boys, rode off to the Thórsnesthing, Kári having carefully packed the chess set. As they approached the site, they encountered not just neighbours but also householders from further away who were all headed in the same direction. There was a great air of festivity about the procession that they formed.

When they arrived, they found that there was already a great throng of people and an air of busyness. Ragnar was pleased to find that the site that he usually took for his booth was still free, and he and the rest of the party made everything secure. When this was done, Ragnar squared his shoulders and drew a deep breath. He turned to Hallgerður. "Best it were done quickly."

"Yes. But try to control your temper. I know it hurts to abase yourself before someone like Gunnar. But you know why you need his help, and you chose him to be your goði after all."

"That I did. But little did I understand how much it meant. I am a free man. In the days of my father and his father, a free man with right on his side did not need the support of a goði and his men. All he needed to do was to appeal to the law, and the Thing would see him right."

"I know. But this is no longer your father's days. Today, justice is counted by the number of men you can bring to the Thing."

"But don't people see that this is bad for us all? When only might is right, right will eventually disappear and might will be everything. Then we might as well just go and invite the King of Norway to come and rule us after all."

"Of course they don't. Nobody wants to see that the path they have chosen is leading to disaster. Now get ready, take the boys with you, and get it all over with. I shall go and speak with some of my friends."

Hallgerður walked off, already calling greetings to friends who lived too far away to visit except at the Thing. Ragnar sighed deeply and called to the boys.

While his parents had been speaking, Kári had ventured outside the booth, trying to see if he could find someone of his own age. It was a beautiful day. The sun was still high in the sky, and it felt pleasantly warm after the long winter. It felt good to be alive. Walking among the nearby booths, he turned a corner only to bump into a girl about his own age who was standing with her back to him.

"Watch where you are going!" she snapped.

"I – I'm sorry", Kári replied. "I didn't see you."

"Then where are your eyes?" the girl asked. Then she looked at him and smiled. "I am Helga. Who are you?"

"My name is Kári. I am the son of Ragnar Snæströnd."

"You look sweet", Helga said. "Come", and she grabbed him by the hand. Kári didn't really care for being called 'sweet', but he enjoyed being taken by the hand. As they walked around the booths, looking at the bustle of men setting up a small town for the Thing, she prattled on about herself and her parents. Although she occasionally asked Kári questions, she never stopped to hear the answers. Eventually Kári gave up trying to reply. When he heard his father calling, he managed to interrupt the flow of words and say that he had to go.

"But why?" Helga asked.

"My father and I have to speak with Gunnar the goði."

"You must be very important for him to speak with you", the girl said.

"I am important", Kári replied, blushing. "I have carved the most beautiful chess set for him. And the ivory was from a walrus that I killed myself." That wasn't really true, but he had killed a walrus, so it wasn't really a lie either. It certainly made the girl's eyes open wider as she turned to look admiringly at him.

"Show me."

"You have to go to Gunnar to see it. And I have to go now", he stressed, as his father's call was heard again.

"Come back soon", Helga called, smiling and waving at him.

Kári felt a glow inside him as he walked back to Ragnar's booth. For the first time, he had met a girl who liked him, and he rather enjoyed it.

When he arrived, his father and brother were already waiting impatiently for him, and both had changed into finer clothes. "Hurry up, get dressed, and get the chess set", Ragnar growled.

Kári quickly changed into his best tunic and, collecting the box with the chessmen, emerged blinking in the sunlight. "At last", Ragnar muttered, while Guðmundr just looked bored. Then they set off towards a larger booth near the centre of the Thing site.

This was surrounded by smaller booths, and a large number of men, perhaps as many as twenty or thirty, lolled outside, talking, drinking and passing the time. As they approached, one of the men looked at them and entered the large booth.

A moment later, a short, stout man with a bald head came out. "Ragnar Snæströnd", he called out in a light voice. "I have been waiting for you. Come inside, my good friend."

Ragnar entered the booth, followed by his two sons. The other man sat down and looked at them. "Your sons, I assume?"

"Yes. The elder is Guðmundr, the younger is Kári. Boys, this is Gunnar, our goði."

Both boys looked at Gunnar, neither knowing quite what to say. The goði cast a glance at them. "Fine lads; you must be proud of them."

"Yes, I am."

"Good, good. Now, we have an urgent matter to talk about. Boys, why don't you wait outside for your father?"

The boys turned, but before they went, Ragnar said, "Kári, stay. Guðmundr, don't go far." Gunnar looked surprised but said nothing.

Guðmundr walked out of the booth. When he came out into the bright light he blinked and rubbed his eyes and looked around. He didn't know any of the men around; they were all rather older than he, at least twenty years old or more. But he couldn't just stand there while his father dealt with Gunnar. And it was annoying to be sent out when Kári was told to stay.

To his right, two girls were looking at him. One was perhaps two years younger than he, but she had a fine figure and carried herself proudly, with red hair and green eyes that stared boldly at him. The other, by contrast, appeared shy and less developed, although she was probably the same age. She was fair-haired, shorter and less pretty than her friend. With nothing else to do, he walked over to them.

"What are you staring at?" he asked.

"What are you staring at yourself?" the redhead replied, while the blonde just gazed at the tall young man. Even at sixteen,

Guðmundr towered over most men, and his beard was already beginning to grow, although as yet it was little more than a light dusting of hair on his face.

"I'm looking at a beautiful gi– woman", Guðmundr hastily corrected himself. He didn't know why, but he suddenly thought that the redhead would prefer being thought of as older than she was.

The redhead smiled. "Look all you like. Looking is free – even looking at me."

Guðmundr smiled. "How about talking? And walking?"

"It depends what you want to talk about. If I find it amuses me, you can talk – and walk with us." When she said this, the fair-haired girl suddenly started and stretched up to whisper something to her friend. But the redhead laughed. "Don't be silly, Ása, what harm can he do?" And without listening to her friend, she turned and began to walk off. Guðmundr lengthened his steps and caught up with them. When he came next to them, the redhead stuck out her hand and took his arm.

Guðmundr was impressed. This was more forward behaviour than he was used to from local girls. He wondered who she was. But for the moment, he was happy to walk with her, and with her friend, feeling the envious stares of even older men around them.

But they had not walked for long before the flap over the entrance to the booth was parted again and Ragnar and Kári came out, followed by Gunnar. Kári looked dishevelled and Ragnar's face was dark with anger. Gunnar, meanwhile, was no longer looking as affable as he had when they first met. In fact, if Guðmundr had not known better, he would have feared that his father and the shorter goði were close to coming to blows.

*

Once Guðmundr had left the booth, Ragnar wasted no time in getting down to the matter at hand. "Kári has something for you", he said, gesturing at his son. Kári understood and brought out the box with the chess set. At Ragnar's urging, he held it out to Gunnar, who took the proffered box and opened it.

As he looked inside at the chessmen, taking out a few of them to study more carefully, Ragnar said, "Kári has carved most of these himself."

"Really? He is a skilful ivory carver. These are beautiful, perhaps the most beautiful I have ever seen. A princely gift, Ragnar, a princely gift."

"Thank you goði."

Gunnar put the box down on the table. "But why are you still standing? Sit down, my friend, sit down. Now, as I said, we have an urgent matter to discuss."

"Thank you. Yes, my case is coming up …"

"Yes, yes. Your case. In due course, in due course", Gunnar waved his hand. "There is something more important to deal with first."

Ragnar looked at him in surprise.

"Forgive me", he said. "I thought we were going to discuss my case. You have indicated that, as my goði, you will support me against Leifur."

"Well, yes. But you understand my dilemma, Ragnar. I personally like you. And, of course, you have the law on your side. But if I support a man who has slighted me, I will lose the respect of my fellow goðar and of all my neighbours."

Ragnar stared at him. "I don't understand. How have I slighted you? Have I not just honoured you, by presenting you with a beautiful chess set?"

"Ragnar, Ragnar, why are you pretending?" The other man shook his head with a sorrowful expression. "You know perfectly well that if a walrus is caught on land or near the shore, half of it belongs to the landowner. Yet I hear that you have killed a large walrus, with the most amazing tusks, on my land and without even letting me know, let alone giving me my fair share."

"What?" Ragnar stood up, refusing to believe what he had just heard. "That walrus was caught well offshore, far away from your land. We caught it outside Kolgrafafjörðr – you don't have any land there."

"That is not what I hear. My friends tell me that you told them you caught it on the coast of Grundarfjörðr, and that is my land."

"That is not true. We were outside Kolgrafafjörðr. Kári here almost died during the hunt. It was nowhere near your land."

"So you say. But why would my men invent such a story? I have known them for years. I trust them. In fact, my son Einar says he saw you himself. Are you slandering him by calling him a liar?"

Ragnar could not believe his ears. He had already handed over a valuable gift to this man for support in a case he should have won anyway. Now Gunnar was trying to steal half the walrus – probably the tusks – from him. But before he could say anything, Kári stood up.

"Your men are lying!" he shouted. "They are liars and you are a thief! My father will not give you anything. If you want to have a walrus, hunt him yourself!"

"I suggest you discipline your son, Ragnar. Otherwise, I may have to do it for you. As for the walrus, can you prove your case? My men will swear oaths that they saw you catch it on my land. Why not simply accept that and give me what I want? After all, you still have your case against Leifur to deal with."

Ragnar regretted having come to Gunnar's booth unarmed, but he was not going to let this stand. "If you touch the boy, you will regret it, goði or not. What he says is true. Your men are lying, and you know full well what the law calls a man who tries to take what is not his and what it calls men who swear falsely." Then he turned to Kári. "Come, son, we are leaving."

A furious Kári looked as if he was going to rush at Gunnar, but Ragnar grabbed his shoulder and turned him around. They both walked out of the booth, Kári spluttering with anger, Ragnar more concerned lest one of Gunnar's men decide to stop them from leaving or worse.

Gunnar followed them out. Outside, the loitering men straightened up. They must have heard the shouting but they were all looking for a command from Gunnar before doing anything. But he was not looking at them. He had spotted Guðmundr and the two girls.

"Jórunn! Leave the low-born boy alone and come here – at once!"

The redhead looked at him. "Yes, Father", she replied meekly, dropping Guðmundr's arm before running up to the goði, with the other girl in tow. Guðmundr looked after her. So she was Gunnar's daughter, and her name was Jórunn. Would he ever see her again? As Guðmundr continued to look at her, she turned around – she was now standing behind her father, who couldn't see her – and winked at him. He thought of winking back but decided that it might be a bad idea. Instead, he joined his father and brother as they began to walk away.

But before they got far, Kári suddenly straightened up and turned around. "Gunnar", he called out, catching the attention of the goði and all his men. "You are a thief and liar. What you did today was wrong and unfair. My father taught us never to endure injustice, and we will not. You will regret this."

The words were so at odds with the thirteen-year-old who spoke them that nobody reacted. By the time they had sunk in, Ragnar and his sons were already so far gone among the Thing booths that any attempt to stop them, or worse, would have been impossible without risking a larger quarrel and a fight.

As soon as the three arrived at their booth, Ragnar sent one of his men to find Hallgerður. He told the others to dismantle the booth. When Hallgerður arrived, it was to find the booth gone and Ragnar waiting impatiently to leave.

She looked at him in surprise. "I understand that something has happened", she said. "And I understand that we are leaving. But I am not going before you have told me what it is. If you are making a mistake, I want to know now so that I can stop you and change your mind."

Ragnar sighed. His wife was a very clever woman, and she certainly had a mind of her own. That was one of the things he loved about her. And she was right. Maybe he was being a little hasty. So although he really did want to leave, he began to tell her what had happened. While he told her, Hallgerður's face darkened as she too grew angrier and angrier. However, before she could say something, an older white-haired man approached. When he was close enough to be sure that they noticed him, he stopped and cleared his throat.

Ragnar turned to him, welcoming the interruption. "Eirík goði", he said.

"They tell me you are leaving the Thing."

"Yes." Ragnar did not want to explain why.

"Before your case against Leifur has come up?"

"It seems the case is lost already", Ragnar muttered.

"Why? You have a strong case. Leifur is a weak and silly man, and everyone knows his case is as weak as he is. And you have strong support."

"I had strong support. It seems I don't any more."

"Really?"

Before Ragnar could stop him, Kári burst out, "Gunnar is a thief and a liar."

Eirík turned and raised his eyebrows at the boy. "I wouldn't perhaps go quite as far", he said. "At least not in public." And turning back to Ragnar, he added, "But you chose him as your goði."

"So everyone tells me", Ragnar said bitterly. "But now it seems he has unchosen me."

"Indeed. Well, you can always choose another goði, as you know. Someone who is able to help you. Not at this Thing, perhaps, but in the future."

"Right now, I just want to go home", Ragnar said.

"Of course. But remember, if your case is not brought at this Thing, you may lose your right to bring it. Leifur has rights too: the right to have his case heard and to clear his name if he can. You cannot hold your case over him for ever. Justice delayed is justice denied."

"What justice? I already told you, my case is lost."

"Maybe not yet."

"What do you mean? Please speak plainly. I am tired of words that do not mean what they say."

"I am speaking plainly. Not all goðar are like Gunnar. Some of us still believe that, as a goði, we have a duty not only to our followers, but also to see the law upheld. A law that applies equally to all and that gives justice not to he who has the greatest strength, but to he who is in the right. That is how it used to be and how it should be. I think you will agree with this."

"I do. But I cannot stay here, and fine words won't help me."

"True, but this may help. You have to leave, I understand that. But I am prepared, with your permission, to speak up for you at this Thing. At least in this way, you do not lose by default."

"And what do you want in return?"

"Nothing. I am only keen to see justice done. Of course, should you in the future decide that you are looking for another goði than Gunnar, then we can at least talk about it."

Ragnar considered Eirík. Maybe not all goðar were the same after all. Of course, Gunnar had also once sounded reasonable. But Eirík seemed to mean what he said. And it was his one hope of still prevailing against Leifur. Eirík was right; if nobody spoke for him at this Thing, he would lose by default.

"Thank you", he said. "Yes, I would appreciate that very much."

"No need to thank me. But remember what I said."

"I will. Thank you again."

They rode slowly away from the Thing site. They had not gone far, when they suddenly heard a laugh. Kári looked around and saw Helga standing by the path pointing at him and laughing. When she saw him looking at her, she stuck out her tongue at him. "Not so important now, great carver", she called out.

On their way home, Hallgerður asked Ragnar what he would do.

"Since Eirík will speak for me, the case will hold until the next Thing. I will not give this up."

"And with Gunnar?"

"What do you mean?"

"You have made a powerful enemy. And so has Kári, although Gunnar may overlook that."

"I will never go back to him for anything. Kári was right. He is a liar and a thief."

"I agree. But he is a powerful liar and thief. Maybe you should listen to Eirík and change goði?"

"But what will that help? Once again, it means relying on

somebody else to help me, instead of trusting the law to get my right. This is not how it should be!"

Hallgerður sighed. Ragnar was a good man, and he was right. But he was also a stubborn man, and he was wrong.

"But it is the way it is. And you know it. Now listen to me. I was not happy when you chose Gunnar. But he was the most powerful goði in the neighbourhood, and I could understand it. But I trust Eirík. He has a good name and reputation. You will need someone's support. At least think about what he said."

Ragnar fell silent. So typical of Hallgerður. She was clever and would give good advice; you knew she was right, even when you wanted to go off and sulk. Finally he said, "I will, my dear. I have already told him that I will."

Kári listened to his parents. The humiliation of the meeting with Gunnar, compounded by Helga's mocking laughter at him, still burned. But more than that, he raged at the unfairness he had witnessed. It didn't even matter if his father's case was right or wrong. The law should be the same for everyone. You should not have to crawl to someone powerful to get your rights. And he never would, he promised himself.

Chapter 2

Spring 1060

When the spring came, the household at Snæströnd busied themselves preparing for the year's trading voyage. Ragnar's knarr had spent the winter protected from the elements in the naust. Now the hull was carefully scraped and the planks impregnated with walrus oil and covered with tar, to protect them against shipworm. Once the tar had dried, the ship had been dragged down to the beach on rollers and floated. It had taken the entire crew of twelve to move the ship. In addition to Kári and Odd, there were five of Ragnar's men, who would man the oars. The other five were younger sons of neighbouring farmers. Their fathers had entrusted Ragnar with goods to sell – and lists of goods to buy abroad – and the sons were sent to safeguard their fathers' interests and also, as rowers, as part payment to Ragnar for taking their goods.

Once the knarr had been safely brought down to the beach, the crew – and their fathers and friends – had been feasted by Ragnar. This had been a tradition at Snæströnd since his own father's days. In those days, Ragnar recalled, there had been more shipowners in Iceland; and his father had always said that in *his* father's and grandfather's days, ship-owning had been common. But somehow, as the years went by, there were fewer and fewer ships around and ever fewer men who went trading afar. Ragnar was proud that he, at least, had maintained the tradition.

This had not been Kári's first feasting, but he was still surprised to see the amount of beer some of the others could drink. There had been toasts to good faring, to high profits, to Ægir and Njörðr the sea-gods, to the White Christ, to Ragnar and to his guests, to Odd and even to Kári. Someone jokingly called him 'the young master' to much ribald laughter.

Kári himself had drunk sparingly, perhaps only three or four horns. There was still a lot of work to do before they would finally set sail. The ship had to be checked to make sure there were no leaks. That didn't worry him, nor did the allocation of rowers to each oar to ensure smooth rowing. Odd would take care of that. No, the real work had to do with loading the trading goods and keeping track of what belonged to whom. And then there was also the issue of supplies to be carried: food for the journey and spare walrus hide and ropes for the sails, extra oars, water and so much more. He had never realised how much work was involved in what he thought of as a simple trading voyage where you sailed out with one load of goods and returned with another.

And the record-keeping. At first, he had protested against being saddled with this, but his father had made it clear that if he ever wanted to be a proper trader, he had to know everything: what was being shipped and traded in his name, and who owned what and how each trade went. On top of that he would have to account for his actions to those who had given him goods to sell on their behalf. Secretly, Kári was rather proud of his ability to read and write well; few people could, even Guðmundr was not quite as comfortable with the letters as he was.

"Of course you can leave all this to others", Ragnar had said. "But all that will do is make you poor and lazy while someone else gets rich at your expense. As long as I live, this will not happen." So Kári had gritted his teeth and learned and now carried a roll of careful notes. But at least he would be spared from rowing this time around. Odd was to steer the knarr, and he was also to teach Kári how to do this as well as how to be a trader.

He had of course learnt how to row. Over the past few years, he had been on board the knarr, and smaller boats, rowing with his father around the coasts, visiting other farms. But now this would no longer be his main task. This was his first real voyage, and as Ragnar's man on board, he was master of the ship. Well, not quite.

In fact, not really at all. The real master was Odd Barðsson. Odd was a few years older than his father. He had worked for Ragnar for as long as Kári could remember, and for many years he had traded on Ragnar's behalf, taking his ship east to Norway or south to Orkney, Scotland, Ireland and England. Ragnar had made it clear that Odd was in command and that Kári should do nothing without his approval. Above all, he should not agree to any trade without having spoken with Odd first. Kári didn't mind. He knew Odd and liked him. He also trusted him, and, more importantly, so did Ragnar. He was sure he could learn enough from Odd so that in due course he could command his own ship and be his own man.

And when he was his own man, he would decide where they went and what they traded. He would be in charge of his own destiny, not just be told by others what to do.

The morning after the feast, Kári was up early and went down to the beach. When he came down, he drew a deep breath. He loved the smell of the sea in the spring, the salty, tangy feeling with its promise of an adventure, something new just beyond the horizon. Today, the smell was mixed with the tar from the knarr lying slightly further away, just offshore to his right. Soon enough the loading would begin. He had drawn up a plan for how to stow the various supplies and goods and discussed it with Odd, who had approved it. Now he just hoped that the others would do as he instructed them. He could already hear noises from the houses behind him, where men were roused after too much beer and too little sleep and told to start carrying goods down to the beach where they would eventually be loaded and carefully stowed on the knarr. They were taking cloth, and walrus hides, ropes and ivory, which he was going to trade in exchange for wood and food and other goods that could not be obtained in Iceland. Soon enough he was busy supervising the stowing, rearranging badly-placed goods and making sure that everything was as well protected against both wind and water as it could possibly be. This was particularly important for the woollen cloth, the wadmal, they were taking to sell.

When he was younger, he used to wonder why anyone would want to buy cloth. He could understand why the ivory, particularly if carved, was desirable. And his father had explained that the walrus oil was even more valuable than ivory, because it was used together with the tar to coat ships and make them impervious to shipworm. Walrus hides were also valuable, and, of course, walrus were not found in Norway or the more southern countries. But cloth? When he had asked Ragnar, his father had explained that even wadmal, which he thought of as ordinary, was sometimes attractive to people in other countries who wanted warmer clothes than they could make themselves. What was common in Iceland was special elsewhere.

It was late afternoon before they were done, but there was still some time until the tide began to turn and they would have to set off. A hand suddenly descended on his shoulder. "Daydreaming about foreign lands, little brother?" Guðmundr asked.

"Not really. I was actually thinking about trading and why anyone wants to buy our wadmal."

"Well, I don't understand it either, but as long as they buy it and we get what we need, who cares? Anyway, people in foreign lands are strange."

"I'm not so sure."

"What do you mean?"

"When Father talks about Orkney and Norway, they sound just like Iceland."

Guðmundr wasn't convinced. True, he had met people from Norway, and they didn't seem so different. But that was probably because they had learned how to behave from Icelanders. Anyway, he didn't care very much one way or the other. Kári was going abroad and he was staying at home, and that suited him just fine.

He turned away from Kári and looked inland. It was getting darker. He wondered if his father would miss him if he disappeared the next day. He had not seen Jórunn for ages and it might be a good day to ride off and bump into her – by sheer accident, of course. It was difficult enough to see her. In the five years since they had met at the Thórsnesthing, they had only managed to meet a few times a year. Never at a Thing; that was not possible any more. Her father and, even more, her stupid oaf of a younger brother,

Einar, watched over her like hawks. And even if they didn't, his own father's enmity with Jórunn's father made it difficult to meet her in case they were seen together. He really wished his father could settle this feud. It was ridiculous that it was still running after five years and seemed nowhere near ending. Oh, Gunnar was a turd and a liar and had insulted and slandered his father and one day he would pay for that. But in the meantime, Guðmundr was unable to speak with either his father or Jórunn's about their relationship or even to see her as much as he wanted.

As much as he wanted – that was exactly it. He knew what he wanted. But what did Jórunn want? When they met, she would laugh, tease him, hug him and occasionally kiss him. Sometimes even more. The last few times quite a bit more, actually. He smiled to himself as he remembered the taste of her lips and, even better, her breasts and her heavy breathing as she became more excited. But all this skulking around and hiding was annoying him. It wasn't what a real man would do. And it wasn't just that. His parents were beginning to pressure him to get married. There were regular visits of neighbours and friends from farther afield, just happening to bring their daughters, all dressed up in their best clothes and wearing as much silver as their fathers could afford. Some of them were pretty enough and some of them were clever enough. All of them showed that they wouldn't mind wedding the handsome son of the wealthy Ragnar. But none of them were both pretty and clever the way Jórunn was. In fact, even her friend Ása was better, and she was nothing compared with Jórunn. For the moment, he was able to say that none of them were for him. But it would become more difficult as time went by. His father really needed to make peace with Gunnar.

While Guðmundr was thinking about Jórunn, Kári's thoughts turned back to the ship. He looked out at the sea again, when from the corner of his eye he caught a movement. It was his father, beckoning him to come. It was time. He started to walk down to the beach but then became more excited at the thought of finally leaving and started to run. When he reached his father and Odd, his mother had also joined them.

Ragnar looked at his son. He felt proud of the boy, going on his first proper voyage at eighteen. Of course, Kári had already proved himself at the oars on shorter voyages, to the farms at Thórsnes and along the coast to the big ice-field at the end of Snæfellsnes that you could see from far out to sea. But this would be his first trading voyage abroad. Ragnar had been the same age on his own first voyage. But he had gone with his childhood friend Odd, who had already been out once. Now Odd was going to teach his son as well. Where had the years gone? And had he ever looked like that – so eager and ignorant at the same time? Of course, there were differences. Kári was short and had dark hair; Ragnar was equally short but much stockier, with hair that had once been fair and was now grey and white. And where Kári's eyes were grey, his own were green.

Kári's hair and eyes were a gift from Ragnar's mother, who had been from Ireland, taken on a raid there. Even to this day, he remembered his beautiful mother, and her burning shame at having been a slave. After his father had freed her, she had refused to let him have any slaves. Ragnar shared her feelings. Having grown up to see their farm prosper on the voluntary labour of free men, he had honoured his mother's wishes by refusing to hold another man in thrall. He hoped Kári and Guðmundr would always feel the same.

Was there anything left to say to Kári before he left? Probably not. He had told the boy everything he needed to know, certainly everything he could possibly remember, and Odd would tell him more. Meanwhile, telling him again would probably just annoy him. Instead, he embraced the boy and then said gruffly, "Say goodbye to your mother as well."

"Yes, Father", Kári replied, letting go of Ragnar and turning to Hallgerður. "Goodbye, Mother. I may be some time."

"As long as you come back", she replied, before also embracing him. For a moment it looked as if she was going to say something else, but she didn't.

"Where is Guðmundr?" Ragnar asked.

"I saw him earlier", Kári said. "We have said our parting words."

"Very well. Off you go then. Fare well on the seas." Then Ragnar turned to Odd and gripped his arm. He felt like asking his friend to take good care of the boy. But this would shame Kári and in any case, Odd would do it regardless of what he said.

Finally, Odd spoke. He had a hoarse voice, almost as if he were whispering. "Best get on board. The wind is right and the tide is turning. Leave now and we will reach the Jarl's seat in Orkney in two days or three at the most."

And with that, he and Kári boarded the knarr. The crew of ten was already raising the sail and manning the steering oar.

Kári had never told anyone, but this was the moment he dreaded. He went to stand in the prow of the boat, looking out across the boundless sea. There was a cold wind that bit his fingers and face, but he didn't care, just as he didn't care about the spray from the waves that splashed him. Behind him he heard the cracking of the sail as it filled and the squeak of the ropes as they took the strain. The crew was quiet and he felt himself all alone with the sea. He loved standing there, watching the waves rise and fall before him as the knarr ploughed on, rising and falling with them. This was the feeling of freedom; one man facing the force of nature, each trying to achieve mastery over the other. In years to come, this would be his favourite spot on the ship.

The reason for his fear was because on his last voyage with his father he had been badly seasick. Ragnar had told him that this happened to everyone sooner or later, but he did not want the others to see 'the young master' weak as a kitten, unable to stand upright and spewing his innards out.

*

Ragnar and Hallgerður remained on the beach, looking after the knarr until it was almost out of sight. Ragnar sighed. Hallgerður looked at him. "He will be fine", she said. "And it was time."

"I know. But I was thinking about the first voyage when I was more than just an oar-rider."

"Was it the same, do you think?"

"I don't know, though I do know one thing: I was not sure if

I wanted to go or not. I went because Odd convinced me to. But Kári really wants to go. I don't know what that means. Oh well, the Allfather will no doubt watch over him."

They turned and began to walk back towards Snæströnd. Today, the beach did not live up to its name; the snow had all melted long since. But it was beautiful even so: the snows had the stark grandeur that Ragnar loved, but the softer green it wore in the brief summer months had their own hold over him. He had built this farm from almost nothing, and although the free-roving sailor in him would never entirely disappear, he was glad it was Kári going off with Odd and that his part was now to stay at home tending the land.

Coming closer to the farmhouse, Hallgerður looked out across the valley and said, "There is someone coming."

Ragnar looked in the direction she indicated. "Yes. And whoever it is, he is important, because it is a large group, and they are all riding."

Hallgerður nodded. "Ten men at least. But they are riding slowly, so they are not hostile. I think you will find that it is Eirík goði and his men."

"I think you are right. But although they are not hostile, ten men will attack our food stores."

"We have enough, even after the winter. Last year's harvest was good. And you may not be a goði, but you are wealthier than many goðar and have your reputation to think of. They will not be disappointed."

When they reached the farmhouse, Hallgerður quickly began to order her servants to clean up from the previous night's feasting and prepare food and drink for the new guests. Ragnar waited outside. He spotted Guðmundr coming up towards the house and beckoned him to come. "I don't know what Eirík goði wants, but I can guess. If I am right, this will concern you too."

When Eirík entered the farmstead, Ragnar saw that Hallgerður had been right. Eirík had nine men with him. Not that he had doubted her – her eyes were better than his. But he was still impressed. It would look good that food and drink had been set for exactly ten guests.

As Eirík and his men dismounted, Ragnar directed farmhands to care for their horses and walked up to the goði. "Welcome, Eirík. I have not seen you for some time."

"Thank you, Ragnar. I come unbidden but there are matters we should discuss before the spring Thing."

"So there are, but before we get serious, you and your men have ridden long and are no doubt both hungry and thirsty. Let us go inside."

When they came inside, Eirík stopped for a moment. Although he had visited Ragnar in the past, he was clearly impressed by the amount of food and drink waiting for him and his men, even though nobody had known they were coming. His followers looked eagerly at the table and even more eagerly at the horns of beer. But before they could sit down, Eirík went up to Hallgerður, who was waiting for him with a horn in her hand.

"Welcome, dear friend. You honour us with your visit", she said, handing him the drink.

"Thank you, wise lady. It is a pleasure to see you and our honour to be greeted by both you and your husband."

"Sit and tell us why you have come."

Eirík and his men sat down, but it took some time before he broached the reason for his arrival. It was clear that he was unwilling to speak while anyone else could hear what he said. So it was only much later, when it was already dark and his men had been shown to the outbuildings where they would spend the night, that he finally turned to Ragnar and seemed ready to speak.

"Five years ago, you were treated badly by Gunnar goði. He went back on his word to support you in your case against Leifur, and he tried to take from you what was your right."

Ragnar nodded. He needed no reminder.

"I suggested you should change goði, and you did. You are now counted as one of my men. This has been good for me as well because you are a man of high repute – not only wealthy but honest and upright. For such a man to change means that his new goði must also be respectable. And I appreciate that."

Ragnar still said nothing. He thought he knew where Eirík was headed, but it was always better to let the other man speak his fill.

"But things are now getting more difficult. At that Thing, your case against Leifur could not be heard because you were not there. Nor could Gunnar's case against you about the walrus be heard. I think he had assumed that you were so keen for his support that you would give in at once, and so he had not prepared the case. Therefore, nothing happened.

"A year later, he was better prepared. He put forth his claim about the walrus and wanted the Thing to fine you the value of half a walrus. At this Thing, I was able to hold the case, again because you were not there and by casting doubt on Gunnar's claim, asking why he had not made it a year earlier. Many of those present were also ill at ease and nothing was decided.

"But at the next Thing, as you know, Gunnar had men swear oaths that he was telling the truth. His son Einar claimed to have seen the walrus with his own eyes."

At this, Guðmundr could not keep silent. "He is lying. He is a snivelling little turd and a liar."

Ragnar put his hand on Guðmundr's sleeve. "I know. But let our guest speak."

Eirík had taken advantage of Guðmundr's outburst to drink some more beer. Now he put down his horn and continued, "I don't think anyone who knows Gunnar or how this whole case came about believes him. Nevertheless, at this Thing, as you know because you were there, he won his case, and you were fined the value of half a walrus, or the equivalent of one and a half cows. You have refused to pay the fine."

"Indeed", Ragnar said. "The case was won by oath-breakers and people who foreswore themselves."

"This may be true. But it is the judgement of the Thing. You appealed the case, but at the next Thing you lost again. You claimed that Gunnar's case was wrong and it was once again held over to the next Thing, where once again you lost. So far, nothing else has happened. In fact, because people know you and know Gunnar, the Thing has also decided that your case against Leifur will not lapse; but it will also not be heard until your fine has either been paid to Gunnar or been declared void."

He stopped and looked at Ragnar and Hallgerður. Ragnar still kept silent, so Eirík sighed and continued. "I now must ask you: what do you intend to do?"

"What do you mean?"

"The Thing has three times decided against you. Will you pay the fine?"

"You already know the answer to that. Gunnar's case is false. I cannot pay him."

"I know that Gunnar's case is false. And I do assure you that most right-minded people do too. But I have to think of many things. As a goði, I have to uphold the law."

"Then uphold it", Ragnar interjected.

"I would like to. But I must also uphold the peace of the land."

For the first time Hallgerður spoke. "You spoke earlier of Ragnar's reputation for honesty. How would this reputation look if he submitted to a false verdict?"

"Hallgerður is right", Ragnar said.

"I know she is. And if the world was a just world, I would not be asking you this. But think: so far, this case has seen no bloodshed. I would prefer that it stayed that way. But the longer it drags out, the greater the likelihood that this will not last. Even if no one wants a fight, it can still happen. And I must also think of others who have a claim on my time. They too have a right to expect their goði to work for them and to give them justice."

"But this is not justice. You are asking my husband to submit to an injustice", Hallgerður said.

"All I am asking is for Ragnar to at least consider paying Gunnar's fine. Yes, you would submit to an injustice. But everyone knows that it is an injustice, and so they would ask why you were submitting. And the answer to that is that there is a higher justice. This higher justice is to obey the law even when it is wrong. Moreover, you would be able to pursue your own case against Leifur at last. Remember, if you refuse to pay a fine lawfully decided by the Thing, even for a wrongful case, Leifur can decide that he will not pay you when he loses his case."

Guðmundr had been silent since his outburst, but now he cleared his throat. "Father, perhaps you should consider doing what Eirík suggests? It is not only about you: I have to live here as well and live with our neighbours. I would prefer that this did not develop into an even longer feud."

Ragnar looked at him. "Peace is good. But justice stands above peace, and he who seeks peace by abandoning justice will find neither peace nor justice. Never forget that."

Guðmundr was silent. He had not meant it this way. He supported his father. Yes, he wanted peace with Gunnar so that he could meet Jórunn. And he did mean what he said about having to live with his neighbours and preferring peace. But not at the price of humiliating his father.

Hallgerður spoke again. "You said that being my husband's goði was good for your reputation. Would not his submission to a false verdict damage your own standing?"

Ragnar looked at his wife and son. He wished that Kári had been there. He was sure that Kári would have supported him. In truth, he too wished that this case was over. But he would not stoop to rewarding a liar. Still, he wanted to be sure that, whatever he did, he would not regret it afterwards. Finally, he said, "Eirík, I hear what you are saying. And I respect you, both as my friend and as my goði and because you are a just man. I will not say either yea or nay tonight. I wish to sleep on this, and tomorrow I shall give you an answer."

"I ask no more than that", Eirík replied. "And I will say to you that, whatever you decide, I will do my best to support you. I have promised to do so, and unlike some other goðar, I will not be foresworn. Let us speak again tomorrow."

That night, Hallgerður and Ragnar lay awake, talking about what to do. In the end, Hallgerður said, "You know I defended you to Eirík. But Guðmundr is also right. Maybe peace is worth this price. After all, it is not as if you cannot afford to pay him." For a moment it seemed as if she wanted to say something more, but then she stopped herself.

"Oh the price is not high. But if I pay, I lose my honour, and that is worth much more. And there is also this: where is the law if it is not a just law? What will happen at the next Thing or the next time a powerful man brings a false case against his neighbour? Answer me that."

"You are a stiff and stubborn man, Ragnar Snæströnd."

"Stubborn I am when my honour is questioned. And as for stiff ... come here, woman, and you'll find out." He stretched his arm towards Hallgerður, who laughed quietly and rolled closer to him.

Afterwards, while Ragnar fell asleep, Hallgerður remained awake, thinking about the day's events. She felt as strongly as Ragnar that submitting and paying Gunnar was wrong. It would also see her proud husband humiliated, something she too wanted to avoid. But there were reasons to consider more carefully what Eirík had said. One thing he said was certainly right: the Thing had made a decision and fined Ragnar. Just or unjust, the law had to be obeyed. If people did not obey the law, or if they chose which laws to obey, they might as well not have any law, and then the only right would indeed belong at the end of a spear. Ragnar was right that seeking peace at the cost of justice would lose you both. But was it right to disobey the law in the cause of honour? Would you then not only lose the law but also peace and honour? And Eirík had rightly pointed out that if Ragnar refused to pay a fine because it was unjust, why would not Leifur or anyone else refuse to pay any fines because they did not like them?

All this she could discuss with Ragnar. But there was a further reason to consider attempting to make peace with Gunnar, which she could not tell her husband. This was Jórunn Gunnarsdóttir. She knew that Guðmundr was seeing the girl. Indeed, once or twice she had sent one of her servants to tell Jórunn that Ragnar was going to be away for some days. She had never asked, but she was fairly certain that her son had managed to meet the girl 'by chance' on those occasions.

She did not really think that Jórunn was the right girl for Guðmundr. Oh, she was clever and pretty, but also too flighty and too spoiled. She would not be a good mistress at Snæströnd. But telling Guðmundr this would only make him desire her more. Better he find out for himself.

And then she finally fell asleep. But in the morning, she made sure to speak with Ragnar before he went to see Eirík. At first he was unwilling to listen to her, but at last he said, "You are right. I will try to make peace – as long as I keep my honour."

As Eirík's men were preparing to leave, Ragnar took the goði aside. "Do not think that I do not appreciate what you are trying to do", he said. "I know you want this issue to be resolved. But I cannot submit to an injustice, and so I cannot simply pay Gunnar. But I too wish to live in peace with my neighbours. So I suggest we try to find a way to resolve this which preserves justice and honour."

"I do not know how we can do that", Eirík replied. "But I said I would support you, and I will. Yet I fear the worst is yet to come."

"Perhaps not. I have listened to my wife."

"This is perhaps something that men should do more often", Eirík said with a smile.

"For the sake of peace, I will do this: I will pay Gunnar the value of half a walrus, as he has demanded."

Eirík looked as if he wanted to say something, but then he realised that Ragnar was not yet finished.

"But I wish to have my say. I wish to speak to the Thing and explain that I am doing this, even though it is unjust, because the law must be obeyed and be equal for all. And I then wish my case against Leifur to be heard at last."

Eirík looked thoughtfully at him. He was pleased that Ragnar had unbent this much. It was probably the furthest he would go. But he also worried that if Ragnar spoke too hastily at the Thing, it might make matters worse, rather than better. Still, this was as much as he could hope for.

"Thank you", he said. "I think this will work. It is certainly the honourable thing to do, and I think you will find that everybody else will agree with me. So let me consider it, and I promise to give you my reply well before the Thing. Until then, let us do or say nothing that will raise further anger."

And with that he mounted his horse and rode off, with his nine men following him.

Chapter 3

Spring 1060

The knarr made good speed westwards along the coast. It wasn't long before Snæströnd was too far behind to be seen. Soon enough – too soon, Kári thought – the sun began to set. As it did, Kári left his place in the prow and walked back to the steering oar, where Odd was carefully watching the coast.

"What now?" he asked.

"We keep going west until we pass Snæfellsjökull, then we turn south and head for Reykjanes. Don't worry, lad, I can do this alone and in the night if I have to. Meanwhile, the wind is good, so we can let most of the rowers sleep. You should get some rest too."

"Are you sure? Well then, wake me up if you need me."

A smile seemed to flicker across Odd's face, as if he thought it amusing that he would need Kári's help. But he said nothing, and having made the offer, Kári was secretly quite glad it had not been taken up – it was already dark, and Odd's advice was good. He went off to the space he had marked out for himself on the deck and lay down beneath a fur.

But try as he might, he could not fall asleep. At first, this was because he was concerned about the ship. Had everything been stowed properly? Should the walrus tusks have been secured better? And what about the wadmal? Was it covered by enough hides to ensure that it wouldn't get wet from the spray or if it rained? And if there was an emergency? Could they bail the ship quickly enough? What about food? And water? Was there enough to last them all the way to Orkney? Should they put into Reykjanes for more water? Odd had told him they had enough. But perhaps he had forgotten how much they needed.

As these thoughts, and others, passed through his mind, he found himself lying on his back looking up at the sky. Far above, stars glittered like tiny pieces of silver on a black cloth. There he saw Bifröst, the bridge of stars on which the gods would ride to and from Valhalla.

He wanted to sleep, but the stars kept him awake. Even when he tried to turn his gaze away, he found that the movement of the knarr and the different noises of men snoring, muttering in their sleep and breaking wind all kept him awake. At one stage, he even thought of getting up and going to speak with Odd again, but he worried that Odd would think him silly.

He thought that he would never fall asleep. Yet all of a sudden he started as a wave broke over the shipboard and splashed his face. When he'd wiped the water away and looked up, he realised that it was beginning to get light. So he must have slept after all.

He rubbed his eyes and stretched his body. Then he stood up, shaking the loose water off his fur and carefully stowing it so that it would stay dry. One of the other men was sitting by his oar, munching on something. When he saw that Kári was up, he nodded at him and reached down, bringing up some bread and dried mutton from beside him. "Breakfast?" he asked.

Kári took the proffered food and thanked him. Still eating, he walked over towards Odd, who seemed not to have moved at all during the night.

"Good morning, young master."

"And to you as well, Odd. Where are we?"

"We have passed Reykjanes. Now we are headed southeast. We'll go west of the Færeyjar, then straight for Hjaltland but turn south well before we get there. We should reach Orkney maybe tomorrow night but probably the morning after."

"That is good. Now what?"

"Now, young master, it's time for you to take the steering oar."

"Now?" Kári had known this would happen at some stage, but

somehow he thought it would not be this soon. What if he did something wrong?

"Now." Odd grabbed Kári's left hand and pulled him towards the steering oar, closing his hand around it. Almost by reflex, Kári put his right hand together with his left, then turned around and faced the prow again, holding on mainly with the right hand. But he still felt apprehensive, and no doubt looked it as well.

Odd grinned. "You have to learn. And best to learn on the open sea, where mistakes won't be so costly. Just hold this course until I come back."

"Where are you going?"

"I need to sleep. Don't worry. You'll be fine."

And he was. True, for a while his grip on the steering oar was almost desperate. But eventually it began to ease, and he felt more confident about what he was doing. The sun was shining, and he knew to sail with the sun slightly to his left until it was high in the sky. Soon he even began to enjoy himself. This was almost as good as standing in the prow – one man, measuring himself against the sea.

He was almost disappointed when Odd eventually came to reclaim the steering oar. The older man looked at him. "How are you feeling?" he asked.

"I'm fine", Kári replied. "Absolutely fine."

And suddenly he realised that he was. It wasn't just that he was fine. He had had so much to think about after they left – his worries during the night and then his concerns about the steering – that he had forgotten to be seasick. For a brief moment, he feared that the thought would make him retch, but nothing happened. He drew a deep breath and realised that there was no danger of being sick. Instead, it was just the same smell of the sea as at home – except deeper, somehow fuller and more … more sea-like. He laughed as he handed the steering oar to Odd and went back to standing in the prow again, exchanging words with the rowers on the way.

It was indeed two days later that they reached Kirkjuvágr in Orkney. They came in on the morning tide. When he saw the town, Kári left his place in the prow and made his way back to Odd, who was once again steering. The sail was down, and the entire crew was manning the oars, rowing slowly.

"This place is huge!" he exclaimed. "How many people live here? And what do they all do?"

Odd laughed. "It is huge, Kári, because you are not used to it. In truth, this is not a big town. Wait until you see Jórvik; that is really large. Kirkjuvágr is quite new, perhaps twenty years old or so. Still, there are probably a hundred people living here, and as many traders or more visiting. As to what they do, some of them serve the Jarl, but fortunately we won't have much to do with them. Most of the others are here for us."

"For us?" Kári sounded bewildered.

"Not for you and me personally", Odd said. "I mean they are here to trade. It is easy to get here from Norway and Denmark, from Scotland, the Suðreyjar, Dyflin, Ireland and England. It is a good place, too, to buy metal tools for the ship and get repairs done, should you ever need to on a future voyage. So traders meet here to buy and sell. Not to mention to eat and drink. We will, of course, do that too – I know a man who sells the best beer in the town."

While he talked, the knarr had smoothly approached a wooden pier that stretched out into the water. Most of it was taken up by other ships, similar to their own, but Odd steered for an empty space. Once they were near enough, he told the rowers to ship oars and the knarr gently glided to the pier, barely bumping it. As soon as they were along the side, two of the rowers jumped ashore with ropes and began to make the boat fast. While they were doing that, two armed men who were standing nearby began to move towards them. As they approached, Kári looked up.

"When I said we won't have much to do with the Jarl's men, it seems I was somewhat hasty. Here come his hirdmen."

"What do they want?" Kári asked.

"Find out who we are, mainly. Now that Jarl Thorfinn has slain his brothers and nephews, he fears no one, so at least they won't suspect us of being enemies."

Odd turned out to be right. The two hirdmen seemed bored with their duty, but one of them asked who they were and from where they came. Odd replied that they were Icelanders from Snæströnd, and with this they seemed to lose interest and went back to leaning on their spears and lazily looking around.

"At least they didn't ask us for silver. Now then, young master, what do we do?"

"What do we do? Do you not know?"

Odd grinned. "Oh yes, I do. But it is for you to learn. So, what do we do?"

Kári tried to think. What should they do? What did he want to do? Although it was early, the sun already shone quite strongly and it was warm. There was a smell, but not the fresh smell of the sea, rather a fetid smell of old rancid food. And the sky was full of seagulls, loudly squawking and from time to time dipping close to the boats or the jetty, presumably trying to find some food to snatch.

He scratched his head. "I guess we should look for some traders", he ventured.

"In due course", Odd replied. "But first, we check the ship for any damage or repairs that might be necessary, and then our stores to see what we need for the onward journey. We will certainly need fresh water and it is probably a good idea to buy some more food. Then the crew will want to go ashore, so we should set up a roster where at least three of them remain on the ship all the time. This may be a good town, and Thorfinn keeps order well, but even so there are men who might be tempted to make off with an unattended ship. And then you and I need to go and get something to eat and drink, and *that* is where we will find traders who will tell us anything we need to know."

Kári's head spun. So much to keep in mind and to do. Now he began to realise how much he really needed to learn – and how fortunate he was to have someone to teach him. He also understood why his father trusted Odd.

Making all the arrangements didn't take too long. There was no need to disturb the trade goods, so he only needed to check that nothing had been spoiled by seawater and that everything was still safely stowed. Arranging for some of the rowers to go ashore had not been difficult, but it was Odd who spoke to them and explained that they were not going to be in Kirkjuvágr long and told them how much time they could spend ashore. Most of them listened impatiently, wanting to get off at once. It was only when Odd told them that "if you are not here when we sail, we will sail without you, and it will be up to you to explain to your fathers why you were not there when we traded their goods!" that they suddenly perked up.

When he had finished, Odd sent four of the men ashore. Kári, having first asked Odd, instructed two of the others to take their empty water kegs in a small skiff to a nearby stream that emptied out into the bay and refill them. Then he turned to Odd again. "You mentioned food and drink?"

"So I did. Let me just make sure I have some silver to pay for it", he said, looking into a purse hanging from his belt.

They left the knarr, telling the men remaining on board when they would be back, and then they set off. Kári felt surprisingly unsteady walking on land again, almost as if the land was moving beneath his feet. Odd had told him that this would happen after a long sea voyage, and he had been expecting it, but it still felt very strange.

While they walked, he looked around. Odd might think that Kirkjuvágr was small, but to Kári it still was larger than anything he had seen. There were certainly more people than he had ever seen in one place except at a Thing. He could see maybe twenty or thirty houses, and slightly further off he saw a large stone building with a tower, which he understood was the church of the White Christ. Everywhere there were people hurrying along in one direction or another. And the smell remained, although it changed from rotten seaweed, as it had been by the sea, to more of a smell of sweaty people, stale beer and piss. The reason for the last was obvious when he saw a man relieving himself against the wall of a building they passed.

They had not walked far before Odd turned towards a house with an open front. There were tables and benches outside and inside, with people sitting and eating and drinking. Women were moving between the tables, carrying mugs of drink or platters of food.

"Who lives here?" Kári asked. "And how can he afford to feed all these people? Do they work for him?"

Odd laughed. "This is an inn, Kári. People come here to eat and drink and also to meet and talk. And they pay the innkeeper for the food and drink. In fact, he probably makes much silver out of this."

"Oh. Is it expensive?"

"Don't worry, Kári, there are many things that are different from what you are used to in Snæströnd. Today you find them strange, but soon enough you will find them perfectly normal. In a place like this, where men show up from afar, you need an inn where they can meet. And so there will be an inn. And if the innkeeper is very expensive, you will find that even in a small town like Kirkjuvágr there will suddenly be more inns as others want to share in the wealth. In fact, I can see that there are more inns than last time I was here, but that is a few years ago. This place was always good in the past, and I hope it will be today as well.

"And one more thing, Kári."

"Yes?"

"Don't speak with the women. Or, at least, don't agree to anything they suggest."

"What? Why?"

"You will see."

As they entered the gloomy room, a small, wizened man who was busy in a corner suddenly looked up. When he saw Odd, he smiled and came running towards them.

"Odd Barðsson! I haven't seen you for a good while! Where have you been?"

"Here and there", Odd replied, "but mainly home. But now I'm back. Is your beer as good as it was?"

"Better", the man said. "The barley harvest was excellent. Wait until you try the winter brew."

"I look forward to it. Tell me, is there anyone I know?"

"Let me see. There are a couple of traders from Dyflin, but you never went there, did you? One or two from Norway and from

Hjaltland. Not many from Jórvik. Times are bad there, they say. You'd better look around for yourself. Meanwhile, who is your friend?"

"You remember Ragnar Snæströnd? Well, this is his son Kári. The young master, out to learn the trade. Kári, this is Harald, the innkeeper. He is from Denmark and he knew your father."

"Any son of Ragnar and friend of Odd is welcome here", the innkeeper said.

"Thank you", Kári replied. He felt bewildered. His father had never mentioned any inn, let alone any innkeeper to him. But when he thought about it, it made sense for Ragnar to have known Odd's friends. And it made sense for him to have known inns in the places he had visited. It was just that it was so new.

He followed Odd as the older man looked around and eventually moved to a table that was already occupied by four or five men but still had a few empty places. Odd sat down after receiving a nod.

A few moments later, Harald and one of the women brought them mugs of beer and platters of meat and bread. Kári tasted the beer. It was nice, and it was certainly richer, somehow, than what he was used to drinking in Iceland, but he didn't think that it was as special as Harald had promised. Odd seemed to like it, though, as he quickly drained one mug and asked for another.

While Kári sat quietly and looked around, Odd began to speak with the other men at the table. Kári was not surprised to hear that they were also traders. They were from Ireland, from Dyflin and one from Cork, but they were all Norwegians. Odd had asked if anyone was from Jórvik, but apparently there were few traders from England in Kirkjuvágr at this time.

One of the Dyflin traders noticed that Kári was not joining in the conversation and leaned over towards him.

"You are being very quiet, friend", he said.

"Yes", Kári replied. "I'm trying to learn."

"Really? This is your first voyage?" When Kári nodded, the man smiled and said, "This must be celebrated. Girl, bring another beer for our young master trader here."

As the woman put another mug in front of Kári, he drained his first mug, then thanked the man.

"Don't mention it. It is my pleasure. Tell me, where are you from and what are you trading?"

"We are from Snæströnd in Iceland."

"Never heard of it. Is it big?"

"It is a big farm", Kári said, slightly offended. "My father is an important man. He owns our ship."

"Of course, of course. I meant no disrespect", the man said. "Let me introduce myself. I am Ivar mac Arailt from Dyflin. A trader, like yourself. And you are?"

"Kári Ragnarsson."

"Tell me, Kári, what are you trading?"

"We bring walrus hides and ivory, and wadmal."

"Interesting. And what are you buying?"

"Anything, really. Wheat, linen. Weapons, tools."

"You won't get much of that here in Kirkjuvágr."

"Oh I know. We are only selling here. We are headed for the big market in Jórvik."

"Jórvik? Why would you want to go there?"

Kári didn't really know. It had just always seemed clear that they were going to Jórvik and he had never thought to ask why. He looked towards Odd for help, but Odd was deep in conversation with the others and didn't even notice. To hide his confusion, Kári drank deeply from the beer mug.

"You shouldn't go to Jórvik, you know. Come to Dyflin. Trade in Dyflin is much better. Jórvik is a bad place right now; trade is bad there."

"I don't know." Kári really wished Odd would help him. He drank some more beer, but this made it even more difficult to think clearly.

"Surely you are the master of the ship. Didn't you say it was your father's ship? You should just tell your fellow there – Odd, was it? – that you've changed your mind. And in Dyflin, I will trade for you. Help you. For a commission, naturally."

Kári didn't know what to do. He stood up, but when he did, it seemed as if the entire room was turning, and he had difficulty standing straight. One of the women working in the inn was nearby and saw him swaying gently and came up to steady him. He leaned gratefully against her. She looked more closely at him and said, "Poor lamb. But you're a good-looking lamb, aren't you? Leave him alone, Ivar", she snapped at the trader who had also risen from his chair.

"Come with me, lamb. I'll show something much nicer."

Kári tried to think. "What do you mean?" he said.

"Oh, you don't know, do you. You'll find out. Just come with me. You will like this."

Kári looked at the woman. Earlier he had thought she looked quite young, but now he could see that she was quite a bit older than he was. Her face was full of wrinkles and there was a greedy look in her eyes. But she seemed to want to help him.

"Thank you, old lady", he mumbled.

The woman's eyes blazed. "Old!" she shrieked. "Who are you calling old? I am no older than you! Twenty summers is all I've seen, I'll have you know!"

One of the men still sitting laughed out loud. "In that case you must have been a babe in your mother's arms when I first enjoyed you", he said. The girl swung around to see who had spoken, but that meant she had to let go of Kári. Meanwhile, Odd had finally noticed what was going on and stood up and came over to them.

"Come, Kári", he said. "I think it's time to go back to the ship." And without waiting for an answer, he took the young man's arm and dragged him along, out of the inn and into what was now a dark night and to the ship. Kári had difficulty walking but tried to keep up.

Odd didn't say anything. When they came to the ship, he suddenly straightened Kári up so that it seemed as if he was walking on his own. Ignoring a question from the one sleepy crew member who was awake and on guard, he led Kári to the prow, where he bedded him down. Then he looked at the younger man and laughed quietly to himself, before he went to his own place by the steering oar and fell asleep.

The next morning, Kári woke up with the worst headache of his life. He stumbled to the side of the ship and was noisily sick into the water. When he had finished, he turned around to find Odd already there, watching him.

"Well?"

"I know", Kári replied. "I may be stupid, but I'm not that stupid. I was drunk. I drank too much beer. And it wasn't even that good. I apologise."

"I rather liked the beer", Odd said. "But you are not stupid. A stupid man would not have realised that he was drunk, and he would not have apologised for it. So you have learned a lesson. Don't worry, there is no harm done. And just so you know – but never tell him I told you – your father did the same on his first voyage."

"My father was drunk?"

"Oh yes. Badly so. You at least went to sleep. He decided that he would walk around, singing in a loud voice to everyone he met."

Kári couldn't believe it. Ragnar singing drunkenly was a sight he had never seen and could barely imagine. It didn't seem like the stern father he had always known. But Odd just laughed. "Happens to all of us. Me too. Just remember, don't do it again. Or if you do, make sure you have a friend with you who is not drunk."

"I will remember that. Thank you."

For much of the morning, Kári remained on board the ship, trying not to move too much. He thought that all the other crewmen noticed and were looking at him, but nobody said anything, so he could not be sure.

Shortly before noon, Odd returned and beckoned him to come over. As he sat down, Odd said, "I have done some trading for us. We have sold some of the wadmal to a group of Irish traders – the ones I spoke with last night – and some of the walrus hides to a Norwegian. They paid well in silver."

"Good", Kári said.

"We need to buy some supplies, so we will stay tonight, but tomorrow we go on to Jórvik."

"Oh!" Kári suddenly remembered. "The Irishman I spoke with. He said we should go to Dyflin, not to Jórvik. He said trade is bad in Jórvik right now."

"He was trying to make you go to Dyflin so that he could profit from your trade. But it may well be that times are bad in Jórvik. Some of the others said so as well."

"Then why do we go there? Let's go to Dyflin instead."

"No. And I will tell you why. First, because your father and I had agreed that we are going to Jórvik. I can change that, but only if I have good reason. And so far, nothing I have heard sounds like a good enough reason, even if there may be some trouble. Second, I don't know anyone in Dyflin, and I don't know if they have what we need. But I have been to Jórvik several times, and there I know people. Even if times are bad, they will give us a good trade. Also, Jórvik is big, much bigger than Dyflin. In Jórvik, there are wealthy people who will pay high prices for walrus ivory. So Jórvik it is."

Kári thought about it. True, Ivar had been trying to take advantage of him, if Odd was right – and Kári was sure he was right. But that need not mean that going to Dyflin was wrong. However, his father had made clear that Odd was really in command, so if Odd said Jórvik, Jórvik it would be. But he did promise himself that – one day – he was going to go to Dyflin. And then another thought struck him.

"That woman, last night. She said she was going to show me something nice. What was she talking about?"

Odd burst out laughing. "Oldest thing in the world, young master. She wanted to lie with you – for silver, of course. In fact, she would have preferred just to take your silver without lying with you if possible, if she could convince you that you were having a wonderful time."

Kári blushed. He knew, of course, what men and women do, and he had occasionally – well, frequently, really – thought of some of the girls on his father's farm or some of the neighbouring girls. It just hadn't happened yet. But with this woman?! That was disgusting. "But she was old!" he burst out. "And ugly!"

"Too many men", Odd said. "Now, are you ready to come ashore to help me buy supplies? Or would you rather stay on the ship?"

"I will come with you."

"Very good. We will make a trader of you yet."

When they were ashore again, Odd mentioned that last time he had been to Kirkjuvágr, the place had been much smaller. He pointed out a few of the houses that had been built since. They were generally larger than the older ones and showed greater sign of wealth. "Kirkjuvágr is growing", he said. "Who knows, when you come back next time there may be as many as five hundred people living here. Still smaller than Jórvik but becoming a big town."

"And all trade?" Kári asked.

"Yes, either with us or for us. I told you, everyone brings things here and sells to others who have brought other things."

"Do they bring the food as well? I don't see any farms."

"Oh there are farms, outside Kirkjuvágr, and of course on the other islands. There are many settlements in Orkney."

Kári thought about it. "If Kirkjuvágr has no farms, then they must all trust each other."

"What do you mean?"

"The traders living here must trust the farmers to bring them food. And the farmers must trust that they will be paid and will get goods they need at a price they can pay."

Odd looked strangely at him. "Did you think of that just now by yourself?"

"Yes. Is there something wrong?"

"No. That is exactly what is happening. But most people don't realise it. If you asked them, traders would usually say that farmers are stupid, and farmers would probably reply that traders are sly tricksters. But their actions show that they do actually trust each other because otherwise neither would get what they want, whereas as it is, both sides do. Now then, where am I supposed to get some salt pork and bread for the onward journey?"

In the end, they spent five days in Kirkjuvágr. On the last day they found a butcher and a baker. Both were prepared to sell them what they needed, although not quite at the price that Odd was prepared to pay. Kári listened carefully to Odd's negotiations with the two men, determined to learn as much as he could. He still felt embarrassed by his behaviour the first evening and was keen to show Odd that he would not repeat it.

The next morning, having received their new supplies, they left Kirkjuvágr.

While the knarr was steering out of the bay and into the open sea, Odd signalled Kári to come and stand beside him.

"Well, young master", he began. "What have you learned from these few days?"

"For one thing", Kári replied, "that it sounds strange when you call me 'young master'. All my life you've called me Kári. Why this change? After all, you are much more the master of this ship than I."

"But one day you *will* be the master. And it is important that the others realise this. They need to respect you. Mind, they won't do it just because your father is wealthy and owns this ship. You still have to prove that you are worthy of their respect and their trust. But they also have to see that I respect you, and part of that means treating you as the master. Do you understand?"

Kári thought about it. "Yes, I think I do. It still feels strange, though."

Odd laughed. "You'll get used to it soon enough – young master. Now then, what have you learned?"

"Apart from getting drunk, you mean?"

"That too. Although I'm sure it will happen again. What else?"

"Let me think. First, I learned that the first thing in port is to decide what supplies you need for your onward journey."

"Good. And?"

"Find other traders? At an inn?"

"What about your crew? And the ship?"

"Oh. Yes, make sure there is always someone on the ship."

"Yes, that too, but there is one more thing that came before even that. We only had a short and safe journey from Snæströnd, and it was unlikely that anything on the ship would have needed repair or replacing. But even so, you remember we checked the ship from stem to stern. You should do this after even the shortest and most uneventful journey – keeping the ship sound is the shipmaster's most important duty of all."

"I understand and will remember. But there is one thing I don't understand. Why did you say 'at least they didn't ask for silver' when we arrived?"

"Because all too often, men like that find that when they have a little power, they will use that to try to enrich themselves. A guard who can allow you to do something or forbid it may decide ask for silver, or maybe part of your trading goods, before granting your request. For instance, to come ashore. Or he may decide that if you don't pay, he will need to question you for hours to 'make sure that you are not an enemy of the Jarl' or something. The more important the man, the more he can ask for."

Kári was shocked. "And you pay?"

"Depends on how much of a hurry you are in, or how powerful your friends are, but, usually, yes."

Kári thought about this. This was just what his father was always so angry about: men in power using their position to feather their nests. That a free man would be forced to grovel for what was his right, was unfair. And it must be bad for everyone, he felt.

"If this happens, if the hirdmen ask for silver to let you land, won't people stop coming? And then they will all get poorer instead of richer?"

Odd was once again impressed. He recognised Ragnar's thoughts, but he had not heard them this clearly expressed by his old friend, nor had he expected a youth like Kári to grasp this so rapidly. There was obviously more to this boy than he had yet seen.

"You are right", he said. "But Jarl Thorfinn is a strong ruler now. He understands this as well, and that is why his hirdmen dare not press traders for silver or anything else."

Chapter 4

Summer 1060

Once he had seen Eirík and his men ride off in the distance, Ragnar returned to Hallgerður. Although he had just agreed to settle the feud with Gunnar and pay him the fine, it gave him no pleasure. Instead, he keenly felt the humiliation of having to swallow his pride and submit to an injustice. What made it worse was that everyone knew that it was an injustice, and there were many who would take pleasure in seeing him abase himself. Ragnar was under no illusions about his reputation. There were some who were his friends, men like Odd. There were some who respected him, men like Eirík. But there were many who envied him his wealth and who felt he was arrogant and haughty and who disliked him for this. He had no doubt that some of the latter had given their support to Gunnar at the Thing simply to see Ragnar suffer. Should he really give them the pleasure of seeing him crawl to Gunnar, begging forgiveness? Far better to avoid the Thing and the whole business! Eirík was sure to understand that he couldn't go through with it.

But when he explained this to Hallgerður, her reaction was not what he had expected. "Eirík may well understand", she said. "He will understand that you are a foolish, stubborn man."

Ragnar was taken aback. Of course, it had been her suggestion that he submit, but even so, he had thought that she would understand his reasons. "My love", he said, only to be interrupted.

"Don't you 'My love' me. Listen to me instead. I will tell you why you should go through with your original thought. It is not because peace is better than feuding, although this is also true. It is not because of what people will think, although you will find that people will think more highly of you for upholding the law, even at a cost to yourself, than for stubbornly standing on a right that can no longer be upheld and the cause of which many have already forgotten. No, you should go through with this in order to show that you do not put yourself above the law. You often say that the law must be obeyed."

"But – but this is not the law. It is the decision of the Thing that is wrong", Ragnar interjected.

"But the Thing made a decision according to law. If the law is wrong, you can try to change it. If the decision is wrong, you can appeal it."

"I did, and it failed."

"Then so be it. Let no one say that Ragnar from Snæströnd only obeys the law and the verdict of the Thing when he agrees with it."

"No one would dare say that!"

"Would they not? Is that not what is happening? You lost a case. The verdict was unfair. Many know this. But Ragnar Snæströnd always upholds the law. Well, show them that you do!"

Ragnar sighed. He knew when he had lost. And he knew that Hallgerður was right. He would do as she said, but it still rankled with him.

He wondered how Kári was doing. They should be well on their way towards Reykjanes now. He hoped the boy wasn't seasick again. And where was Guðmundr?

During this time, Ragnar was still from time to time afflicted by doubts about what to do. But Hallgerður remained steadfast in her views and when he had brought the issue up with Guðmundr, the boy had said that whatever his father decided, he would support him. But privately Guðmundr felt that his mother was right.

Soon enough the time for the Thórsnesthing approached. A messenger had come from Eirík saying that he agreed with what they had said at their parting. By this time, Ragnar realised that changing his mind would cause a bad break with Eirík and decided that he would have to carry it through after all.

In due course, Ragnar and his household rode to the Thing plain. There was already a busy throng there when they arrived; it seemed that attendance this year would be very good. However, they had no problem setting up their booths at the usual spot, and then Ragnar went to look for Eirík. He found the goði engaged in speaking with a group of strange men. When he spotted Ragnar, he interrupted what he was saying and beckoned him to come closer. "Friends", he said, "this is Ragnar Snæströnd, who I have told you about. He is an upright man of strong principles with a great respect for the Law. Welcome to the Thing, Ragnar."

"Thank you, Eirík. You flatter me."

"Not at all. I have asked my friends here, who rarely attend the Thing, to join us this year because I want them to meet you."

So Eirík had brought his friends to make sure that they had a large group supporting them. That was presumably good. But it was Ragnar who was going to be humiliated, not they. Best it were done quickly, in that case.

"What will happen?" he asked Eirík.

"Tomorrow morning I will address the Thing and ask them to listen to you. Then it is all up to you. Are you ready?"

"As ready as I will be", Ragnar replied. "But –"

"Excellent", Eirík cut in. "In that case, I will see you in the morning."

Ragnar was taken aback by the interruption. It seemed so unlike the ever-friendly and mild-mannered Eirík. Maybe Eirík just wanted to make sure that he would stick to their agreement. True, he had wavered, but no longer.

When Ragnar returned to his booth, he only saw Hallgerður. "Where is Guðmundr? I wish to speak with him."

"He must be meeting friends", Hallgerður replied. "He has not been to a Thing for some years, so he probably has a lot of people to greet."

"Hm. As long as he is present tomorrow morning."

Guðmundr had indeed gone out to look for someone. He was sure Jórunn would be at the Thing. It might be dangerous to try to sneak a tryst with her here, but his heart ached for her, or even just the sight of her flaming red hair – he hadn't seen her for far too long now.

He would need to find her away from her father or her brother, though. That meant away from their booth, and probably somewhere in the market that always took place at the Thing. He walked around the booths aimlessly, attempting to avoid anyone who might want to talk to him and at the same time trying to keep an eye out for bright red hair. He was so intent on Jórunn and her hair colour that he didn't notice another girl until he bumped into her and almost tripped over her. He reached out to steady himself and grabbed her. It was only when he managed to rebalance himself that he recognised Ása. She recognised him at the same time and blushed.

"Oh, it's you", he said.

Her smile faded. "Yes."

"Is your friend here as well?"

"Yes, Jórunn is here."

"Ah, you wouldn't know where she is?"

Ása looked at him. "What is it worth to you?"

"What do you mean?"

"Never mind. Yes, I know where she is", she replied tartly. "Come with me and I will take you to her." And she took his hand and dragged him off.

Guðmundr was surprised at how warm her hand felt. It felt rather pleasant, actually. Ása was nice, of course, but she didn't have the spark – that something – that Jórunn had that made him want to be with her all the time.

Ása pulled him along through the maze of tents and booths. After what seemed like an eternity, he suddenly spotted Jórunn, sitting with some other young men and women, chatting and laughing. The danger of a meeting with his love melted in the face of Guðmundr's need to speak to her.

He turned to Ása. "Can you go and tell her that I am here? I would prefer that people not know that we meet."

Ása stared at him, with a mixture of pity and what looked like contempt. But she released his hand and nodded. Then she went up to Jórunn and whispered something in her ear. Jórunn seemed surprised and didn't move, so Ása whispered again, tugging at her. Now Jórunn did say something to the others, laughed and then left, following Ása.

Guðmundr had retreated behind a booth, out of sight of Jórunn's friends. When she and Ása came around the corner, she looked around, at first not spotting him. Then she saw him and smiled. "Guðmundr."

"Jórunn! I haven't seen you for ages." He made to embrace her, but she held him off. "Not here. Come."

The sun was beginning to slide towards the horizon as Jórunn led him away from the market, away from the booths and to a nearby hill. Ása was still trailing along, until Jórunn turned to her and said, "Thank you Ása. We don't really need you now."

Ása didn't say anything, just looked at them, turned and left.

They followed a winding path through the undergrowth until they had turned a shoulder of the hill and came to a grassy glade, well back from the path. As soon as they were out of sight of any chance observer, Jórunn threw herself at Guðmundr. "Have you missed me?" He didn't reply, trying to kiss her. At first she laughed and pretended to fend him off, but soon she started plucking at the laces of his tunic instead. He was tearing at her clothes, trying to kiss her everywhere, on her lips, her eyes, her neck and moving down to caress and kiss her breasts as they became visible. She tasted of honey, he thought. He heard her breath becoming more ragged and felt her nipples stiffening under his mouth. Her own hand was urgently feeling inside his trousers, where he rapidly responded to her touch. They sank down into the grass, still trying to caress and fondle every part of the other's body, rolling round until they were finally rid of enough clothes. Guðmundr was on his back when Jórunn gave a little laugh and sat on top of him, slowly sinking down as he penetrated her. Then she started riding him, slowly at first, but picking up speed until with a moan he spent himself in her.

Afterwards, they lay side by side in the grass. They had barely spoken since Ása had left them. "Yes, I missed you", Guðmundr said. "I miss you all the time. I go mad when you are not with me."

"That is how I like you", she replied, leaning over him and biting his ear gently.

"Did you miss me?" he asked.

"Do you want me to?"

"Of course I want you to miss me."

"Well, let me think. Maybe. A little bit. I am sure there must have been some day in the winter when I had nothing to do and suddenly thought of you. If there was, then I am almost sure, yes quite certain, that I probably missed you." She laughed again.

Guðmundr sighed. She was always like this, teasing him when they were alone. Why couldn't she say something straightforward for once? He knew what he wanted; he wanted her. But what did she want? As long as their fathers were enemies, this was the most he could have. But hopefully this would now change. He was tempted to tell her what would happen the next day, but his father had impressed on him that nobody must know. He didn't fear that Jórunn would tell her father, but if she did let something slip and it turned out that it came from him – well, better not to think about that.

"What now?" he asked instead.

"Now", she said, "I will carefully smooth out my clothes and then go and meet my father. He will ask what I have been doing. I will tell him that I just bedded Guðmundr Ragnarsson."

"What?!"

"Don't be silly. Of course I won't. I will tell him that I spent the evening with Ása and my friends. After all, I did spend the evening with friends. Are you not my friend?"

She leaned over and kissed him deeply, pushing her tongue into his mouth. But just as he began to respond, she suddenly rolled away and stood up, brushing grass off her skirt and trying to bring some order to her hair.

"We don't have time. I am sure your father is looking for you as well."

"When will I see you again?"

"Tomorrow. Or maybe the day after. Or the next day." And before he could stop her, she ran off, laughing aloud.

Muttering darkly to himself, Guðmundr also got up and rearranged his clothes. Then he walked back through the market stalls, enlivened now with the sounds of people eating and drinking, of friends reunited. When he approached the Snæströnd booths, he saw Ragnar sitting outside, with a mug of beer.

"Where have you been?" his father asked.

"With friends", Guðmundr replied.

"Yes, your mother said you would be. Well, make sure you get some sleep. I want you along tomorrow morning. It is important."

"Yes, Father. Good night."

"Good night." But Ragnar did not go to sleep for a long time. He remained with his beer, thinking about what the morrow would bring. He hoped he was doing the right thing. But he still had difficulty accepting the humiliation it would entail, even for the sake of peace. Was there another way? Probably not. Anyway, it was decided. Above him, the sun had finally set for the short summer night. He looked up at the stars and wondered what they were looking down at.

The next morning Ragnar still felt uneasy about what was to happen. However, one look at Hallgerður made him realise that even broaching the subject with her would be worse than useless. Instead, he carefully weighed out the right amount of silver, which he put into a purse and then tied to his belt. While he was doing this, Guðmundr joined him and asked "Is it time?"

"It is time", Ragnar affirmed. And then they walked out to the Thing plain. After his talk with Eirík the previous evening, he was not surprised to see the plain more crowded than ever before. For a brief moment he thought of just flinging the silver to the ground and disappearing in disgust, but he fought down the impulse and walked up to Eirík, even stopping on the way to greet the odd acquaintance. There were others he did not want to acknowledge. Nearby he spotted Gunnar, sitting, he felt, like a fat slug, surrounded by his hangers-on, including his son Einar and Leifur.

Eirík turned to welcome him. "Just in time", he said. Then he turned to face the Thing.

"Men of the Thing, there is a matter that needs resolution. The noble Gunnar goði has told you of his case against Ragnar Snæströnd, and the Thing has decreed that since the noble Gunnar does not, of course, lie, then his claim is good. But it has not been paid. This pains me, for all men must see the true worth of the noble Gunnar's claim. So I have spoken with Ragnar, and he now asks to speak to the Thing."

There was a murmur of excitement and then the Thing quietened as all eyes turned to Ragnar, who stepped forward to stand beside Eirík.

"Men of the Thórsnesthing, hear me", he began. "You know very well the matter between me and Gunnar." Eirík might refer to Gunnar as 'the noble Gunnar', he thought, but Hel would take him before he used that term.

"You know that I disputed his account. When the Thing found in his favour, I disagreed. I appealed, and the Thing once again found in his favour."

To the side he could see Gunnar leaning forward and whispering something to Leifur, who laughed. He was sure they were enjoying this.

"Now, there are those who would simply ignore the ruling of the Thing. They do this because they have sufficient might to do so, knowing that to force them to comply is beyond the powers of the Thing. This is tempting. Why should I submit to a ruling which I know is false, if I am able to ignore it? And yet, we all know that this is wrong. By submitting to a ruling, even if false, a case is closed. By refusing to submit, events can grow, and soon men will turn from bad words to harsh words and from harsh words to the duelling ground."

He swallowed.

"But it is not just that. We Icelanders are proud of the fact that we have no king. We have that which is greater than any king – we have our Law, the Law that is read every year at the Althing by the Lawspeaker to remind us. But for the Law to work, everyone must accept it. Nobody should say 'I am above the Law.' Because if that happens, soon everyone will be above the law and what would we then have? No, everybody has to obey the law and submit."

Ragnar paused again. Now he had to say it. He suddenly realised that he had been hoping for something – anything – to happen that would make it unnecessary, but now there was no longer any delay possible.

"And so, Men of the Thing, I stand here and say that I submit to your verdict."

There, now he had said it. Curiously, he felt lightheaded, as if finally saying it had made it go away. It was almost as if a pain he had expected never actually materialised.

"I am ready to pay Gunnar the fine decided by the Thing, and I will do so now."

He stopped and began to walk towards Gunnar, who stood up with a wide smile on his face. As Ragnar approached him, a steady murmur of approval began to be heard from the assembled Thing.

When Ragnar was close enough, he untied the purse from his belt and handed it over, saying "Gunnar, as agreed by the Thing, herewith the value in silver of one half walrus. And I hope this now sets matters aright between us."

Gunnar held out his hand weighed the purse. Then he said, "I accept this, as is my right." The words were fair, and yet Ragnar felt that it was almost said grudgingly, as if Gunnar had expected or even hoped that Ragnar would never pay him. Then Gunnar continued, "Fine words, Ragnar. But the world would be better if men used fewer fine words and instead honoured the decisions of this Thing willingly and upheld the law."

For a brief moment, there was silence. Then a voice shouted out from somewhere behind them, "It would be better, Gunnar goði, if men did not abuse the law for personal gain!", followed by much louder sounds of approval from the assembly.

Ragnar did not trust himself to say anything. Instead, he turned around and walked back to Eirík, looking neither right nor left. Eirík gripped his arm and leaned closer. "Well said, Ragnar. Well said and even better done!"

"Thank you", Ragnar mustered. But he really did feel as if a weight had lifted from his chest.

"Will you stay?" Eirík asked.

"I think I would prefer not having to watch Gunnar gloat, if you do not mind. Is there any reason why I cannot leave?"

"None. But stay until the Thing is finished."

"I will."

As they walked off together, Guðmundr was clearly trying to say something. Ragnar waited, and eventually the younger man said, "Thank you, Father."

"Why?" Ragnar was puzzled.

"For what you did. It was the right thing."

"Oh. I am glad you approve. At least now you will be able to live in peace with your neighbours."

But Guðmundr was not thinking about that. His thoughts were rather with his own future. With Gunnar and his father no longer enemies, the time had surely come for him and Jórunn to be more open about their relationship. He wanted to run off and tell her, but first he felt he should follow his father back.

"As for me", Ragnar continued, "I hope it will be a long time before I have to see Gunnar again, or speak to him."

Guðmundr felt a twinge when he heard this. His father would not be happy if he knew of his hopes for Jórunn. But he would just have to accept it. And surely now that he had settled his feud with Gunnar, he would eventually relent on this as well.

Hallgerður was waiting for them outside the booth. She didn't need to ask – she could see that things had gone well. She had been worried that Ragnar would baulk before going through with the plan, but it was clear from both men – Ragnar looking dissatisfied and yet relieved, as if a weight was off his mind, Guðmundr looking pleased – that this had not happened.

She moved forward to meet them and held out her arms to embrace Ragnar. "Well done", she said.

He sighed and held her close. Then he stepped back and his face suddenly lightened as he said, "Well, that's that."

While his parents embraced, Guðmundr decided that this was a good time to disappear. Even though he was keen to find Jórunn, at first he wandered aimlessly among the booths. Then he finally decided he could wait no longer and started out in the direction of Gunnar's booth. All things considered, it was probably still best to come there while the Thing was still deliberating and both Gunnar and Einar were away.

In the end, he didn't have to go all the way. As he had half suspected would be the case, Jórunn was walking through the market with Ása. He hurried up towards them. Ása spotted him first and said something to Jórunn, who turned around. When she saw him, she smiled and dismissed Ása. The blonde girl looked sullenly at her friend but walked off.

Guðmundr came up to Jórunn. "Let us go somewhere else. I have something to say to you."

"I hope it is something nice", the girl laughed.

"Oh yes, it is nice." He took her hand and led her back to the glade where they had spent the previous afternoon. He had only intended to bring her there because the spot was secluded. But once they were there, the memory of the previous day's events came flooding back. He turned to Jórunn and kissed her. She tried to fend him off at first but then began to respond. Between the kisses, she said, "Weren't you going to tell me something?"

"That can wait", he muttered, lifting her skirt.

This time their coupling was even faster than before. It was not long before they were lying in the grass, tearing at each other's clothes. Suddenly she bit his lip. He could feel the blood running down his chin. She licked it up and laughed.

When they were finished, Guðmundr looked at her. She never seemed more desirable than at times like these. Her red hair was in disarray, but her face looked like a cat who had just licked a whole bowl of cream. Her clothes were dishevelled, with one breast exposed and the other half hidden, while her skirt was dragged up well above her thighs. For that matter, his own clothes were not particularly decent either.

"Was this what you were going to tell me?" she asked, arching her eyebrows.

"No, no. This was what your presence does to me."

"I like that", she laughed. "I clearly need to be in your presence more often."

"Now you can."

"What do you mean?"

"Don't you know what happened today at the Thing?"

"No." She looked at him and wondered why he was suddenly looking so serious and solemn. Then she suddenly realised and started to speak.

But before she could say anything, Guðmundr spoke rapidly: "My father paid the fine he owed to your father. This means the feud is over. We can tell them how we feel. My father can speak to your father, and we can be wed. The sooner the better." His face glowed with pleasure and he reached out for her.

"Guðmundr, wait."

"What?"

"Just wait a moment."

"But why? Don't you love me?"

"Let me speak." She moved away from him and tried to arrange her clothes. This was not something to be said half-naked. Guðmundr looked at her in surprise and with some apprehension. He tried to move closer to her, but she held up her hand.

"Stop. Please sit and listen." He looked bewildered but stopped and waited obediently.

"Guðmundr, I like you. I really like you. I enjoy what we are doing. Nobody brings me pleasure as well as you."

"Then what –"

"Please don't speak. As I said, I really like you. But there are two problems here. The first is that my father would never dream of letting me marry you, feud or no feud."

"Why not?"

"My father is a goði. Your father may be rich, but he is not a goði, and your family came well after the Settlement. Yes, my father may not be as wealthy, but he will not let me marry anyone who is not from another goði family, or maybe a noble from Orkney or Norway.

"But this is not the only reason."

"What do you mean?"

"Guðmundr, this may be difficult for you to understand, but – I actually don't want to marry anyone."

"What?"

"I don't want to marry anyone. If I marry someone, what will happen? Oh, I will become the mistress of a farm somewhere, yes, maybe a large one, but still. My life will be all about the farm, going from sowing to harvest, supervising farmhands and maids, making butter and cheese and counting the newly-born lambs. I will be expected to birth children regularly and to listen to and obey my mother-in-law and my husband."

"But – what is wrong with that? This is what women do."

"This is what some women do, Guðmundr. This is not what I do, nor what I want to do. I am a free woman. I see who I want to, I do what I want to, I even bed who I want to when I want to. I do not wish to give this up, nor do I see why I should."

"I don't understand." Guðmundr really did not understand what she was saying. What did she mean? This was what people were supposed to do. It was as if he had suddenly said that he did not want to be a farmer.

"I thought you loved me? I love you!"

Jórunn sighed. How could she explain to him if he didn't want to understand? Then she smiled and caressed his cheek. "I know you do, Guðmundr. And I think this is sweet. And I like you. Maybe I even love you. But not enough to marry you, even if it were possible, and it is not."

"Does this mean that I will never see you again?"

"That is up to you. I told you, I like you and I enjoy what we do. I will see you again. But only if you forget all thought of wedding me."

Guðmundr just stared. Of all the possible answers to what he had to say, this was one he had never expected. He shied away from her caressing fingers and straightened his clothes. Then, without a word, he turned and rapidly walked away.

Jórunn looked after him. Should she call him back? Part of her wanted to. She had told him the truth. She really enjoyed what they did, very much so. But if she called him back now, would he not just believe that everything she had said was meaningless? Before she could finish her thoughts, he had disappeared over the hill.

Once Jórunn was out of sight, Guðmundr began to run. Somehow, he felt that running would clear away what had just happened. He still couldn't believe that Jórunn had turned him down, certainly not for those silly reasons.

He ran through the market and past the Thing plain, which was now emptying as the day's business was over, and towards the booths. He could already see Ragnar's booth ahead when he suddenly hit someone. Both he and the other person fell. Guðmundr began to snap something, when the other cried out, and he realised it was a woman. He stopped himself and got to his feet, holding out a hand to help her as well. "Why don't you look where you are going, you clumsy oaf!" she exclaimed.

"Ása?"

"Oh. It's you. You should still look out. I hope I haven't torn any clothes."

He looked at her but, not knowing what to say, stayed silent. When she stood up she looked at him, noting his dishevelled state. "What have you done? Where is Jórunn? I thought you were with her."

He suddenly found his voice. "Don't talk to me about her", he muttered. "Look, Ása, I'm sorry. I apologise. I didn't see you."

"Well, that was clear. But what happened to you? No, don't tell me. I know. Jórunn told you, didn't she?"

He did not pretend not to understand. "You knew?"

"Of course I knew. She thinks I am a little mouse to whom she can say anything and who doesn't have any thoughts of her own except what she tells me to have. Oh, I knew that this would happen."

"You are not a little mouse!" Guðmundr was surprised by his own vehemence.

"Perhaps. But Jórunn thinks I am."

"Why did you not tell me?"

"Would it have helped? I knew you were besotted by her. Oh, I wanted to tell you long ago that you were far too good for her. She doesn't deserve someone like you."

Now Guðmundr was surprised by her bitterness. "I thought you liked her?"

"We were close friends when we were little girls. And since then, we have continued to be with each other when we meet. I do like her – but I know what she is like."

"Oh. I had no idea."

"It is not easy if your father is not wealthy or a goði. You take what company you can."

Guðmundr had never heard Ása speak like this; indeed she had seldom spoken much to him at all. He realised that he didn't even know very much about her or her family.

He didn't know what to say. Instead he thought about what Ása had just said. "What do you mean, I am far too good for her?"

"Look at you: you are handsome, you are the son of the wealthy Ragnar Snæströnd, you are kind and a good man. Anyone would wish to be with you. But you go to the one person in Iceland who will never be yours."

Once again, Guðmundr was taken aback. "I didn't know you thought this", he said. "Um, are you hurt? Do you wish to go and sit down somewhere?"

"I am fine. You can leave me."

"No, I don't want to." Guðmundr wasn't sure why he said this. But Ása was Jórunn's friend; or at least she knew Jórunn better than anyone else he knew. Maybe she could explain why Jórunn had behaved so strangely.

"I want to make sure you are not hurt", he said lamely. "You might have a swelling or something. Let us go and sit somewhere until you are sure you are well."

"Thank you. I think I hurt my foot when I fell. Can you hold me?" She did not wait for an answer but leaned against him as they walked a short way to a little dip that was a bit more secluded. Ása sat down and indicated that Guðmundr should sit next to her. She had put on a show of limping a bit; she was indeed slightly hurt, though perhaps not as much as she was pretending, but this was the first time she had been alone with Guðmundr and she was not going to let that go to waste. She had seen enough of him when she had been with Jórunn to know that he really was not only good-looking, but also a good man. Jórunn might think she was a mouse, but she herself knew this was not true. And so although Guðmundr had thought of finding out more about Jórunn from her, he found himself instead telling her about himself, about his family, about Kári and about Snæströnd. It was only much later that he managed to ask her questions, and then he felt that first he should ask her about herself. By then, he had already realised that he liked speaking with her. So much so that they continued talking long after the sun had finally set and most others had left to retire to their own booths. He even forgot to ask her if she was still in pain. And somehow they never got on to the topic of Jórunn, although Guðmundr constantly kept thinking of bringing it up.

When Guðmundr had left them, Ragnar was silent for short while. Then he asked Hallgerður to bring him something to drink. It was only after he had drunk his beer that he sat down and told her what had happened. Hallgerður listened in silence and then asked, "How difficult was it?"

Ragnar thought for a while before he replied. He remembered his feelings at the time. "It was worse before it happened", he finally said.

"It always is. But you know it was right. Now what?"

"Now we wait until the Thing is over, and then we go home and wait for Kári to come back. I wonder how he has fared."

"So do I. But I meant right now?"

"Right now", Ragnar said, "I think I need more beer."

"If you are going to drink more, I think you should go to the market." Ragnar looked at her, but Hallgerður was already pushing him away from the booth in the direction of the market, and he knew better than to argue when his wife was in her determined mood.

When Ragnar had gone, Hallgerður sat down to think. Peace with Gunnar – that was good, always assuming it would hold. But now the issue of Guðmundr and Jórunn was bound to come up. She guessed why Guðmundr had disappeared, but when he came back, she wanted to hear from him first. If Jórunn had agreed to wed him, she would have to think about how to ensure that Ragnar would accept it.

Ragnar walked over to the market where he found the aleman and asked him for a beer. He didn't want any company, so he made sure to sit in a corner with his back turned to the entrance, drinking first one mug of beer and then another few. He thought the beers would make him feel better about what he had done, but they didn't seem to help much.

While he was sitting there, the sun moved slowly across the sky and eventually began to sink closer towards the horizon. It was clear that the Thing deliberations had ended because the tent was filling up with noisy men discussing the day's business. Suddenly he thought he heard his name mentioned behind him and to his right. He did not want to turn round but leaned in that direction to hear better.

"Ragnar Snæströnd? Why do you ask? I've never liked him."

"Neither have I. Thinks too much of himself and doesn't mind showing it."

"True." There was a pause, probably due to the man drinking. "But, I have to say that today he behaved well."

"I agree. He may be proud, and rather too eager to prove he is always right, but he showed himself to be a man of honour."

"Yes. I used to think that all his fine words about 'no one being above the law' and 'everybody equal before the Law' were just words. But today he showed that he meant it."

"I don't know if I would have done the same."

"What do you mean?"

"Everybody knew that Gunnar's case was weak and probably based on a lie. Why would someone pay a fine that is clearly unjust? Would you?"

"Maybe." Another pause for drinking. Ragnar was trying to identify the voices, but they were not familiar enough, and the beers he had already drunk made it even more difficult to think straight.

"Probably not", the man resumed.

"See what I mean? Ragnar did. I think he really means what he says about the law. Maybe it is not all for show after all."

"Like I said, he showed himself to be a man of honour, and I think a lot of people agree."

"Yes, I think you are right. They say Gunnar didn't like it, but he certainly needs the silver."

"I thought he was rich?"

"He wants people to think that. I have heard from people who know that he is badly in debt."

That was interesting, Ragnar thought. Was that why Gunnar had started this whole case, which both of them knew was based on a lie? Because he needed silver? True, he had never heard that Gunnar had been a successful trader, but he had a large farm and his wealth must come from somewhere. But what did this matter to him? He drained the last beer in the mug and put it down, wiping his mouth and standing up. He would have liked to know who the two men were, but when he turned around, the seats where they must have been sitting were empty. By now the sun had just set and he began to walk somewhat unsteadily back towards his own booth. Thinking about what the men said made him feel better and he suddenly remembered a drinking song that he had known in his youth. He wondered if he still remembered it. How did it go? Something, something, beer, something something, gods, something, rowing. It came to him and he began to sing as he walked back.

*

The next morning, Ragnar woke with a headache. Hallgerður seemed strangely unsympathetic, merely asking if he wanted to sing some more for the benefit of everyone in the vicinity. Ragnar decided that the best thing to do was to ignore her, so he walked over to the Thing plain again. By the time he arrived it was already mid-morning, and it was clear that he had missed something important. When people saw him there was a murmur, and while some men stepped out of his way, others made a point of coming up and greeting him. In truth, the way his head felt, he would have preferred if no one had done so, but he forced himself to be polite and speak a few words with each one who addressed him. When he finally reached Eirík, the goði turned to him and said, "Ragnar! I was worried that something had happened to you. I was so sure that you were going to be here as soon as we began."

Ragnar felt confused. "Why? Surely we dealt with everything yesterday."

"We did, with Gunnar. But have you forgotten your case against Leifur? Once you had paid your fine to Gunnar, you were free to proceed against Leifur. Surely you knew that."

Ragnar groaned. He did know. Or, rather, he had known. How could he have forgotten? If only the sun would kindly shine a little less strongly in his face, he could think more clearly.

"I am sorry", he finally muttered. "Completely forgot. Am I too late?"

"Not at all. Fortunately, you had given me the right to bring this case. And several people told me that they had seen, actually, heard, I think they said, you last night. So I decided to move without you. After all, it is an old case and everyone knew what it was about, so there really was no need for further speeches."

"Oh." Ragnar felt confused. He shook his head to try to clear it. "What happened?"

"I think you impressed the Thing yesterday. Anyway, they found in your favour. Leifur has been told to pay you a fine to settle. The fine is half again as much as you paid Gunnar."

"What?"

"Yes. In truth, it is quite high. But I think it was a combination of people respecting what you did yesterday, annoyance with Gunnar for bringing a case that most of us knew was false, and a desire to honour you and strike at one of Gunnar's supporters."

"I don't know what to say."

"My experience", Eirík said, "is that saying nothing is sometimes the best course. And that is what I think you should do right now. In any case, Leifur hasn't paid yet and we will see if he does. I expect he will appeal."

"Yes", Ragnar said. Then he thought for a moment. "I want you to know, this was not why I did what I did. The silver is not important."

"I know", Eirík replied. "And so does everybody else. You could not know how this would turn out. And you made very clear yesterday why you paid. I don't think anyone doubts that. Some people may not like you, but I think everybody respects you and knows now that you uphold the law."

'Some people may not like you', Ragnar thought. Yes, that was what he had heard last night. And at other times in the past. But that was not important. He would do what he felt was right.

He decided that he would stay until the end of the Thing. Like Eirík, he very much doubted that Leifur would pay the fine, but he did not want him to have an excuse to avoid paying. As expected, however, nothing further happened that day. Leifur was nowhere to be seen.

That evening, Gunnar sat down with his son. Events had not gone the way he desired at this Thing. At first, Einar was puzzled.

"Why are you not happy? Ragnar paid up and you have more silver today than you had yesterday. Surely that is good?"

"Have you not been listening for the past five years? Of course, the silver is welcome."

"Then why did you not force Ragnar to pay you earlier?"

"Because in the first place, this wasn't really about the silver. And in the second place, yes, I can persuade people to support me with their words at the Thing, but when it comes to supporting me with their swords to enforce the Thing's decision, it is another matter."

"I don't understand. Why is that?"

"Because everyone knew that my case was false. Therefore, it was not about the silver, which I never really thought Ragnar would pay anyway. I can certainly put the silver to good use. But there are more important things going on."

"You mean Eirík? Is that why you brought a false case?"

Gunnar sighed. His son really was stupid. Why could not Jórunn have been born a man instead? She was clever and he would not have had to explain to her, certainly not after discussing the issue so many times.

"Yes, Eirík. Because of him, I initially supported Ragnar against Leifur because Ragnar had a better case and he is rich. But Ragnar is not well liked, and in any case, he is not free with his wealth. Oh, he is always ready to disperse advice and talk about the Law and of how proud he is that he still owns a ship 'like Icelanders of old'. But he holds tightly to his silver. Leifur is poor but has many friends. So by supporting Leifur, I gained followers, but not wealth. I guessed that Eirík would try to gain Ragnar's allegiance in return for his support – they are both of the same mind, with their loud reverence for 'the Law'. But as long as Ragnar refused to pay, Eirík's position was also weaker. But now Ragnar has paid. And worse, the Thing liked him and he won the case against Leifur and much honour besides. Not only that, he gained more silver. So Ragnar has gained and Eirík has gained. Leifur has lost, and even though I gained some silver, I too have therefore lost. Now do you understand?"

"Well, yes. But surely this was just one case. You still have a larger following than Eirík."

Gunnar wondered why his son couldn't understand. It was not enough to leave things be. If you wanted to be powerful, you always had to make sure that your power increased. If it didn't increase, it would sooner or later shrink. Surely that was obvious?

"Let me try to explain. I did not bring a false case because I like doing that. The times are changing. Iceland is changing. It is important that people who understand this change can help to guide it. Eirík and his friends – people like Ragnar – they think life can always remain the way it was. Now, I'm the first to say the old days were good. But they do not last forever."

"I don't understand what that has to do with Eirík?"

"When change comes, there are three types of men. There are those who resist it; there are those who accept it; and there are those who try to lead and control and guide the change, for the benefit of everyone else and for their country. Do you understand that?"

"I think so."

Gunnar sighed again. "Well, Eirík and Ragnar, they are the type of man who talk about the old days, the Law, the traditions. They resist any change at all cost. And by doing that, they cause harm, because change cannot be resisted. So they create discord and strife."

"But is all change good?"

"No. But a clever man, a great man, can discern when change is good and when it is necessary."

"I see. But you said three types of men?"

"I did. The second type, as I said, is the one that accepts change, but doesn't know how to guide it. He doesn't know how to ensure that it turns out for the best. And then there is the third kind of man, men like us. We are the ones who see change coming and who spend time pondering how to make use of it and to ensure that it is good for everybody. And when change comes, we try to ensure that it is smooth and trouble-free. But to do that, we cannot have men like Eirík and Ragnar standing in the way. This is why we need to diminish the influence of people like them. And so, therefore, we must from time to time do things which we would not otherwise do and which lesser men might think are shameful if they do not understand the reasons why."

"But what are these changes?"

"Can you not see around you? The power of the White Christ and his church is growing. So is the power of kings. How long can Iceland remain alone in the sea without a strong man to lead us?"

At this point, the entrance to their booth was flung open and a tall, thin man with a pockmarked face strode in. He blinked to adjust his eyes to the darker interior, then he spotted Gunnar and Einar.

"This is your fault, Gunnar!" he shouted. "Now you have to help me out!"

Gunnar looked at the newcomer. "Leifur", he replied, "how good to see you. Do come in and have a seat. Einar, please pour some beer for our guest." The younger man stood up and Leifur flung himself down in his place. His face was red and he seemed ready to burst.

"Calm down, my friend", Gunnar said. "What can be so upsetting?"

"Calm down? That is easy for you to say. The rich and powerful Gunnar goði can afford to calm down. But I can't. You saw what happened today. I lost my case and now I have to pay that self-satisfied fool from Snæströnd more silver than I have ever seen. Where will I get that from? No, this is all your fault."

Einar reappeared with a mug of beer, which the other man drained in two gulps before handing the mug back and saying "More!" Einar looked as if he was going to say something, but his father waived at him to get more and returned his attention to Leifur.

"Come now, you are overwrought. Why is this my fault?"

"You said you would support my case. This was why I was prepared to swear that you were right in your case against Ragnar, even though I knew you were not. You told me that Ragnar would never pay and so his case against me would never go anywhere. Well, you were wrong! Ragnar paid and now I have to pay him."

"Not yet, you don't. Let us begin by appealing. After all, Ragnar did not pay for many years."

"Yes, but now he has paid. And the Thing thinks he was in the right and gave him victory in my case. Anyway, I do not have the silver. You will have to give me money."

Gunnar thought that the last thing he was going to do was to give this fool the silver he had just received in order to see it go back to Ragnar and to Eirík. But softly, softly. It would not do to have Leifur also deciding that perhaps another goði would be of greater help to him.

"Let us not be so hasty", he said. "At the moment, no one is paying anybody anything. The Thing concludes tomorrow. We will have plenty of time to think about how to deal with this afterwards. But rest assured that I, your goði, will look after your interests and help you with this."

"You had better", the aggrieved Leifur replied. "If not – well, who knows?"

Time, Gunnar reflected. First he needed to gain some time. And then he would think of another way of hitting back at Ragnar and weakening Eirík. Maybe the White Christ would help him; people said that he helped those who prayed to him and who were his friends and those of his church. And, of course, he was a good Christian – had always been, in fact.

Chapter 5

Summer 1060

They continued to be lucky with the weather, including a steady breeze which meant that little rowing was necessary. While they sailed along the coast, Odd told Kári about the lands they passed, first Scotland and later Northumbria. From time to time they would spot towns on the coast, but apart from mentioning their names, Odd ignored them. "We're headed for Jórvik and that's where we will go", he said.

They finally reached a river mouth half closed by a long sand spit, and there Odd told them to take down the sail and start rowing west and up the river. "This is the Humber", he said. "We go up the Humber until we reach the Ouse, and then up the Ouse to Jórvik. This is hard rowing, but it'll be worth your while, lads. The beer in Jórvik is better than in Kirkjuvágr."

It took them another two days at the oars to reach Jórvik. When they reached the city, the densely-packed houses spilling out beyond the city walls, Kári was amazed. Now he fully understood what a big city really was like and why Odd had been so disparaging about Kirkjuvágr. In front of him, to his right as they rode up the river, he saw the large church that Odd said was called the Minster. But it was not the only one. He could see the towers of other churches all around him, on both sides of the river.

And the people! Everywhere, throngs of people, coming or going, just standing, talking to each other. There were soldiers as well. Not like the two sleepy hirdmen in Kirkjuvágr; these were alert guards, patrolling in groups of five or six. When they reached the bridge over the river, they saw larger groups of soldiers on each side. Once they were within earshot, one of them called down, "That's far enough. Who are you and where are you from?"

Odd ordered the rowers to back water, while he looked at Kári, who swallowed nervously. Was he supposed to reply? What if the soldiers asked for silver?

He opened his mouth, but couldn't make any sound. Then he closed it, breathed deeply and tried again. "We are traders from Iceland", he shouted up.

"What?" the soldier shouted down. "Speak clearly so I can understand you."

Kári had some trouble understanding him as well. He tried again. "From Iceland", he called out, slowly and carefully. "Traders."

Now the soldier seemed to understand. He said something to his comrades, who laughed. Then he called down, also speaking slowly. "Find a berth along the quay. And wait there."

Kári turned to Odd. "You heard him. Let's find a berth."

"Very good, young master", Odd said, grinning as he instructed the rowers.

When they had secured the knarr along the stone quay that lined the riverbank, Odd and Kári waited while five soldiers, led by the man who had spoken with them, approached.

"From Iceland?" he said, still speaking slowly. "What are you carrying?"

Now that he was closer, Kári found that he could understand the soldier more easily than he had thought. Nevertheless, he decided to speak slowly and carefully as well. "Walrus hides and ivory and wadmal, to trade for wood and other goods."

The soldier also seemed to find that he was picking up the Icelandic accent. "Very good. Do not remove anything from your ship. A representative of the Jarl will come on board and assess the value of your load and your taxes. Two of my men will remain here and hold you until you are free to come ashore."

When he had disappeared, leaving the two guards, Kári looked at Odd, raising his eyebrows.

"No, this is different", Odd replied. "This is a tax we pay

to be allowed to trade freely in Jórvik and to benefit from the security here."

Kári felt confused. How did this differ from the extortion that Odd had talked about earlier? It was still the case that someone felt the right to take the traders' money because he was stronger. He said this to Odd and the older man tried to explain. "The difference is", he said, "that this is not whatever the guard fancies that day. It is decided by the Jarl or maybe the King. They say it is to pay for their rule and for the guards and the upkeep of the walls and the quays and everything else they do. And it doesn't change because someone wants more money on a particular day."

But Kári did not seem convinced, and Odd felt that the more he attempted to explain, the less convincing it sounded even to himself. What *was* the difference, really? Finally, he gave up, ending lamely, "Well, we still have to pay, yet it shouldn't be so bad. Maybe five silver pennies, seven at the most. Now we'd better see what we need for the ship while we are here."

It was well past noon when a richly-dressed man appeared, flanked by a group of guards, and demanded to be let on board. When his guards also attempted to board, Kári tried to stop them, but the man waved him aside. "Young man, these are my guards and my goods inspectors. If you want to trade here, step aside. Otherwise, you can return to whatever grubby hole in the ground you crawled out from."

Kári blushed and instinctively reached for his knife. But a look at the guards, armed with swords or spears, who looked at him with contemptuous stares, almost as if daring him to draw the knife, managed to halt him. With an effort, he swallowed and stepped aside. But he didn't trust himself to speak.

The man ignored him and walked over to the bales of goods stowed in the knarr, where he began to poke and lift the packs, looking inside and underneath. When he spotted the walrus tusks, his face lit up and he said, "Trying to hide something, I see. That will cost you. Jarl Tostig doesn't like cheats."

"We're not cheats!" Kári burst out. But before he could continue, Odd spoke up.

"We are hiding nothing. The ivory is under the hides and packed to be safe from water damage."

"So you say", the man sneered. "Would you have admitted to carrying valuable goods if I had asked? I am sure not. All traders are trying to cheat. It is time we put an end to that. But that is not for me to do. I am only here to assess your tolls. Thirty silver pennies."

Odd was astonished. That was far more than he had expected and more than four times what he had paid on his previous trading voyage to Jórvik with a similar cargo.

"You cannot be serious!" he exclaimed. "That is robbery! In that case we will leave, rather than stay and trade."

The man looked at him. "Leave or stay, that is up to you. But whatever you do, you will pay thirty silver pennies before the sun has set. If you have not paid by then, your goods will be sold and the fee taken from the price. Should there be anything left, you will of course receive it. Or pay up what is lacking."

Odd did a quick calculation in his head. They could still make a profit if they paid. Small, yes, but at least a profit. And they would have to sell all the goods they had brought and at the best price. But better that then leaving with less silver and no trade. He swallowed.

"We will pay."

"I thought you would", the man said. "Thirty pennies. Plus five pennies to compensate for the insults I had to suffer. And proper coinage, coinage of our King Edward."

Odd could see that Kári was about to burst, so before anything further happened, he counted out thirty-five silver pennies from his purse and handed them over with ill grace. The man took the money and left without another word.

When he was gone, Kári turned to Odd. "Thirty-five silver pennies! That's worth more than the half walrus that Gunnar tried to steal from my father. It is more than three sheep in value! You said five or seven!"

"That's what it should have been", Odd replied, conscious of the stares from the rest of the crew, who had followed the exchange. "I'm afraid we will all suffer from this. Everyone's profits will be lower. But we were in their power. What could we have done? And you will notice one thing: although the sum he named is high, it is not so high that we will not make a profit, so we will come back. Nor is it so low that we think nothing of it."

"Had we known, we should have hidden the most valuable parts of the cargo."

"He would have found them, and then we would have had to pay more."

"And you still want to come back to Jórvik?! We should have gone to Dyflin after all."

"Perhaps", Odd replied. "But now we are here. And do not think that I am unmoved or unsurprised by this. Things have happened since I was here last, and we now need to find out what they are and also where and with whom to trade."

"Another inn?" Kári asked.

"No. We will visit an old friend. But first, let's see what the ship needs."

It was dark before they had finished checking sails and ropes as well as the boat itself. Odd repeated that there was still no reason to expect anything to be fraying or breaking but that it was a good idea to always do this when you came to port.

As in Kirkjuvágr, the crew was then divided into three groups, and one of them drawn by lot sent ashore for the evening. Seeing the eagerness in their faces, Odd told them to be careful and not to drink too much. He reminded them that if they ended up in trouble with the locals or with the guards, any fines would be deducted from their father's profits, and then he let them go. Seeing them rush off, laughing and talking excitedly among themselves and staring at the city (while pretending not to), he sighed. "At least one of them will get drunk and end up fighting someone", he said.

"Which one?" Kári replied.

"If I knew, I would have tied him to his oar. It's just that it always happens. Now, you and I are going to visit Master Hákon."

"Who is he?"

"He is an old friend of mine – and of your father's. His father was from Norway, but he was born here. Both I and Ragnar usually trade with him. But above all, he knows everyone in Jórvik and also everything that happens."

Kári was glad that Odd was with him. If he had been alone, he would surely have been lost after all the twisting and turnings of the streets. Odd explained that it was easy enough to find your way once you knew where you were going, but that, in any case, all you needed to do was to remember where the Minster was. This, Kári felt, would only be helpful if you could see it. But it was dark and the houses frequently blocked the view of anything except the night sky directly overhead.

Soon, however, Odd stopped in front of an impressive-looking building. It had two floors, the lower one built from stone. He pounded on the door and, after a short while, a voice from inside asked nervously, "What do you seek?"

"Tell Master Hákon that Odd Barðsson from Iceland is here to see him."

"Wait."

But they didn't have to wait long before the door was opened and a young man, presumably the one who had spoken through the door, asked them to step in.

"Come with me", he said and led the way inside and up a staircase. Kári marvelled when he saw it. He had never seen a staircase inside a house previously, and precious few outside. It felt strange, but it was just as easy to use as an outside one.

They were ushered into a room lit with a large fire and some torches on the walls. A large man with a flowing white beard stood up to greet them. "Odd, my friend! I have not seen you for many years. What brings you to these shores? And this young man is your son, presumably?" Hákon spoke just like the soldier they had met when they arrived, but Kári soon found that as long as he listened carefully, he could understand him with no trouble.

The two men embraced, and then Odd said, "Not mine. This is Kári Ragnarsson."

"Ragnar's son? I knew your father very well. How is the old bear? You are welcome, boy – Kári, I should say. No longer a boy.

My son gets very annoyed if I call him a boy. Is that not so, Alfred?" he asked of the young man.

"As you say, Father", Alfred replied wearily, implying that he had heard this many times before.

"Bring ale for our guests, Alfred. And you two, sit down near the fire. Now, why are you here?"

As Alfred returned with mugs of ale, Odd replied "We are here to trade, what else?"

"I understand. But why now?"

"What do you mean?"

"Hmmm. Let me see, how long is it since you were last in Jórvik? More than five years?" Odd nodded.

"Well, we have a new jarl. Tostig he is called."

"Yes. We heard his name mentioned earlier."

"Not in a way that you liked, I'm sure", Hákon said. "To cut a long story short, he is a bad one. He loves money and the power it gives. But he doesn't have much money, so he is using the power he has to get more. You never know when there will be another new tax or toll imposed, or a 'voluntary contribution' called to cover the Jarl's expenses. In the beginning, we just paid, of course. But having paid doesn't mean that you are left alone. On the contrary, Tostig feels that those who can afford to pay must be wealthy, and so he revisits them with new demands. Not all the time, you understand. He is clever enough to leave you alone for a while so that you can make some more profit. Then he – or his men – come and take that. It is never enough to make you do more than protest and hope that you will be safe for the future, but always enough that you feel the loss."

"I know what you mean", Odd said. "They did it to us as well."

"Tolls at the river?"

"Thirty-five silver pennies!" Kári exclaimed. "Odd thought it would be five or maybe one or two more. And we were lucky that it wasn't even more."

"Yes, you probably were. I'm afraid that is what is happening now. And they are getting greedier. Two years ago it probably would have been fifteen silver pennies."

"What if we had not paid?" Kári asked. "They threatened to take our goods if we didn't."

"They would have. And you would have been lucky to escape with your freedom. I'm telling you, it is a bad city now."

"But if this is going on, why do traders still come here? Is it still worth their while? Who will trade in a city like this?"

Hákon smiled. "I can see you are Ragnar's son", he said. "The truth is, there are fewer and fewer coming. Some refused to pay and lost their goods, some were forced to pay. There was a time when dozens of ships would come to Jórvik every season. Now we are lucky to get a handful. Almost nobody from Denmark and Norway anymore, although there are some Flemish traders who are coming."

"This is truly bad", Odd said. "Will we find someone to trade with?"

"What do you have?"

"The usual. Walrus hides and ropes, walrus ivory, carved and uncarved. And wadmal."

"And buying?"

"Linen and wheat. And wax and tar if we can find any."

"Let's see. I will trade with you, of course. And I know some others who will as well. The Flemish buy cloth; they will buy your wadmal. You should be able to both sell and buy everything you need."

"At what prices?"

"Well, that is the strange thing. Because fewer traders are coming, the prices are good. In fact, you have probably never sold for these prices. Of course, what you want to buy is also more expensive, but I think you will find that, overall, your profits – and Ragnar's – will increase. But what is good for you is bad for us."

"Then why do you suffer this?" Kári asked.

"What can we do? Tostig has his housecarls, his armed guards. Of course, we all have arms. But it is one thing to wield a knife or a sword against someone trying to steal your purse or waylay your wagons on the road. It is something completely different to fight these men. And even if we did, what good would it do?"

"You would be rid of Tostig."

Alfred suddenly spoke up, having remained silent while his father talked. "No Kári, unless we kill him, we will not be rid of him. And whether we killed him or not, we would be rising against our King. He might agree that Tostig deserves it. But his writ doesn't run here. The real rulers here are Tostig's brothers – Harold above all. And they would be happy to destroy Jórvik."

"But then things can only get worse."

"You are right. Unfortunately, the strong do what they will, and the weak suffer what they must. I fear that Jórvik is dying. But we are not dead yet. Let us have some more ale and talk about trade matters instead."

While Odd and Hákon discussed trade, Kári drank the ale – which was far better than what he had drunk in Kirkjuvágr, or anywhere else for that matter – and listened. Occasionally Alfred would make a comment, but it was mainly the two older men who made plans and discussed prices.

It was late by the time they came back to the knarr. That night, Kári slept well. Even better, he found that he woke up without a headache. Maybe the ale here really was better than the beer at home. It certainly was better than the one in Kirkjuvágr. But why would it matter where the beer came from? Could it be the water? Or was it the grain? Or perhaps just the way it was brewed? Maybe Odd would know.

But when Kári got up, he found that Odd had already disappeared, leaving word that he had gone back to Hákon to discuss trade and leaving instructions for Kári to once again check their trade goods.

*

In the end they remained in Jórvik for more than two months. From time to time Odd would bring a stranger on board and show him what they had to sell. He would also go to other traders' houses to see what they had to offer. He would always bring Kári along, and whenever they left another trader or their visitor had left the knarr, he would sit down with Kári and go through what they had discussed. At first, Kári had some difficulty keeping track of all the details, but soon he began to find that he not only remembered, but that he liked it. He enjoyed comparing prices, discussing the quality of the goods he was selling or buying and trying to match his needs with those of others. And he found an even greater pleasure in finally agreeing to a trade. He realised that for all the arguments had when bargaining, in the end, a trade would only be struck if both buyer and seller felt that they did well out of it. More than one of the men they dealt with said at the end, "Look me up when you are next in Jórvik" or "when you come to Dyflin or Heiðabyr or Niðaros or Bergen". At first he feared that he had been taken advantage of and that they wanted to trade again because he was easy to fool. But he knew that he had made good deals.

The first time this happened, he asked Odd, who told him that they wouldn't say this if they had cheated him. "Someone who cheats you will try to avoid you in the future. Sooner or later, unless you are very stupid, you will realise that you were cheated. By letting people know, you will ruin the cheater's honour and trade. So he will do it once and hope you never see him again. If someone says they want to continue to trade with you, that is a compliment. It shows that they respect you. And it shows that they are satisfied with the trade. And you know that you traded well too. No, this is good for you. Make sure you remember who they are, where they come from and what your trade was. All of this will help you next time and the time after that."

There was only one episode where Kári felt he had made an embarrassing mistake. Early on, he had questioned the scales one of the traders used for weighing his silver. The man had looked at him scornfully and said, "Young man, if you had any experience of trading, you would know that you do not question a trader about his scales. Either you trust him or you don't. Let me tell you that if I cheated or if my scales were false, everyone would know soon enough. If you were older, I would tell you that a trader is always prepared to fight for his scales. But since you are still wet behind your ears, let me say this instead: we will weigh the silver which I pay you and the ivory which you sell me on the same scales. Then if my scales were false, they would play us both false by the same amount."

Kári listened to what the man said and blushed. "I meant no disrespect", he said. "You are right, this is my first trading voyage and I have much to learn. I apologise for causing any offence and thank you for the lesson you taught me."

The man laughed and clapped Kári on the shoulder. "Very good, young man. At least you know when you have made a mistake. Now we will forget this ever happened."

But when they left, Odd turned to Kári and said, "I thought better of you than that, Kári. You are lucky that he was in a good mood. Others would have thrown us out and just as soon made sure that nobody would trade with us. You do not insult traders if you want to keep a good name! What would you say if someone accused you of cheating or false trading?"

Until now, Kári had never seen Odd angry. This was a different side to his father's friend. But it also made him realise what a foolish thing he had done. "I am sorry", he said. "It will not happen again."

"Our friend here told you to forget it. I will tell you never to forget it. And you are right; it will never happen again."

Odd never spoke about this again, but Kári would from time to time think about it with embarrassment.

Most of the traders they dealt with were Norwegians or Danes or even English. But at least once, Kári was surprised when Odd brought two men on board and started speaking with them in a language that Kári could not understand at all. When the two had left again, Odd turned to Kári and said apologetically, "I realise you didn't understand. But these were Frisian merchants, and the only way we could speak with each other was in Latin."

"I didn't know you spoke Latin", Kári said.

"Oh yes. When I was very young, my father thought I should become a priest of the White Christ. He sent me to study, so I learned reading and writing and Latin. It is very useful."

"Oh." Kári once again thought of how little he knew about not just Odd but also his father, people he had spent his entire life with. Was this true of everyone he knew? But another thought was more urgent. "Should I learn this as well?"

"It will certainly be helpful to you. And you can at least read and write already. But you should know that the runes we use are different from the letters used in Latin. So it won't be easy. But yes, it is a good idea."

After twenty or twenty-five days, there was a change in their daily work. Traders would appear with bearers in tow. Kári and Odd would already have divided their goods according to their agreements with different merchants, and Kári had also begun to plan how to stow their purchases. So when buyers arrived, Kári would look at his lists and then he and some of the rowers would pick out the right goods and hand them over, in exchange for silver. Others would arrive with men carrying goods Kári and Odd had bought and would receive silver in return. After some days of this, all the trading goods they had brought were sold, with one single exception. This was a small piece of walrus ivory that Kári had found and begun to carve in the likeness of the knarr. When Odd had noticed, Kári had grinned sheepishly and said "I haven't carved ivory for so long, I thought I would try again. It is from my father's store, so I am sure he will understand."

But though their goods were gone, the knarr was not empty. In fact, it was if anything packed more tightly than when they came, with linen and beeswax, and also with wheat, carefully packed to keep it dry and ensure it would not spoil. Then there were some iron tools, from a trader who had been keen on getting walrus ivory but did not have enough silver to pay for his purchases and offered the tools in part exchange.

They had also bought supplies to last them on the way home and made arrangements to replenish their store of water.

When the knarr was finally full, Odd sat down with Kári and went through all their trades and accounts. It took time, but when they were finished, Odd looked pleased. "We have done well. *You* have done well, young master. Even counting the thirty-five silver pennies we had to pay here, our profits are higher than I had hoped."

"That is good", Kári replied. "But why?"

"I think there are two reasons. The first is that there are indeed fewer traders in Jórvik, just as everyone has said. So people who do come can get a better price. But the second reason is that you have shown yourself good at negotiating. I will tell Ragnar, and I am sure your father will be proud of you."

Kári glowed. Praise from Odd was praise indeed.

But their conversation was interrupted. Two soldiers appeared on the quay, dragging a man with them. Kári recognised one of the rowers, but he seemed the worse for wear, hanging from the arms of the soldiers. One of the soldiers called out "Are you Kári, from somewhere in Iceland?"

"I am he", Kári replied.

"Then this is one of your men." And they threw the rower on board, where he landed with a thud on a pack of linen.

"What is wrong with him?"

"Can't hold his beer. And tried to fight with everyone in the inn and with three men from the Jarl's hird." Now that Kári looked at the rower he could see that his nose was bleeding and one of his eyes was swollen shut. There also seemed to be more blood coming from a wound in his arm.

Odd spoke up. "Thank you for bringing him to the ship. Allow me to offer you some thanks." A silver penny suddenly showed up in his hand.

One of the soldiers came closer and the penny moved from Odd's hand to his. "Just make sure he doesn't do it again."

"Oh we will, have no fears."

The soldiers looked at the knarr and laughed. Then they disappeared. Odd and Kári went to look closer at the rower. But first Odd looked around. Seven of the crew had already come on board. With the drunken man back, that left two ashore. He called one of the men over and said "Find the other two and bring them back at once. Hurry!"

The man nodded and ran off towards the nearest inn. Kári looked at Odd. "We must leave!" Odd said.

"But –", Kári began. Then he shut up and nodded. Instead, he quietly ordered the remaining five crewmen to prepare the knarr and be ready to man the oars as soon as the missing men came on board.

And then he and Odd started to wash the blood off the drunken man. To their relief, his wounds didn't seem too bad. A broken nose, which Odd reset while the man was still unconscious, although he moaned with pain when it happened. A nasty cut to the arm, which they bound up. "You will have to row, young master", Odd said. "It will be some time before this fellow can man an oar."

"I know how to row. And I assume we are leaving because we do not wish to be fined for this fellow's behaviour?"

"Of course. Remember, I told you one of them would drink too much. At least it was only one, and at least he was good enough to wait until the end. If this was Kirkjuvágr, I wouldn't be that worried. We would be told what the damages were and would pay them. Then we would get the money back from this man's father and that would be the end of that. Next voyage he would have learned his lesson. But here, I am not so sure how fair the fine will be, and I'd rather not wait to find out. We need more water, but we can get that downriver, enough to get us to Kirkjuvágr where we can get more."

"Very good. But I feel bad about leaving Hákon without saying farewell."

"I agree. Still, we have time. We cannot leave until everyone is back on board, and the missing two may take some finding. And we need to wait for darkness to fall. I suggest we go to him at once. But not for long. As soon as we can, we set off."

Odd left instructions to the crew, and then he and Kári stepped on to the quay. But they had not got far before they spotted the large shape of Hákon hurrying towards them, with Alfred by his side. When they met, he said, "Word flies quickly. I heard you had trouble with the watch?"

"One of the crewmen got drunk", Odd said. "It was bound to happen."

"Yes, I'm sure it was." Hákon looked around to see that no one could hear them, then he lowered his voice. "I think you should leave."

"We already are", Kári said. "But thank you for coming to tell us."

"Odd is my friend, and so is your father. And you too, Kári Ragnarsson, I hope I can count you as my friend?"

"I would be honoured to be your friend, and doubly so after tonight. Thank you Hákon."

"You should thank Alfred as well. He happened to be in the inn when your crewman was boasting about Iceland just before he started fighting. You are the only Icelanders in Jórvik, so it was easy to know which ship he was from."

"Thank you, Alfred", Kári said, Odd echoing him. "Hopefully we will meet again in better times."

"It is in the hand of the Norns, I mean in the hand of God", Hákon said. "Now go."

When Odd and Kári returned to the knarr, the missing crewmen were already back, grumbling about having been dragged from their beer. There was a tense wait until Odd ruled that it was sufficiently dark, then they cast off and carefully began to row south, trying to make as little noise as possible.

Nobody tried to stop them and the knarr made good speed rowing downriver. By the morning they were well downriver, and by late afternoon they were close to where the Ouse ran into the Humber. There Odd stopped to fill their water casks before continuing. But both Kári and Odd were happier still the next morning when they cleared the mouth of the Humber and reached the open sea to turn north.

There they caught a southerly wind, which allowed the rowers to rest. Kári was going to stand in the prow of the knarr, when Odd asked him to come to the steering oar.

"Do you want me to steer?"

"No. I want to ask you what you think about your voyage so far."

"Hmm. I enjoyed the trading. But I did not like Jórvik."

"Go on."

"Oh, the city was impressive. But there was too much fear, too much worry. We traded well, but that was because everyone else was doing badly."

"You mean they were disappointed with their trades?"

Kári frowned. "No, not that. Then they wouldn't have traded with us, I think. No, it was just a feeling that prices were high because trade is bad and nobody comes there. And they are worried about the future." He thought for a while, then added, "Kirkjuvágr was small by comparison, but it was a better place."

"Ah", Odd replied. "Remember what I said. Jarl Thorfinn is a strong ruler, who keeps order."

Kári gazed thoughtfully across the sea before he replied. "No, that is not the reason."

"What do you mean?"

"A ruler can be strong and just or strong and unjust. Thorfinn is a strong ruler and perhaps he is just – I do not know. But in Jórvik, it seems that Tostig is also a strong ruler and he is unjust. And King Harald Fairhair was a strong ruler of Norway, yet it was because of him that so many people left for Iceland. Maybe a weak ruler is better than a strong one, or even no ruler at all, like we have in Iceland."

Odd listened. Once again Kári surprised him with the way he thought of things. "Then what do you think it is that makes a good place for traders?" he asked.

"I am not sure. I think there are many things that are important. Trust between the traders is important. Being able to trade without the jarl or his men standing over your shoulder and counting your silver with a view to by hook or by crook make it their silver. Remember, Hákon and many of the others told us how things change all the time, with new tolls and duties to pay. I think there should be one set of rules that do not change and that are equal for all. In Iceland, the law protects everybody equally – but not in Jórvik."

"Is that all?" Odd wasn't sure quite what to make of Kári's words.

"I don't know. But I do know this: Kirkjuvágr was small but everybody came there and traded freely; Jórvik is big and rich but its trade is drying up. That has to be bad."

"That is certainly true", Odd said. "Now go get some rest. I will wake you up when it's time for you to steer."

But Kári couldn't rest. Instead, he went back to the prow and stood there, looking out across the sea as the waves rose and fell and the knarr plowed on. Far off the port he could see land, with seabirds swarming above. On starboard, the sun continued to rise. This was how it should be. A free man, sailing where he wished, master of his own destiny.

When they arrived in Kirkjuvágr, Odd said that they would only stop to pick up more supplies. They had been lucky with the weather so far, and he wanted to return to Snæströnd before their luck ran out. They still spent two nights in the small town, as Kári now found himself thinking about it. But rather than letting the men go ashore, Odd kept the crew on board by telling them that they needed to be present for the reckoning of the trades and for him to set out what they should each report to their fathers. Kári wasn't sure if this was the real reason, or if Odd was merely making sure that no one was tempted to get drunk and misbehave. In any case, it worked. Kári and Odd sat down with each man in turn, carefully detailing what each one had brought, for how much it had been sold, what they had bought in return and how much silver was owed to them – or rather, to their fathers. Since profits had been higher than expected, there were generally happy faces – the man who had been fighting in Jórvik was the only exception. When told that one silver penny would be deducted from his father's profits, he protested that he had not agreed to this and nor would his father.

"Your father will agree once he is told what you did", Odd said. "Or if he doesn't, you can find a silver penny somewhere and pay him back. But for me, this is what will happen."

They had contrary winds from Kirkjuvágr, so from time to time they had to row again. The journey that had taken them three days on the outward run took six days back. But on the afternoon of the fifth day they rounded Snæfellsnes, and the next morning they could see Snæströnd to starboard. They had been away for just over three months.

Chapter 6

Autumn 1060 – Autumn 1064

That autumn, much happened at Snæströnd. Kári's return and his success in his trading were celebrated not just by his family but by many of their friends. For some time he and his father would travel to neighbouring farms and sell some of the goods he had brought back and also arrange for the next summer's trade. Because he had shown himself a skilled and successful trader in spite of his youth, men were eager to make sure that they could send goods with him again and also have their sons in his crew.

Ragnar took great pride in Kári's success. But for much of the time he remained gloomy. Even though men told him that he had come away from the Thórsnesthing with much honour, he himself was torn between a feeling that he had done right to obey the law, however unjust the verdict, and a nagging thought that he had still betrayed something he deeply believed in. True, everyone around him, including Hallgerður and Guðmundr, kept saying that he had done the right thing. And it was certainly true that with the profits from Kári's voyage he was wealthier than before, even if Leifur never paid him what the Thing had decreed. In fact, Ragnar was certain that Leifur would attempt to avoid paying for as long as possible. But it had never been about the money, it had been about what was right; and this was where he still felt uncertain. It did not help that he was increasingly finding that his body ached when he rose in the mornings. He had not hurt himself and he was puzzled why he would feel the pain. When he spoke with Hallgerður he feared that she would laugh at him and say that he was only imagining it. Instead, she smiled at him and said, "It happens to us all, my love. You are getting older."

Guðmundr found that he spent much time riding to visit Ása. At first, he told himself that this was because he hoped to meet Jórunn there or at least ask Ása about Jórunn. But as the days turned to months and the number of his visits grew, Jórunn never appeared, and her name did not really come up much either. He found himself enjoying Ása's company; she was calmer than Jórunn, but the more he saw her, the more he realised that she was by no means less clever, and she was in some ways even more strong-willed. This became clear at the end of one particularly enjoyable visit when he was leaving and he said, "I will be back."

"Why?"

The question took him aback. "What do you mean, 'Why?'?" he asked.

Ása looked him straight in the eyes. "I mean exactly that. Why will you be back? Why are you coming here?"

Guðmundr felt confused. "Well, um, that is to say, well …" He fell silent. But Ása said nothing, merely looking at him and clearly expecting an answer. He tried again: "Well, I like coming here", he finally said.

"That's very nice to hear. And why do you like coming here? Because of the beautiful landscape, perhaps?"

And then Guðmundr realised what she was asking. He might be a little bit slow at first, but he was not *that* stupid. "I like coming here because I like meeting you, Ása."

"Because I am Jórunn's friend?"

Now why did she have to bring up Jórunn's name? They had not spoken about her lately. He tried to picture Jórunn in his mind's eye. She had red hair, of course, and green eyes. And her laughter … But even as he did, the picture slowly faded and was replaced by that of the fair-haired girl who was looking intently at him. He swallowed.

"No. I like meeting *you*. To be with you gives me pleasure." And as he said it, he realised that it was true. Yes, she was not Jórunn. And he and Ása had not lain with each other, as he and Jórunn had done so often (and even as he thought that, he felt something stirring). But he did like her.

"I like being with you", he said, this time with a firmer voice.

Suddenly she smiled. "That is good. Because I like being with you as well. Now, what are you going to do about this?"

This time he was faster to grasp her meaning. "I think", he said, "that the time has come for me to speak with my father, and for him to speak with your father."

Ása did not pretend to be surprised. "I think that is a very good thought. And I also think that you should do this sooner rather than later."

"I will." He was going to ride off, but she came closer. Although she was shorter than him (and shorter than Jórunn, but why did he suddenly think about her again?) there was not much distance between their faces and, before he stopped to think, he leaned down and kissed her. He was not sure how she would respond, but the passionate reply was not at all what he had expected. The kiss lasted long, and when it broke off, he found himself having to take a deep breath.

"Now go", the girl said. "And be back soon!"

On the ride home, he could smell the scent of newly-mown hay, and it seemed like the setting sun glowed redder than it ever had before. He would indeed speak with his father as soon as he got home. And with his mother. Hallgerður would be sure to agree, but what would Ragnar say? Ása was not wealthy – would that matter to his father?

*

During the summer Thór Egilsson, one of the local goðar whose farm was close to Snæströnd, had openly proclaimed his faith in the White Christ and had built a small church on his farm. In most other Christian churches, the priests were members of the farmer's family, but this one was different. He was from a great city that he called Arelat in the lands of the Burgundians, where he had studied for the priesthood in a school run by the Archbishop himself, or so he said. He was a tall man, with shaven head, whose name was

Willibald. It was said about him that he was not content to only serve as priest for one farm but wanted to spread the faith of the White Christ to everyone, even though most Icelanders felt that a man's faith was his own, and indeed many of them would from time to time worship the old gods as well as the new one they all professed to follow. For this reason, he would frequently travel to Skálholt to meet with the Bishop there.

Willibald did not yet speak much of the Danish tongue. But he had somehow found out that one of Ragnar's men spoke Latin. Since then, he had frequently come to Snæströnd to meet with Odd. They could often be seen wandering across the fields, deep in conversation. At first, Willibald had tried to persuade Odd to come regularly to church and also to bring Ragnar and the household at Snæströnd with him. But Odd early on made clear that this would not happen and that it would be better for their friendship if the priest never brought this up again. Odd could see that this was not an answer the priest liked to hear. But few men in Iceland spoke Latin, so Willibald held his tongue, and they talked about other matters. Odd found that he enjoyed speaking Latin, and Willibald learned much about Iceland from him.

That autumn, when the harvest was being celebrated at Snæströnd, Ragnar announced the betrothal of his son Guðmundr to Ása Alfsdóttir. Guðmundr's concerns about his father's reaction had been unnecessary, both because Hallgerður quickly showed her approval and because she had, after first swearing him to secrecy, finally told Ragnar about Guðmundr's friendship with Jórunn – adding that, in her view, Ása would make a much better wife for Guðmundr and in time be a good mistress of Snæströnd.

But if there was joy in Snæströnd, the news was not received with pleasure everywhere.

"How *dare* he! How dare *she*, that miserable little mouse! That traitor! They will regret this! If it's the last thing I do, I'll make them regret this. Hel will be too good for them."

The outburst was followed by a pot being hurled to the floor so that it smashed into pieces – not the first one, either, judging by the shards already lying on the floor.

From a safe distance, Einar Gunnarsson was watching his sister's outburst. As she turned around, looking for something else to destroy, he laughed. The sound brought her up sharply.

"What are you laughing at? Do you think this is funny?"

"Calm down, sister. Of course I don't think it is funny. But I must say that I did not know that you were so fond of Guðmundr. Did you not tell me that you refused to wed him?"

"That is not the point!" Jórunn spat.

"Then what is the point? Please explain to me."

"I'll tell you what it is. That little mouse. I took her in, I let her be in my company. I was kind to her. Where would she be without me? Sitting on some small farmstead with three children and a useless husband! And now she is stealing him from me."

"But she isn't. You just said that you did not want him. What are you complaining about?"

Jórunn wasn't listening. "And he! Who does he think he is? Betraying me with that little, little, ugly – mouse!" Once again she looked for something else to break, but Einar grabbed her hands.

"Stop. I've heard that now. She is a mouse. You seem very fond of calling her that. And he is betraying you. But how, exactly, is someone who is not your man betraying you with someone else?"

"You're a fool, Einar."

"Very well. I'm a fool, she is a mouse, he is a traitor. Now can you please explain what is going on!" By now Einar was almost shouting, and he was so near Jórunn's face that her hair flew back. This brought her up short and she stopped struggling against his grip and calmed down.

"Be quiet and listen, then, Einar. Yes, Guðmundr Ragnarsson asked me to wed him and I said no. I do not wish to marry anyone. But he is still my man. I may not want him, but nobody else should have him either – least of all someone who pretended to be my friend and who went behind my back to snatch him. I will not let her have him! Now do you understand?"

"Very good. You will not let Ása –"

"Don't mention her name!" Jórunn interrupted.

"You will not let the mouse have him. May I ask how?"

"I don't know yet."

"Well then, do you wish to hurt him or her?"

"I don't care. Both of them."

"Last question. Should we go and speak with Father about it?"

This brought Jórunn up short and she had to think about it. Should they speak with Gunnar? He was hostile to Ragnar and therefore no doubt to Guðmundr as well. But would he help them? You never knew with her father. He might come up with a plan. But he might also be annoyed with her and tell her that it was her own fault and that he was not going to waste time cleaning up her mess. But what could she do on her own? She thought some more, conscious of the fact that Einar was watching her. Then she decided.

"No. I don't think we should bother him with this. We can deal with it ourselves."

"Ourselves?" Einar looked at her.

For a brief moment, her temper flared again. "You will help me, brother, otherwise —"

But before she continued, he held up a hand. "Yes, yes. I will help you. Now tell me what you have in mind."

As Jórunn told him, Einar's face showed different emotions. But finally he said, "Yes. I think this will work. And I will help you. But are you sure you will meet him?"

"Trust me. I know what he does when he is at home."

"In that case, well and good. When do we do this?"

"The sooner the better. They will both regret what they have done."

"Very good. Then let us ride tomorrow. Today it is already too late."

*

Some days later, Guðmundr was walking around the boundaries of Snæströnd. He would do this every so often, partly to see that boundary markers were set and maintained, but mainly because he enjoyed the long walks around the property and being alone. The beauty of the landscape never ceased to beguile him, whether in the winter or in the all-too-brief summer. He would be away from the farmhouse for more than a day, sleeping in a shepherd's hut or, if the weather was warmer, in the open. Occasionally he would find lambs that had been separated from the flock and return them or meet neighbours walking the boundaries of their farms. He knew that one day, when Snæströnd was his, he would not be able to do this as often, as there would be much to do that would keep him tied to the farmstead. But for as long as he could, he would keep taking his walks.

His path took him through a shallow valley between two hills. It was already after noon and the sun would be setting in a few hours; soon he wouldn't be able to see the hills anymore, and he knew he needed to find somewhere to spend the night. But right at the moment, he was thinking about his forthcoming marriage.

The world was strange, he thought. You never really knew what the Norns would spin. He was marrying Ása, but it was only half a year ago that he had thought that he would be marrying Jórunn. He wondered what she was doing right now. Strange, when he thought about her, it was almost as if he could see her in front of him, the red hair framing her face, the green eyes sparkling and her wicked smile.

"Hello Guðmundr."

That shook him. It wasn't a vision. It really was Jórunn, standing in front of him. She was wearing a fur cloak, but it was open in front and he could glimpse a blue tunic and a grey skirt underneath. He swallowed.

"Jórunn. What are you doing here?"

"Aren't you going to greet me properly?" She came closer. But as she approached, Guðmundr backed away and she stopped.

"What are you doing here?" he repeated.

She laughed. "What a question. I heard you have been betrothed."

"Yes."

"And to Ása. I never thought that she was your type. Is she?"

"What do you mean?"

"Surely you have lain with her. What is she like? Is she better than me? Everyone else tells me she likes to do strange things."

Guðmundr looked at her. "What strange things?"

"Hasn't she shown you yet? Have you not bedded her?"

"We haven't –" He stopped himself. Why were they talking about this?

"Poor boy. You'll find out soon enough. But in the meantime, you must be feeling terrible, without a woman for so long." She approached him again, but Guðmundr once again backed off.

"Jórunn, this is not a good idea."

"Why not? I thought you liked it?"

"I did. But I am betrothed to Ása, and –"

"Don't you dare mention her name!" she spat.

"Now, look here, Jórunn –"

"And don't you 'look here' me. And let me tell you one thing, you traitor: nobody treats me like this and gets away with it!"

"But, but … I asked you to marry me. You said no." Guðmundr was thoroughly confused. From being sweet and seductive, Jórunn had suddenly turned into a furious shield-maiden who seemed ready to strike him dead.

"Who cares what I said! You scorned me, and I won't allow that. And as for that little mouse, she will regret her behaviour."

"Now, wait a moment. Don't speak like that about Ása."

He took a step towards her, only to recoil when she suddenly cried "Rape! Rape!" in a loud voice and began to tear her clothes and loosen her hairbands.

Guðmundr didn't know what to do. He turned away from her, pleading, "What are you doing? Put your clothes back on. And stop shouting." But Jórunn continued to scream, shouting 'Rape!' and calling for help.

Before Guðmundr could decide what to do, he suddenly heard a rustling noise from the bushes beside the track. Before he could turn towards the noise, he felt a sharp point pricking his neck and a voice hissing, "Trying to rape my sister, are you? Well, well, the great Guðmundr Ragnarsson. Who would have thought it?"

"Einar? Are you mad? I am not trying to rape your sister. She started tearing her clothes and screaming. I was nowhere near her."

"So you say. But I saw you. I know what you did. And you will find out what happens when you attack a woman. Coward!" And the sharp point stabbed just a little deeper, not deep enough to draw blood (he thought), but deep enough to be felt and to show that it could draw blood at any moment.

"This is not true. I am innocent", he protested. "And you know it."

"I don't know it at all. Sister, did he hurt you badly?" Einar asked.

"Oh Einar. I'm glad you are here. Where did you come from? He was trying to force me, and I couldn't resist."

Guðmundr's head swam. What was going on here? But before he had time to think, the point of what he assumed was Einar's sword jabbed him again.

"Walk."

"Where are we going?"

"We are going to the nearest farm. Not to Snæströnd, where your father would only listen to your lies. We are going somewhere where honest people will listen to my sister. Now stop talking and walk. It is easier if I don't have to cut you, but I will if I have to." And once again the point was at his neck, now tracing a line under his chin.

Guðmundr swallowed and began to walk in the direction Einar indicated, from time to time prodded by the sword. They walked up the low-lying hill to the east. When they reached the crest, Guðmundr was surprised to see two horses grazing on the other side. He looked at them and at the two siblings – Jórunn had not bothered to do up her clothes apart from fastening her fur cloak around her neck. When Einar saw his glance, he said, "You are lucky, sister, that I followed you and spotted your horse here so that I knew where you were."

"What? Oh. Yes. Thank you, brother."

And then Guðmundr realised that this was all an elaborate plot. They had planned it together, to trap him. But why? And where were they going? But he was not going to give them the satisfaction of begging for answers. He would find out soon enough.

Einar and Jórunn mounted their horses, and, with Einar still prodding Guðmundr with his sword, they set off towards the nearest farm. Guðmundr knew that it was not far away, but by the time they had reached the horses, the sun was already setting, and Einar and his sword ensured that they went at a brisk pace; the walk would be more difficult once the sun had fully disappeared and they could no longer see so easily where they were going.

While he walked, he kept thinking about how he could prove his innocence. And why had Jórunn done this to him? He thought she liked him. In fact, she had said so, even when she said she would not wed him. As for Einar, he was a loathsome toad and nothing he did would surprise Guðmundr. He would have liked to hear them talking to each other see if he could learn something, but it seemed that they were not in the mood for speaking either, so they continued across the cold, dark landscape in silence.

It was late when they reached the farmhouse, but, even so, there seemed to be a lot of people moving about, and there was light and noise and smoke from a large fire coming from the house. When they approached the house, a dog began to bark and a man came out, challenging them.

"Who are you and what do you want?"

"I am Einar, son of Gunnar goði, and this is my sister, Jórunn. She was attacked by this man. I bring him here so that you can witness my accusation."

The man peered at them through the darkness, but eventually called for someone to take care of their horses. "Come in", he said. "You are fortunate. I am Thór Egilsson goði, and this is my farm. Even more fortunately for you, we also have another goði here visiting me today. Between us we will hear your grievance at once.

While he was speaking, Thór led the three into the house. Inside, a group of men were sitting around a table. They looked up to see what was happening, and one of the men stood up and exclaimed, "Guðmundr? And Einar Gunarsson? What is this about, Thór?"

Einar's heart missed a beat. Eirík! What was he doing here? He would not prove easy to persuade and would be scrupulously fair to Guðmundr – if not biased towards him outright. But that could not be helped. They would have to continue with the plan; or admit to their deception at once. And who knew what the consequence of that would be? He thought fast, and before Thór could say a word, he cut in, "Eirík goði, this man tried to force himself on my sister. He attacked her. It was only by pure luck that I happened to arrive in time to stop him."

Guðmundr wanted to interrupt but realised that if he did, things could quickly turn into a shouting match, where nobody would listen to him or to anyone else. At least Eirík knew him and would in due course let him say something in his defence. But the goði barely glanced at him before turning his gaze back to the two siblings. "Is this true?" he asked, not of Einar or of Guðmundr, but of Jórunn.

"Are you calling my brother a liar?" she asked.

"No", Eirík replied mildly. "But claiming that someone attacked you is a very serious accusation. It requires proof – as I am sure you understand."

"Look at the state of my clothes. They were almost torn from my body when he threw himself at me. Had it not been for Einar, he would have forced himself on me against my will."

"Where did this happen?"

"There is a dale on the Snæströnd farm, close to the border with this one."

"And why were you there so late in the day?"

"Why are you asking me all these questions?" Jórunn demanded. "Who is the guilty one here?"

"I am only trying to get at the truth", Eirík replied, still speaking mildly. "I am just surprised that you would find yourself alone on the borders of Snæströnd farm this late in the day, so far from your father's holdings."

"I have nothing to hide", the young woman said. "You may not know this, but Guðmundr and I have been seeing each other for some years." It was clear from Eirík's widening eyes that he had been unaware of this. "He wanted to wed me, but his parents are making him marry Ása Alfsdóttir. He sent me a message saying that he wanted to see me. When we met, he told me that he did not want to marry her; that he only cared for me. I explained that I did not love him and did not want to marry him and that his parents were only thinking of his own good. I thought he would understand, but instead he told me that we should go away together, even leave Iceland. When I said I was not going to go with him, he threw himself on me, telling me that it was not my choice. That is when Einar appeared and saved me. We could not go to Snæströnd, because his father would not believe us, so we came here."

"I see. Thank you for explaining this. Guðmundr, what do you have to say?"

Guðmundr was silent for a moment. He knew that whatever he now said would determine not only what happened next but maybe the rest of his life. He had to make them believe him.

"None of this is true. No, wait, some of it is. Jórunn and I have been seeing each other. But that came to an end at the Thórsnesthing this year. I did ask her to marry me, and she said no. Since then, I have, as you know, become betrothed to Ása Alfsdóttir, but that is *my* choice, not my parents'. As for the rest, none of it is true. I met Jórunn in the dale, but I had not asked her to come there. She seemed to want me to lie with her, but when I refused her, she suddenly tore her own clothes and started to scream for help. I did not touch her."

"Hm. Are there any witnesses to this? Apart from the three involved?" Eirík asked.

All three shook their heads.

"Hm. I do not wish to be too hasty. Yet this should be cleared up quickly, lest it grow. Thór, what is your thought?" The two men started whispering to each other. From time to time they looked up at the three young people. While they spoke, Jórunn and Einar looked defiantly around at the rest of the group, who were watching them. Guðmundr saw how men who had been standing next to him shifted slightly further away, as if they feared to be tarnished by his presence. He had hoped that Eirík, as his father's friend, would believe him, but the goði had shown no sign of trusting him more or listening less to Einar and Jórunn. Yet they were the children of his enemy Gunnar. How could he listen to them? With a sinking feeling, Guðmundr remembered that one reason his father had become Eirík's thingman was the goði's strict respect for the law.

While the whispering was going on, there was a sudden movement at the door and some more men came in. One of them was taller than many Icelanders. When they came in, he started to greet Thór, when he suddenly spotted Guðmundr, Jórunn and Einar.

"Vide!" he exclaimed. "Illi sunt."

"Quid?" a hoarse voice replied.

"Hi tres sunt quos iam vidimus."

The men in the house had all turned to look at the newcomers. Because they stood in the way, Guðmundr and the two siblings could only see the taller man, but Guðmundr recognised the hoarse voice and began to hope again.

Before he had time to say anything, however, Thór spoke to the tall man. "Scis hos juvenes?"

"Non, sed hos iam vidi."

Thór seemed to want to speak more, but Eirík interrupted him. "Perhaps you can explain what is going on?" he asked.

"Forgive me, Eirík. This is my priest, Willibald. He says he saw these three."

Eirík stood up. "Really? When? And where? And does he know them?"

"He said he doesn't know them, but that he saw them. I have to ask him more. Please wait."

While the rest of the men waited, Thór began to speak with the priest. But it became clear that from time to time his Latin was not good enough and the man with the hoarse voice, who could still not be seen, had to help him out. Eventually, Thór turned back to Eirík.

"Willibald says that he saw them at different times today. Earlier in the day, he saw the young man and the young woman riding together. They tethered their horses and sat down and waited. He did not think this was important, so he continued as he was meeting a friend. But when he and his friend came back, they saw them again. No, not them, only the woman. She was alone and she was meeting the other man."

"What happened?"

There was a further exchange of Latin between the three men.

"He says they were quarrelling. Then suddenly the woman began to tear her clothes off."

"Is he absolutely sure about this? She did it to herself?"

"Yes. He says they were surprised to see it."

"What did the man she quarrelled with do? Did he attack her?"

"No. Willibald says that the other man was too far away to touch her, and that anyway he turned around so that he would not see her when she began to scream. He says they never really saw his face, but he recognises the red-headed girl and is certain of this. And then the first man appeared with a sword and attacked the man she quarrelled with."

"And he will swear to this?"

"Yes, he will", Thór replied "He says that he will swear on the Holy Book. He would not dare to lie after taking such an oath."

"I would swear too", the hoarse man said. "I did not see the two together at first, but everything else is as the priest has said. I saw it as well."

"And did anyone see you?"

"I don't think so."

Suddenly Willibald spoke again. "Hi qui sunt?"

"He is asking who these people are", Thór translated.

"Does he really not know?"

"He wouldn't", Thór said. "He only knows the people on my farm and those who come to his church and very few others."

"Please tell him what has happened and who they are. But above all, thank him for helping us to clear this up so quickly."

While Thór turned back to Willibald to tell him what had happened, Eirík turned back to Jórunn and Einar.

"You have heard the priest", he said. "Do you have anything to say before I pronounce my decision?"

Jórunn just lifted her head haughtily, but Einar blustered, "He is lying. They are both lying."

"Be careful who you call a liar." This was the man with the hoarse voice, who suddenly came into view.

When Guðmundr saw him, he felt weak with relief. Finally, he was certain that this was over. "Odd! I knew it was you. Thank you."

"Do not thank me. Thank Priest Willibald. If he had not suggested that we should meet at the border of the farms, we would not have been there to see what happened."

"I will."

But before Guðmundr could say anything else, Eirík stood up. "This is my decision", he said. "Guðmundr is clearly innocent of the charges. I find that Einar and Jórunn have conspired to slander him and to make a false accusation. If Guðmundr so wishes, he can now bring a case against them." And he looked expectantly at Guðmundr.

Guðmundr felt uncertain. Should he? Would it not be best if this entire event were forgotten? "I would speak with Jórunn alone", he finally said.

Einar looked as if he was going to say something, but Jórunn walked away from him to a corner of the room and Guðmundr followed her. The other men in the room moved away and turned their backs towards them.

When they reached the corner, Jórunn turned around and faced Guðmundr. "Say what you wish to say, and then let me go."

"Jórunn, why? Why did you do this?"

"I have nothing to say to you."

"Nothing? I don't understand."

"That is perfectly clear. Are you done?"

"If you will not say anything, then, yes. But you must realise that I will not forget this day."

Jórunn returned to stand with Einar, while Guðmundr went to Eirík. "I do not wish to bring a case against them", he said. "Everyone here knows that their accusations were false, and it would be better if this did not become widely known."

Eirík sighed with relief. He had worried that Guðmundr would bring a case against the siblings. If he had, Eirík would have been bound to support him. They would have won, of course, but it would have widened the conflict between him and Gunnar, and he preferred that this did not happen. "You are doing the right thing", he said. "Well done."

Before Einar and Jórunn left, Odd went up to them. "You do not know how fortunate you are", he said. "If Guðmundr had brought a case against you, you would have been shamed in front of everyone you know. I very much doubt that your father would thank you for this. Now you are escaping the consequences of your foolishness, and few people will hear of this. But do not think that it will be forgotten. And this I promise you: if I ever see you again unbidden anywhere on Snæströnd, I will have you whipped. Now crawl back to where you came from."

At first, Jórunn and Einar rode back through the night in silence. But as the sun rose, Einar said "This was a bad plan."

"You agreed to it", she replied.

"How was I to know that there would be witnesses? And that one of them would be a priest?"

She sighed. "Well, what is done is done."

"Not necessarily. We will see what Father says."

"You intend to tell him?"

"Of course. First, because he is bound to find out anyway, and better he hears it from us. Second, because we may still salvage something."

"What? And how?"

"I don't know. But Father will know."

In this, Einar was mistaken. When he told his father what had happened, Gunnar thought less of how to help his children than of his fury at their behaviour. "How could you even be so stupid? Don't you ever stop to think of where your actions will lead you?"

"We couldn't know that we would be seen", Einar muttered.

"But you had to think that you might be. When you plan something, it is not enough to assume that everything will go well. You also have to consider what might go badly. What were you thinking of, Jórunn? I had expected better of you."

Gunnar looked at his daughter, but Jórunn remained silent. He didn't know if this meant that she had nothing to say. But knowing that she was clever, he thought that it was more likely that she realised that for once she had acted thoughtlessly. Einar had, he thought, almost certainly just been led by his sister.

"We will not speak of this again. It is bad enough that it happened. Others will know, and I may lose some thingmen to Eirík. It is not good, but I can live with this. What is worse is that it binds Eirík and Ragnar closer together, and I would have preferred to avoid that somehow. In any case, neither of you will do anything of this sort again without speaking with me in advance. Is that clear?"

When neither of his children replied, he raised his voice: "I said: IS THAT CLEAR?"

"Yes, Father", Einar mumbled, while Jórunn just inclined her head minimally.

*

The following spring, Guðmundr and Ása got married at Snæströnd. Their wedding was celebrated with much feasting and merriment. Guðmundr had worried how his mother and his wife would get along, since both were headstrong and minded to get their own way. But Ása accepted that her mother-in-law was the mistress of Snæströnd, while Hallgerður knew that someday she would no longer be and that Ása would take her place. And so they got along well with each other. It also helped that, later that year, Ása became pregnant.

Kári, Odd and Ragnar talked much over the winter about where to go trading. It was clear that they could not go back to Jórvik. Kári suggested trying Dyflin, but Odd was not happy with this idea. In the end they decided to try to make two trading voyages that year. One would be to Suðreyar, the southwestern islands that were ruled from Orkney by Jarl Thorfinn. Here they could sell walrus meat and hides and buy wood. They would then do a second voyage to Scotland, where they would also sell wadmal and buy grain and beer. They could go twice in the summer because the sailing distances were shorter, and this could perhaps compensate for the fact that there would be less silver from each journey.

In the spring, therefore, Kári and Odd rode around to the neighbouring farms, asking for men to join the crew. Because the previous year had been profitable, they had no problem finding five men to join them, together with five farmhands from Snæströnd, and they had to turn away some who wanted to join. Instead, Kári promised that, in future years, he would go twice and that he would only take rowers on one voyage each, so that more could join him at least once a year. This also pleased the neighbours, since they could more easily afford to spare their sons for a shorter voyage.

He asked Odd if they should perhaps take more rowers from other farms, but the older man cautioned against this. Kári said that taking more men from other farms would leave more to work at Snæströnd.

"This is true", Odd said. "But I would still say no, and for these reasons. First, the men who work for your father are the friends who you grew up with. They trust you and you trust them. Others may learn to trust you in the future, but they will never be as close to you as these. This also means that they will stand by you. They know how to sail and row your knarr. They will not be lured by another trader in Kirkjuvágr or Jórvik to leave you and travel somewhere else. Next, they will always be available to you, whereas a neighbour may one year decide that he does not wish to go trading or send his son with you. And lastly, there is not very much for the farmhands to do in the summer between sowing and harvesting – as you well know."

Kári felt abashed. "I should have thought of that."

"Never mind", Odd replied. "You cannot think of everything. But you are learning quickly. And this may yet come to be a good idea."

"Yes", Kári said. "And meanwhile it will be good to have men with me who want to be on the ship. Our farmhands are good, and they will not let me down, but they are with me because I demand it and they cannot say no. But a man with me of his own will – he will see things differently. Men will work harder, and their success taste sweeter, when they are free to decide for themselves."

Over the next five years, Kári would sail twice a year trading. And it turned out that he enjoyed much success in his trading and was usually lucky with the weather; only once did he run into a storm on the way back to Iceland which was so bad that they had to jettison much of their cargo. When they came back to Snæströnd, Kári gathered his men and told them, "The loss from this voyage shall fall on me alone. For everyone else, it shall be as if you had not lost anything." For this he gained much honour and reputation, and more men clamoured to join him on his voyages.

The feast at the annual launching of the knarr was more and more attended by Kári's friends and fewer of Ragnar's, who were also growing older. There was now a core of four or five regular crewmen who came on every trip with him. He much enjoyed their company, and to them he gave the assurance that there would always be a place for them on the ship if they wanted it. Although Kári was not a goði, these men began to think of themselves as his men and of him as their leader.

Yet although he was successful, Kári still wanted to do more. He kept carving walrus ivory and bringing it for sale, but only once did he sell some for a good price. This was to a Scots earl who bought an intricately carved box as a reliquary for his king, Máel Coluim, who was a devout Christian. Kári found that he liked the beer in Scotland well enough, but he still hankered after going elsewhere – even to Jórvik. The name Dyflin still lured him, and sometimes he found himself thinking of sailing to more distant places still, places no one from Iceland had yet visited.

When he brought this up with Odd, the older man would still dissuade him. "But", he said, "you are no longer the 'young master'. You are already the master. And you should make these decisions regardless of what an old man thinks."

"You're not old", Kári protested.

"Old enough", Odd replied. "Fear not, I will still come with you. But you have now done enough voyages to no longer need my advice. I am proud of you, Kári. If I had had a son, I would have wanted him to be like you. And if truth be known, I enjoy trading without being the master. It is better to be the master's friend."

Kári felt touched by the older man's words. "Thank you, Odd", he said. "And I shall indeed always be your friend. But I also hope that I will still have your advice?"

"That you will. So, what will you do about Dyflin?"

"Dyflin can wait for another time", Kári replied.

*

When Guðmundr had been married for two years, Ragnar spoke with his sons and told them that the time had come for him to divide his property between them. Guðmundr and Kári were surprised and asked why.

"I have become older", Ragnar said. "This happens to everyone. But it is also that I no longer wish to attend the Thing or play a part in other men's lives. I tried once, and it brought me no joy."

"But Father, you did the right thing with Gunnar", Guðmundr said, while Kári nodded.

"I know. So everyone tells me, and so my head tells me as well. But my heart still dislikes what I did. Yet this is not my only reason for doing this. You are both still young and strong. And both of you are successful. Guðmundr, you are wed, you have a daughter and will have more children, and it is time for Ása to be the mistress of Snæströnd." He held up his hand as Guðmundr opened his mouth. "Your mother agrees. Kári, you are already much travelled and a successful trader."

He paused and then continued, "All of this is good, and I am proud of both of you. But you should know that not everyone sings your praises. Not everyone is happy at your success. Where there is good fortune there is jealousy; where there is jealousy there will be men willing to see you harmed. You may need the help of others to withstand attacks, and I cannot guarantee to continue to protect you. You need to build up your own friendships. And for this it will help you to be seen to be masters of your own actions."

Both boys were silent. Was their father trying to say he would leave them? Was he ill? Ragnar sensed their unease and smiled. "No, you will not be rid of me just yet. I will still be here."

"What will you do?" Kári asked.

"I shall remain on Snæströnd."

"Why don't you come with me? Come and trade. Odd would want you to come, I am sure. So would I. You used to trade, and you could meet your old friends again."

Ragnar shook his head. "No more. And I think you are taking for granted that the knarr will be yours."

Kári looked surprised, but his father laughed. The sound was so rare from the stern Ragnar that both sons at first looked puzzled and wondered again if their father had taken ill.

Finally he stopped laughing, but he had seen the boys' reaction and thought to himself, am I so grim that they think I cannot laugh? I used to laugh all the time when I was young. Hallgerður liked my laughter. She said it sounded like a stream coming down the mountain in the spring. Where did that go, that my sons do not even recognise it?

"No", he said. "You already know what I will do. Guðmundr, you are my eldest son and a good farmer. You will inherit Snæströnd. Kári, you are a successful trader. You shall have the knarr. But there are conditions."

"Speak", Guðmundr said, while Kári chimed in "I listen."

"Guðmundr, you will allow Kári to take the usual men from the farm to man the knarr every summer."

Guðmundr nodded. "Willingly."

"Kári, you will compensate Guðmundr for the use of the farmhands."

"Of course."

"Make sure you always stand united. You may quarrel. Brothers do. But always remain united against others."

"We will", the boys said at the same time.

"I also charge you to become thingmen of Eirík goði and to support him. He is a good man, a good goði and he has been our friend. But only do this as long as he continues to defend our freedoms and uphold the Law. Remember, the goði is there for us – we are not there for him. Yes, we support him but not in the way of the men of Norway who have no choice but to support their king. We choose our goði, and if he is unfaithful to us, we can choose another."

Kári and Guðmundr nodded again.

"And fear not. I do not intend to die just yet. I will still be here, and, in the way fathers do, I will help you and also point out your errors." He laughed again.

This was now how life at Snæströnd proceeded for the next two years. Kári and Guðmundr prospered and grew wealthier. Both of them pledged their support to Eirík, and both began to attend the Althing as well as the Thórsnesthing. This was easier for Guðmundr, who stayed in Iceland, but Kári would also come whenever he was not away trading. For Eirík, the presence of Ragnar's sons lent him much honour, and he asked Guðmundr to become one of his advisors in the Lögrétta, the Law Council of the Althing. This displeased some of his friends, who felt that he should have chosen them instead, but Eirík defended his choice, saying "The sons of Ragnar are young, but both have already proven their wisdom. By asking Guðmundr to advise me, I benefit not only from his advice, but also from that of his father and his brother. When I heard that Ragnar wanted to stop coming to the Althing I was disappointed, but his sons are well able to support me in his stead. There is also this: I know I can trust them to be loyal because we have in many ways the same thoughts. And that can be very important."

On the rare occasions that he attended the Althing, Kári found that there were many people wanting to talk to him. His skill as a trader was becoming known, and his wealth – and his generosity to his friends – ensured that he was seldom short of company as the business of the day gave way to the more social side of the annual gathering. It was at one such evening that Kári met a man from Greenland, who came to seek him out.

"Are you Kári Ragnarsson? I hear you are a great trader", the man said. "People tell me you travel at least twice every year to buy wood and grain."

"Many people buy those", Kári replied.

"Yes. But few go more than once a year, and that shows great spirit", the man said. "I do not mean to offend you."

"I am not offended. Maybe puzzled."

"Oh. My name is Snorri Ingolfsson, but people call me Snorri Vínlandsfarer. You have of course heard of Vínland?"

"I have not."

Snorri looked surprised. "I thought everybody knew of Vínland. You do know of Greenland, at least?"

"Of course. But tell me about this Vínland?" Kári was still not sure what the stranger wanted of him, but he had learned that if you ask questions, men will talk and that it was better to listen patiently than to rush into a conversation if you wanted to learn something.

"Well, Greenland is half a moon's sailing west of Iceland. This you know."

Kári wasn't sure if he knew how long this journey was, but he nodded.

"Another half-moon on from that you reach a wonderful land, a land full of grapes and wheat and forests. This is Vínland."

"I see."

"I knew you would see. Now, what do you say?"

Kári looked at him. "What do I say about what? What do you want me to say?" He could not understand what Snorri meant.

"To go there, of course. Listen, Greenland has even less forests than Iceland. We need much wood. Some of us go to Vínland to get it. But it is not enough. You could bring your ship and we could all go to Vínland. Together we would find enough wood there to bring to Greenland, and you could also bring wood back to Iceland. Remember, nobody lives there but skrælings, so you would not have to pay for the wood."

Kári thought for a moment. Maybe some years earlier he would have been excited at the thought of going to a land nobody had heard of and trading there. Sometimes the thought of doing so still lured him. But he had also learned one or two things. And so he replied, "Snorri, I am honoured that you ask me to join you. But think of this: If I were to go to Vínland with you, from what you say it would take at least one month to go there, maybe more, and the same to return. And then we would have to cut down trees and chop them up to load on the ships. So we would probably have to winter there."

"You could winter in Greenland", Snorri interjected.

"Maybe, but that is not much better. It would still mean that instead of making two voyages in the year, I would make one voyage over two years. And you said that the – did you call them skrælings? – will not trade with us, so I gain no profit from bringing goods there."

"Oh." Snorri looked crestfallen.

"But I thank you for asking me, and I would like to hear more about Vínland if you would tell me."

But apart from going to Vínland to get wood, Snorri did not have much to say about the country. It was warm and beautiful, but the skrælings were hostile (Kári noted that he had not said that from the beginning). Some Greenlanders had tried to settle there but had returned. The more Kári heard, the more he thought this sounded like a bad proposition, but Snorri must have done well out of it, for the man seemed wealthy enough. Kári thought that if he had not had any responsibilities, he would have liked to go there. But this was no longer possible. Still, he enjoyed hearing about distant lands, and the knowledge could always become useful one day.

Although both Guðmundr and Kári prospered and became well known and respected, there was this one difference between them, and it became greater as the years passed. Kári found great pleasure in what he was doing. He was happiest at sea or trading in foreign lands, where he was master of his own destiny, and where success or failure was due only to him. He enjoyed coming back to Iceland, and each time he saw Snæströnd from afar he wondered how he could ever bear to leave it again. But in Iceland, for all his wealth and honour, and for all that there were men who looked up to him, he knew that he was not a goði, and there were always others who would think him a lesser man for that reason.

But Guðmundr was not content and grew less so as the years passed. He himself did not know why. He had married a woman who loved him with a fierce, possessive love that seemed to grow stronger as the years went by. He had a little daughter who adored her father, and after some years Ása was once again big with child. And yet there was something missing. He was wealthy and master of a rich farm, and people respected him. His reputation grew when Kári decided after some years to take three men from Snæströnd instead of five on his voyages, so that he could take more of their neighbours' sons, and Guðmundr could then lend the extra farmhands to his neighbours. But here too, something was missing. Even advising Eirík in the Lögrétta paled for him.

Guðmundr worried about this nagging unhappiness. When he was younger he might have asked his mother for advice. A few years ago, earlier in their marriage, he would have asked Ása. But now he did not really feel he wanted to do that, and moreover he did not know why. He tried to put the thoughts out of his mind, but they kept returning. And strangely, from time to time he began to think of Jórunn again. He did not understand why, after the way she and Einar had treated him, but he did. He would sometimes spot her at a Thing, but he never spoke with her and she pointedly ignored him.

There was one thing which Guðmundr did see as the cause for his unease and which rankled with him. This was his father. Although Ragnar had divided his property between his sons and told them that they were now masters of their own destinies, this did not seem to apply to him. Ragnar would still rise early each day as he had always done and tour the farm, speaking with the farmhands. So did Guðmundr, of course, and sometimes they would go together. But Guðmundr felt that his father still made decisions, sometimes without informing Guðmundr and sometimes reversing decisions that Guðmundr had made. At first, he had said nothing. His father's instincts might well be right and he still felt that he had much to learn about running a farm as large as Snæströnd. But after some time, he began to feel that the father's behaviour belittled and criticised the son. The farmhands occasionally asked Guðmundr, "Who do we obey, you or your father?"

Ragnar would also frequently ask Guðmundr how things had gone at the Thing and what advice he had given Eirík, and then his father would tell him what he should have said instead.

Finally, Guðmundr decided to speak with Ragnar about this.

"You said I was to be master of Snæströnd and master of my own destiny, Father. Yet you do not allow me to be."

Ragnar was surprised. "I am merely trying to help you. This was my farm for many years and I know it better than anyone else. Don't you want my help?"

"It is not your help that is the problem", Guðmundr said. "It is that you are still trying to be the master. Snæströnd can only have one master; if it is you, then it cannot be me. And the men know it. If you wish to give me advice, that is well and good and I appreciate that. But not in this way."

Ragnar couldn't understand. Surely Guðmundr realised that his father only wanted to do what was best. And wasn't it better to make changes at once if something was wrong, rather than to wait until he could find Guðmundr and then ask him to do it? Why could not Guðmundr see this?

But when Ragnar tried to explain this to his son, Guðmundr refused to listen. The more Ragnar spoke about the right way of doing things, the more impatient Guðmundr became, until he finally burst out "So the right way always has to be your way, does it? Snæströnd is managing very well right now. The farm is no poorer than it was when it became mine. But you never give me any credit for this. I never hear a word of support from you, and yet it is I who work hard to give you your daily food."

Ragnar was taken aback. Why didn't the boy understand? "All I am saying is that there are good, trusted ways of doing things. You should not change everything we do too hastily."

"Really", Guðmundr spat. "I didn't hear you say this to Kári when he changed how he traded. Of course, everyone knows that Kári is your favourite, the wonderful trader who can do no wrong."

Ragnar stuttered, "This … this isn't true. I try to advise him as well."

"Well, then he is fortunate in that he is not here to hear your advice. And I wish I wasn't either." And with that Guðmundr stalked off, leaving Ragnar to look bewildered after him.

After this, relations between Ragnar and Guðmundr deteriorated. Ragnar took enough heed of what had happened to stop changing Guðmundr's instructions, and for some time he tried to avoid commenting on how Guðmundr ran the farm. But the two would now never ride together around the farm, and as time went by, Ragnar began to hope that his son's rage was over and that he would again appreciate his father's advice, and so he began to speak again about what to do. But Guðmundr was rarely in the mood to listen, even when he would afterwards realise that his father might sometimes be in the right.

*

In the winter, three years after Ragnar had divided his property between his sons, a man came riding to Snæströnd. He was not from that part of Iceland and was not known to either Guðmundr or Kári. When he arrived at the farm, he was met by both brothers and by their father. When he had entered the house and been given warm ale to drink, he asked, "Is this Snæströnd? And is one of you Kári Ragnarsson?"

"I am he", Kári replied. "Who are you?"

"My name is Bjarni. I have come from Orkney."

"You sailed in the winter?" Kári was impressed.

"Yes. And I hope never to have to do so again!"

He paused, and Kári and Guðmundr waited.

"In Kirkjuvágr, I met a man known to you. His name was Alfred Hákonsson, from Jórvik."

"Alfred? Of course I know him. How was he?"

"He was well. He bade me tell you that Tostig is no longer jarl in Jórvik and that he and his father would gladly see you return there, and the sooner the better. He said that there will be much and good trading."

"And you sailed to Iceland during the winter just to deliver this message?" Guðmundr asked.

"No, no, I had other reasons to do that. But when I came here I thought I should deliver my message."

"You have my thanks", Kári said. "And I think you are welcome to stay the winter at Snæströnd, unless you have somewhere else to go with another message."

As Guðmundr and Ragnar both nodded, Bjarni said, "I do not, and I would be glad to stay here until the spring."

Chapter 7

Winter – Summer 1066

That winter Kári spent much time visiting neighbouring farms to arrange the crew for the voyage to Jórvik. Because it was now six years since they had been to Jórvik, and because of Bjarni's message promising much trade, many clamoured to send their sons with him. As was now his custom, he decided to take just three farmhands from Snæströnd so that they could take seven of those who were by now calling themselves Kári's men. Odd had offered to stay at home to make room for one more, but Kári had not accepted this.

"I have only been to Jórvik once", he said, "and you know the sailing there far better than I. Also, I think that Hákon would be pleased to see you – and you would probably like to see him as well."

"Both of those things are true", Odd whispered with a grin. "But I thought you wanted as many as possible from the other farms."

"Seven will be enough. After all, we will go back to Jórvik in future years. But I want your opinion on another matter."

Odd looked at him. "This sounds important."

Kári looked hesitant. "I am not sure. But my thought is this: for many years now we have traded the same goods. We sail with wadmal and walrus hides and meat; and we return with wood and grain and beer. This is all good and we make a profit, but the profits are always small because the goods we sell do not give us much silver. Now, the way things were going in Jórvik when we were last there, they will not have had much trade in the last few years, so they will have been unable to buy many things. I was thinking that we should bring much more walrus ivory, both carved and uncarved, than we usually do. That will sell for more silver, and even if we buy as much grain as we can carry, we will still come home with more silver than usual. What do you think?"

"Why are you asking me this?"

"I would hear your views."

"I do not think you need those anymore. But, since you ask, I think this is a very good idea. And this will bind your friends even more firmly to you, since they will make more silver with you than their fathers ever did or thought they would. But I will now ask you a question."

"Yes?"

"You are planning this voyage in great detail, which is good. The old Kári would have rushed to get the knarr into the water as soon as he could and not thought as much about what to carry as about getting to Jórvik first. What happened to him?"

Kári smiled ruefully. "The old Kári, as you call him, is still there. The temptation to rush, to act first and think later, is always with me. But I have you and my father to teach me otherwise, and so I try to rein him in."

Odd laughed and clapped Kári affectionately on the shoulder. "I am glad to hear that. But do not let the old Kári disappear. Sometimes, acting before thinking is also good."

"I will remember that too", Kári said.

When the spring came, the knarr was carefully prepared with walrus oil and tar, and the oars, ropes and sails checked for any damage over the winter. The ship was launched and loaded with as much ivory as Kári and his friends could gather together. The launch party was more raucous than usual, as men drank to the profitable journey, with many toasts drunk to Kári, 'the master trader', as his friends now called him. Ragnar and Guðmundr also took part in the feast, but once again Guðmundr found that he was not happy. He did not know why. He did not want to go abroad to trade. Was he jealous of Kári, who was surrounded by friends who admired him? He didn't think so. Guðmundr knew that there was no lack of men who envied him, but he was not sure there were many who liked him. But he didn't think he cared. He drained another mug of beer and lay down on the grass instead, looking up at the stars. They certainly didn't care either.

The next day, the knarr set sail and, as they had done so many times before, went west towards Snæfellsjökull and then turned south to Reykjanes. Once again, the wind was with them, and on the third day they reached Kirkjuvágr. Nowadays Kári and most of his men were used to the small town, but there was still a feeling of excitement when he – or Odd – steered the knarr into the bay and he saw, rising over the houses, the tower of the church after which the town was named. Of course, he thought with a wry smile, the excitement quickly disappears when one is hit by the smell from the harbour. But reaching the first port away from Iceland was still exciting; a sign that now they were abroad and that the game of trading could begin.

Once they had made the knarr fast, Kári went through the routine of inspecting sails and ropes to make sure nothing needed repairs. He and Odd had previously divided the crew into three groups and the first group was already leaving the ship, heading for the nearest place where they could find ale and women. As Kári knew from experience, for men with silver in their purses, it would not take them long to find what they wanted.

As for himself, he and Odd would do what they always did the first day in Kirkjuvágr. They would go to the inn of Harald the Dane and find out all the news that traders needed to hear.

When Harald saw them, his face broke into a smile. The short man had seemed ancient to Kári six years ago and he still seemed ancient now, but he did not seem to have aged.

"I thought I would see you early in the trading season", he said. "As long as Bjarni's ship did not founder, the message would get you here quickly enough. Now sit down, have some beers and some bread and fish, and I will join you soon." He disappeared, but soon one of his serving women (Kári blushed as he remembered the first time he had been there) showed up with large mugs of beer and a platter of bread and salt fish.

Kári had once asked Odd why the fish was so strongly salted. "Easy", Odd replied. "Salt fish makes you thirsty. So you order more beer. That is why the fish is cheap and the beer expensive."

After a short time, Harald came back and sat down with them, with his own mug. Kári noted that the Dane drank heartily, but carefully avoided the salt fish.

"So you will go to Jórvik", he said. It was clearly a statement, not a question.

"Yes", Odd replied. "But the message was very brief. Can you tell us what happened there?"

Harald drank some beer and thought for a moment. "I am not sure how much I know. I do know that everyone – merchants, priests and nobles, citizens, Danes and English – were getting more and more fed up with Tostig, who kept raising taxes and demanding more money. And then they rose against him and forced him out of the city. Everyone feared that his brothers would destroy Jórvik in revenge, but they didn't – they exiled him instead. Now there is a new jarl, but I forget his name. He is not one of the brothers, though. But that is not the biggest news."

"And what is that?" Kári asked.

"That is that their king died shortly after Christmas. And the new king is none other than Harold Godwinson, Tostig's brother."

"Oh. So is Tostig coming back?" If he did, Kári thought, maybe they should have rushed to Jórvik after all, in order to do their trading and be away before Tostig was once again in power. But he realised this would not have been possible, without braving the sea in mid-winter.

"Not at all", Harald said. "Tostig is still in exile somewhere – Flanders, I hear. There seems to be little love lost between the brothers nowadays. But Harold's crown is still not safe, I hear. People say there are others who want to be king, and Harold has called out the fyrd and is preparing for war."

"War is bad for trading", Odd said. "Will it happen?"

"Nobody knows. But you are right that it would be bad, and many people are worried. I dare say your friend Hákon will tell you more."

Although Kári and Odd tried to find out more, there were many rumours but few hard facts or certain knowledge. Therefore, they decided that it was better to spend as little time as possible in Kirkjuvágr and instead proceed directly to Jórvik. Two days later, they set sail south again, with a grumbling crew that had hoped to spend more time ashore. But both Kári and Odd told them that they would have plenty of time to lose all their silver in Jórvik.

Once again, the journey to Jórvik – down the coast of Scotland and England and rowing up the Humber and Ouse rivers – went smoothly. Kári wondered what would happen when they reached the city. If things really had changed, the first sign would be how much silver the guards demanded for letting them enter. He was less worried that they might be recognised by someone; after all, it was six years since they had been in Jórvik, and it was unlikely that the same men would be on duty and also remember one drunken Icelandic sailor, especially since Tostig had been expelled.

When they approached the Humber, there was another surprise: at the mouth of the river was a warship with alert soldiers who demanded to know who they were and where they were sailing. They didn't ask for any silver, but two of them kept a lookout at the knarr until it had continued well past them. When they rowed up the Ouse the next day, they would from time to time spot other groups of soldiers, either encamped or watching the banks of the river. No one stopped them, but it was clear that their passage was noted. Another difference from their previous visit was that they saw other ships headed in both directions. When Kári remarked on this to Odd, the older man grinned. "Some of them were here last time", he said. "You were so preoccupied with everything that you probably didn't think about them. But it is true that there are more of them now."

When they finally arrived in Jórvik, the sun was already setting. They were challenged from the bridge again, but the challenge was friendly, and they could enter. Kári was standing at his preferred spot at the prow of the knarr and found a space along the stone quay where they could moor, and Odd steered them in. By the time all was made fast, there was already a group of soldiers waiting for them. They were not alone. Kári's heart sank when he recognised the same man who had extorted thirty-five silver pennies from them six years ago. But the man did not seem to recognise them. He asked who they were, where they were from and what they were trading, but did not seem particularly interested in the answers. Instead he yawned and said, "Five silver pennies in toll. And make sure that they are valid coins in good condition, not shaved or clipped."

Kári was not going to ask whether the man recognised him or why the toll was so much lower. Instead, he opened his purse and sorted through his coins; he carefully picked out five English silver pennies with the picture of King Edward that seemed the least worn and handed them over. The man cast a quick glance at them, then handed them to one of his men and disappeared without a word.

Kári didn't say anything either, but he turned a quizzical look at Odd, who merely winked at him.

When they had finished inspecting the knarr for any damage or wear since Kirkjuvágr and had once again let part of the crew ashore, Kári and Odd finally set off on their business. While they walked through the dark streets towards Hákon's house, Odd suddenly asked, "Were you surprised by the lower tolls?"

"No, not really", Kári replied, "This was what you said last time that it should be. But I was surprised that it was the same man who took so much more last time and yet did not even try anything this time."

Odd laughed, but it was a mirthless laugh. "You will find men like him everywhere. They do as they are told. Maybe he enjoyed taking a lot of silver from us, maybe he felt embarrassed. Most probably he didn't think about it at all. But there is a new jarl, and clearly new orders. So the toll collector will be polite and will charge a fair amount. But if tomorrow Tostig is back, you will find that this man is once again arrogant and will demand thirty or even forty pennies."

"This should not happen", Kári said angrily. "How do they expect traders to come back if the rules change at the whim of the ruler?"

"They don't", Odd said. "They don't, because they neither understand nor care. Then, when traders no longer arrive and their flows of silver suddenly dry up, then they care. But most jarls and kings do not think in terms of what is good for traders or for their own merchants. They want their money, true enough. But they don't know how to ensure that they get it by fair means. They think it easier to take by force and not to worry about the consequences."

By now they had arrived at Hákon's house. A servant opened the door to their knock, and, hearing their names, let them in at once, taking them to Hákon's room. Everything looked so similar to last time that Kári was shocked when he realised that the shrunken old man who rose to meet them was Hákon. Alfred was at his father's elbow to help steady him.

Odd too looked taken aback. Hákon noticed and smiled ruefully. "Yes, I have aged. All men do. And I have been ill. But I am still glad to see you."

Odd tried to speak, then swallowed and tried again. "And we to see you. Thank you for your message."

"I wasn't sure that you would get it", Alfred said. "But it was worth trying. Both to get you to return and to give you a head start on other traders."

"We appreciate that", Kári said. "We came as fast as we could."

"Do not thank us. This is what friends are for. Now, let us have some beer." At a sign from Alfred, the servant disappeared, only to return shortly afterwards with four large tankards of beer, while Alfred carefully helped his father to sit down again.

After they had drunk, Odd turned to Hákon again. "It is good to drink Jórvik beer again. It has been far too long. Don't you agree, Kári?"

"It is certainly much better than the beer in Scotland, if that is all you have had", Hákon interjected. Alfred smiled.

Kári said, "I would not presume to judge. But this is good beer, that is true."

"Now", Odd said, "we heard some news in Kirkjuvágr. But they did not know very much. What happened here?"

Hákon and Alfred looked at each other. "It is a complicated story", Hákon said. "Maybe Alfred should tell it – he knows it better."

"I will try to be brief", Alfred said. "I don't know how much was planned, but people were tiring of Tostig and his constant demands for more money and higher taxes. Finally we chose a new jarl, Morcar, the brother of the Jarl of Mercia. Tostig tried to stand against him, but his brother Harold, who is now king, supported us. Tostig left, but he is back from time to time, raiding the coasts. There is talk that he will join forces with the Count of Flanders, or the Duke of Normandy, or the King of Denmark or of Norway – anyone who will give him his lands back and let him kill his brother."

"Will anyone support him?" Kári asked.

"I don't know. We are all happy with Morcar. He keeps the peace and he keeps the taxes low. But there are rumours of war. The Duke of Normandy claims that Harold had promised to support him as king. He is threatening to invade. I am sure you saw plenty of soldiers on your way here?"

Kári nodded. "And warships too, on the Humber."

"Well, nothing has happened so far, and we all hope nothing will happen. But when earls and dukes fight to be king, the one thing you know is that it is a bad time to be a merchant."

"It is a good thing that in Iceland, we do not have either dukes or jarls or kings then", Kári said.

"You are right. Now then, what did you bring us and what do you want to buy?"

Kári noticed that this time, it was Alfred who was doing all the talking. Hákon nodded as his son spoke, and there was no sign of dotage or not understanding. But it was clear that, as his father had aged, Alfred was now making the decisions. He sighed. Was this not also what Ragnar had said a few years ago?

"We bring much walrus ivory. We thought you would not have seen any recently if no traders from Iceland had come. Also some walrus hides. And we would buy grain, as much as we can load. We have been bringing wood from Scotland these last few years and don't really need that as much now."

"Ivory is good", Alfred replied. "I am sure you will get a good price for it. And I will start finding out who now has grain to sell."

While the two of them began to talk about the details and of names of traders to approach, Odd and Hákon were engaged in a different conversation.

"But you cannot just leave", Odd protested. "What about your business?"

"Oh, my business", Hákon replied. "You can see what's going on. Alfred is making all the decisions nowadays. And he's good, mark my words. No, this is my last chance to not just trade with the world, but to see it as well."

"But Rome? How are you going to get there? And what will you take to sell – and what do they have to sell you?"

"Odd, I am not going to Rome to trade. Going to Rome is a holy journey. I am going on a pilgrimage. Listen, now is a good time to go. The country is at peace. Whatever others say, Harold is safe on the throne. Neither Tostig nor anyone else can topple him, because he has the support of all the great men. And we are happy with him too. And as for how to get there, pilgrims go to Rome all the time. Why, only a few years ago, the Scots king, whatever his name was, went. King Canute went once. You know, even Tostig, our late earl, went. Mind you, he got robbed, so he can't have been a true pilgrim."

"What do you mean?"

"A true pilgrim could not be harmed on his pilgrimage. God would surely not permit it."

Privately, Kári was not so sure about the White Christ's protection of pilgrims. But he did like the thought of the rapacious Tostig being robbed.

"Anyway", Hákon continued, "I am going. And you should come with me."

"Me?" Odd was surprised.

"Yes, you. Why not? You are a Christian. Don't you want to see where Saint Peter himself trod and founded the Holy Church?"

Odd thought about it. Was he actually a Christian? He knew that everybody in Iceland really was supposed to be Christian. And, true, he had once studied to become a priest, but that was long ago and he had never finished his studies or shaved his head.

Since then, he hadn't thought much about what he believed in. When they launched the knarr each year they would drink to all the gods, to Njörðr and Ægir as well as to the White Christ, but did he believe in one more than the other? Of course, the Christian priest had been very helpful when Einar had accused Guðmundr of assaulting his sister, but that was because it was the right thing to do, not, presumably, because his God told him to intervene.

"I don't know", he finally replied.

"How can you not know?" Hákon said. "What about Kári? Kári, surely you are a Christian?"

Kári was surprised by the question. "In Iceland we are said to be Christian", he replied. "But this is not something we talk much about, and it is not something you ask of men."

That seemed to surprise Hákon in turn. "But what about your salvation? What about your soul? If you do not believe, you will not be saved!"

Now Odd spoke again. "I would have called myself a Christian once", he said. "That is certainly true. But now? As I said, I don't know."

"Then even more reason that you should come with me to Rome", Hákon said. "It is for your own good."

"Let me think about this", Odd replied, and nothing more was said about the subject.

*

Kári and Odd remained in Jórvik for two months. During this time, they sold all their walrus meat and much of their carved ivory. Hákon bought a beautiful box that Kári had carved and said that he would take it to Rome to fill with holy relics. Kári, who was already working on another box, asked how he would know which relics were true and holy, and Hákon replied that no one would dare forge such holy objects, for fear that the saints would strike them.

They bought as much grain as they could, but they still had plenty of silver left. Almost all the payment for their ivory was in King Harold's new coins, which had recently begun to be minted in

Jórvik. Kári was impressed with the beautiful coins, silver pennies with the picture of the King. Previously, almost all the coins he had seen had been worn by long use or even shaved or clipped. That was why it was always better to weigh the silver than to trust the face value of any coins.

When the time for their departure approached, Odd drew Kári to one side to speak with him privately.

They were standing on the stone quay, looking at the bustling scene, with ships coming and going and men carrying loads to and from moored ships. Odd seemed to have difficulty in saying what was on his mind. Kári was puzzled, but then he understood.

"You wish to go to Rome with Hákon", he said.

"Yes."

"Can I ask why?"

"Not because I have become a Christian again. But something Hákon said is true for me as well. All my life I have traded and sailed in these parts – Orkney, England and Scotland, and sometimes even to Norway. I would like to see more of the world. And they say Rome is a great and noble city. Compared to Rome, Jórvik is a poor little village, less significant than Kirkjuvágr."

"I understand", Kári said. "But we need you."

"No, you don't. You already know that. You didn't even need me for this voyage, but you let me come because I wanted to see Hákon again. He is an old friend. We still have much to talk about, and maybe on the way to Rome we will manage to speak of it all."

Kári thought for a while, then he said "Are you decided?"

"Yes, I am."

"Then I will give you the silver that is due to you, because I am sure you will need it. And I will miss you."

"That will be helpful", Odd replied. "And I will miss you too. But do not think that I will be gone for ever. I will come back to Iceland, this I promise you."

"I will hold you to it", Kári said. And then the two of them embraced.

Some days later, Odd and Hákon left, with Hákon showing great pleasure that his friend was coming with him. Kári felt a brief pang of jealousy. He too would have liked to go to Rome and see the amazing city. But he was happy for Odd to go and looked forward to his return.

Before leaving, Kári had a long talk with Alfred. During this stay, the two of them had spent much time together and had become good friends. It was clear that Alfred was not as hopeful as Hákon.

"My father is a very shrewd man", he said. "But sometimes he takes what he wishes to be and decides that this is also how things really are. He is not worried about war. But I will tell you that not only am I worried, most of my friends are as well. You know that while you have been here, Tostig has been raiding the coasts."

"Yes, but he was driven off by your new jarl."

"He was. But we fear we have not seen the last of him. Listen, we were concerned when his brother became king, but so far he has been a good king. But every day we hear new rumours of war. If war comes, it may come in the south, where Harold is; or it may come here. But wherever it comes, it means no trade, and sooner or later it means that a king or a jarl comes and tells us to give him money and to give him men who will fight for him and get killed. You are a trader, Kári, surely you too prefer peace to war?"

"I have no experience of war myself. But yes, even so I know that peace is better, that is certainly true."

"Maybe we are all too worried. Too much has happened over the past years. We could now do with a few years of stability, of good trading and above all of peace and low taxes. But I and many other merchants fear that we will not be granted this."

"I hope you are wrong", Kári said.

"So do I. But I will be glad if next summer we can talk about this again and my gloom has proved unnecessary."

*

The next day, Kári and his men began to row downriver. The weather was still good and they sailed up along the coast with a good southerly wind, which sped them on towards Kirkjuvágr.

As they approached Orkney, however, the sky began to darken and the wind shifted from south to west. At first Kári was not very concerned, but the wind gradually grew stronger and soon rain began to fall, at first lightly and then ever heavier. It did not take long for what had been a strong wind to become a storm, with a rising sea that made it difficult to control the ship. Kári had kept the sail up as long as he could, reducing it to a mere scrap, but now he had to shout at the men to take it in and to ship the oars as well, and to tie themselves to a stay so that they would not be washed overboard. He lashed himself to the steering oar and tried to maintain a northward course, but this became impossible, even when one of the other crew members tried to assist him. Squalls of rain came sweeping in over the knarr, which lifted and plunged terrifyingly as the huge waves passed under the hull.

As it grew darker still, Kári could barely see beyond the prow of the ship. By now he was wet all through and so cold that his fingers were locked round the steering oar. He could taste salt water on his lips from the spray that was flung up every time the ship crashed into the troughs between the waves. At first he had worried about the cargo, but soon he realised that this was the least of his worries. The knarr was a sturdy ship and well built, but it was taking a tremendous thrashing. As they were tossed hither and thither, Kári lost all sense of direction; he hoped that the wind would stay in the west, for he knew that he had sea room to the east. He did not know how long the storm had lasted or if it was day or night, there was just mind-numbing fear, and the mighty power of the sea and the wind.

Much later – how much, Kári neither knew nor cared – there was a brief lull in the storm. The skies remained dark, and the ship still rose and fell wildly on the foaming seas, but the wind abated from its dreadful scream and at least the crewmen could call to each other and have a break from the bailing. Kári was heartened to hear that they had lost no one. But he felt exhausted, with every bone in his body aching, and he assumed everyone else on board felt the same. He told the men to drink something and to try to get some rest before the storm hit again, as he was sure it would.

This might only be his second storm – and much worse than the first – but he had heard enough stories from Odd and from other older men that he feared the wind and high seas would last some time yet before they abated. He could only hope that they would survive the second half of the storm.

In the end, he managed to snatch a little sleep, still tied to the steering oar. But then the wind picked up again and the noise increased. The knarr sped along, although in what direction, no one could have said; the bow was pushed one way and another as it rose on the crest of one wave, only to plummet to the bottom of the next one, while the seas repeatedly sprayed them all.

The storm continued to rage and Kári gave up any pretence of trying to measure time or to steer. There was lightning too, and he could see most of the men lying supine on the knarr, not even attempting to move.

Eventually he became certain that the frenzied note of the wind shrieking through the rigging was dropping. And indeed the storm quieted and the waves, though still huge, were less confused, and the knarr rode them more smoothly. It was still very dark, though gradually Kári began to see some stars through rifts in the clouds.

And then the sun rose in front of them, and in its light they could see that they were headed towards a coast. They were still too far away to see much beyond the mountain peaks that were rising high above the water. But since the sun rose above the mountains, Kári knew that they were at least headed towards the east. That could mean Norway or Denmark. But he had never heard that Denmark had any mountains, whereas everyone always spoke of the mountains in Norway. So this was almost certainly Norway. In front of him, the men were already, unbidden, getting their oars out. But not all the oars; Kári saw three of the men looking ruefully at the remains of oars that somehow had been broken during the storm. He called out to them to raise the sail as well. That was hard and heavy work, with the sail sodden and stiff, but at least they still had both a sail and a mast.

As they approached the coast, he could see that it was broken by many inlets. He did not know which to steer for, but when they came even closer, he thought he could spot some ships slightly to the north, so he altered course towards them.

They sailed in this direction for some time, until they approached the mouth of a large fjord. As they rounded a promontory, Kári suddenly drew breath sharply. In front of him, he saw hundreds of ships, lying in the sun. Many of them were longships, and from the reflection of the sunlight on their decks and the shields along their sides, he realised that they had warriors on board. There were also smaller ships, knarrs and other smaller trading and fishing vessels. In front of them was a large and exceedingly beautiful ship, with a carved and painted dragon's head at the prow. This was the largest ship Kári had ever seen, and surely the most beautiful as well. He realised that only a great sea captain or a king could own such a ship. On the shores of the bay he saw what seemed to be a huge city of tents, certainly bigger than Kirkjuvágr, although not as big as Jórvik. This was surely an army, perhaps even the King's host.

Even as he thought this, a smaller boat approached the knarr. Once they were within earshot, a man stood up and called out "Who are you, and where do you come from?"

"We are Icelandic traders", Kári replied. "I am Kári Ragnarsson and this is my ship. We come from Jórvik and were blown here by the storm. Where are we?"

When he said Jórvik, the man started. Then he replied, "Jórvik, eh? You will now follow us into the bay and wait where I show you."

"We need supplies and repairs", Kári called, but the man just repeated what he had said.

Kári ordered the men to reef the sail again and then row slowly after the small boat, which was clearly trying to find a place where they could moor the knarr. It was not easy, because every spot seemed to be full of ships or tents or men, but finally they found some space between two ships.

The pilot rowed away, but the man called out once again, "Wait here. Do not go ashore, and do not try to leave."

Once the knarr was safely moored, Kári and the men began to go over the ship. The sail was unfurled and laid out to dry in the sun. The ropes were inspected; most were in good condition, but some were clearly fraying. And both the cargo and the hull were carefully inspected. They had been fortunate, Kári realised. The hull was still intact and did not show too much damage, though they would need three new oars. However, it turned out that in spite of careful stowing and fastening, they had lost some of the cargo.

Once they finished with the ship, Kári told the men to have some food while they waited. Some time later, a group of soldiers approached them in a small boat. The man who had hailed them earlier was with them. When they were close enough, he called out, "Who is the master of this ship?"

"I am", Kári replied.

"Come with me."

Kári sighed. He had expected as much the moment he saw the fleet, but he was not going to submit tamely. "Where to? And why? And where are we?"

"As to why, because I say so", the man said. "And I say so with the power of these ships and these men. As for where to, King Harald wishes to see you."

"The King?" Kári was bewildered. But at least he now knew where they were. Harald meant that they were definitely somewhere in Norway.

"So I said. He heard that you have just been to Jórvik and would speak with you. Now come, or would you wish my men to come and get you? Oh – it would be a good idea to bring him a gift."

"A gift?"

"A gift. It is always wise to bring the King a gift when you meet him."

Kári thought back to his first visit to Jórvik. There it had been the guardsmen who demanded extra silver. Here, apparently the king did it directly. But the pattern was the same: you are in my power, I have the might, I will take something valuable from you. Inwardly, he cursed this king and all his greedy men. But he knew that, once again, he had no choice.

"I will come", Kári said. Turning to his crew, he said to one of the men from Snæströnd, "Hallvarðr, you are in command until I come back. Do not let anyone leave the ship." Then he went to the prow of the ship, where he kept his own things. He had heard that King Harald was a fervent Christian, and he knew what the 'gift' would have to be. Sighing, he took out the ivory reliquary, the pair to the one that Hákon had bought, and brought it with him. The Norwegian looked at it but said nothing. They walked along the shore in silence, but when they mounted a small hill, Kári once again saw the beautiful longship and stopped for a moment to look at it. At this, the Norwegian and his men stopped too.

"Impressive, isn't it", he said.

Kári nodded. "Beautiful", he replied.

"That is the *Serpent*, the King's own ship. It is the biggest in the fleet", the Norwegian said.

They continued and came to a large tent. Outside was a group of guards and another group that was more richly dressed. After they had taken Kári's dagger from him, they stood aside to let him and his guide pass. One man standing at the opening of the tent turned inside to say something, and then Kári and the Norwegian, whose name he still did not know, were signalled inside.

It took Kári a few moments to adjust his eyes to the darkness in the tent. Then he saw that there were some chairs and a large table inside. No one was sitting down, but a very tall man, a man who topped Kári by at least two heads, was standing by the table. He was fair-haired and had a long lip-beard and, strangely, one of his eyebrows was higher than the other. When they entered he turned and looked at them.

"Lord", Kári's guide said. "This is the man from Jórvik. Kári Ragnarsson."

"Not from Jórvik", Kári said. "We are Icelanders."

"But you just came from Jórvik, did you not?" the tall man – King Harald, Kári realised – said.

"We did. We were blown here by the storm."

Harald sat down. "Sit", he said. "Tell me about Jórvik. But wait – there is someone else who needs to hear." He made a sign to Kári's guide, who disappeared.

Kári turned to the King. "Lord", he said, "I hear that you follow the White Christ."

"I do. Surely you do too?"

Kári didn't know what to say, then replied "In Iceland, we have decided to do so."

Harald nodded.

"I have a gift for you, Lord. A token of gratitude for your kindness in letting us resupply and sail unharmed." Best get that said at once, he thought. Then he held out the reliquary.

Harald seemed impressed and took the box. Kári had decorated it with figures of the White Christ, such as had been described to him by Odd, and also with pictures of other holy men he had been told of.

Harald looked at the carvings. "This is a princely gift, Kári. I thank you. Now as to resupply and sailing, we must discuss this. But first, I would hear what Jórvik is like. What do men say, what do they think?"

Before Kári could say anything, the entrance to the tent opened again and two men entered. Neither said anything and the King waved at them to sit down and signalled to Kári to continue.

Kári said, "What do you want to know?"

"First tell me what they are saying about their new king and their new jarl."

"They are pleased that Tostig is gone. They say the new jarl is a better ruler. He doesn't ask for more money and higher taxes all the time." Kári thought for a while, then continued, "I think they like their new king as well. They say he is fair."

One of the two men who had joined them snorted. "Fat merchants! All they think about is their money." Kári was surprised to hear that he was not Norwegian but English. And he was annoyed by the man's comment.

"Those 'fat merchants' are the ones who provide you with the money you spend. Where else would you get it? They are worth ten times such as you!"

The man flushed, but Harald laughed. "Well replied, Kári. What else do they say?"

"They worry that there will be war. The Duke of Normandy says he should be king instead of Harold."

"Would they support him if he came?"

"I don't think so. Some said that he claimed a better right to be king than Harold, but I think that what the people of Jórvik want more than anything else now is peace. They had a bad time under Tostig and want to recover. A friend there said to me that they now want good trading, peace and low taxes."

Harald smiled. "We will give them peace and good trading. As for low taxes – we shall see. How about their king? Can he defend his realm?"

"That", Kári replied, "I do not know. There were more guards, both in the city and on warships in the river, than I had seen before."

"And where is he?"

"I do not know that either. But men said he is in the south, for that is where the Duke will attack."

Harald sat back and glanced at the other two men, who rose and left the tent. Kári was not sure what he was supposed to do so he stood up and waited. The King looked at him quizzically.

"Lord, may I go back to my ship? We need repairs and supplies, but then we would like to return to Iceland as soon as possible with the grain we have bought."

"Ah. I'm afraid that is not so easy, Kári. I cannot let you leave right now. I'm sure you understand why."

For a moment Kári considered pretending that he did not know what the King was talking about. But he did not like to pretend to be stupid, and he doubted that Harald would believe him. "You intend to attack Jórvik", he said, "and you fear I would warn them."

"Would you?"

"Yes I would. I am not your man and I have friends there."

Strangely, the King did not seem angered by the reply. "That is an honest answer", he said. "It is what I thought you would do, and in your position I would do exactly the same, though I might not admit it so openly to the King. But that is also why I cannot let you go. Oh, and you are wrong. I am not just aiming to attack Jórvik. I intend to become King of England."

"What? Why?" Kári exclaimed before he could stop himself.

"England is mine by right. My nephew Magnus made an agreement with Harthacanute that whoever survived the other would inherit his kingdom. Well, Harthacanute died first and so Magnus should by right be king of Denmark and of England as well as of Norway. And, of course, I inherit his rights. I am the rightful King of England and I will make it so in fact as well as in name. Now you know why I cannot let you go just yet."

Kári was not happy, but he knew that Harald would not care much about that. "Well, then, will you allow us to trade here until we can leave?"

"No, I don't think that is possible either. We need all the supplies here for the fleet." Harald was quiet for a moment, then he continued, "Unless, of course, you agree to become my man."

"I am not one of your men, Lord. I am a free Icelander."

"Yes, yes, I know. But see here, Iceland was settled by Norwegians. We are kin. You have already proven yourself a friend by your generous gift. Why not join me?"

"I am not a soldier, Lord. And I wish to return to Iceland." Kári did not say it, but he thought that if he returned as a king's man, not only would he lose much honour, but his father and brother would be furious with him. But, most importantly, he did not wish to be one of Harald's men or that of any king or other ruler.

"Because you have already done me some good service, Kári, I will be generous to you", Harald now said. "All I ask is that you become my man as long as you are in my kingdom. What you do elsewhere, I neither know nor care. And, if you do, I promise that you will be allowed to trade without tolls wherever I rule. Now, what do you say?"

Kári thought about what Harald had said. He still did not want to become a king's man, but he knew that he needed some agreement in order to repair his ship.

"I will promise not to oppose you as long as you live and I am in your realm", he said.

"That is good enough", Harald said. "Now, as my man and since you will not oppose me, you understand that I will need your ship and your grain for my fleet."

Kári realised at once that he had been tricked. He began to feel a red rage, greater than ever before. He had come to the King's presence without a sword, but for a brief moment he felt an overpowering urge to throw himself at the tall man and strangle him.

Then Harald laughed. "Come now", he said. "If I wanted to kill you and take your ship, I would have done so already. And if I wanted you dead, it were easily done." He looked towards the entrance of the tent, and Kári followed his gaze. He had forgotten about the two guards who were standing there. They did not move, but their eyes were locked on Kári, and he did not doubt that if he had followed his urge, he would have been dead before he could take one step towards the King. His shoulders dropped and he tried to force himself to relax.

"It is not as bad as you think", the King said. "This will not take long. I will be crowned in London before Christmas. You will have your ship back, I will pay you handsomely for your grain and you will trade freely in Norway, England and anywhere else where I rule. And remember, that may one day mean Iceland as well. When I do, I will have need of good men there too. In the meantime, here – see how this will fit your arm." And he removed a golden arm-ring that he had been wearing and tossed it over to Kári.

Kári caught the ring. Harald's words had sounded fair enough, but he realised two things. The first was that the moment he put the ring on his arm, he would mark himself for everyone as a king's man. And the second was that, beyond the golden ring, Harald had no intention of paying him for his grain. For a brief moment he contemplated throwing the ring back in the King's face. What joy it would be to see his smile disappear! But the guards were still watching him, as was Harald. He didn't trust himself to speak, but he slid the ring on his arm. The King nodded and turned away, and Kári understood that their talk was finally over. He left the tent and, after retrieving his dagger, walked back through the camp to his ship, dark thoughts chasing each other through his head.

Finding a man with a small boat, he asked him to take him out to his ship. The man agreed immediately, and Kári was initially rather surprised at the deference he was shown, until he realised he was still wearing the golden arm-ring and so marked out as important. Useful, he thought, but it did not in any way change his view that it was not a treasure but a fetter.

When he came back to the knarr, his men looked at him. "What is wrong, master?" Hallvarðr asked.

Kári didn't say anything. Instead, he boarded the knarr, removed the ring from his arm and hurled it on the deck. Then he went to the prow, signalling the crew to gather around him. Then he said, "The Norwegians will come and take our grain. You might as well take the gold ring – it is all we will ever get for it. As for me, I will not take that man's gold!"

Some of the men started to object, but he held up his hand. "That is not the worst of it. That turd, that disgusting lying scoundrel, Loki would have been proud of his trickstering, he is going to attack Jórvik. And we have to go with him!"

Again, the men began to ask questions, but one or two of them also looked around to see that they could not be overheard. At first, Kári did not reply. Once again, he felt the rage building up in him. "I would have killed him if I had carried a sword. Useless, disgusting coward. He's a dog. Less than a dog; a dog's turd."

Then he explained what had happened, interspersed with further insults to Harald and to all Norwegians. When the crew heard, the men from the other farms all said, "We have to fight. This king and his slaves shall not steal our goods." But the three men from Snæströnd looked at each other. They had heard similar curses from Ragnar in the past.

"Master, we agree this is wrong", Hallvarðr said, while the other two nodded. "But we cannot fight all the Norwegians at one time. Instead, we should plan what to do now and how to get away."

Kári looked at them all. He really wanted to go back to Harald's tent and kill him. But he knew that he would not get far before he was killed himself; and even if by some miracle he managed to kill the King, it would not help matters. He and his crew would all be killed. He was the ship's master, and the crew's – his men's – lives were his responsibility. He took a deep breath and held up his hand. As the men quietened down, he said, "We will not fight. Fighting will not achieve anything. But nor will we agree to everything they wish. I have promised to not oppose King Harald while he lives and I am in his realm. But that promise was forced from me and I do not feel bound by it. This is therefore what we will do. First, if they come to take our grain, we will hand it over. We will remember who took it and how much, and we will ask for payment. I doubt that we will get any, but we will deal with that in due course. What is more important is, can we somehow send a warning to Jórvik?"

Some of the men grumbled at his words, although eventually they all agreed that what he said was right. But try as they might, no one could think of any way to evade the Norwegians and send a message to Jórvik.

They remained with the Norwegian fleet for some time. Kári did not see any more of the King, but their grain was taken, and they could see more and more ships and men arrive in the fjord. That apart, and except for the occasional trip ashore to find water or buy more food – at a price – they were largely left alone and heard little of the King's plans. But they knew they were watched and there was never any chance of an escape. At least Harald ran a good camp, though, and it was easy to get new oars for the boat and material for the other repairs made necessary by the storm. But other than that there was very little to do, or to keep the crew occupied, and the men clamoured to go ashore.

At this, Kári told his men "I will not stop you from going ashore. But you should be aware of the dangers. On this ship, you are free men from Iceland. But once you step on the land, the King does not see you that way, nor do his men. What they see is a ship they want, a cargo they have taken and men who would make good soldiers. Some of you may like that. That is up to you. You have to decide your own life. But this is the advice that I would give you. Be careful ashore. Never go alone. Make sure you come back in the evening – do not spend the night away. And never get drunk with the King's men, lest you wake up the next morning and find that you have agreed to join his host."

Some of the men grumbled when they heard this and said that they were not his thralls or his children. To this, Kári replied that they were right. He was not telling them what to do, only suggesting what they should do if they wanted to remain in his crew. "For on the ship, and as long as we are at sea, I am the master and I command", he said. "But I do so because you wanted to join my crew. I did not force you to come with me, nor will I force you to remain with me here."

The men thought about what he had said and discussed it among themselves. Kári did not say anything more, nor did he ask them what they wished to do. But it came to pass that when the time came to sail, all his men were still with him.

As summer turned to autumn, they saw more activity on the other ships, until one day they saw tents being struck and groups of men boarding the ships. A group of fifteen armed men appeared alongside; their leader said that they had been allocated to Kári's ship "for his protection" and would sail with them. Kári noted grimly that they had brought very little food with them but before he could say anything the leader spoke again. "And don't worry about feeding us. Those fat English farms will soon provide more than enough for us and you too."

And so they sailed for England.

Chapter 8

Spring 1066 – Spring 1067

At Snæströnd that spring, things were not well. The farm was still prosperous, but Guðmundr found himself spending much time riding alone to the neighbours or around the farm. Where once he had been known as a cheerful man who often smiled and who liked to be surrounded by friends, now, even when he was at home, he would prefer to spend time alone. Not even his children, Guðrún and Eirík, could do much to make him smile.

At first, Ása had not said much. She remembered how close they had been at the beginning of their marriage and hoped that Guðmundr would return to being the same man again. But as time went by, this did not happen and she saw him growing ever more distant and unhappy. Her parents lived too far away to be of help. Instead, she spent more time with the children.

Yet after some time, Ása decided that she had to speak with her husband. At first, Guðmundr tried to behave as if nothing was wrong, but Ása persisted. "You did not marry a stupid woman, even if Jórunn thinks so", she said. "Something is wrong, and I want to help you."

Guðmundr did not like her speaking about Jórunn, but only said, "This is something you cannot help me with."

"How do you know if you do not give me the chance to try?" she replied.

"Perhaps you are right", Guðmundr said. And so he told her about how his father still tried to decide everything and how he had quarrelled with Ragnar and how this made him feel that his father would never see him as a man and how Ragnar always favoured Kári.

"Are you jealous of Kári?"

"No. This is not my brother's fault. But he is away and doesn't have Father always looking at what he does and finding fault with him."

Ása thought about this and said, "I fear this is often the way with people. Your father is a strong-willed man. He was successful in many things, but he now sees that you are surpassing him, and maybe it makes him feel smaller. And so he feels that he has to show that he still knows a thing or two. It also makes him feel useful in his old age."

"But what should I do?"

"For the moment, say nothing. You love working on the farm and you know the men want your leadership. Show them that you, not Ragnar, are their leader. Not by quarrelling with him, but by being with them. And if you are here more and doing the things that need doing on the farm with them, they will get used to you making the decisions. In this way, you will become their leader and the master of Snæströnd in fact as well as in name, and yet you will spare your father's feelings. And if you spend more time on the farm, you spend more time with me and with Guðrún and Eirík, and that is also good."

Guðmundr felt embarrassed but saw the wisdom in her words. "You are right, and I will take your advice", he said.

For some time after that, Guðmundr felt much better, and his relations with Ása improved. But eventually the dark thoughts returned and the two of them frequently quarrelled. These quarrels were often started by trivial matters, but they continued for a long time and, since both of them were proud people, it was ever more difficult for them to be reconciled. Almost the only time they would not quarrel was when they lay with each other, and this they still did often enough. But where Ása continued to love Guðmundr and hope that he would return to her, he found it difficult to rekindle the love he had once felt.

Ragnar and Hallgerður saw what was happening. Ragnar thought of speaking with Guðmundr, but Hallgerður felt he should not do this. "This is between man and wife", she said. "You can speak with our son, and maybe he will tell you what is wrong. But it will be difficult for you to make him change his behaviour. That is something he must decide himself."

"I know my son", Ragnar replied, "and I fear that he is too stubborn to change on his own. Like his father, perhaps", he added with an attempt at a laugh.

"Don't say that; this is not a laughing matter. And though you say you know him well enough, the question is whether you know yourself." Hallgerður said.

"What do you mean?"

"I mean that Guðmundr may now have problems with Ása, but it is possible that his unhappiness comes from you."

"From me?"

"You are not letting him grow up. He is a grown man and should be allowed to run his life and Snæströnd the way he wishes. Is this not what you always talk about? The freedom to take responsibility for your own life?"

"Yes, of course, but …"

"But nothing. If you would destroy your son, then speak with him. But you will regret it."

"I do not agree", Ragnar said. "Nevertheless, in this I will be guided by you, at least for the time being."

But although Hallgerður had seen why Guðmundr was unhappy, in one aspect of the matter, Ragnar was right. Guðmundr felt trapped. He knew he was dissatisfied and that he was at fault but did not know what to do or how to behave differently. Instead, he continued to spend as much time as he could away from the farmhouse, leaving early in the morning and returning home late in the evening. Then he would often sit up all night, drinking alone and disappearing again the next morning before anyone else had woken up.

One evening, when he came home late and was as usual sitting and drinking, Ása came to sit with him. At first she did not say anything and so he took no notice of her. But after some time, she began to speak. "How long will this continue?"

"What do you mean?" Guðmundr replied.

"You know full well what I mean. You are rarely home and when you are home, you are never with me, nor with the children. I married the man I loved, yet now I find that I might as well have married a ghost or be a widow since I never see you. I thought this had passed, but I see that it has not."

"You exaggerate", Guðmundr said, but he knew that what she said was true.

"Do I? When did you last play with your children? Guðrún is old enough now to know who you are, but only two days ago she asked me who the strange man is who comes and sits here at night and if you are a ghost."

"Then it is your fault for not teaching her better!" Guðmundr snapped before taking a long draught of beer.

"How can I teach her when you are not here? Guðmundr, what is wrong with you?"

Guðmundr slammed down the beer mug so hard that it spilled on the table. "You do not understand how difficult it is to run a farm this size!" he said.

"Then tell me. How can I understand if you don't want me to help you? I love you, Guðmundr, I always have since the day we met. But you must speak to me. I want to help you." Ása had tears in her eyes and even Guðmundr could hear the despair in her voice.

Guðmundr looked at her. Suddenly he thought she had never looked so beautiful. The candles flickered and cast shadows on her face, and her shadow danced on the wall behind her. He could not understand why he didn't love her the way she deserved and the way he thought he once had. Suddenly he held out his arms to her and she came to his embrace. He kissed her mouth hungrily and began to tear at her shift. She responded eagerly and they fell to the floor. He was biting her breasts while she was trying to unlace his trousers. He helped her to remove them and pushed himself into her. Their lovemaking was more excited and urgent than it had been for a long time. For Ása, it felt as it had when they were newly wed. She moaned his name and felt both her and his breathing become heavier. Suddenly he arched his back and climaxed, exclaiming "Jórunn!"

For a blink of an eyelid, Ása froze. Then she pushed him away from her and stood up, gathering her shift around her again. Guðmundr looked at her, appalled at what he had done. He had not meant it. He really wanted her, not Jórunn. Or did he? He didn't know anymore.

Ása looked at him, with a look in her eyes and a face he had never seen. He began to stammer, "Ása, I –", but she cut him off.

"This will not be forgotten", she said in a voice cold as ice. Guðmundr tried to say something, but she continued without listening. "When you are here, we will share a bed. This is your home and my children are also your children. But I will not lie with you again."

"But – you are my wife", he spluttered.

"Am I? Then whose name did you just call out? Maybe you married the wrong one after all. Perhaps you should go back to her."

And then she turned around and left him. Guðmundr felt a mixture of shame and anger. Most of all, he was angry at himself for his stupidity. But the anger also grew at Ása, and as he stood up and fastened his trousers, he called after her, "Maybe I will do just that." Then he walked out, slamming the door behind him.

For the remainder of the spring and early summer, Guðmundr rarely came home. When he came, he would speak politely with Ása and he would try to be friendly to his children. But although no one knew exactly what had happened between them, the state of their relationship soon enough became common knowledge.

For Hallgerður and Ragnar, this was a source of great sadness and Hallgerður admitted to Ragnar that she should have let him speak with Guðmundr. But although Ragnar now tried, his son made sure to stay away from him as well.

As for Guðmundr, his self-loathing grew. He did not know where he had gone wrong, but he felt that everything he had touched had turned to ashes and dust. That others envied him his wealth and his influence only made it worse, and the more he thought about this, the darker his thoughts became. At first, he had thought of trying to beg Ása for forgiveness, but soon he began to blame her instead. This situation lasted until it was time for the Thórsnesthing.

*

And so the time came for the Thórsnesthing, and Guðmundr and Ása remained very distant from each other. At this year's Thing, there were not many important disputes to be settled. True, Leifur had not yet paid his fine to Ragnar, but that was because he had appealed to the Althing, so this issue was not discussed here. What little there was to decide was dealt with by the goðar alone. Eirík had spoken with Guðmundr. He, like everybody else, had heard about the events at Snæströnd and had asked if there was anything he could do to help.

When Guðmundr remained silent, Eirík said, "I am your friend, Guðmundr. I would like to help you, if I can. You are too important for me to see you like this without offering my support. But I will not push you to accept it."

Guðmundr realised that Eirík was being friendly, but still did not feel that this was something he wanted to talk about with the goði. Instead, he said, "Goði, I thank you for your concern." But then he said no more and took his leave. Eirík watched him go. He worried about his friend. But he also wondered what this meant for him. He had come to respect Guðmundr for his thoughts and to rely on him for much advice. Without Guðmundr by his side, things could only become more difficult.

Guðmundr walked away, and for some time he wandered aimlessly through the booths that made up the Thing market. He found some beer and walked along, drinking. As the day wore on and evening began to fall, he found himself outside the market and walked up a small hill and down the other side, where he sat down. Then he suddenly laughed a short, bitter laugh. This was where he had lain with Jórunn the last time, the time when she told him that she would not wed him or anyone else.

He lay down in the grass and looked up at the stars that were slowly beginning to appear in the twilight. He drank more beer and thought, what would have happened if I had married Jórunn instead?

"Well, you certainly wouldn't be lying here, all alone", a voice said.

"Huh! What?" Too late, Guðmundr realised that he must have spoken those words aloud. Had he really drunk as much as that? "Who's there?"

When he heard the laughter, he knew. He should have known anyway. "Jórunn! What are you doing here?"

"What are you doing here yourself?" she replied. "Or maybe we are both here for the same reason. To be away from other people. May I sit down?" Without waiting for an answer, she sat down next to him.

Guðmundr tried to sit up, but the effort was too much, and he lay down on his back again. He really must have drunk a lot, he thought, but he couldn't remember doing so.

For a moment neither of them said anything. Guðmundr found it hard to collect his thoughts properly, and Jórunn did not know quite what to say. In truth, she didn't really know what to think of him either.

At one time she had certainly enjoyed being with him. He was handsome and he made her feel good. If only he had not started talking about being wed. But why did he then have to go and marry the mouse? That had been the start of all her troubles.

She knew that it was jealousy that made her concoct the wild plan with Einar to accuse Guðmundr of attempted rape. But Einar was a fool, incapable of doing anything right. He should have made sure that there were no witnesses! At least Guðmundr had not brought a case against them in return. Maybe he did still care for her?

But since then, things had got worse. Although the whole matter was supposed to remain secret, people had of course talked. And so she found that those who were previously her friends had begun to shun her. People who did not know who she was looked strangely at her or tended to avoid her once they heard her name.

Even her father was changing. Previously, he had always indulged her. True, she was a daughter and it was Einar who would inherit the goðorð and the farm. But Einar really was a fool, and her father knew that. If he needed advice, he would ask her, not her brother. And he had accepted that she did not want to get married, at least at first. But this too had changed. Now he would frequently bring home men who clearly were intended as possible husbands for her. She had changed too. Maybe marriage would not be such a bad thing after all. At least, if wed, she would become the mistress of a farm – and if she knew her father, it would be a rich farm. Instead, she found herself at home, with a father who no longer indulged her and instead tried to rein her in; and a brother whom she despised, but who would in due course also try to run her life. But the men her father brought home all seemed scared of her. It seemed that none of them wanted a woman with a mind of her own, someone who could answer back and tell them if they said something foolish. When she was younger, people had liked that. Now it seemed that they were put off instead. And although Jórunn was still not keen on giving up her independence, she was beginning to realise that not being married and growing old alone on her father's farm – or worse, when it became Einar's farm – was not very attractive either.

Should she have accepted Guðmundr that day so many years ago? She didn't really know. But she did know that her father would never have agreed to it, so what did it matter?

Suddenly Guðmundr sighed. Once again he tried to sit up, and this time he succeeded. "What do you want?" he asked.

"I wanted to be away from all the people at the Thing", she said. "Why are you here?"

"So did I. I couldn't bear listening to them talking about their silly concerns, coming to ask me questions about matters I didn't care to talk about. But you were always with so many people?"

"That was long ago", she said sadly. "Now, no one wants to be with me any more."

Guðmundr didn't know what to say. Without thinking, he put his arm around her and pulled her closer to him. She leaned against him and for a brief moment it felt like old times. "Thank you", she said.

"What for?"

"For not bringing a case against us – that time. And for being here, now."

He didn't say anything, but continued to hold her close. Then he sighed.

"What is the matter?" she asked.

"Everything." And suddenly Guðmundr found himself talking about his unhappiness, in a way he had never been able to talk to Ása. He told her about how his father did not leave him alone and how he felt that nothing he did was ever good enough. He did not tell her about his quarrels with Ása, but Jórunn had already heard some rumours, and she also realised that one reason he was speaking with her was because he could not say this to his wife.

She put her arm around him and embraced him. "Poor boy", she murmured, "my poor boy."

Then she let go of him again and said, "I want you to know one thing. What I did – that time – I did it because I was jealous, that is true. But I never intended for you to get really hurt. I wanted to scare you and punish you. But I really didn't want you to get hurt."

Was that true? By now, she didn't really know. But she was glad that he was there with her now.

And so was Guðmundr. He had felt bad when he had called her name with Ása. But, truth to tell, having Jórunn there now made him feel much better.

They sat there for another while, neither of them talking, both of them feeling comforted by the other's presence.

Much later, Guðmundr stood up, still somewhat unsteadily, and Jórunn also rose. "I have to go back", both of them said at the same time. Then they both burst out laughing.

Guðmundr stopped first and said "I cannot remember when I last laughed! I am glad I met you and that we spoke. I now feel much better."

"And so do I", she replied. "But it is perhaps best if no one else knows that we have done so."

"I think this is right."

And so they separated and went back to the by now dark and quiet Thing booths.

For some time after this, they did not see each other. Guðmundr returned to Snæströnd, but there he found life even colder than before the Thing, with little to please him. After a month or so, he saddled his horse and rode away. At first, he thought that he did not know where he was going, but soon enough he realised that he was riding towards Gunnar's farm. He didn't really know what he would do there. He certainly could not appear at the farm and ask to meet Jórunn. But he could at least go to the neighbourhood and see what would happen.

The first time he did this, he rode aimlessly around for a day and then finally returned to Snæströnd, having neither seen nor spoken with anybody. But a few days later he repeated the ride, and this time, close to Gunnar's farm, he saw Jórunn, also riding alone. He reined in his horse and waited to see what would happen. At first, it seemed that she had not seen him. Her horse continued to walk through the fields. But as he waited, he saw that she was gradually changing direction and coming closer to him. He nudged his own horse forward and down into a shallow dell, and there he dismounted and waited for her.

After some time, he could see first her and then her horse cresting the hill. As soon as she was on his side of the hill and could no longer be seen from the other side, she began to ride faster. Very shortly she was next to him. She slid off her horse and tethered it next to his. Then she turned to look at him. Guðmundr's heart began to beat faster. He knew that what happened next might change his life for ever, but he did not mind. Indeed he was almost excited at the thought.

If Jórunn had any similar thoughts, she didn't show them. Instead, she flung herself into his arms. He pulled her tightly to him and eagerly began to kiss her. As they tore at each other's clothes, he suddenly broke off the kiss and looked around.

Jórunn laughed, the old wicked laugh that he remembered. "I am alone", she said. "I promise." Then they embraced again and fell to the ground, moaning and trying to touch every part of each other's bodies. Finally they managed to get halfway undressed. He was nuzzling her breasts when she suddenly turned him over and mounted him. This had always been their favourite way of making love, and all of a sudden, the memories of all those previous times came back to him. It seemed to Guðmundr as if their lovemaking lasted forever, longer than ever before, and he felt stronger than he ever had felt.

When they were finished, Guðmundr felt completely drained. He looked at Jórunn and said, "I have missed you."

"So have I", she replied, and she realised that she really meant it. When she and Guðmundr had been friends and enjoyed just being together, life had seen so uncomplicated. Why couldn't things have remained like that?

For a while, they were both quiet. Then, as if by unspoken agreement, they reached for each other again. This time, they took it more slowly in the beginning, but as their excitement grew, so did the pace of the lovemaking until it was almost as frenzied as the first time.

Afterwards, Guðmundr said, "I really needed that."

Jórunn looked at him and replied, "Yes, I could feel that." She smiled tenderly. "I knew you would. I could have told you the mouse was not enough for you. In fact I think I once tried to."

When she spoke of Ása, Guðmundr felt a twinge of bad conscience. But then he thought, why? This is all her fault as well. Still, he preferred to avoid this topic altogether.

Instead he said, "What will happen now?"

Jórunn did not pretend to misunderstand him. "This is what will happen", she said.

"What do you mean?"

"I mean that this is what will happen. We will meet – here, if you want, or somewhere else where we are away from prying eyes."

"But then what?" he persisted.

For a brief moment Jórunn felt annoyed at his persistence. Why did men insist on planning the future in detail? Could they not just appreciate the present? She didn't know what was going to happen. No one did. In truth, she did not want to think of the future, for fear that she would not like the way it would be – whether the fates would have her married or not. Neither held out much joy for her.

Instead of saying anything, she leaned over and kissed him. This time, it was a slow, lingering kiss, as much to savour the moment as to silence him and stop any further questions.

After this, Guðmundr would frequently ride out from Snæströnd to meet Jórunn. Each time they met, they would arrange where and when they would see each other again. At first, he tried to vary the days of their meetings, so that he would not be suspected of anything, but soon enough it became so that he would leave every eight or ten days and spend as much time with Jórunn as possible. As for Jórunn, she enjoyed being free, away from a brother she despised and a father she had begun to dislike, and the feeling of deciding her own destiny gave her great satisfaction. Still, whenever Guðmundr attempted to talk about the future, she would always stop him, and he soon decided not even to try.

Although Guðmundr at first felt an excitement and a thrill at seeing Jórunn and enjoyed their lovemaking, after some months his unhappiness returned. This time, it was not because of his father. Instead, he found it difficult whenever he returned to Snæströnd to face Ása. Things were still cold between them, yet it was clear that she was pained by this. She always treated him as the true master of Snæströnd and made sure the farmhands did too. And it was clear to him that, in spite of her words, she still loved him.

And so Guðmundr began to loathe himself and what he was doing. He would avoid Ása as much as he could, and even when he was not seeing Jórunn, he would try to be away from Snæströnd. He also stayed away from many of his friends, and it was only because it was not possible to do otherwise that he would still meet Eirík goði regularly. But when they did meet, he rarely had much to say, and Eirík began to fear that he would lose Guðmundr's advice. He wanted to speak with his friend again, but he also felt deeply that each person makes their own destiny and that if Guðmundr was not prepared to speak with him, then he could not force the issue. He also wondered if he should speak with Ragnar about his son, but here, too, he was not keen to intrude into what could be a family quarrel.

That was how matters continued for some months, as the summer turned to autumn and then autumn to winter and spring. In late autumn, it was clear to the people at Snæströnd that Kári would not be returning until the next summer at the earliest. This saddened Ragnar and Hallgerður, but Guðmundr also felt concern. Kári was the one person at the farm that he felt he could truly speak to about everything, and now he sorely missed him. Instead, when the days became much shorter and darker, Guðmundr's mood also turned darker. When he saw Jórunn, they would still make love, but he would also start talking about how badly he felt. At first, Jórunn ignored his moods, but, as time went on, she began to tire of listening to him. She had gone back to Guðmundr for many reasons. When they had first seen each other, he had been funny and witty and pleasant, always laughing and joking. Now that her own life had turned more lonely and bitter, she did not really want to hear about his feelings towards his wife and how he treated her badly.

She had hoped that his mood would lighten in the spring, but this did not happen. Finally, at one of their meetings, her patience ran out. "Guðmundr, what is wrong with you?" she asked. "When you are with me, all you talk about is Ása. Yet you say that when you are with her, all you think about is me. Can you not make up your mind?"

"This is not true", Guðmundr replied. "When I am with you, I only think about you and you know it. But this is much easier for you; you don't have someone for whom your behaviour will cause sorrow."

At this Jórunn felt her patience almost breaking, but she only replied, "Listening to you like this does not make me very happy either."

"You forget that I am still the master of Snæströnd and responsible for all who live there. And that includes Ása and my children as well."

At this, Jórunn said nothing, but their parting was the coldest it had been since they first met. As she rode home, she thought about everything that had been said and that had been left unsaid. She was angry with Guðmundr for his moods, but most of all she was angry at the fate spun her by the Norns. By the time she came home to Gunnar's farm, she had worked herself into a rage that only needed an outlet to burst forth.

When she entered the farmhouse, her brother spotted her. "What is wrong, sister?" he asked. "Did you fall off your horse?" He laughed.

Jórunn looked at him. You are a fool, she thought. This time, I will speak with Father. But she only smiled as if appreciating the joke and said, "Come with me."

Gunnar was sitting by the fire as his children approached. As he grew older, he had come to appreciate the warmth of the fireplace in the winter.

"Father, I need to speak with you", Jórunn said.

Gunnar looked at her and understood what she meant. He turned to the other members of his household who were busy with various chores around them. "Leave us", he said. When they had all gone and only the three of them were left, he turned back to Jórunn. "Speak."

"Do you still wish to bring down Eirík?"

"What do you mean?"

Jórunn sighed. What was it with men that they didn't listen? "I said, do you still wish to bring down Eirík goði?"

Gunnar thought for a while. What was his daughter up to? But he nodded and said, "Yes."

"Then I can help you. I can show you how to hurt him through Ragnar and Guðmundr at Snæströnd."

Gunnar looked at her. "You are seeing that man again, aren't you?" he asked suspiciously.

Jórunn was taken aback. She had assumed that her father would be pleased to hear what she had to say, not start to challenge her.

"So what if I am? What is that to you?"

"I told you not to do this again! Do you not recall how much damage you caused us in the past with him? You are supposed to be the clever one." Gunnar was almost shouting, his face red with anger. Beside Jórunn, Einar looked as if he wanted to say something, but his father waved him to silence. "Why do you not listen to what I say?"

Jórunn swallowed. "You are right, Father. But listen to me. This time, I can help you. I really can."

"Like last time? Remember how it went", Einar said with a sneer. He did not like to hear his father always calling Jórunn clever. Why did Gunnar never call him clever?

Once again Gunnar signalled his son to be quiet. Then he thought for a while. His power had lessened in recent years. True, he was still the most powerful goði at the Thórsnesthing, but Eirík and Thór had enough supporters combined to almost outnumber his own. Much of their strength in recent years had come from Snæströnd. Maybe the girl did have a better idea this time. At least she had shown good enough sense to come to him, instead of the stupid way she had tried once before. And of course, if her plan, whatever it was, was successful, it would not only increase his local power but also his influence at the Althing. It was at least worth listening to her.

"Very well", he said, "speak on, I am listening. And you Einar, be silent."

Chapter 9

Autumn 1066

The King's fleet was an impressive sight as it sailed out from the fjord, led by the *Serpent* and with at least two hundred longships and numerous trading vessels. Kári's knarr was at the rear, and from where he stood at the stern, steering his full ship with an even heavier heart, it looked as if the whole sea was covered with ships. The sun glittered over the water and its rays were reflected in steel and gold from the ships, while sails in bright colours filled out overhead.

On his own ship, Kári watched his crew setting about their tasks, while the soldiers they had taken on board were sitting in small groups, cleaning their gear or in some cases sharpening their axes and swords with whetstones. One of them, squeezed in near Kári, had just finished working on his sword. When he noticed Kári's gaze, he said, "Show me your sword."

Ever since their unwelcome guests had come on board, Kári had taken to wearing a sword at all times and told his men to make sure they were never without arms. He did not think that they could resist for long if the Norwegians tried to take the ship, but he did not intend to give it up without a fight, if that was what it came to. So far, though, the soldiers had been almost friendly. He still didn't like to hand over his sword, but he did not know how to refuse. The soldier looked at the sword and carefully felt the edge. "This is not good at all", he laughed. "See, it's notched, and there is rust in places. This won't help you much when you're up against the English. Here, take this and try to keep it in better shape in the future", and he returned the sword, hilt first, together with his whetstone.

Kári sighed. "Thank you. I will do as you say as soon as I am not steering."

"Oh", the soldier said. "Give it back then, I'll do it for you." Then he called out to his fellows, "Comrades, better help the traders sharpen their swords, otherwise they will do no more damage than if they tried to hit the English with a dried herring." The soldiers all laughed, but Kári saw some of them speaking with the Icelanders, either handing over whetstones or taking their swords and beginning to sharpen them. He also saw the look on his men's faces – for some of them, this was clearly the first indication that this was serious and that they really were expected to fight, and kill, when they reached England.

Kári swallowed, then said "Thank you" again.

"Don't thank me", the Norwegian replied. "The more of us there are that fight, the less likely it is that we will become food for the eagles. Oh, and I hope you have something else to wear in battle than a tunic?" Kári shook his head. "Then why didn't you get something before we sailed?"

"I – I didn't think about it", Kári replied. He was furious with himself, realising that he should have thought of this. It was a pity Odd was not with them; he would have known. "Are there any spares?" he asked.

"We don't have any", the Norwegian replied. "After the first battle, there will be plenty. But if you don't have anything now, you may not be around by then. But don't worry, wherever the fleet lands first, you should be able to round something up. There is always someone who has a spare shield or an extra leather jerkin and helmet. Mind you, it will cost." He laughed. "Fighting men always like to gather silver before a battle, although what use it is to them if they do not survive is beyond me. They say that in Paradise there is no need for silver – nor for fighting, for that matter." He seemed pensive.

Kári was surprised. "You are a Christian?"

"The King is, and he wishes all his men to be. But it must be said that some of us wear both a Cross and a Hammer under our tunics. And Valhalla sounds a better destination for a fighting man than Paradise. Mind you, they say that there is a great champion of God called Michael, who is a mighty warrior indeed."

*

Although the whole fleet had set out together, Kári was not surprised to find that many of the ships got separated from each other as they crossed the North Sea. He tried his best to keep in with a large group of longships and traders, but each morning there were fewer ships that could be seen from the knarr. Not few enough, though. When they set out, Kári had hoped that somehow they might be able to slip away from the fleet and sail directly to Jórvik to warn the city, but he soon realised that this would not be possible. Even if he did manage to steer away from the fleet, one of the longships would easily have overhauled them. In any case, they would somehow have had to overpower the Norwegian soldiers they had with them first, and he could not see how that would be possible. The only other hope he had was for a storm to sink most of the fleet, but the sea that had been so turbulent on the previous crossing and the wind that had mercilessly blown them to Norway were both on their best behaviour.

It was clear from the sun that they were not sailing straight to Jórvik. Kári asked the soldiers where they might be headed, but they had no answer and just told him to follow the fleet. That was not very helpful since that was what he would have done anyway. However, he kept a careful eye on the position of the sun and did his best to estimate their speed, and so he was not surprised to find the islands of Orkney rising out of the sea in front of him and the ships ahead of him turning south into the bay of Kirkjuvágr.

Kári ordered the men to man the oars and row slowly towards the town. They would have to find a place next to another ship; the quays of Kirkjuvágr were already full and longships were already lying three or four abreast, moored to each other. But it was also clear that a large part of the fleet had not arrived yet; if it had, he doubted whether they would even be able to find a spot anywhere near the town. At least he knew where he would be able to find fresh water without entering Kirkjuvágr itself. That knowledge might come in handy.

Finally, they found a spot next to a longship. After Kári had asked and received permission to moor alongside it, he gathered his crew. "We won't be going ashore", he said. "Not unless we stay here for long, and I doubt that will happen. But we will need fresh water, and I need to find a helmet and a leather jacket."

One of the crew members, a man from a neighbouring farm, asked "What about us?" The others, both the farmhands from Snæströnd and those from other farms, nodded and looked at Kári.

Kári looked at the Norwegian soldiers, but they were all gathered around their leader and could not hear what he was saying. "Hallvarðr, you and the others from Snæströnd are not taking part in any fighting. You will remain on board to guard the ship whatever happens. As for you others, I am not telling you whether to fight or not. I must go, because of my oath; but that only binds me and I will not command you either way."

The seven men from neighbouring farms looked at each other. Then they nodded to each other, and one of them spoke: "We have already talked about this. This is not a fight we would have chosen. But we are your men, Kári, and other men would speak ill of us if we did not follow you now."

Kári felt a warm glow when he heard this. He knew that many of the crew had already been calling themselves 'Kári's men' for some years, but that was when they were only trading. To hear them now say that they would also follow him into battle was something else, and for the first time he really felt that he was their chief. But he also realised that he was now responsible for much more than simply making sure that they traded well.

"I hope you will not regret this", he replied, "but I am glad to hear it. Now we must find more helmets, I think."

He told his crew to inspect the knarr's gear and made his way to the Norwegian soldiers. Their leader, the man who had sharpened Kári's sword for him, looked at him.

"I will need to find some fighting gear for my men", Kári said. "Where do I go?"

The Norwegian thought for a moment. "You may find that some of the other ships have some spares. But remember what I said: it will not come cheap until there are plenty of dead men who won't be needing their armour any longer."

Kári thanked the man and went back to where he stowed his own belongings. Asking Hallvarðr to stand so that none of the soldiers on board or from the other ships could see what he was doing, he opened a small box and took out a purse which he filled with silver coins and tied to his belt, before carefully putting the rest back. Then he stood up and, asking two of his men to follow him, made his way to the side, where he carefully asked permission to board the longship next to them.

At each ship they came to, Kári asked to speak to the captain, but no one had any spare gear they were willing to sell. It was only when he came to the fifth ship, a longship that seemed more battered than most of the others, with a dragonhead at the prow that was clearly in need of repainting, that he had more luck. Here, one of the men said that they had enough, both helmets and leather jerkins, and even one or two shields to sell, if Kári was interested.

Kári bought eight leather helmets with iron bands, eight leather jerkins and two shields. When he was told how much silver he would have to part with, he swallowed, but eventually weighed out the amount and handed it over. The ship's master laughed and said, "We raided in Scotland on the way here. They killed some of our men, but that is good news for you and better for me. I get more silver this way than they would manage to get for me had they remained alive."

Kári didn't comment, but merely thanked the man. Then he and his men took their purchases ashore and began the walk back to their ship. One of his men said, "I know you, Kári. You did not like to part with your silver."

Kári replied, "I do not mind parting with silver. That is what it is there for. But I prefer to buy goods that I can sell or goods that are useful. I do not enjoy having to spend this much silver on something that can be used for one thing only."

"Still", the man replied, "in battle you may well be glad that you bought it."

"That is true", Kári said. "But I would have liked it better if we were not going into battle. And if greater scarcity makes men ask for a higher price, I prefer to be the seller than the buyer."

But even that joke did not lighten his mood.

They returned to their own ship, clambering back over Norwegian decks as they made their way from the shore. Looking about him as he went, Kári noticed something strange on a longship moored a little further along the quay. A man was standing by the mast, looking out over the bay. That was not strange. What was strange was that in his hands he held a rope, the other end of which was tied around the waist of a woman who was sitting on the deck.

When they were back on their own ship, the men started to sort through what they had bought and try on the leather jerkins and helmets, each trying to find the best fitting one. But Kári did not join them; instead he returned to the quay and walked over to the other longship. There he stopped and looked at the man, who glared back at him.

"Is it customary among Norwegians to tie their women up?" Kári asked.

The man looked at him again. "Mind your own business, Icelander", he snarled.

All of a sudden Kári felt his heart fill with rage; rage against the Norwegians and their king, rage against this stupid war that he was being dragged into and now rage against this foul-mouthed lout. For a moment, he wanted to jump into the longship and run his sword through the man. Then, with difficulty, he calmed down and said, "I was curious. This is a Norwegian custom I had not heard about."

The man shrugged. "I am not Norwegian", he said. "We come from Mann, to help King Harald. As for the woman, she is my thrall. I captured her on a raid in Ireland. She says she is the daughter of a king or chieftain or something. More likely, her father was a stablehand."

The woman seemed to sense that they were talking about her, because she stood up and looked at the two men. She was tall, Kári saw, taller than he was. Her hair was dark and her eyes were green. It was difficult to say how old she was, because her hair was unkempt and her face was dirty.

"How do you deal with your own thralls?" the Manxman went on.

Kári still felt the rage inside him and wanted to say something to rile the man. "I do not have any", he said. "Some Icelanders do, but I never will. My father's mother was Irish. She would have died rather than remain a thrall. I think she would have killed any man who treated her like this."

The man laughed. "Would she indeed? Well, I dare say this one would like to kill me. Isn't that so?" he said and suddenly jerked the rope taught. The woman stumbled, but quickly regained her footing. She stared at her captor and her face was transformed. Her eyes turned black and Kári suddenly realised two things. The first was that if eyes alone could kill, the woman's captor would already be dead. The second was that she was the most beautiful woman he had ever seen.

The man laughed again. "Glare all you like, pretty Maebh", he said. "Once I have had my sport with you, I may decide to let you keep your eyes. Or maybe I'll pluck them out to remind you that you should behave." He pulled at the rope again, and the woman fell to the deck.

For a second time, Kári was tempted to draw his sword and lunge at the man. Part of him realised that he would almost certainly be killed, but he wanted to release the anger he felt at everyone around him. Before he could move, however, he felt a grip on his arm. He looked around and saw a Norwegian soldier, one of the men who sailed on the knarr, whose second hand was now holding Kári's sword.

For a moment they stood there with their eyes locked, but then Kári's tension left him. When the Norwegian felt Kári go limp, he released him, but he didn't move. The Manxman had not noticed anything, but the woman – Maebh, apparently – must have seen something, because as she rose to her feet, she looked at Kári with a strange expression. Then her owner walked away, still laughing and dragging her behind him.

"I don't know what you were thinking of", the Norwegian said. "But know this: if he had not killed you – and he would have – then we would have had to. King Harald prefers that his men die facing the enemy. He is not keen on them fighting each other, and anyone who does will find his life forfeit."

Kári stood silent for a while. Then he forced his face into something resembling a smile and said "I thank you."

"Don't mention it", the Norwegian said. "We need someone to steer your ship." But he smiled to show that he meant no offence and walked off.

Over the next few days, the rest of the fleet gathered. Kári heard that some of the ships had made landfall in Hjaltland first before sailing south to Orkney. As soon as the entire fleet had arrived, they left Kirkjuvágr and set sail south for England. The King's strength had grown in Orkney, since many from the islands, including the two new Jarls of Orkney, had joined him with several ships. Nor was this all; on the way south they stopped in Scotland, where men sent by the Scots King joined them. In addition, Jarl Tostig had arrived with a large number of ships and a great host of followers.

While they were sailing down from Kirkjuvágr, the leader of the Norwegian soldiers on board the knarr would often come and sit in the stern, where Kári was steering. At first they would talk of the sea and where they were headed and the battles to be fought. But after some time, the Norwegian began to ask questions of Kári.

"I do not understand", he said. "Everyone tells me that Iceland was founded by Norwegians. Yet you do not willingly obey our king, nor do you have any kings of your own. How is that possible?"

"I thought everyone knew this", Kári replied. "In Iceland, we tell our children these stories so that they will not be forgotten. Iceland was founded by men who left Norway after the Battle of Hafrsfjord because they did not want to live as thralls under Harald Fairhair."

"Yes, but that was long ago. Fairhair has been dead for two hundred years."

"What does that matter?" Kári asked. "It was not just that king. We want no king over us. We are free men."

"But how does that work? Who tells you what to do? How can you have order without a king?"

"No one tells us what to do. We have a Law that everyone knows, because it is recited by the Lawspeaker. All free men meet at the Thing to hear and decide cases. And apart from that, each one does what he wishes, as long as he does not break the law or harm anyone else."

"I still don't understand", the Norwegian said. "How do you know if a man is a free man or a thrall, a noble or a farmhand?"

"We don't. Because it does not matter. Look at my crew. Three of the men are farmhands from my brother's farm, Snæströnd. The other seven are sons of neighbouring farmers. Can you see the difference between them?"

"No I can't. They all seem content with what they do, and they all seem equally independent-minded. And I have wondered how come they came to sail your ship."

"If I did not know them", Kári smiled, "I would not be able to tell the difference either."

The Norwegian thought about this for a while. Then he said, "But this is unnatural. Things cannot work this way!"

"Why not? After all, they do work for us, so it must be possible."

"Yes, but don't you see? Look here, Kári, everywhere in the world it is the same. There is a king and he has his nobles. And the nobles have their farms and their farmhands, and at the bottom are the thralls."

"Not in Iceland."

"Everywhere. Are you a Christian?" Before Kári had time to answer, he continued, "In Paradise, God Himself is King, His Son Christ is the Jarl, and there are his nobles who are Saints and Angels. And Kingdoms on earth should try to be mirrors of the Kingdom of Heaven."

Kári smiled. "In Iceland we are all supposed to be Christian. But this is not a question we ask each other."

"But even if you follow the old gods, surely you know that Óðinn is the King of the Æsir of Valhalla, with Freya his Queen. It is the same thing."

"So you say, but do you actually know this?"

The Norwegian laughed. "Everybody knows this."

"Well, maybe. But all I can tell you is that in Iceland, yes, some men have thralls. And some men are wealthier than others. But apart from the thralls, we are all free men. No one tells us what to do. Some men are good and others are evil, but the most important thing is that we are free. And we wish to retain that freedom. The men on this ship join me because they know that I am a successful trader and good at gathering wealth, and so manning my ship means they will get some of that wealth for themselves. If I forced them to come, would they be willing to help me succeed in my trading? Or would they prefer to see me fail so that they would not have to come along another year?

"And your brother's farmhands? Can they do what they want?"

"No, as long as they work for him, they must obey him. But they can leave him if they want to. And they have chosen to come on the ship. I would never take someone who was forced to come. I must be able to trust everyone I sail with. Is that not the same for you?"

"I don't sail", the Norwegian said. "Oh. Yes, I see what you mean."

"I'm sure you do", Kári said. "When you are standing in a shield wall, who do you want next to you? Someone who is there by his own free will, or someone who was forced to go by some king and who would prefer to run away at the first possible opportunity?"

"You are right there", the Norwegian said. "But when he stands next to me in the shield wall, I also want to know that he will obey his captain's commands."

"And on my ship, I want to be certain that the crew will obey my commands as well. But they join the crew knowing that this is the case. But at any time they are free to leave me, back in Iceland or in another port. I neither can, nor would I try to stop them."

"But you mentioned the law and the Thing. What if someone refuses to obey the Thing's verdict?"

"That happens", Kári admitted. "But when it does, men will appeal, and the matter will continue to be discussed. And his friends and neighbours will try to persuade him that in the end he should submit."

"And if he still refuses? Do you not have fights in Iceland, and blood feuds?"

"We do. Sometimes men refuse to obey and refuse to be reconciled, and sometimes we have long feuds. This is a problem. But does this never happen in Norway? I have heard that even your kings fight about who should rule the land."

"Yes, this is true", the Norwegian said.

"When men fight in Iceland", Kári said, "their fight only involves them and their kin. When kings fight in Norway, is it the same?"

"No. When kings fight, things in Norway are bad. And it gets worse when they ally with the Danes or the Swedes in the hope of defeating their rivals, as the Jarls of Lade did." He spat as he mentioned the two neighbours. "Then we could all end up as thralls of foreigners."

"This would not happen in Iceland", Kári said. And then nothing more was said about this topic.

*

Up until now they had not witnessed any fighting, but once they were sailing down the coast of England, this began to change. They sailed slowly, and in many places Kári saw longships peeling off from the fleet and sailing towards the shore. The main body of the fleet would keep sailing, but soon they could see smoke rising behind them as farmsteads and villages were being put to the torch.

Kári and his men did not know how the fighting was going, although the fact that the ships continued seemed to mean that there was not much resistance. But when they had sailed maybe two-thirds of the way down towards the Humber by Kári's reckoning, things changed. There was a large town on a headland, and here the English were apparently resisting strongly. Soon the command came for all the fleet to turn in towards the coast.

Once they were near enough, they saw men wading ashore from the ships and forming up on the beaches. The Norwegians on the knarr also jumped into the water and joined the rest of the host, but Kári and his men stayed on board. He might have to fight, he decided, but he was not going to join a battle unless someone told him to do so.

In the end, there was no need for this. The English had fought bravely, but once enough Norwegians were ashore, the defenders retreated into the town. Kári wondered what would happen – whether the English would surrender or whether the Norwegians would storm the town. While he and the rest of the crew, and many from the other ships in the fleet, were trying to understand what was happening on the shore, they suddenly saw a fire light up the sky from a hill overlooking the town. Some wondered if it was a building set on fire, but Kári thought that it might be a beacon, lit to warn other towns of the Norwegian attack. Yet, try as he might, he could see no other beacons being lit in the distance. After some time the fire seemed to dwindle again and it looked as if some brands were falling towards the town below. Kári was beginning to turn away, when one of his men called out, "Look! The town! It's burning!"

It was difficult to see, but it looked as if the man was right. Soon the light from the fire grew brighter and Kári and the others realised that the town really was burning. When Kári understood what was happening, he was once again filled with anger towards the Norwegians. "Why are they doing this?" he muttered. "I thought he wanted to become King of England. Now it looks as if he wants to become King of Corpses."

After the town had burned down, the Norwegian soldiers began to return to the ships. When the men who had sailed on the knarr clambered on board, Kári saw that they were all back and none of them even wounded. He asked their leader what had happened. "Oh nothing", the man replied. "By the time we were ashore, the

English cowards had already fled to the town. So we built a fire and burned it. I never even drew my sword."

"And what about the English?"

"They are dead. Most of them probably burned with the town. Who cares?"

"But – wouldn't it have been better to let them surrender?" Kári asked.

"Maybe they were told to surrender and didn't. I don't know", said the Norwegian. "But what I do know is that you will see many towns and villages who will now surrender, rather than suffer the same fate."

And so it proved. From then on, although longships would still occasionally turn to shore and land groups of soldiers, there were no more burnings. From shouted conversations with nearby ships, it was clear that those who went ashore soon returned with much booty, surrendered by scared farmers who hoped thereby to save their lives.

Soon after this they reached the mouth of the Humber, where they turned in. Kári remembered the warship he had encountered when they came in the summer. He wondered if it was still there, but even if it was, there was precious little it could do against the Norwegian fleet. Far better that they flee and join whatever force the English were assembling. At least the English could no longer be taken by surprise; there must be enough refugees from the coast fleeing to Jórvik to sound the alarm both there and elsewhere.

Whether in fact the warship had been there or not, Kári never found out. Certainly, by the time the knarr turned the headland and entered the river, it was not there.

The fleet continued into the Humber and turned north up the Ouse. From time to time Kári would hear the noise of fighting as they encountered scattered resistance, but he rarely saw anything.

When they approached Jórvik, though, it was clear that things were going to be different. Kári was astonished at how quickly rumours spread through the fleet. He never saw anyone come close to the knarr or speak with the soldiers on board, yet by the time the ships had all been beached along the riverbank, everybody knew that there was a host of Englishmen, led by Jarl Morcar, that was ready to do battle with them. And this time, it was clear that Kári and his men were expected to take part in the battle.

The Norwegian soldiers watched the Icelanders getting ready, donning their unfamiliar helmets and leather jerkins and grabbing their weapons. Then they all joined the host that was forming up ashore.

Kári and his men stuck to the Norwegians from their ship. For some time they remained standing, and Kári wondered why nothing was happening or why they were not moving. But when he asked the Norwegian leader, he just laughed and said, "This is your first lesson of warfare: you wait. The waits always seem long, but when the fighting begins you will wish that the waiting had lasted longer."

Now there was movement throughout the host. Kári could not see what was happening, but overhead banners suddenly appeared and he saw a priest walk out in front of them. Kári saw that other priests were standing further along the line. The men all turned quiet and then the priest began to preach. The wind meant that they could not hear everything he said, but so much was clear – he was telling them to fight hard for their King and for the White Christ and that anyone who fell in battle would go straight to Paradise. Kári could see how many of the men made the sign of the Cross over their face and chest as they listened. But others, and not only a few, made the sign of the Hammer, and many clutched amulets hanging around their necks. Kári didn't wear one but wished he had – Cross or Hammer didn't matter, as long as it afforded some protection.

He looked towards the centre of the line, where he assumed the King would be. There he saw Harald's banner, the flag with a raven, which men called the Land-waster. Even from this distance, it looked as if the raven was flapping its wings. Then something above the banner caught his eye. He looked up and saw the figure of a man who seemed to be floating in the air. He was huge, with a long beard and wearing armour and a cloak. On each of his shoulders sat a black raven, and when he turned his face towards

Kári, it was clear that he was blind in one eye. He looked both ways over the host, then a smile seemed to flicker across his face and he nodded, and then the figure dissolved.

Kári continued to stare at the spot where the figure had appeared, until suddenly someone nudged him and pushed him forward. He turned to one of his crewmen who was standing next to him and asked, "Did you see him?"

"Who?" the man replied.

"The man floating in the sky."

"That's no man, that is the King's banner", a Norwegian soldier interjected. "Can't you see the difference between a raven and a man?"

Kári shook his head. Had he really seen something or had he imagined it? He didn't know, but now the whole host began to move forward and there was no time to think about it.

They did not have far to move. The host soon divided into two parts. The greater part stood with the King on a low ridge running alongside the river, while the rest of the host formed a line inland to the right towards a deep swamp. That was where Kári and his men stood.

Soon they could see the English army approaching from the north. To Kári it seemed as if it was a glittering dragon that approached inexorably, with the sun reflected in the mail and weapons of the front line. He hadn't even noticed, but he had drawn his sword and now gripped it so hard that his knuckles turned white. In his left arm he held the shield he had bought, but this was already weighing him down, and he wondered if he would be able to hold it high enough to protect himself.

Even while the Norwegians were still attempting to form their line, the English approached. When the two sides were within earshot of each other, men began to call out insults and shout at their enemies. Soon the English were so close that Kári could see the faces of the men opposite him. He felt strange. Until then, he had felt that although he was in the Norwegian host, he had no share in this fight. In fact, part of him wanted the English to win. The men in the English army were just men on the other side. But now, seeing them advance, weapons ready, screaming, he suddenly felt that these men were indeed the enemy. They were not just coming to fight the Norwegians who were attacking their land, they were coming to kill Kári and his men from Iceland, men who had done them no harm. Without realising how it happened, he found himself screaming wordlessly, giving vent to his rage. Alongside him his men were doing the same, shaking their swords and yelling at the English. He felt the urge to rush forward and stab and hack at the faces on the other side, wanting to see them bleed and fall for his sword.

Suddenly the distance between the two hosts dwindled to nothing, and Kári found himself being shoved backwards by the pressure of the English attack. He pushed back, still screaming and flailing with his sword. He tried to remember to keep the shield up, but it was difficult to hold it and at the same time wield the sword. In front of him, a blond man with a beard seemed to be shouting something and raising an axe with both hands above his head. Kári followed his instincts and stabbed towards the man's face. He felt the resistance when his sword hit and the point entered the Englishman's eye. The man screamed and dropped his axe, trying to grab Kári's sword, but he pulled it back, seeing blood spurt out from the wound. The man disappeared, and from the corner of his eye, Kári saw a sword descending towards his left side. He managed to get the shield up and felt a jar along his arm as the sword connected. A Norwegian on his left thrust his spear towards the new attacker. Kári did not see if he was hit or not, but in any case he disappeared.

Then the pressure eased as the English fell back. Kári felt drained and leaned forward, trying to support himself with his sword. But there was not much time to rest, because with a shout the English attacked again.

This time, Kári did not have time to think. The fighting was getting more confused, with swords and axes hacking and spears stabbing. He felt a crack on his helmet, but it was only a glancing blow and, instead of pain, he felt anger at whoever had hit him. But although he and the others in the line fought with all their strength, it was clear that the English were steadily pushing them back, and step by step they retreated. At one stage Kári found himself slipping, and when he managed to cast a glance down, he found that he was stepping on a face. He hoped the man was dead, but he really didn't care as long as he himself did not fall. If fighting standing in a battle line was difficult, it was much more difficult to do so when being forced backwards.

Suddenly an English warrior seemed to rise up before him and a sword came down towards his head. He held up the shield but not quickly enough, so instead of taking the blow on the shield, the sword bit into the edge and got stuck. The Englishman tried to wrench it loose, but Kári dropped the shield and flailed at him with his sword. The Englishman fell, but Kári wasn't even sure if he had hit him. Much later, he was asked how long this fighting had lasted, and he would always say that he didn't know, but that it felt as if it lasted for ever.

Around him, the Norwegians were becoming more silent, fighting now with growing desperation, while the screams of the English began to sound triumphant. Then suddenly there was a sound of horns from their left, and when Kári looked up, he saw the English advance wavering. In the distance he thought he could see a banner approaching. Beside him, a Norwegian called out "It's the raven. Óðinn's raven!"

Now more Norwegians took up the chant and screaming "Óðinn! Óðinn!" they began to surge forward at the enemy. The English, who had pressed them so hard, found themselves pressed from their right and their rear and began to waver in turn. This time, things moved faster. As the Norwegians pushed forward, the English retreat became more rapid and confused, and soon many of them were fleeing as quickly as they could. But some still stood and fought, and the Norwegians pushed against them, treading on bodies everywhere so that it was more like dry ground than a marsh.

Kári and his men were advancing together with the Norwegians. From time to time they had to stop to fight small groups of Englishmen who attempted to make a stand. During one of these fights, Kári slipped as he tried to avoid another English sword. He tried to grab on to something but at the same time felt a sharp pain in his left arm and fell heavily into a pool of water. As he tried to get up, he leaned on his arm and fell again. Before he could rise for a second time, something landed on his back. He felt a sharp blow, and everything turned black.

*

When he came to, he was sitting up. Someone was trying to tie a rag around his arm, but he could see the rag quickly turning red with blood, and the man was busy ripping a tunic apart to get another rag. "What happened?" Kári asked.

"You fell, and a spear pierced your arm", the man replied.

Another of his men standing nearby added, "They were trying to get at you, so I covered you with my shield and they hit that instead, but it must still have knocked you out."

"Thank you", Kári replied.

The man laughed. "Aren't you glad that you bought two shields, after all?"

Kári tried to laugh too, but his head hurt too much. "Yes, that was silver well spent. Perhaps there is some use for shields and helmets even for a trader."

A second rag was now tied around his arm and seemed to have staunched the bleeding, but the wound still throbbed painfully. He looked around, but everything seemed quiet. "Where is the battle?" he asked.

"Oh", one of the others replied. "It's over. We won. Someone said that we were a trap to lure the English on, and then the King and all his host fell upon them from behind. Most of the English are dead and the rest have fled, pursued by the Norwegians."

"You did not follow them?"

"We are your men, Kári. When you fell, we stayed with you."

"Thank you. I am grateful. I was grateful that you came to fight with me and I am now glad that you did and that you waited here."

"Just remember that next time we wish to go ashore in a new port", the man replied, and they all laughed.

Kári now tried to stand up, but when he did he felt dizzy and had to sit down again. Two of his men came to help him, and, leaning on them, he managed to stand up. When he did, he looked around and asked, "Is everyone here?"

"Yes", one of them replied. "This was not our day to die."

"And wounds?"

"Some, but yours is the worst."

At this Kári suddenly felt weak again and almost fell to the ground. When his men saw this, they exchanged worried glances, and two of them cut branches off a nearby tree and made a stretcher with their cloaks. Then, although Kári protested and said that he could walk, they put him on the stretcher and took turns to carry him back to the ships.

When they had marched up towards the battle, the distance had not seemed so long. But going back, it seemed to take for ever. At first two men would carry the stretcher, and then others would take their place. But after they had covered some distance, four of them would carry it and the other three would quickly rotate to relieve them. In this way, it took them a long time to get back to the knarr, and by the time they had reached it, Kári was drifting in and out of consciousness.

They carried him on board as gently as possible. The men from Snæströnd, who had been left at the ship, prepared a bed of furs for him on the deck of the knarr and laid him down there.

There Hallvarðr changed the bandage on his arm, but he could see that the wound was not healing and was if anything looking worse. He wished he knew more about tending such wounds. Also, Kári was drifting in and out of consciousness, sometimes sounding lucid, sometimes raving. At times he shouted for his sword, at other times he was yelling that they should set course for Dyflin.

While this was going on, the survivors of the battle continued to drift back to the fleet. It was clear that many had fallen in the battle and that many more of the survivors were wounded. Yet they seemed to be in a good mood, some of them singing or chatting as they returned. But one group was missing. However long they waited, none of the men from Norway who had sailed with them on the knarr came back. The Icelanders never found out if this was because they were all dead or if it was that they went to another ship. But since some of their belongings were left on the knarr, they thought it more likely that the Norwegians had all died in the battle.

As the sun set, Kári's men began to worry about him. Although they had cleaned his wound as best they could and were constantly bathing his face with cool water, he seemed to grow more feverish. Nor was there anyone they could ask, as the Norwegians seemed busy with the aftermath of their victory and preparing for the surrender of Jórvik and took no interest in the Icelanders.

Kári continued to grow worse during the night, often shouting at the top of his voice. The men took turns sitting with him. In the middle of the night, Hallvarðr was just going to relieve one of the other men, but first he needed to empty his bladder. As he stood at the stern of the knarr, he suddenly heard a voice from the longship next to them.

"You! Icelander!" It was a low voice, barely more than a whisper. For a moment, Hallvarðr wasn't even sure if it came from the ship or if it came from the river, maybe a sea creature that was trying to lure him to its deep. He looked around but saw no one. Then he heard the voice again.

"You! On the trader. Are you an Icelander?" This time the voice definitely came from the longship. He turned and peered at the ship trying to see who was talking.

"What do you want?" he called.

"Shh. Keep your voice down. Are you from the Icelander ship?"

"Yes I am. Who are you?"

"Listen to me. Is that your chieftain who is calling out? Is he sick?"

"He was wounded in the battle", Hallvarðr said. "The wound is infected."

"I can heal him for you. But you have to help me."

"Who are you? How can you heal him? Show yourself", Hallvarðr demanded.

"Do you have a knife?" the caller asked. "Throw it to me."

In retrospect, Hallvarðr could never say why he had obeyed the request – to throw his knife to a stranger was such a stupid thing to do – but the voice was strangely compelling. He took his knife and, gauging where on the longship the speaker seemed to be, threw it. It clattered as it fell to the deck, and Hallvarðr froze. He waited for a few long moments. Then first a head and then the rest of the body came into view over the side. "Help me into your ship", the speaker whispered.

Then the other person lowered himself into the water between the two ships. Hallvarðr signalled to one of his men to come and hold him steady as he leaned down and stretched out a hand. He felt his arm gripped and he began to pull the person out of the water. Then he suddenly loosened his grip and almost dropped the person. "You're a woman!" he exclaimed.

The woman's grip tightened. "How clever of you to notice", she hissed. "Now, are you going to help me on board? I told you that I can save your chieftain."

Hallvarðr pulled the woman on board. For a moment she stood, dripping seawater on the deck. "Who are you?" he asked.

"Wait", she said. "Answer me this: does your chief have any thralls?"

"What? Why? No, he doesn't think people should be thralls."

"Good. Then this is the right ship. Now take me to him. And make sure no one can see me from the other ships."

Hallvarðr didn't know why he obeyed the woman, but there was something in her voice which showed that she was not prepared to argue. He even forgot to ask for his knife back.

When the woman saw Kári, she turned to Hallvarðr again. "Bring some fresh water and some clean cloth. And do you have a fire on board? Bring a torch. And a piece of wood."

Hallvarðr still felt puzzled but did as he was told. Then the woman knelt down by Kári and removed the bandage on his arm and cut away the sleeve of his tunic. "Hold him!" she told two of the other men, then told a third to clamp Kári's jaws around the piece of wood. She quickly cleaned the wound again and then took Hallvarðr's knife and stuck it in the fire. Then, before the men could stop her, she began to cut away the flesh around Kári's wound. Kári bucked and moaned, but the men held him, and the wood in his mouth dampened his cries. And then he fainted.

When she was finished, she cleaned his wound again and bound it up. Then she washed her hands in the water and stuck the knife in a rope she had tied around her waist like a belt.

"Give me something to drink", she commanded. One of the men brought her a mug of beer, which she drained. Then she said, "I will now go to sleep. Wake me up if he wakes up, or else just before the sun rises. Make sure no one knows that I am here."

The other men looked at Hallvarðr, but he only nodded at them to do as she said. Then he sat down next to Kári and tried to make sense of what had just happened. At least, he thought, Kári seemed to breathe more evenly.

He sat there until the east slowly began to turn red with the rising sun. Then he told one of the other men from Snæströnd to take his place and went to wake the woman. When he touched her shoulder, she suddenly turned around and, before he knew it, she held a knife – his knife, he realised – at his throat. Then she smiled. "I apologise", she said. "I forgot where I was. How is your chief?"

"He isn't really our chief", Hallvarðr began. "He is the owner of this ship and we are his men."

"Yes, but how is he?" the woman replied, annoyed at the explanation.

"I think he is better."

"Take me to him."

When the woman saw Kári, she knelt down by his side. She removed the bandage on his arm, smelled the wound and then washed it again before tying another bandage.

"I wish I had other things to heal him", she said. "Some cobwebs would be good, or some moss. But even without them, he should improve."

"Thank you", Hallvarðr said. "But – who are you, and why are you doing this?"

"When he wakes up, I will tell you", the woman said. "Meanwhile, has anyone asked for me?"

"No, I don't think so."

"Good. Remember, no one must know that I am here. Do you have a cloak I can use?"

When Hallvarðr brought her a cloak, the woman wrapped herself in it, making sure that it covered her head and face. Then she sat down and waited.

When the sun had risen enough, Hallvarðr noticed a commotion on the longship next to the knarr. Men were shouting and cursing. Then one man appeared on the side nearest to them and shouted: "You there!"

Hallvarðr stood up and approached the side. "Yes?"

"Have you seen a woman?"

Hallvarðr was conscious of the men watching him and even more of the woman next to Kári, who was hunkering down, trying to seem inconspicuous. He didn't know what was going on, but the woman had so far been of help to Kári and that was what mattered.

"What?" he called back.

"A woman! Have you seen a woman?"

"A woman?" Hallvarðr had long ago learned that if you did not want to answer a question, it was good to appear stupid; the easiest way to do this was to pretend not to understand, and the best way to do that was to repeat questions.

"Yes, a woman! Have you seen her?"

"Where would she be?" he called back.

"I don't know", the man bellowed. "If I did, would I ask you, you stupid fool? Have you seen her?"

"We haven't seen her", Hallvarðr replied. "Who is she?"

"Never you mind", the man shouted back. Then he turned around and said something to someone else on his deck about "stupid Icelanders".

Hallvarðr went back to sit by Kári and the woman. He didn't look at her for fear that the man from the other ship would notice something. But from underneath the cloak, he heard a whispered "Thank you."

Kári continued to sleep until noon. When he awoke, he at first tried to sit up but fell back again. The woman had already prepared some warm broth. Now she moved closer towards him and began to feed him. "Lie still", she said. "You will get better soon, but right now you should not move."

Kári dutifully drank the broth, but then looked at her. "Who are you? What are you doing here?" he asked.

"As for what I am doing here", she replied, "I am healing you. And who I am?" She looked around to see that no one could see her and pulled the cloak back from her head and face. Then she quickly hid her features gain.

Kári stared at her. "You! You are –", he started, but before he could finish, the woman put her finger on his mouth and hushed him. He nodded, then whispered "You are the Irish captive! Maebh."

She nodded. "I am glad to see that you remember me."

Kári tried to smile. "It was my arm that was wounded, not my head", he replied. "How did you come here?"

"Our ship is next to yours. I recognised you when your men brought you back from the battle. One of them helped me on board when I said I could heal you."

"Can you?"

"Yes. But first, I want to ask you some questions."

"What, before you decide if I am worth healing?" Kári felt puzzled.

"When you spoke with the man who captured me, you said that you do not have any thralls and that you do not hold with those who do. Is this true?"

"Yes. My father's mother –" Kári began.

"I remember", Maebh said. "Was she really Irish?"

"Yes."

"What about captives?"

"I have never captured anyone. But I am a free man from Iceland. If I owned thralls, would I not be the same as any king or lord, forcing people to do my bidding? There are Icelanders who hold thralls, but I think it wrong and I never will. As for captives, I suppose if I ever captured someone, I would let them pay ransom and go."

"Good", Maebh said. "Now listen to me. I am the daughter of an Irish chief. I was taken by the captain of the Manx ship. I made the mistake of trying to kill him on the first night. I should have waited until he thought I was too tame to harm him. But I would rather die than live as a thrall."

"So would my grandmother", Kári said.

"So you said. For your grandmother's sake, will you take me back? You will be richly rewarded."

"Where would you go?"

"I come from Cork and that's where I would return."

"Where is Cork?"

"Have you never been to Ireland? I thought you were shouting about Dyflin."

"Was I? No, I haven't. But I would like to go to Dyflin, that is true."

"Cork is a town southwest of Dyflin. Take me back there."

Kári smiled weakly. "Right now I cannot take you anywhere", he said. "We are in the middle of a Norwegian fleet and they won't let us go. Also, I have sworn an oath to do nothing against their king while he lives. But you have already done me a good service, and this I promise you: you will remain on my ship and nobody will give you away. And then we shall see."

Maebh thought about it, and then she nodded. "For now, that is good enough. Thank you." And she smiled.

"No", Kári said. "I thank you." Then he leaned back again, exhausted.

For the next three days, Maebh stayed hidden on board the knarr. She rarely left Kári's side, daily cleaning his wound and changing his bandages and feeding him, and under her care, he quickly grew stronger. The rest of the crew were busy inspecting the sails and oars and rearranging such goods as they had on board. They didn't know what to do about the gear belonging to the Norwegian soldiers, but Kári decided that they should keep it. If the men came back, the knarr was the most likely place they would come to retrieve their property. And if they didn't, this would have to be payment for their passage.

They heard nothing more about the search for Maebh. But they did hear other things. The battle had seen a great slaughter of the English, and Jórvik was now defenceless. The Norwegians had marched against Jórvik, and the leaders of the city had met them outside the walls and offered to surrender in return for being spared. King Harald had accepted their offer, and it was agreed that he and his host would enter the city on the fifth day after the battle.

On the morning of the fifth day, the King sounded the horns and ordered the host ashore. Kári's men stayed on their ship, but they watched what was happening. Later they heard that the King had divided his army. Two men out of every three were to follow him to Jórvik, and the third would remain by the fleet. The English who had followed Tostig were to join the King, but the two Jarls of Orkney and some others, including King Harald's son Olav, remained with the fleet.

It was a beautiful day and the sun shone. Most of the men left their mail-shirts at the ships and marched off with sword, shield, spear and helmet, and some of them also carried bows and arrows. They were in high spirits and were joking about the feasting that would await them in Jórvik.

After they had left, those who remained went back on board their ships. Some remained on shore, cooking food by campfires, others were inspecting ships and gear for damage.

Thus the morning went. But as the sun continued its rise and had already passed its peak, sharp-eyed observers suddenly saw three men come riding at full speed towards the ships. Kári and his men were too far away to hear what was happening, but it was clear that this was not good news. Horns were sounded and men were mustered. This time, the men must have been told to wear their mail-shirts, because the host glittered in the sun. As soon as it was assembled, the horns blew again and the men started moving northwards at a run.

Kári was by now strong enough to stand up, and he and his men watched the departing Norwegians. "I don't know what has happened", Kári said, "but I can guess. And my guess is that the English in Jórvik decided that they were not going to surrender after all."

"How could they do that?" Maebh asked. "Their host was destroyed."

"Yes. So the only reason that they are not surrendering is if another host has come to their aid. And that means that the English King himself must have arrived. I think that the Norwegians will now find it more difficult to enter Jórvik than they thought, and the welcome they get will be rather different from the feasting they expected."

As he said this, he looked away towards the line of ships along the riverbank. Suddenly, he saw the same sight he had seen before the battle. Over the centre of the line, a giant figure of a man appeared. It was the same man, the bearded one-eyed man with the ravens. But this time, his face was not smiling. Now he shook his head and turned away from the ships. Kári made the sign of the Hammer. He wanted to tell the others about the figure, but before he could do so, it dissolved. Instead he turned to Hallvarðr. "This will not turn out well for the Norwegians. I think it would be a good idea to prepare the knarr for departure." Hallvarðr nodded and quietly began to tell the rest of the crew. Maebh looked questioningly at Kári. He smiled at her and said, "I don't know what is happening, but when we leave, you can come with us."

Maebh nodded and smiled back. This was the second time she had smiled at Kári, and when she did, Kári felt as if the sun had descended from the heavens and come to rest in her face.

They waited again for much of the afternoon. Then they began to see small groups of men come back from the direction of Jórvik. When they were close enough, men began to shout questions at them. Kári sent one of the men ashore to find out what had happened. The man ran off, but quickly came back. As he climbed on board, he gasped, "There has been a big battle. I don't know much, but this is already known: the Norwegian King is dead. He fell in the beginning of the battle."

When Kári heard this, he straightened up. "Listen", he told his men, who all turned to him. "You know that my oath was tricked from me and unwillingly given. Still, I did not want to be foresworn. But my oath was to King Harald personally and only for as long as he lived. Now we hear that he is dead. My oath is void, and this is no longer our fight. Man the oars. We are leaving these Norwegians to look after themselves."

One of the men said, "What if they try to stop us?"

"I think they have other things to think about", Kári said. "But if they do – we fight. I am tired of obeying king's men. We are free Icelanders."

And with that, the men quickly slipped the mooring ropes, manned the oars and began to row the knarr downstream. As Kári had expected, the Norwegians were not interested in what they were doing. Instead, more men were leaving the ships and streaming ashore. Even so, he felt much better when the swift current had carried them around a few bends in the river and they were out of sight from the Norwegian fleet. He felt even better when the sun set and darkness began to fall, hiding them from anyone but the closest observers on the riverbanks.

They continued rowing through the night, carefully keeping to the middle of the river. It was not something Kári would have chosen to do, but he was keen to put as much distance between the knarr and the Norwegians as he could. He did not really think that they would care particularly much about a small Icelandic trading ship disappearing. Certainly, if they had lost a battle, they would be more concerned with escaping the wrath of the victorious English, who would now wish to avenge the harrying of their coast. But there was always the risk that a single longship captain might decide that even a little booty – from a knarr, say – was preferable to returning to Norway without any booty and with the King slain.

They were fortunate, however. No one challenged them, and after another day of rowing, they reached the Humber, where they turned east. The wind was westerly, so they could set the sail and Kári could let the men rest. A day later they reached the mouth of the river and finally the open sea lay before them. Kári drew a deep breath, savouring the salty tang in the air.

Hallvarðr turned to him. "Where are we sailing, Kári?"

Kári looked beyond Hallvarðr towards Maebh. "We sail for Ireland."

Chapter 10

Autumn 1066 – Winter 1067

Once they had turned north with the coast of England on the port side, everyone on the knarr felt much relieved. It was still possible that they could be overtaken by a longship fleeing from the battle at Jórvik, but the further they sailed, the less likely this seemed.

Kári continued to strengthen and recover under Maebh's care. But his arm was still weak, and he was unable to either steer or row. The other crew members took turns steering, while Kári spent much time standing at the prow looking at the sea. It was getting late in the autumn now, and the air felt chillier, but he still loved the wind and the salty spray from the sea in his face. Maebh had taken to standing with him and they spent much time talking. Kári told her about his life and his family in Iceland. She seemed particularly keen to hear why he did not like having thralls and kept asking him to explain this and what he meant by being a 'free man' or a 'free Icelander'.

Kári liked speaking with Maebh. But he was surprised by one thing. This was the second time in a short while that someone had asked him about Iceland and freedom. Much as he felt that life in Iceland was good, he had seldom had to think much about what made it good and why the absence of kings and the presence of freedom were so important to him. He had simply taken it for granted. Yet finding that people in other countries knew little about Iceland and seemed puzzled by it, he had to think about what to say about his home. He also realised that if he wanted to explain to someone else why it was better to be free in a way that they could understand, he would have to think more carefully about it. It was not just a question of saying that having no king made things so much better.

He also asked Maebh about Ireland. It started when she asked him why he wanted to go to Dyflin.

"On my first voyage, in Kirkjuvágr, I met a trader from Dyflin. He wanted me to go there. We didn't, but for some reason I have dreamed about it ever since. Have you been there?"

"No, but I have heard about it."

"Tell me what you know. More knowledge in advance is always good for a trader."

"What would you know? Dyflin was founded by men from Norway. Men say that it was fought over by Norsemen and Danes and Irish chiefs for many years. Then, a long time ago, well before I was born, there was a big battle where the High King of Ireland defeated the men of Dyflin. But now, it is said that Norsemen and Irish live in peace and trade with each other there, and many ships come there from other lands to trade."

"What do they trade?"

"Everything. Linen and wadmal and silk, gold and silver, weapons and grain and even slaves."

"Hmm. You mentioned a high king. Does he now live there?"

"I don't know, but I do not think so. I don't even know who is High King now. We have so many kings in Ireland."

This was news to Kári. "How can you have many kings?"

"Because in Ireland, anyone who has a farm or two will call himself a king and make war on his neighbours. Some are more powerful than others, and they try to keep hold of their power. Others are trying to become powerful and are therefore always keen to fight."

"This does not sound like a good country for traders", Kári said.

"In some places it is", Maebh replied. "But it is true that we do not have much peace. You told me that in Iceland, you have one law and no king. In Ireland, we have many kings and no law. And when I hear you talking, it is clear to me which is better."

Kári thought about it. "It is strange", he said. "In England they have one king, in Norway they have one or two and in Ireland you have many. A Norwegian tried to explain to me that it was only because they had a king that they had order. Yet it seems to me that in none of these places is there as much obedience to the king as we have to our law, nor is there as much peace as we have in Iceland. Maybe as soon as you have a king, he thinks that he is above the law?"

"I am sure that's true", Maebh said. "Certainly, neither my father nor any other king thinks they should obey any laws."

Kári was surprised. "Your father really is a king? I thought that was your captor mocking you."

"Oh no", she said. "My father is indeed a king. But you heard what I said. He is king over a few farms and a small village or two. But he calls himself a king and will fight anyone who disputes that."

"But he is not powerful enough to protect his daughter?"

"What? Oh. No, I was taken from a nunnery. I was staying there to learn Latin. My father thought this would make me attractive enough to become a high king's queen, or maybe even be sent to England to marry someone powerful. And if no one would wed me, then I could be left there out of the way. The nunnery was looted by the men from Mann, and I was taken. I told them I was a king's daughter because I hoped they would let me be ransomed. That was a mistake." She fell silent.

"Because your father would not ransom you?"

"No, because the Manxmen thought it fun to have their sport with a king's daughter. I should have told them I was a scullery maid; they might perhaps have let me go when they were satisfied."

"Well, at least you can now go home", Kári said.

"Perhaps. But to what? I don't even know if my father is still alive or if he has been killed in some pointless battle."

For the first time since they met, Kári felt a twinge of jealousy at her words. He suddenly realised that he didn't want her to go back to her father. Did that mean that he wished her father was dead? He preferred not to think about this. For the moment, he did not know what else to say, and so he fell quiet and gazed out at the sea. It was already dark, and the stars were appearing overhead.

In normal times, Kári would have put in at Kirkjuvágr before rounding the north of Scotland and proceeding down towards Ireland. But he was still concerned about meeting remnants of the Norwegian fleet, and so they avoided making landfall in any settlement, only trying to find small streams where they could take on fresh water. This, and contrary winds, meant that it took them ten days to reach the coast of Ireland. There they had to stop and ask for directions, and so it took them another two days before they reached a settlement at a river mouth. This, the men thought, must be Dyflin on the Liffey river, and when they hailed a small fishing vessel coming out and asked where they were, they found that they were right.

When they entered the city and moored the ship, Kári went through the usual routine with the crew. This was the longest period they had ever spent at sea without making landfall, and it was also their longest time away from Snæströnd ever. The wear and tear was beginning to show on sails and ropes and oars, and Kári made careful notes of everything that was going to need either repair or replacement. By the time all this was done, it was already late and dark, and Kári told the crew that they should try to rest. They would be able to go ashore the next day.

By now Kári's bandage did not really need to be changed, but he liked when Maebh did it. While she was cleaning his wound, she asked, "What will you buy here?"

"I don't know yet", Kári replied. "I need to see what they have to sell. But I still have much silver left from Jórvik. This year, we took a large amount of walrus tusks to sell. I fear we may have to winter here, although I would have preferred not to. If we buy grain now and keep it on the boat for four months, it will spoil. Maybe the best thing to do is to buy something that will be expensive in Iceland. Because it is clear to me that this time, instead of two trading voyages in one year, I will end up with one in two years only, and it would be best if it were profitable."

"What is expensive in Iceland then?"

"Everything", Kári replied. "But I think if we can buy silk here, that would be good."

"We can find out tomorrow", Maebh said. Kári raised his eyes swiftly to her face. This was the first time she had shown that she felt herself to be part of his company and he wondered if it meant something. He wanted to ask her, but could not find the words. Instead they both sat silently for a while.

The next day, the crew drew lots to see who would go ashore first. Those with the longest straws set off in high spirits to see what the town had to offer them, silver jingling in their purses, and accompanied by much ribald laughter from their mates. Later, Kári and Maebh went ashore. Hallvarðr watched them go and smiled to himself, but said nothing. Kári would find out soon enough, he thought.

While they walked through the town, Kári looked around. It was bigger than Kirkjuvágr, but much smaller than Jórvik. There was a large marketplace, though it was mostly empty and there was a poor selection of trade goods available. But he did see one thing that puzzled him. At one of the stands where a merchant was selling bolts of silk and linen, Kári saw three men with dark skin. At first he thought they might have a disease, but he noticed that nobody avoided them, so they clearly were not sick. When he looked more carefully at them, they seemed almost like normal people, except that their skin was dark and their hair was short and curly.

The merchant noticed him staring and said, "Never seen those before, have you?"

"No", Kári said. "What are they? Are they men?"

"Oh, they are men like us except for their colour. They are blue-men slaves from Særkland. I bought them in Lishbuna."

"Where is that?"

"It is a great trading city in the south, where we get silk and gold and slaves."

Kári looked again at the dark-skinned men, and one of them looked back at him briefly. There was a look in his eyes that surprised Kári; it was not quite one of anger, nor yet one of despair, but it was certainly not one of submission, and there was an intensity behind it that could not be ignored. Kári was unsettled by it; he never liked seeing men enslaved and this blue-man, although he looked different, was surely entitled to freedom too.

While Kári was speaking with the merchant, Maebh was looking at the fabrics on sale. When Kári turned from the blue-men and began to inspect the goods, Maebh took him firmly by the hand and led him away. They passed other merchant booths. Some sold more fabrics, but although Kári wanted to stop and look at them, Maebh kept pulling him away. He could have stopped anyway, but that would have meant letting go of her hand, and he didn't want to do that.

Later, there were other booths where merchants sold such goods as Kári needed for the knarr, and there he was allowed to stop and purchase ropes and wool and leather strips for the sail, as well as food for the crew. He found prices higher than he had hoped for, but Maebh helped him bargain and in the end he paid little more than he would have had to in Jórvik or Kirkjuvágr.

When they approached the knarr, Kári halted and turned to face Maebh. She looked at him, waiting to hear what he had to say.

"I did not want to start quarrelling in the market", he said. "But I would like to know why you didn't want to let me look at the silk that was for sale. When did you become the owner of the knarr?"

The question brought a smile to Maebh's face. "Not yet", she replied with a laugh. "And there are many reasons why. First, the silk here is no good. And anyway, if you show interest, the merchant will raise his prices."

"This I know very well", Kári interrupted her. "But if I want to buy, I do have to show interest at some stage."

"This is true, but that was not my most important reason. I don't think you should buy silk in Dyflin at all."

"Why not? It will sell well in Iceland."

"So you said, and I believe you. I did not say that you shouldn't buy silk, only that you should not do so here and now."

"I am listening, Master Trader", Kári said. Maebh smiled again.

"Think", she said. "You have seen that there are not many people trading here. This is because we have arrived late in the year. The best quality of everything, including silk and linen, will already have been sold to traders who left long since in order to get home before the winter. So what the merchants have left is what they could not sell. And while they would probably gladly sell it now, they would soon notice that you know little about silk and would take advantage of that."

Kári admitted to himself that she was right, marvelling at how much she knew of his world and wondering where she had learnt it. Not even with Odd could he have had such a conversation. "But if I want to wait for better goods to come, I will have to winter here, and I have already told you I would prefer not to do that."

"I remember", Maebh said. "And this is my third reason for taking you away from the market. I have a much better plan."

Kári did not say anything but nodded at Maebh to continue. He noticed that when she became more animated, her eyes seemed to sparkle.

"I think", she said, "that we should go to Lishbuna."

"To Lishbuna?" That took Kári aback.

"Yes. Think about it. First, it means we go south, where it will be warmer, and we will winter there."

"How much warmer?"

"Much warmer, trust me."

"What is this, Muspelheim, the realm of fire? If it is too warm, how can people live there?"

"Oh, people live there. You heard the cloth merchant. Lishbuna is a great trading city, he said. So people clearly live there. Did you not tell me that you want to see faraway places? This will be farther than any of your neighbours in Iceland have ever been, I think."

"Perhaps", Kári said, but he remembered the Vínlandsfarer.

"Also think about this: if we go there, you will be able to have first choice of everything you wish to buy, and you will not have to pay the merchant to bring it from Lishbuna to Dyflin. And we can then go straight back to Iceland and arrive early enough in the year to sell before anyone else is back from their trading."

"We? I thought I was taking you to Cork?"

Maebh blushed as she realised her slip of the tongue. In truth, she had spent so much time close to Kári that she had begun to assume that they would remain together, but she had not yet thought of how this would work if she returned to Cork.

"I meant you."

"Then what about Cork?"

"We – you – can pass Cork on the way back from Lishbuna. Listen to me; you need me. I told you I speak Latin. There will certainly be people in Lishbuna who speak Latin, but you will not find anyone speaking Norse. I will help you trade."

"If you help me, I will pay for your help", Kári said.

Maebh looked at him. "You are a strange man, Kári Ragnarsson. I do not want your silver. I am helping you because you saved me and helped me."

"Is that the only reason?" Kári asked, looking at her. He thought Maebh would blush, but she looked him straight in the eyes.

"That is something you will have to find out in time." But she smiled while saying it.

"I accept your help", he said, smiling back. "And that you are coming with me of your free will is worth much more to me than the silver I will gain. But now I think we have another problem to solve."

"You are wondering how we will reach Lishbuna."

Kári was again impressed. That was indeed what he was wondering, but he had not thought that she would realise that. He nodded.

"Let me see what I can do", Maebh said. "I think I may have an idea." But however much Kári pressed her, she refused to say what it was. The only things she told him were to make sure that the knarr was ready to sail and to spend no money on trading goods in Dyflin.

Kári took her advice. And he thought to himself that, so far in life, he had met few people whose advice he would trust almost immediately. Odd, of course, and usually his father. But he realised that Maebh was another one. For a moment he wondered if this was because of her eyes and her smile, but the more he thought about what she had said to him, the more he realised that her advice was good. Once he had come to this conclusion, he stopped worrying about how they would get to Lishbuna. Maebh would arrange it. Instead, he thought of what a strange year it had been, with the storm, the time with the Norwegian fleet and the battle outside Jórvik. And now, not only was he in Dyflin where he had so long wanted to go, he was going to travel to a place he had previously never heard of and didn't even know where it lay. The Norns certainly spun their threads in strange ways.

For the next three days, Maebh would disappear every morning and return in the evening. Kári had attempted to ask where she went and whether she wanted someone to come with her – to protect her, as he put it. She had laughed and said that he would find out the one and that she had no need of the other. He briefly wondered if he should follow her but decided that she could probably avoid him if she wanted and would almost certainly be annoyed with him if she spotted him. And this he preferred not to happen. Instead, he remained by the knarr. The crew enjoyed the stay and spent as much time ashore as possible, losing a good deal of their silver to the pleasures of the town. And in the meantime, Kári's arm continued to heal, so he knew that when the time came to leave, he would be fit to steer again.

On the evening of the third day, Maebh did not return alone to the ship. With her she brought an older man, perhaps twice her age. He wore a dusty tunic of white wool, over which he had a cape with a hood that was currently folded down. On his feet he wore leather sandals, and in his hand he held a staff and a small bag. His head was strangely shaved, with a three-cornered bald patch, pointing forwards and to each ear. Kári had never seen such a strange head.

The man hesitated when they reached the knarr, but Maebh boarded the ship, dragging him along, and took him up to Kári.

"This is Aidan", she said. "He is a monk and he wishes to go in pilgrimage to the tomb of the Apostle Jacob."

Kári nodded, uncertain what this meant but unwilling to show his ignorance.

Maebh looked carefully at him, puzzled by the lack of response. Then she suddenly realised why he was saying nothing. She was beginning to find Kári more and more impressive. Someone else would have asked her questions by now, showing his ignorance, but he didn't. He was wise. And, yes, she realised, of course she liked him because of what he had done for her, but there was more to it than that. There was something else about him, something she could not quite explain to herself. All she knew was that the choice between leaving him and travelling to her father's farm in Cork, or going with him to a strange place, was an easy one. And after that, she would see.

"The Apostle is buried in Compostela in a country called Galicia, as I am sure you already know." She flashed him a brief smile. "There are one or two ports that are nearer, but Aidan says that he is happy to go to Lishbuna and travel on his own from there."

Now Kári understood. He nodded again and turned to the monk.

"Welcome on board, Aidan."

The monk nodded, but before he could say anything, Maebh continued. "Aidan has travelled widely. He has been to Rome once and to Compostela twice. And he was once a ship's master. He knows how to sail to Lishbuna."

That was much more than Kári had dared hope for. It was all very well to have someone on board who knew where they were going, but someone who actually knew how to get there was much, much better.

"Thank you, Maebh", he said. "And you, Aidan, are even more welcome than I just said."

"Thank you, my son", Aidan replied. "When do we sail?"

"As soon as the tide is right", Kári replied. "That, and when I have my crew back on board."

"Good. The sooner we leave, the better. You do not wish to sail these seas in the winter, and we are getting perilously late in the year as it is. But I think that the tide will be headed out tomorrow morning, so that would be a good time to leave."

That night, after the crew had all come back and Kári lay down to sleep in the stern of the ship, Maebh came and sat with him. At first, she only sat there, as if waiting for him to speak, but Kári seemed content to say nothing until she spoke. Finally, tiring of the game, she broke the silence.

"There is one more thing you have not asked me", she said.

"And what is that?"

"How Aidan is paying for his passage."

"I thought he was paying by guiding us there?"

"Yes. But I thought you might want some silver too?"

"His guidance will be worth more than any silver, I think", Kári said.

"That's what he thinks too", Maebh replied. "But he meant his heavenly guidance. He offered to pay in blessings and prayers for us."

"What did you reply?"

"I said that this was all well and good, but in that case, he would have to bring his own food, since I doubted that the blessings would be nourishing enough."

When Kári heard that he burst out laughing, and before he knew what he was doing, he embraced the Irishwoman. She stiffened for a brief moment but then quickly relaxed and put her arms around him. They held each other and then, as if realising what they were doing, drew slightly apart, looking into each other's eyes. Then their faces moved together and lips met in a kiss, slowly and almost hesitantly at first, then more intensely and almost frantically, as if they had held off doing this for so long and were now trying to make up for lost time. He touched her hair and her face and tried to kiss her everywhere at once, her neck, her throat and her eyes, but always returning to her mouth.

When they eventually stopped, Kári's head spun. He opened his mouth to say something, but Maebh stopped him by kissing him again, this time more gently. Whatever Kári had thought of saying disappeared as he gave himself up to the sensation.

Finally, they stopped again. This time, Kári held up a hand to make sure Maebh did not interrupt him. "I think", he said, "that this is where we should now stop."

Maebh raised an eyebrow at him. What was suddenly wrong with him? she thought. He clearly wanted her as much as she wanted him. Or had she misjudged things? She didn't think so.

"Wait", Kári continued. "All I mean is that there are ten other men on board –"

"Eleven", she interrupted.

"Eleven other men on board. This may not be the best place. And I think going ashore and finding a dark, cold corner somewhere next to a house is not what you deserve."

"What do I deserve?" she whispered.

"I do not know. A king's dwelling in Lishbuna perhaps? If you can wait that long? If not, we will go ashore now."

For a brief moment, Maebh was tempted. But she knew Kári was right. "I can wait", she said.

"Thank you", Kári replied. He swallowed nervously, before adding, "my love." He felt strange. He had never felt like this before.

Maebh leaned over and kissed him again, but lightly this time. Then she stood up and made her way over to her own sleeping berth.

The next morning, they sailed out of the Liffey and, following Aidan's instructions, turned south.

Kári would always remember this journey fondly, even though it was difficult for him and for Maebh. They did not wish to let the crew know what had occurred between them, so they kept apart and rarely spoke, only looking towards each other from time to time.

They stopped once more on the Irish coast to take on fresh water. But after that they set sail due south towards what Aidan said was called the Cantabrian Sea.

Aidan would stand next to Kári by the steering oar. At first, he was quiet, only telling Kári if they needed to alter course. But soon Kári began to ask questions about the monk's past life and about his experiences. When Aidan seemed little pleased to talk about that, Kári asked him instead why he was undertaking his journey.

"I go to Compostela to honour the Apostle Jacob."

"Yes, but why?"

"I wish to pray for forgiveness for my sins."

"And will he grant your prayer?"

"If it is a true prayer and I am truly repentant, yes, he will assuredly grant it."

"You must be a very sinful man."

Aidan sighed. "More than you know, Kári, more than you know. But is this so obvious?"

"No. I only thought that you must be if you have made so many pilgrimages."

"All men are sinful, Kári. We are born in sin."

"Are we? Why?"

"What do you mean, why?"

"Why do you say that all men are born in sin? Or are sinful? I had a friend on this ship, we left him in Jórvik because he wanted to go on pilgrimage to Rome. But he was not a sinful man."

Aidan looked at him. "But surely you know this, Kári. You are a Christian."

Kári stroked his beard and laughed. "In Iceland, this is a question we do not ask. Yet on this journey, it seems everyone wants to know if I follow the White Christ. In truth, I do not know, although in Iceland we are all supposed to follow him. Why does everyone keep asking me this?"

Now Aidan looked at Kári with horror in his eyes. "But surely you must be a Christian, Kári?! You seem a good man. You cannot be a heathen!"

"I don't know what a heathen is", Kári replied, "and as for being a good man, I hope I am. But what do these two things have in common?"

"Wait, let me ask you something first. I thought Iceland was a Christian country?"

"We are. Many years ago, the Lawspeaker decided that we should follow the White Christ. For a time, anyone who did not wish to do so could continue to follow the old gods in their own homes. This is no longer the case, but we still feel that what each one does is nobody's business but his own."

"But – but how can you have such a system? Don't you understand the dangers?"

"It works in Iceland", Kári replied. "This way, there is no strife between such followers of the old that remain and the followers of the new. And that is good."

"Yes, but don't you see? Your immortal soul is in danger. If you are not Christian, you will go to Hell, you will not be saved!"

"What is that to you? Why would you care?"

Aidan sighed, more deeply than before. "Kári, it is not I who care. No, that is wrong. I do care. But I care because my Lord cares. He cares for everyone, Kári, and he wants you to be saved."

"Your Lord? I thought you were a monk. Who is your Lord?"

"My Lord is Jesus Christ, my Saviour – and yours and everyone else's."

"How can he be my saviour if I do not follow him?"

"Kári, Jesus cares for everyone. Jesus suffered on the cross and died so that we can all be saved. All you need to do is to believe in Him, and you will be saved. After you die here on earth, you will go to Paradise and live in eternal bliss. But if you do not believe in Him, you will be cast in Hell and suffer the torment of the damned for eternity."

"Everyone I know who follows the White Christ tells me that he is a mild and forgiving God?"

"Oh, He is, Kári, He is!"

"But how can he then condemn people to the eternal torments you talk about? Should he not forgive everyone if they are good men?"

"In order to be saved by the Lord, Kári, you must believe in Him. Baptism will wash away your sins and make you worthy to be saved. Look, Kári, you are a good man, I can see that. How can you not be a Christian?"

Kári smiled. "I know many good people in Iceland who almost certainly are not. And I know Christians who are not good people. The King of Norway who was killed in England, he was a Christian. He wanted all his men to be Christian as well, although I saw many of them wear Hammers and call to Óðinn in the battle. Their king was a bad man, Aidan, greedy for gold, a liar and a trickster. And in battle, some of the men who called on the White Christ fell, and others who called on Óðinn survived."

"I did not say that all Christians are good men. There are bad men everywhere. But through Christ they may change their ways.

Look at other people. Your friend Odd is a Christian; is he not a good man? And what about Maebh? Would you cause her to sin?"

"I don't know how much of a Christian Odd is", Kári replied. "And as for Maebh, why would I cause her to sin?"

Aidan looked him straight in the face. "Surely you must know that for a Christian woman to wed a heathen man is one of the greatest of all sins, one impossible to wash away even for the most powerful of saints?"

Kári was taken aback by the monk's words, but he tried not to show it. Instead, he thought about what Aidan had said. Previously, he had not known much about the White Christ apart from what he had picked up in Iceland, which was little enough. Although much of what Aidan had said impressed him, he also thought to himself that, after all was said and done, this White Christ was just the same as any other lord – he wanted to interfere in Kári's life and control him. True, it might be with good intentions, but the effect was the same, that Kári would be unable to follow his own wishes. The old gods might have their failings and often behaved capriciously, but at least they generally left their followers alone.

He was more impressed by what Aidan had said about the White Christ caring for everyone, even those who did not follow him. And although Aidan had said of himself that he was full of sin and in need of forgiveness for his sins, Kári had come to understand from his stories that he was a genuinely good man. Of course, his words about Maebh had also made an impact, although Kári realised that until then, he had not really thought of her as a wife. But the more he thought of that prospect, the more attractive it sounded.

Aidan frequently offered to baptise Kári, but although Kári was ready to hear more, he was not prepared to let himself be doused with holy water.

Meanwhile, their journey progressed. Aidan expressed surprise at how good the weather was. He earnestly explained to Kári that this was because God was looking favourably on his pilgrimage. Kári nodded but thought that it was far more likely that they were just lucky. Since he had already had his full share of bad luck this year, it stood to reason that he was due some good weather. And whether it was divine help or luck, he would accept it – and the warmer days that, just as Maebh had promised, they were now enjoying. But he did take careful note of everything that Aidan told him about directions, since he realised that he would have to steer back to Ireland on his own unless they somehow managed to find someone headed in that direction.

During this journey, Maebh spent much time thinking about what had happened with Kári. Although she had already realised that she liked him, the intensity of her feelings when they kissed had come as a surprise to her. In one way she was glad that they were in a small space with many other people. She realised that, before they returned to Cork, she would have to decide what she wanted to do. Kári seemed a good man, and she felt that much of what he said was things she agreed with. But although what he said about Iceland sounded good, it was also clear that it was a poor country. Was she prepared to leave her family and go with him, to live on his brother's farm? That was certainly not the future she had envisaged for herself. On the other hand, would it really be so much worse than staying in Ireland and ending up marrying someone picked by her father because he ruled over three farms instead of two? In the end, she decided that she would let matters run their course, at least until they returned to Cork. After all, it was only there that she would have to make a final choice. In the meantime, whatever happened would happen.

Soon after crossing the Cantabrian Sea, they reached a coastline which they followed to the west. Aidan told Kári that they would actually pass close to a small port called Vigo. "This is the closest to the tomb of the Apostle", he said, "and one of the last ports in Christian hands on this coast." Kári understood what this meant; Aidan had already told him that Lishbuna was not a Christian city, although who exactly lived there was not quite clear to him, except that they were hostile to the followers of Christ.

Now he asked, "Will it be dangerous for you to travel through other lands?"

"There is danger everywhere, my son", the monk replied. "I will go where my Lord leads me."

"We could stop at Vigo. Then you would be in a Christian country."

"I have promised to take you to Lishbuna, Kári, and that I will do. What would Christ think of me if I abandoned you and broke my promise?"

Once again, Kári was impressed with Aidan and his faith, as the monk was willing to put himself in danger for the sake of a stranger he barely knew.

When they finally reached Lishbuna, Kári and his crew were amazed. This was a city much larger even than Jórvik. As they sailed eastwards up the river that led to the city, the sun shone on white buildings ranged along the northern hillside. There was a fortress by the port, and all over the city slender spires topped with green stretched towards the sky. Aidan noticed Kári's look and explained, "Those are the temples of the unbelievers." The harbour seemed full of ships and of bustle.

Kári was not surprised when they were hailed by two warships. He could not understand what they said, but when the soldiers on board realised this, there was a pause, and then someone came to the prow and began to shout in different languages. Eventually, Aidan understood and replied. Maebh stood next to Kári and he asked her, "Is this Latin?"

"Yes. He is explaining who we are. Oh, he doesn't know that I understand Latin. Do not tell him, nor anyone else."

"Why not?"

"You never know. But having a knowledge that is not widely spread is often an advantage, in trading and otherwise."

Kári nodded. Meanwhile, Aidan turned to them and said, "We are to berth by a pier and wait there."

Lishbuna might be larger than Jórvik, Kári thought, but it seemed to be the same as everywhere else. If you come, you pay. He wondered how much they would have to pay this time.

The men were manning the oars now, following Aidan's instructions to a stone pier, where they moored the ship. But at least they did not have to wait. When they arrived, there was already a small group of soldiers there, with a man who, to Kári's relief, spoke Latin with Aidan. After a brief exchange of words, Aidan turned to Kári. "He is asking for five dirhams", he said. "I have told him that we do not have any dirhams but that you will pay him the same weight in silver."

Kári nodded. This was about what he had expected. Wordlessly he handed over a handful of silver coins to Aidan, who passed them over one at a time to the other man, who was busy setting up a small scale. When he had put three coins on the scale, he turned to Aidan and signalled that it was enough.

Once the soldiers were gone, Aidan turned to Kári again. "I shall leave you now. Many thanks for the passage."

Kári was surprised. "Are you leaving at once?"

"Why not? There is still a little sun left in the sky. I have a long way before I reach Santiago, so I might as well get started. May God and His Son the Lord Jesus Christ watch over you, Kári, and show you the light."

Kári felt strangely touched. "Thank you", he replied. "And – and may they both be with you as well, Aidan."

Aidan took his staff and his bag and climbed ashore. Then, without looking around, he set off towards the city. Kári watched him go, realising as he did so that, short as their acquaintance had been, he would miss the monk and their talks.

Then he felt a hand on his arm and turned around. It was Hallvarðr.

"I know what you want to say", Kári said. "We should start inspecting the ship and decide who gets to go ashore first. But surely you know whose turn it is?"

Hallvarðr smiled. "Not this time, Kári."

"What do you mean?"

"I mean that this time, we will check the ship tomorrow, when it is properly light. Right now, we are all going ashore. So it would be a good idea if you could give the men some silver. They are going to need it if they are not coming back until the morning."

"What?" Kári didn't understand what Hallvarðr was talking about. "Why would we all go ashore. Who will guard the ship?"

Hallvarðr's smile grew broader. "I didn't mean we would leave the ship alone and unguarded! You, Kári, are staying on the knarr with Maebh. But all of us, the whole of your crew, we are going ashore."

"What are you talking about?"

"Kári, I may be your brother's farmhand, but I am also your friend. I am not stupid, nor are the others. You may think that we see nothing, but we all know what is going on. So we are leaving the ship to you and Maebh tonight."

"Why?"

This time Hallvarðr laughed. "I think you know. And if you don't, I can assure you that she does and that it is about time you found out. Now, will you give me some silver, or do I have to wrest it from you?"

Kári did not know what to say. He blushed, but he had enough sense to stop arguing. Instead, he opened his purse again and poured out some silver coins in his hand and gave them to Hallvarðr. Then he thought for a moment and added some more. "You may need to drink more than usual", he said.

"We will certainly drink your health", Hallvarðr replied. Then he turned around and whistled at the crew, who had all been watching while pretending to be busy about their tasks. Some of them nodded at Kári, and one or two winked at him. Then they all climbed onto the quay and disappeared, leaving Kári and Maebh.

When the crew had left, Maebh slowly came up to Kári, looking at him with her eyebrows raised.

"I – I …". He tried again, "I did not know that this would happen."

"It seems your men are cleverer than you think", Maebh replied. Then she looked around the knarr. "This is not quite the king's palace that you promised would await me in Lishbuna", she said.

Kári felt himself blushing furiously. "I'm sorry", he stammered.

Maebh laughed. "I think that even so, I will make do. We will make do. There are bound to be some soft furs somewhere." And now she came closer to Kári, once again smiling.

Kári thought of something to say, but decided that, at this point, silence was better. Instead, he held out his arms and embraced her and felt her body melting against his.

They did not go to sleep for a long time that night, but when they finally did, they did not complain, and they slept very well.

Chapter 11

Winter – Spring 1067

The next morning, Kári was surprised to find that the sun was already quite high in the sky, and it was very pleasantly warm. He found it hard to guess how late in the morning it was, but in Iceland, even in the middle of the day in high summer, he rarely felt the sun's warmth like this, and it made him feel good.

But that was not the only reason for his contentment. He smiled to himself as he turned and looked at Maebh, who was still asleep, breathing gently. He didn't want to wake her up but carefully and lightly touched her body, savouring the softness of her skin. He still found it difficult to believe what had happened. Not their lovemaking – that, he realised, he had somehow known would happen. No, it was meeting someone like Maebh. She was different from the Icelandic girls he had known. She was not just clever – Jórunn, for instance, was probably equally clever. But Maebh was wiser. He laughed. For one thing, Maebh thought about both of them, while Jórunn seemed only to think of herself.

The laughter woke Maebh. She stretched her arms over her head and turned her face to look at him, smiling as she did so.

"Good morning", he said.

"Good morning." She moved closer to him and rested her head on his arm, one hand running through the hair on his chest.

"I think I could lie in the sun like this all day", Kári said.

"Only because of the sun?"

"No, because the most beautiful woman in the world is by my side", he replied.

"I wonder what your men would think of that?"

His men! Suddenly Kári remembered that the crew could return at any time. In fact, he was surprised that they had not yet returned. He shot up and began to scramble around for his clothes, tossing Maebh's shift to her. When she didn't move to put it on, he opened his mouth to say something but stopped when she laughed.

"Why are you laughing?"

"Because of your fears. Your crewmen know what we have been doing. After all, that is why they left us alone. They don't want you to be embarrassed by them coming back early. So you can rest assured of two things. First, that they have spent a very pleasant night with other women. And second, that one of them will be somewhere where he can see us, but not so close that he can see us clearly. And the moment we get dressed, we need but show ourselves, and they will all soon show up. Probably joking with you when they come."

"How do you know this?"

"I don't. But I think I know how most men think, and your men like you, Kári. They respect you. And so this is what they would do. And that means that we are in no hurry."

He stopped what he was doing and looked down at her. "In that case?"

She laughed again and shot him a wicked look, suddenly sticking her tongue out at him.

For the rest of his life, Kári would remember that morning in Lishbuna, the sun shining on them as they continued their love-play. He would remember the smooth roundness of her shoulders, her pert breasts, and her smell mixing with the smell of the knarr and the furs they were lying on. Above all, he would remember the feeling of having all the time in the world to do nothing but be with Maebh.

By the time they began to dress, the sun was already past its zenith and beginning its slow descent. When they were finally dressed, Kári went and stood at the prow, looking out over the harbour and towards the city. Once again he was struck by the blinding whiteness of the buildings, but now he also saw that there was plenty of lush greenery. It was different from the green colours of Jórvik, more intense somehow.

Maebh came and stood next to him, and he pulled her closer, savouring the feeling of her presence. "What are you thinking about?" she asked.

"I am thinking that this is a very good place for us to spend the winter", he replied.

She did not reply, because while they were standing there, the crew suddenly appeared. It was easy to see that most of the men had spent the night, and probably the morning as well, drinking. Some of them smiled as they saw Kári and Maebh, but nobody said anything beyond wishing them a good day.

Kári had been prepared for some teasing from the men, at least from the seven neighbours, but he was pleased that they restrained themselves. Instead, once they were all on board, they began the usual harbour routine. Only this time, none of the crew went ashore. Instead, Kári and Maebh asked Hallvarðr a few questions about what they had seen the previous night and where they should go, and then they left the knarr and crossed the busy harbourfront towards the town itself.

Kári noted that many of the buildings had only a door but no window. He could see trees growing above their roofs, so he guessed that there must be gardens behind the blank front walls. Also, once they had moved away from the salty, fishy reek of the harbour, he began to pick up other smells, ones he could not identify but which he certainly liked. He could see that Maebh was similarly affected because everywhere they went she seemed to be sniffing the air, turning her face this way and that and exclaiming with pleasure when she spotted a beautiful flower.

Maebh did find the city exhilarating. In the past, she had never thought much of travelling, but since she had been captured by the Manxmen and taken to Kirkjuvágr and then Jórvik, she had discovered that there was a much larger world around her than she had ever envisaged in Ireland. True, it was better to travel of her own free will than as a captive, but she now knew that she liked seeing new places. And Lishbuna was certainly different from anywhere she had ever seen or could have imagined. There were trees she had never seen before and flowers she could not recognise. And wherever they went they were surrounded by people, people wearing strange dresses and looking even stranger. They even saw more blue-men, but here they didn't seem to be captives as some of them were armed and walked in groups like soldiers. But one thing puzzled her. Once they had left the port, they did not see any women anywhere.

After they had walked around for most of the afternoon, Kári's growing hunger reminded him that neither of them had eaten anything all day. He cast his eyes up and down the street, looking for an inn. When he could not immediately spot one, he began to look around for someone to ask, only for it to strike him that neither of them could speak the local language. For a moment he hesitated, not certain what to do. A thought made him start walking back towards the port area. When they had walked past a few houses, Maebh put her hand on his arm. "Shall I tell you what we are doing?" she asked, smiling.

Kári was happy for her to tell him anything, as long as she kept smiling, so he just nodded.

"You are looking for an inn, and you have realised that there must be some at the port. Am I right?"

Kári burst out laughing. This was one of the reasons he loved her, he thought. She knew what he was thinking, without him having to say anything. "Is it so obvious?" he asked.

"No, but I was thinking exactly the same thing. It makes sense, and I'm getting hungry."

He laughed again and gave her a quick embrace, causing some of the passers-by to stare disapprovingly.

Then he took her hand and they continued to walk. Once they were down by the harbour, they followed the noise and the smell until they came to what had to be an inn. People were sitting outside, eating and drinking, speaking loudly and playing games of different kinds. Kári was surprised to see that there were two or three chessboards. At least, that was what they looked like, although the pieces looked different from the ones he had carved so long ago in Iceland. But as he stopped and observed the games, he realised that the moves were the same.

He would have liked to continue watching – he had not played chess for a long time – but their desire for food and drink took over. They found a table with free spaces and sat down. Even before they could try to see what others were eating, someone came and put plates and a platter with bread and what looked like little green and black fruits on the table. He also asked them something, but Kári just shook his head and mimicked eating and drinking. The man nodded and disappeared. When he had gone, they tried the food. The bread tasted good, but it was different from bread at home, whiter and flatter. The black fruits were quite tart, while the green ones were slightly salty. Maebh bit into one only to cry out when she realised that it contained a large stone. But once they knew this, they found the fruits very pleasant. Shortly afterwards, the man reappeared with a steaming bowl full of something that smelled of fish and a jug and two mugs. He waited expectantly by the table until Kári opened his purse and began to take out coins. He only had silver pennies, but one of those seemed to satisfy the servant as he took it and disappeared.

Kári and Maebh enjoyed the food. It was some kind of fish stew, although the taste was one neither of them had ever encountered. But when Kári poured them drinks from the jug, he was surprised. The liquid was clear, but when he tasted it he spluttered. "It is water!" he exclaimed. "Strange-tasting, but water."

Maebh took a sip from her mug. "Yes. Water with some kind of flower, I think."

"Don't they have beer or mead? Or even wine? Surely they must have something else than scented water. The crew did not get drunk on water last night!"

Maebh smiled again. "I rather like it", she said. "For tonight. Not for every day. But for tonight it is good. As for tomorrow, we can ask Hallvarðr what they drank when we return to the knarr."

It was dark by the time they returned to the knarr. Kári was not surprised to find that most of the men were already fast asleep.

What did surprise him, though, was to find Hallvarðr sitting on the quay, speaking with a stranger. Perhaps twenty years older than Kári, he was dressed like a local, wearing the white full-length cloak that was so common in the city, but he was tall and fair-haired whereas most of the local people seemed to be shorter and darker.

As soon as Hallvarðr saw them approach, he stood up, and the stranger did the same.

When they came closer, Hallvarðr stepped forward. "Kári, this is Ingjald. He is a Swede. He wishes to speak with you." At this, the stranger – Ingjald – placed his right hand on his heart and bowed. Then he straightened up and turned to Kári.

"I am honoured to meet you", he said. "You are the first men from Iceland I have seen. I think you are the first Icelanders ever to come to Lishbuna."

"Thank you", Kári replied. "We are glad to meet someone who speaks Norse. But how came you here?"

"It is a long story", Ingjald replied. "But the short version is that I sailed east from Sweden. I was captured in Særkland and became a slave. I was a slave for many years, following my master, a trader, on many journeys, learning to speak his language and that of many others as well. Finally, one day, we came through Nörvasund to here, and then my master died. He left me some money and I decided to stay."

"You are a slave?" Kári was astonished. He could see that Ingjald wore gold rings on his fingers and he seemed well fed.

"No longer. I took on their faith, and that made me a free man. I am now called al-Shamali. It means Northman. Now I live here, where I help foreign traders who do not speak Arabic. Most of them are Irish or French. But now, a ship from Iceland. Marvellous are the ways of Allah!" He fell silent.

Kári understood most of what he had said, but there was some of it he did not. However, his first thought was that this was a piece of luck indeed.

"I am pleased to meet you, Ingjald. Al-Sh –. I am sorry, how do you say this?"

"Al-Shamali."

"Al-Sha – Shamali. Yes. I am indeed glad to have met you and would speak longer with you. But it is late and you are no doubt tired. May I suggest that you return to us tomorrow in the morning and perhaps we can discuss our business then?"

"This is good and I will do so", al-Shamali (as he clearly wanted to be known) replied. After bowing again, he left for the city.

It was only now that Kári turned around and saw that Maebh was missing. For a brief moment he feared something had happened, but then he spotted her on the knarr. When she saw him looking at her, she approached the quay. "Since Hallvarðr spoke with him, it was clear that he spoke our language", she said. "But I think it better for the moment if everybody thinks that I am your servant girl."

"Why?"

"Like I once told you, knowledge is a good thing to keep hidden sometimes."

*

The next morning, al-Shamali returned.

Kári had originally thought of going with him to an inn, but Maebh suggested that they speak on board the ship so that she could listen to the conversation without the Swede being aware of it. Kári found this good advice, and so he and al-Shamali made themselves as comfortable as possible in the stern, while Maebh sat some way off, and the other crew members were busy with their tasks.

Al-Shamali looked at the ship. "I have not seen a knarr for many years", he said, "but some things never change."

"There is little reason to change if it is a good design", Kári replied. "Unless you can somehow make it better."

"This is true. Now, tell me, how can I help you?"

"I will", Kári replied. "But first please explain something to me. Yesterday, in an inn, instead of beer we were given water. A strange-tasting water, but not unpleasant. Why is this?"

"Ah. Yes. So, we do not drink anything that intoxicates us. This was ordained by our Prophet, peace be upon him. So you were given rosewater. Water which was scented with rose petals. It is most refreshing."

"It was. But I don't understand. Who is your Prophet? Is he the same as the White Christ?"

Al-Shamali laughed. But when he saw Kári's face darken he hastened to apologise. "Forgive me, I meant no offence. I was laughing at myself, not at you", he quickly said. "I have lived so long among the Faithful that I forget that not everyone knows this. So, the Prophet was a man named Mohammed, peace be upon him. He was a Prophet of God. God revealed to him how the Christians and the Jews have distorted the true faith. He wrote down everything God told him in our Holy Book, the Quran. The Faithful are those who listened to his teachings and have submitted to God, who in their own language is called Allah. And one of the things he forbade us was to drink wine or any other drink that makes us drunk."

"The monk who guided us to Lishbuna called you unbelievers", Kári said. "I did not understand that then, but now I think I do. You are not followers of the White Christ."

Al-Shamali grimaced. "They are infidels who have perverted the true faith, idolators who claim that the son of Mary is God. There is often conflict between us and them."

Kári thought about this and then said, "In spite of what you are saying, some of my men had definitely drunk beer when they came back to the ship yesterday."

"Not everyone in Lishbuna belongs to the Faithful", al-Shamali replied. "There are also Jews and Christians. They are allowed to drink whatever they want. Your men were probably lucky and found an inn catering to them."

"I thought you said there is hostility between you and the Christians?"

"Often there is. But there are still some of them living here. As long as they pay the tax and behave properly, they are allowed to live in peace and follow their own faith, false though it is."

Kári thought that this sounded much like Iceland, where one man's faith was not his neighbour's concern, although he disliked the reference to other faiths as false. "I see. Now, let us talk of other matters. We are here to trade. Are you able to help us?"

Now al-Shamali smiled. "I most certainly can. And you are very fortunate to have found me. I know many merchants in the bazaar. What do you need, what can you sell and how long will you stay?"

"I hope to stay over the winter. We cannot sail back to Iceland until the spring, and we have business to conduct in Ireland on the way as well. As for selling, we do not have much, except some carved walrus ivory, but we have silver to pay for our purchases. We will need supplies for the ship and for ourselves while we stay, and I have been told that there is a good market in silk?"

When he heard the word silver, al-Shamali's face brightened even more. Now he looked very pleased. "It seems that Allah himself has been gracious enough to smile upon you. And upon me, of course. Let us first talk about your supplies, and then we will speak of the silk. I think I know where you will get the best price, both for your sales and for your purchases. But may I suggest something else?"

"Of course."

"You have arrived late in the year and wish to stay over the winter. This is the right thing to do, not least because you will then be here when ships begins arrive from the east and caravans from other parts of al-Andalus with new goods to trade early in the year. But do you really intend to stay on your knarr the whole time? Or would you prefer to rent a house in the city for yourself and your crew?"

Kári was surprised by the question. He should have thought of this, he realised. Not just for himself and Maebh, but for all of them. He really could not expect the crew to spend the next few months on the ship. However, he tried not to show anything and merely nodded, saying, "That was my thought. Can you help with that as well?"

"Of course, of course", al-Shamali replied. "I know just the place. It will cost you, of course, but you said you had silver. And you do understand that I will charge a fee for my services. Perhaps we can discuss this first? Payable in full weight coins of good silver please, neither shaved nor clipped."

Kári knew that he would have to pay al-Shamali for his services and did not mind doing so. But during the negotiations, he found himself occasionally repelled by the Swede's greed. This puzzled him. Al-Shamali had something to sell that Kári wanted to buy, and he was probably the only one in Lishbuna who could sell this. And like any trader, he would want a good price. After all, that was what Kári himself would do. Yet there was something in the man's face whenever their talk turned to silver that disturbed him.

However, although the man drove a hard bargain, he also provided the services he promised. The next day al-Shamali asked Kári to bring one of his crewmen to follow him, and he led them to a modest house near the harbour. When they entered, Kári realised that his first impression of the houses had been right. Inside behind the blank front wall there was a verdant courtyard, with strange trees growing above the roof and shading the interior. There was enough space for the entire crew, with a separate room for himself and Maebh. The house was inhabited by an old woman. Al-Shamali explained that she would stay while they lived there and was also prepared to cook for them. "But no pork", he added.

"Why no pork? Are there no pigs in this country?" Kári asked.

"No, it's not that. But the Prophet, peace be upon him, has forbidden us to eat pork", al-Shamali replied.

"So no beer or wine, and no pork", Kári said. "Has he forbidden you anything else?" He meant it as a joke, but al-Shamali clearly took umbrage and snapped, "Nothing that would concern an infidel!" Then he composed his face again and said, "By the way, the woman wants her rent paid now. You can pay me back later." And without waiting for Kári's reply, he opened a purse he was carrying and counted out a few coins for the woman. When she saw them, she grimaced and spat at the coins, but she took them even so.

Afterwards, the crewman was sent back to the knarr to tell Maebh and the others to come ashore and bring their gear to the house. Kári had already arranged with Hallvarðr that two men would stay on the ship as guards at all times and that one of these would always be from Snæströnd.

Meanwhile, al-Shamali took Kári to another part of the harbour area, where they found the ship-chandlers. Although al-

Shamali tried to push Kári to make his purchases there and then, he demurred, saying that he had not yet completed his inspection of the boat after their voyage and still did not know exactly what would be needed to make good the sail and rigging or whether any of the ropes and oars required replacing. Also, he was not in any hurry to leave; he enjoyed walking around, listening to strange voices speaking an unknown language, seeing a mixture of known and unknown goods, yet smelling the same smells that you always encountered in a port, overlaid everywhere with the heady scent of flowers.

In the afternoon, al-Shamali led Kári back to the knarr. He tried to make arrangements for coming back the next day to take Kári back to the market, but Kári was reluctant to do so. "I wish to wait a few days", he said. "We are all tired and need some rest. And you said yourself that new goods for trading will not arrive for some months yet."

"You will not wish to delay buying equipment for your knarr until then. Remember, they will need such things for their ships too."

"I understand that. But for now we will rest for a few days."

"In that case", al-Shamali said, "why don't I come and meet you at the house in four days? And if you need me before then, just say my name to the old woman. She will know where to find me."

"This is good", Kári said. "And I thank you for your help today."

When al-Shamali had gone, Kári spent a few moments with the two men who were guarding the knarr. Then he slowly walked back to the house. He had been worried that he would not be able to find it, but as he walked, he found that his feet took him there as long as he did not think too much about it.

At the house, the rest of the crew were lounging in the courtyard. It was still warm and many had removed their tunics, enjoying the warmth of the setting sun on their bodies.

Kári was not sure what the old woman would cook for them or how well, but in the evening, he was pleasantly surprised by a fish stew, similar to what he and Maebh had eaten on their second night.

After dinner, Kári spoke for a while with Hallvarðr and the others. Some of the men grumbled that there had only been water to drink, so Kári told them that the next day, they would try to find an inn that would sell them beer. "Or wine", one of the men, who had clearly developed a taste for this drink, interjected.

Kári then went to the room that was set aside for him and Maebh. When she saw him enter, she smiled and took his hand and led him to a large bed that took up most of the small room. "This is still not a king's palace", she said, "but it is much better than the ship."

For the next three days, they carefully inspected the knarr and noted what needed to be repaired or renewed. Kári and Maebh also spent much time walking around the city. At first, they tended to stick to the harbour, but after a short while they began to venture further into the city, enjoying the busy public squares and exploring the narrow alleys between the tall windowless buildings. There was much to marvel at, thought Kári. Large buildings, larger than many he had seen in Jórvik even, and large parks with streams of water running through them. In front of what Aidan had said were the temples, there would be throngs of men sitting or standing around, chatting to each other. Often men turned and stared at them, although Kári assumed it was more to look at the beautiful woman by his side than at him. Often, also, they spotted men sitting by pools of water and washing their feet, something they both found puzzling. Other strange signs were men wholly wrapped in fabric so that nothing could be seen of their faces or bodies, often escorted by armed guards. Both of them wondered at this strange sight. Suddenly Maebh giggled and turned to Kári. "These are not men. They are women", she exclaimed.

"How do you know?" Kári asked.

"Just look at the way they are walking", she replied. "And think about it – how many women have you seen outside the harbour? I am the only one walking around without a guard. This is why they stare at me."

But Kári was not convinced. Rather, he thought it was men who were suffering from some disease that made them wrap up their bodies and who were guarded so that no one would approach them.

On the third afternoon, they chanced to pass by the same inn that they had visited on their first evening ashore. Once again, there were men sitting outside at tables, playing different games. Kári spotted an elderly man with a grey beard sitting by a chessboard all by himself and wandered over to look at the pieces. The man noticed his interest and spoke with him. When Kári shook his head to show that he didn't understand, the man smiled and spoke again, saying something different. Kári looked helplessly at him while the man tried different sentences. Then suddenly he heard the voice of Maebh behind him. "Ita", she said, and the man gestured to Kári to sit down on the opposite side of the board.

Before he could do anything, Maebh spoke again, and the man looked at her and replied. They continued to speak for a few moments, and then she held up her hand.

"He asked if you play chess", she said. "I told him you do. He wishes to play with you."

"Thank him from me", Kári replied. "Who is he?"

"He is a Christian priest. He told me his name is Sancho and he lives here. I have told him your name and where we come from."

That afternoon and evening, Kári and the priest Sancho played many games of chess. Occasionally they would try to converse, but it was tiring to have to rely on Maebh translating everything, and so they concentrated on the game. In Iceland, Kári had been accounted a good chess player, but, in truth, he had not had occasion to play very often. Now he found that this was a completely different kind of opponent, and although he won the odd game, Sancho generally managed to best him, luring Kári into making overconfident moves that suddenly would cost him a rook or expose his king, and then the game would soon be over.

Maebh sat by the table, watching the two men play. This was yet another side of Kári that she had not previously seen; the man who thought long and hard and tried to plan ahead yet who clearly enjoyed the game for its own sake. Where men she knew would have been angry at losing game after game, Kári just smiled and picked up the pieces, ready to try again. And she also noticed that he was clearly trying to learn from his mistakes, again something many men never seemed prepared to do in her experience.

Sometimes, while Kári was thinking over his next move, Maebh would ask Sancho questions about Lishbuna. Thus she found out that, as al-Shamali had already told them and as Sancho himself was proof, there were Christians and others in the city who did not belong to the faith of the Moors, as Sancho called them. They were safe and were treated well as long as they paid a tax for their protection, but they were subject to other rules. They could not live in tall buildings, their churches could not have bells and they had to show respect for the Moors by stepping out of the way when they encountered them. And they could not carry weapons. He also told her where they could find several inns around the harbour and elsewhere which served both wine and beer. He confirmed that the Moors were forbidden from drinking wine, but said that many of them did so anyway, though he warned that it was safer to drink in places for Christians.

When the sun finally set, Sancho asked Maebh to tell Kári that they would have to stop playing, but that he would usually be found at the same place most afternoons except on Fridays and Sundays, these being the holy days for Moors and for Christians, and that he would be happy to play anytime Kári so chose. For this they thanked him and then returned to the house.

On the way back, Kári listened to all that Maebh had learned from Sancho. Then he said, "It is good that we met this priest. Both for the chess and for the information. But one thing this tells me: henceforth, I shall wear my sword when I go out."

Maebh looked at him. "Why?"

"I do not quite understand why the Christians are not allowed to wear weapons, but I do understand that it shows that they are subservient. And I am not, not to any man." From that day, he always carried his sword when he went out in Lishbuna.

The next morning, al-Shamali appeared as agreed. When he saw Kári's sword, his eyes widened slightly, but he said nothing. Instead, he took Kári and two of the crew members back to some of the merchants he had earlier shown Kári. Then he waited, patiently translating as Kári and his two men discussed the strengths of the various ropes, the quality of cloth for the sail and whether one barrel would hold fresh water better than another one.

Once they had decided what they needed, al-Shamali said to Kári that he would negotiate payment. Kári was not happy with that, but when he saw how long the negotiations took, he was glad to be out of it. And when al-Shamali told him how much silver he owed, he was pleasantly surprised. It was clear that the Swede had agreed a good price for what he already knew were high-quality goods. Even so, he made a show of reluctance when he opened his purse and began to count out the silver pennies. As he did so, al-Shamali grabbed one of the coins and looked at it, saying, "What are these? I have not seen their like before. They are Christian, of course, with the cross, but whose is the picture?"

"They are coins of King Harald of Norway", Kári replied. These were coins that had originally belonged to the men who had sailed on board the knarr to England. When they had not come back from the battle, Kári had decided to keep them as payment for their journey.

When he paid over the coins, he noticed that the merchants just weighed them. For a moment he had wondered if they were going to spit at them the way the old woman had spit at the coins paid by al-Shamali. He meant to ask al-Shamali about this, but as they were making arrangements for the purchases to be delivered to the knarr, it slipped his mind. However, as they walked back to the house, he once again encountered one of the cloaked and guarded women. Kári remembered his argument with Maebh and asked al-Shamali about them.

"Your woman is right", the Swede replied. "These are noble women or the wives of merchants or holy men."

"But why the guards, and why do they hide their faces?" Kári asked. "I saw women in the harbour who do not walk around like this."

"Disregard such women; they are to be despised", al-Shamali said. "No good woman would allow herself to be seen by any other man than her husband, nor would she venture outside the house except under guard."

"And they are content with this?"

"Of course!" al-Shamali snapped. "A woman who shows her face to another man, or walks freely around the city, this would bring shame on her husband. How could he let it happen? And how could she do this to him?"

Kári was puzzled by the man's vehemence. "I don't know what things are like among the Swedes", he said, "but this I can tell you: in Iceland, no woman would let herself be locked up and only allowed out if cloaked and guarded."

"What you do in your own country, among the heathens and infidels, is up to you. I am telling you what it is like here."

Kári was beginning to get annoyed by the man's self-righteousness. For a brief moment he was tempted to make an equally sharp retort, but he remembered that he needed to be on good terms with al-Shamali as long as they remained in Lishbuna; the man had after all already shown himself to be useful. Instead, he said, "I am not criticising you or the customs here. But in Iceland, we value our women highly and listen to their advice. My father would not have run Snæströnd as well as he did without my mother's help. Certainly, he would be very careful about doing anything of which she disapproved." He thought to add that nor would he have managed to get to Lishbuna without listening to Maebh, but he felt that this was none of the other man's business.

However, al-Shamali was not mollified. Instead he muttered "It is forbidden to look at a woman or speak with her unless you are one of her close relatives."

That would be difficult in Iceland, Kári thought to himself. He knew enough strong-willed women who ran farms when their husbands were away or had died. Anyone trying to tell them that they must sit at home and never speak to anyone would surely be given short shrift. True, a woman could not be a goði, but they could certainly inherit the goðorð, and more than one man was swayed in his decision at a Thing after listening to a woman's voice.

*

For the next few months, they remained in Lishbuna. The knarr's deficiencies were made good, and they all enjoyed the warm weather. Kári and the crewmen took to walking around bare chested in the house and garden during the day and soon noticed their skin turning brown from the sun. They always dressed when going outside, even when they found it too warm. In this, they differed from the inhabitants of Lishbuna, who seemed to find the weather freezing, dressing in thick linen cloaks and shivering when they could be seen outside, even in the brightest sun.

Kári spent most afternoons playing chess with Sancho. Although he improved, the priest would still beat him more often than not. He did remember to ask Maebh to ask the priest about the coins. Sancho replied that, once upon a time, the land of the Moors had had one strong ruler. At that time, coins did not need to be weighed but could just be counted. "Everyone knew how much a gold or a silver coin was worth", he said. "And the Caliph would ensure that the coinage was not shaved or clipped, on pain of death. In those days, there was peace in al-Andalus. But now, there are so many kings, each ruling their own little kingdom. They all need money. So they melt down coins and mint them again with less gold or silver. By now, gold coins are almost all silver with no gold in them, and silver coins are made of copper. But they still want us to believe that they are full value and force us to take them at that value, lest we be punished."

"But how is this possible?" Kári asked. "How do you know if the coin you received is good or bad?"

"You do not", Sancho replied. "And so all the merchants are angry, and everyone else is too."

While Kári played chess, Maebh had taken to spending much time with the old woman who owned the house. Although they could not speak with each other, Maebh would go with her when she went to the market and also spend time with her when she was cooking. Between them, they took pleasure in introducing Kári and his men to new and strange foods. There was a round fruit the colour of the sun, which when peeled yielded a tart but juicy flesh; and another one, bright yellow, which was more bitter. Others were softer and to be eaten with their skins, and there were red and green grapes, large and succulent. But his favourite was a round, red fruit that contained hundreds of small and sweet pips. Most of the food was fish of some kind or other, but there seemed to be many ways of cooking it and of adding flavour through the use of spices that none of them had encountered before. After some time, Kári ruefully noted that his stomach was getting larger, and so were those of his crew.

Maebh and Kári spent much time exploring Lishbuna, alone or together with Sancho. They would also go with al-Shamali to visit traders, although when they were with him, Maebh would pretend to be Kári's servant. She behaved as if she were easily beguiled by pretty clothes or jewellery and would rarely comment on anything else.

Maebh would also visit Sancho's church for Mass. This was different from the Mass she had attended in the convent in Ireland. Oh, the words were the same, but although Sancho said that it was much smaller than the great churches in the north where Christian princes ruled, his church was much bigger than the chapels she was used to. True, there were no church bells rung, but there were more worshippers, and listening to their singing, in some ways she felt nearer to God even than she had been at home in Ireland with her own family priest.

When Kári asked her why she went to church, she at first tried to explain. But when she found it difficult to make him understand, she said, "Why don't you join me?"

"Is this possible?"

"Of course it is. Why wouldn't it be?"

"I don't know", Kári replied. "I just thought it might not be possible to come if you are not Christian."

"I assure you, anyone can come", Maebh said.

And so Kári joined Maebh the next time she went to Mass. Afterwards, she tried to ask him what he thought about it, but he was strangely reticent, and Maebh realised that it was perhaps better to leave this until he felt that he could talk about it. The truth was that Kári had been much more impressed than he thought he would be. The only churches he had seen were Thór Egilsson's tiny church in Iceland and the churches in Kirkjuvágr and Jórvik, but he had not entered into any of the latter ones. This time, he was not only impressed by the size of the church, but also by the solemnity of the Mass, even though he did not understand any of it. The only thing he said to Maebh afterwards was, "I would like to come again."

*

When they had been in Lishbuna for some months, al-Shamali showed up one day and asked Kári, "Are you still interested in buying silk?"

"Yes, why?"

"Because the merchants are now beginning to count the days until the caravans arrive. Now is the time when we should speak with them and ensure that you get your choice of the best quality available."

"Thank you. This is a good thought."

Kári and Maebh followed al-Shamali to the covered market. When they first arrived, he had shown them different merchants and discussed each one – who would offer what quality and at what price. Now he led them to one of those, saying, as they entered the man's store, "This is Khalid ben Omar. He has heard that his caravan will come in among the very first. Now he would like to show you samples of the silk he can offer."

The first time they had visited this merchant, he had briefly shown them some of his samples. But now, he asked them to sit down at a table, where he had spread out a large number of swathes of silk. Kári was overwhelmed by the riot of bright colours, ranging from red to yellow and blue to green, with some white and black and even purple fabrics, some only showing one colour, others in brightly woven patterns.

Khalid began to describe each sample, translated by al-Shamali. Kári listened as the Swede talked about 'first-class Andalusian silk from mulberry trees', 'half-silk from Palermo, interwoven with linen', 'three-coloured striped silk' and 'Greek imperial silk patterns with gold and silver threads' but found it difficult to differentiate between them. He knew he would have to rely on Maebh to tell him which was the better quality and what would likely sell best. He was tempted to buy the most expensive, but he realised that this might be difficult to sell in Iceland.

Meanwhile, Maebh, acting her role as the ignorant servant girl, was touching and caressing each sample, exclaiming with delight at each new colour or pattern, but above all trying to assess the quality as best she could. Although she knew more about silk than Kári, she soon realised that she was also out of her depth. Instead, she concentrated on a few of the samples, plain ones in red, green and blue, which Khalid had claimed were of the best kind. At least she knew that they were of good quality.

Kári understood her meaning and eventually indicated to al-Shamali that he was interested in buying those fabrics only. As to how much, he indicated that this would obviously depend on the price and on the capacity of the knarr, but he wanted to buy as much as possible.

Previously, when buying equipment for the knarr, he had been content to let al-Shamali negotiate for him. While he had no reason to regret this, this time he was determined to play a bigger role in the bargaining. The Swede might know what silk cost in Lishbuna, but he had no way of knowing how much Kári could sell it for in Iceland. Nor did Kári intend to tell him. They had agreed that part of al-Shamali's fee was determined by Kári's payment for the silk, but he now realised that this gave al-Shamali an incentive to agree a high price, and he also resented any loss of control over his dealings. He had discussed this with Maebh, who agreed and urged him to be wary of al-Shamali or indeed of anyone who would find out too many of his business secrets.

This meant a drawn-out negotiation, where everything had to be translated and explained and then renegotiated, always interrupted by Khalid offering plates of sweet dried fruits or small cakes and scented water. But by the evening they had finally agreed on the number of bales of silk – to be delivered to the knarr no later than two days after the silk arrived in Lishbuna, carefully packed to withstand the sea journey – and on the amount of silver to be paid for it. When Kári tried to calculate how much it would cost, he realised that this would take almost all the silver he had left from Jórvik. He did not mind, since they would be sailing back to Iceland and he would only need what was necessary to take on supplies in Cork and Kirkjuvágr on the way back. But he was not keen to hand over all his silver before he had his purchases in hand, even though al-Shamali pressed him to pay there and then, saying that Khalid needed to pay his supplier. In the end, it was agreed that Kári would come back and complete the payment once he was told that the silk had arrived in Lishbuna, but still before it was delivered to his ship.

After they had returned to the house and al-Shamali had left, Kári told the crew that they would probably be leaving Lishbuna in the near future. He was not sure how they would react. Some of the men clearly enjoyed the stay in Lishbuna, not just because of the heat, but because they had also found themselves women who, he feared, they might not wish to leave. He need not have worried; his announcement was greeted with cheers.

The next few days were spent carefully going over and preparing the knarr. On Maebh's insistence, Kári also gave the old woman who owned the house some of his few remaining silver pennies. The woman looked suspiciously at the coins, but once she had felt their weight, she smiled, and letting out a stream of words, she kissed Kári's hand, much to his embarrassment.

Once the ship was ready to sail, there was nothing left but to wait for the silk. Kári resumed playing chess with Sancho, but his mind was more on planning the voyage home and he played worse than ever, suffering defeat after defeat. But he did not mind; the thought of soon going home was increasingly dominating his thinking. And meanwhile, the priest was pleasant enough company.

One day al-Shamali came to see him and told him that the silk had arrived and that it was time to pay. Together they went to Khalid ben Omar, where Kári handed over a heavy bag with almost all his silver, to the merchant's evident satisfaction.

It was while Kári was away one afternoon that a line of men carrying burdens appeared at the knarr. Maebh and Hallvarðr went to speak with them, but none of the porters spoke Latin. Hallvarðr told the crew to start stowing the silk properly, but Maebh asked him to wait for a moment.

While the porter headman fretted, she opened one of the packages. When she saw the contents, her eyes widened slightly and she insisted on opening two more. Once she had inspected the cloth, she turned to Hallvarðr.

"This is not the silk Kári agreed to buy. Do not take it on board."

"Are you sure?" Hallvarðr asked, puzzled.

"I am certain. I was there. I am telling you that this is not what he bought! Do not let this on board!"

She and Hallvarðr tried to stop the porters, and Hallvarðr called on the rest of the crew to help them. But the porters pushed forward and once they reached the knarr, just threw their burdens over the railings and onto the deck, before running away.

When Maebh realised what was happening, she snapped at Hallvarðr, "Come with me! And tell the men to cast off and move the knarr out into the harbour and not let anyone on board except us or Kári!"

The crew stared at her and Hallvarðr opened his mouth to speak, but Maebh stamped her foot and repeated the order. When Hallvarðr saw her face, he turned to the crew and said "You heard the lady. Move!" Then he jumped onto the quay and followed Maebh, who was already running towards the inn where Kári and Sancho would be playing chess. As Hallvarðr ran, he suddenly thought back to the first time he had encountered Maebh after the battle near Jórvik, and how even then he had found it impossible not to do what she said.

Kári was deeply engrossed in losing yet another game of chess when he saw Sancho look up with a surprised expression. He turned around to see what had agitated the priest and saw Maebh come running, Hallvarðr still trying to catch up with her. When she reached them, she was out of breath, gasping, "The … the …".

Kári held her hands and said, "Take a deep breath, then tell me what is going on."

Maebh tried to collect herself, then blurted out, "The silk. They sent us bad silk. Cheated you." Her words still came out in fits and starts. But Kári had heard enough. Blood rushed to his head and he burst out swearing. It was of course al-Shamali, or rather Ingjald as he had secretly thought of him all along. He disliked and distrusted him from the start – he never trusted Swedes – but he had never been able to pinpoint exactly why. Maybe he had been too helpful, but also too greedy? He had picked the merchants they had gone to, and Kári had not been able to know what they were saying to each other. No matter, he was tired of being taken for a fool by other people, be it the King of Norway or a Swede in Lishbuna.

While all this ran though his head, he had already started to run from the inn, grasping hold of his sword. He was certain that he knew where the Swede was.

Behind him, Maebh wanted to run after him, but Sancho grabbed her arm. "What is happening?" he asked. Maebh tried to break away, but he held her arm in a surprisingly strong grip. "You must tell me what is going on!" he repeated.

Maebh took another deep breath. Then she called to Hallvarðr, who was anxiously waiting, uncertain what to do. "Go! Quickly. Follow Kári. And stop him from killing anyone! Hurry!"

Hallvarðr shook off his paralysis and ran off after Kári. Meanwhile, Maebh tried to explain to Sancho what had happened, all the while pulling him along after Kári and Hallvarðr. But it was not easy for her, because the priest was not only older but also rather stout and had difficulty running as quickly as she wanted. Also, although she had learnt Latin, it was difficult to remember all the words like 'cheating' and 'scoundrel'.

Kári ran faster than he had ever done before. He did not have far to run before he came to the covered market and very shortly to Khalid ben Omar's shop. One of the merchant's men stood at the entrance, but one look at Kári's face and the drawn sword he now carried in his hand made him stand aside. Kári pushed through the door. When he burst in, he was not surprised to see Ingjald and Khalid sitting, laughing and clearly enjoying their good fortune. They turned but barely had time to see who it was before Kári's sword descended on the table between them with such force that the table almost broke in two, and dishes of fruits and drink clattered to the floor.

"Laughing at me, are you?" Kári shouted at Ingjald. "Did you really think you could trick me that easily?" Khalid tried to creep beneath the table. Ingjald attempted to fend off the sword that Kári was stabbing in his direction, but could not avoid receiving a shallow gash on his arm from which blood soon began to flow. But now Khalid was screaming, as was his assistant outside. Suddenly there was more noise from the outside, loud voices and before Kári had time to think about what to do next, Hallvarðr rushed in and grabbed Kári's arms. He was shortly followed by a group of armed men who crowded the small room. Both al-Shamali and Khalid yelled at them, and they surrounded Kári, pointing spears at him. He dropped his sword and stood still, while Hallvarðr carefully stepped away from him.

Al-Shamali turned to Kári, clutching his wounded arm, and sneered, "Not so high and mighty now, the great Icelandic trader? Wait until you see what we do to criminals in Lishbuna."

Kári spat. "You are the criminal. A cheap swindler, you and your friend Khalid. You will get your punishment!"

Al-Shamali laughed. "You are a pagan dog. Do you really think anyone will listen to you against the word of one of the Faithful?"

It seemed that the little room could barely contain those who were there, but now Maebh and a sweaty and breathless Sancho also entered.

The armed men who held Kári were speaking with Khalid. After he had replied to their questions, suddenly Sancho spoke up. Al-Shamali and Khalid both began to shout at once, trying to drown out his words, but a bellowed order from the leader of the guards caused them to fall silent. He listened to what Sancho said, then he shrugged his shoulders and gave an order to the others. Khalid tried to protest, but both he and al-Shamali were seized and all three prisoners were hustled away. Maebh tried to ask Sancho what was happening, but he was busy speaking with the guards and could not spare her any time.

Once the guards and the prisoners were gone, however, Maebh grabbed Sancho's shoulder. "Now", she said, "tell me what is happening?"

"Oh", he said. "It is simple. They will be taken before a qadi, a – a judge. The merchant and the interpreter are accusing Kári of attempting to murder them. I managed to say that this was not true, that they had attempted to swindle Kári. That was why the other two were also taken away."

"What will this judge say?" Maebh asked.

"If he finds Kári guilty, he will be killed. But don't worry. The courts and the laws in this country are fair, even to outsiders."

This failed to reassure Maebh. She agreed to meet Sancho the next day, and then she and Hallvarðr returned to the quay, where they signalled the men to bring the knarr back to its previous berth.

Once on board, Maebh explained to Hallvarðr and the rest of the crew what Sancho had told her. That night, she could not sleep, yet try as she might, she could not think of any way to save Kári. But just in case, she did tell Hallvarðr to get the men to stow the silk so that it could be brought out quickly.

The next day, Sancho had no news, but he carefully questioned Maebh about all the dealings Kári had had with Khalid. Then he sighed. "It is a pity that you are a woman. It means that your testimony is worth less than that of a man. We need something more to save Kári."

Three days later, however, Sancho told Maebh that the court would convene the next day, and that she should come, together with Hallvarðr.

When the three of them arrived, they found Kári, standing alone, guarded by two men, while another three men guarded al-Shamali and Khalid, who were standing some distance away. There was a desk in the middle, and behind the desk sat a man who, Sancho whispered to Maebh, was the qadi. Next to him were two scribes who took down the proceedings.

The qadi cleared his throat. "Bismillah-ir-Rahman-ir-Rahim", he said.

"He is calling on God", Sancho whispered to Maebh, earning an angry glance from the qadi.

Before the qadi could continue, al-Shamali pointed at Kári and said something. The qadi looked annoyed at the interruption but spoke to Kári. When Kári looked helpless, the qadi turned back towards Sancho and addressed him. Sancho replied at length, while al-Shamali tried to interrupt him until one of the guards slapped his mouth to silence him.

Then the qadi and Sancho spoke again. When they had finished, Sancho seemed to ask a question at which the qadi nodded wearily and motioned to him.

"He understands that Kári does not speak Arabic and has agreed that I can translate to you and you to Kári. But we have to be brief, because he does not wish to spend too much time on this case."

"But what did al-Shamali say?" Maebh asked.

"He said that Kári was a pagan and therefore not entitled to a hearing in this court. I replied that this was wrong, that Kári is a Christian who has come to my church many times for Mass and that therefore he is entitled to the protection of the law."

Maebh sat silent. She hoped that nothing would come up that contradicted Sancho's words. If he thought Kári was a Christian and if that was important, then well and good. But was he? She wasn't sure, but she feared not.

The double translation meant that the proceedings took a long time, but the facts of the case were soon clear. Khalid claimed that Kári had come to his shop, accompanied by al-Shamali. They had discussed a large purchase of silk. After discussing various prices, Kári had said that he wanted more rather than better and had settled for a larger amount of plain low-quality silk, interwoven with wool. He had paid an agreed amount and the silk had been delivered. The next thing he knew was that Kári had appeared in his shop, raging like a madman, and had tried to kill him and al-Shamali. He testified that al-Shamali was an honest man who had lived in Lishbuna for many years and was often used as an interpreter by foreign merchants. None of them had ever complained of his behaviour before. On his part, al-Shamali explained that he had met Kári's crew in the harbour, and that he had realised that they were from the same part of the world as he. Since no one else in Lishbuna would speak their language, he had offered his services, and they had accepted. He swore that everything Khalid said was the truth.

When he had finished questioning them, the qadi turned to Sancho. Maebh had already told him everything about the trade, so he conceded that everything al-Shamali had said about how they had met and his services to Kári was true. The only thing that was not true, he said, was the silk purchase. Kári had agreed to buy best-quality silk and paid an agreed price in silver for this, a much higher price than Khalid had stated. It was clear that Khalid and al-Shamali had tried to cheat him by taking the money but delivering inferior goods. Kári's actions in wounding al-Shamali were deplorable but due to their behaviour, and he deeply regretted them.

The qadi looked at Kári, who did not seem to regret anything. In truth, not being able to understand anything that was being said, Kári had found himself thinking of Snæströnd, wondering what was happening in Iceland and if he ever would see the farm again. How strange he felt. He had often spoken about freedom and how proud he was of being a free man or a free Icelander. Yet, in truth, he had always taken this for granted. But on this journey, he had twice been deprived of his freedom. First he was forced by the King of Norway – and he still scowled at the thought of the man – to join his fleet, and now he was imprisoned in a place he had not even heard of a year earlier. Now he really knew what it was to be unfree, and he promised himself that he would never again take freedom for granted.

The qadi had asked if either side had any witnesses. Khalid and al-Shamali had each other. Sancho explained that Maebh was his witness. The qadi listened to what she had to say via Sancho's translation. Al-Shamali replied that as a woman her testimony was worthless and as a servant girl doubly so. When Sancho translated this, she asked him to reply that she was, in fact, not a servant girl but a king's daughter. At this, the qadi briefly smiled, but it was not possible to know exactly why nor if he believed her.

At midday, the qadi broke off the proceedings. Maebh and Sancho asked permission to speak with Kári, which was granted. But here, too, the translation made everything take much longer, and finally Sancho said to Maebh, "See if you can think of anything and just let me know. But we do not have much time."

Kári had listened gloomily to Maebh's explanation of what was going on. Then he said, "I do not see what we can do. They do not listen to you, because you are a woman. If we cannot prove what we bought or how much we paid …"

"But how can we do that?" Maebh said. "It is their word against ours. And we do not know what Ingjald said to Khalid. Maybe he tricked him too?"

"That is unlikely. There is no profit for him in that case, because I paid all my silver to Khalid. No, they both planned this."

Maebh sat silently for a while, thinking. Then she said, "Did they count your coins?"

"No. I gave Khalid a bag of silver and he weighed it and was content. Why?"

"I may have an idea." But she said no more.

When the court resumed, Maebh spoke with Sancho. He listened intently, then turned to the qadi and asked if he would allow him to ask some questions of Khalid and al-Shamali. When the qadi agreed, Maebh whispered, "Ask them how Kári paid for the silk and to repeat how much he paid."

When the two men had replied, she then said, "Ask them how they can say this, when Kári gave them three times as much silver as they claim."

The question surprised Khalid, but al-Shamali replied at length. Sancho translated, "He says that this is not true. Khalid no doubt has more silver, but Kári is not the only person who buys from him. Many people from many lands do.'

Maebh said, "Ask him what the coins that Kári paid him with look like."

When the question was translated, al-Shamali laughed before he replied, holding up a silver coin and handing it to the qadi. When he was finished, Sancho said, "He says that they were paid in silver coins from the far north, Christian coins with a cross on them. Like that one."

"In that case", Maebh said, "ask the qadi to seize Khalid's strongbox. Ask him how come there is a large amount of silver coins in it, coins to the amount and weight that Kári says he paid, coins that are not from the far north but from England, and that do not bear a cross. Coins that show the face of a man who only became king a year ago, so there is no possibility that they would have received them from anyone else but Kári."

When Sancho translated the question, there was an uproar, with both Khalid and al-Shamali shouting, trying to drown out the priest. The qadi looked for a moment as if he was going to say something, but instead he signalled at the guards, who gagged both men. Then he said something else, which made two guards disappear together with one of the qadi's scribes.

While they waited, Maebh could barely stand still. So much could go wrong. What if Khalid had moved the coins Kári had paid him? Or what if he had already paid them to someone else?

But when the scribe and the guards returned, the guards were bent almost double as they carried a chest of impressive proportions. When Khalid saw it, he tried to say something, but a threatening gesture from one of the guards silenced him before he had begun. The chest was put down on the floor in front of the qadi, and at a command, one of his soldiers broke the lock with his sword. As the chest was opened, the qadi murmured "al-hamdu lillah" and stroked his beard. Then he turned to Sancho and asked something.

"He wishes to know if you can show one of the coins you claim Kári paid with."

For a brief moment, Maebh panicked. Then she remembered that she did have one of the English coins that Kári had given her long ago for when she went to the market. She handed it over to Sancho, who gave it to the qadi. He inspected it carefully, then looked into the chest, rummaging among the coins until he found a large bag. He gave an order and one of the soldiers picked it up and emptied it on the table. The qadi took up a few coins from the mass of silver that spread out and compared them to the one Maebh had given him. Seemingly satisfied, he gestured at the guard who put the coins back in the bag. A scale was produced and the bag was weighed.

The qadi now turned his attention to the three prisoners and spoke at length. While he did so, both Khalid and al-Shamali paled. Then the qadi turned to Sancho, who had been listening carefully, and nodded at him. Sancho said, "This is his verdict. Kári did attack Khalid and al-Shamali and wounded al-Shamali. For this he is fined one pound of silver, to be paid to them in compensation."

Maebh began to protest, but Sancho held up his hand. "Wait. This is not all." Then he continued, "Khalid and al-Shamali clearly tried to cheat Kári. They are fined the same amount, to be repaid to Kári. In addition, Khalid must provide Kári with the correct amount of high-grade silk. And finally, both he and al-Shamali will be caned, for besmirching the reputation of the city of Lishbuna and of the Faithful."

When Maebh heard this, she made to embrace Sancho, but he gently fended her off. "I think there is someone else you should embrace", he said. "And I think you should tell him what has happened."

That evening, the crew feasted Kári in the house, with Sancho as the guest of honour. When the toasting, cheering and singing were finally over, and Kári and Maebh were alone in their bedchamber, Maebh said, "You were fortunate to have those new English coins. Otherwise, I do not know how we could have proven the truth."

"You are right. Not just that I had them, but also that they were new, not shaved or clipped until there was nothing to see. But two other things were even more fortunate."

"What?"

"The first was that we received justice. Remember what al-Shamali, what Ingjald said. As a pagan, I would not get justice in a court in Lishbuna. He really believed that. And yet, I did. I do not know many other places where this would happen, except in Iceland, that the foreigner would be given his right."

Maebh was silent for a moment, then she said, "I think I must tell you something. At the beginning of the case, al-Shamali said that you did not have the right to justice in that court because you were a pagan. Sancho told the judge that this was not true, that you are a Christian and that he knew because you often came to Mass at his church. Otherwise, I do not know that you would have been listened to at all, let alone given a fair hearing."

Kári looked at her. "Is this true?"

"Of course it is true. Why should I lie?"

"This is then the third time that a priest of the White Christ does me or my kin a good turn, even though we do not follow him. First there was Willibald, who helped my brother when he was unjustly accused of rape; then Aidan helped us to get to Lishbuna; and now Sancho has saved me. Perhaps it is a sign that the White Christ really means well to all men. Maybe I should become a true Christian after all."

"Do you want to?"

"Perhaps. Do you want me to?"

Maebh thought about it. "I would like you to, but this is your decision. And between us, nothing will change whatever you do."

"I will think about this."

"And what is the last fortunate thing?" Maebh asked.

"The last is that I had you. Because if I had not, no one would have thought of the coins, and even if we had, we would not have had Sancho there to help us, nor even been able to speak with him."

Maebh kissed the tip of his nose. "This is true too, and you will do well to remember it in the future."

The next morning, a train of porters arrived at the house, together with a guard from the court and Sancho. Sancho explained that the porters had brought the silk that Kári had paid for. Maebh insisted on opening the parcels to inspect the cloth, even though Sancho told her not to worry. Once she was satisfied, they led the porters to the knarr, where they took possession of the previous packages and the new bales were carefully stowed.

While this was going on under Hallvarðr's supervision, Kári took Sancho and Maebh aside. "Please translate everything I will say", he told Maebh, who nodded. Then he turned to Sancho.

"I understand that you told the qadi that I am a Christian?"

After Maebh had translated, Sancho nodded. Kári continued, "In truth, until yesterday, I did not really know, even though in Iceland we are supposed to be Christians. But I would not wish you to be forsworn. Therefore, I would like you to pour the holy water over my head, so that I shall in truth be one of you."

When Maebh translated this as well, Sancho smiled broadly. He put his hand to Kári's head and murmured something. "He is blessing you", Maebh quickly whispered. Then Sancho spoke some more. "He is asking if there is anything else we wish him to do?"

"What?" Kári said. But Maebh just smiled.

That evening, Maebh and Kári went with Sancho to his church and Sancho baptised Kári. Afterwards, Maebh asked how he felt. "I do not know", Kári replied. "We will just see. But I am glad that it is done."

"So am I", she said.

He gave Sancho some silver coins as a baptism gift and asked Maebh to thank him again for everything. The old priest was moved and embraced them both as they said their farewells. Then they returned to the house for the last time.

The next morning, Kári and the crew went down to the harbour, boarded the knarr and began to row out into the river mouth. There they soon picked up an easterly wind and raised the sail. When they reached the sea, Kári turned the ship to starboard and then called Hallvarðr over. "We are headed north, north to Iceland, north to home", he said. "Keep that bearing". He handed the steering oar to Hallvarðr and went up to the prow and drew a deep breath, savouring the smell of the sea. The smell of freedom, of being once again master of his own destiny. This, he knew, was where he belonged.

Chapter 12

Winter – Summer 1067

For the remainder of the winter, Jórunn did not see Guðmundr. Had she wanted to, she could have made sure that they met, a chance meeting somewhere between Snæströnd and Gunnar's farm. The reasons she avoided him were many. One was to punish him for slighting her. Another was to make sure that his desire for her and eagerness to see her again would increase and bend him more to her wishes. In this way, she planned to help her father encompass the downfall of Eirík goði by removing the support he received from Ragnar and Guðmundr.

For Guðmundr, the winter months became a time of much reflection. He tried to spend as much time as he could outside, but this did not amount to much. The weather was colder than it had been for some years and when it was not cold, snow would fall for days without end, and it was both very difficult to go outside and even more difficult to explain why he was doing so. Although he and Ása would now speak with each other, their relationship remained cold. But he saw much more of his children and also of his parents, and he noted with some envy how they would all spend time together. This made him think about the time that had passed since he and Ása had been wed and all that had happened with Jórunn as well. The more he thought about these things, the more he was sickened by what he had done.

He knew that what was done could not be undone. But although he now wanted to show Ása that he regretted his behaviour and wanted to make amends, he found it difficult to do so as long as the house was full of people. This was not a subject he wanted to discuss in front of his parents or any listening servants. And so many days passed with Guðmundr trying to avoid speaking with anyone. Instead, he took to spending as much time as he could with his children. In their company he could forget the thoughts that tormented him; and more than once he thought he saw Ása watching the three of them and smiling.

It was well after midwinter that Guðmundr found Ása sitting in the seat that had been his father's and was now by right his, the seat of the master of Snæströnd. The snow had stopped falling and his parents had taken the children outside where they played in the drifts. There were two servant girls with Ása, but Guðmundr realised that if he did not speak with his wife now, he probably never would.

When he approached her, Ása looked up. She did not know what he wanted to say, but she realised that if, after such a long time of silence, her husband wanted to speak with her, it would be important. While he hesitated, she turned to the servants and said, "Leave us. And make sure no one enters before I say so." The girls stood up and left.

Guðmundr was still standing in front of Ása, unsure of how to start. Ása put her handiwork on the table and waited. She had already decided that this time he would have to take the first step. If he did, she would help him, but only with the second one.

Guðmundr remained standing for a moment, then he flung himself to the floor beside her and rested his head on her lap. Almost automatically, she put her hand on his shoulder and felt his body shaking. To her surprise, she realised that he was crying.

It took Guðmundr a few moments to stop, but the tears seemed to have broken the wall he had built up around himself and finally he began to speak rapidly, almost as if he feared that if he did not say the words quickly enough, he would not be able to say them at all.

It took a moment longer for Ása to make sense of the torrent of words, but what she then heard did not surprise her as much as it once would have.

"I have been a fool", Guðmundr said. "I have dishonoured you and myself and I am unworthy of you. I have hurt you and my parents and everyone else around me."

"If all this is true", Ása said, "why are you telling me this now?"

"Because I want you back. I want things to be as they once were."

"Saying this cannot have come lightly to you. And I want it too. But if it was not easily said, it is even less easily done."

"I know", Guðmundr sobbed. "But I am begging you to take me back. I know that I don't deserve this, but I promise you that if you do, I will never hurt you again."

"This is all well and good", Ása replied. "But how can I trust you? And what is it that you have done?"

When Guðmundr heard this, he realised two things. The first was that he must now tell Ása everything that had occurred between him and Jórunn, from the day they had first met and sparing nothing, not even their most recent quarrels. He knew that she already knew much of this and that what had happened before they were wed was not important. But he wanted to tell her everything so that she knew he was being honest. And the second thing was that if Ása asked how she could trust him, it meant that she was prepared to take him back.

Ása listened to everything Guðmundr had to say. When he told her that Jórunn had complained that he only spoke of Ása when he was with her, she smiled bitterly. When he had finished, she asked, "How long is it since you last saw Jórunn?"

"Not for many months", he replied.

"Is this your doing? Or hers?"

Guðmundr swallowed, but he realised that he had to tell the truth. "I … I – at first I wanted to see her. This was her doing."

"But?" Ása asked.

"But as time passed, I thought much about everything and realised that I am glad not to have seen her. I no longer wish to see her. Odd once said that if he spotted her unbidden on Snæströnd's land, he would have her whipped. I now swear to you that I will do the same."

And then Ása knew that Guðmundr really meant what he said and for the first time in many years she felt glad and allowed herself to hope that things now really would become better between them. But she also knew that this might quickly change. So although her heart felt as if it would burst with happiness and longing for Guðmundr's change to be real, she remained wary. All she said therefore was, "I once told you that I have always loved you, Guðmundr. This is still true. I hope you mean what you say, and I want to believe that you do. But I need to be shown that I can trust you."

Guðmundr looked her in the eyes and said, "I will do anything you want."

"For now", Ása replied, "all I ask is that you behave once more as my husband and as the father of my children."

"I will. I promise you that I will. And you will not find me lacking in any way."

They remained like that for a while, neither of them speaking but both thinking of what had been said and what they hoped would now happen. Eventually Ása stood up, and, pulling Guðmundr to his feet too, embraced him and then went to the door of the house and opened it. Outside she found Guðrún and Eirík with their grandparents, complaining that they were cold and wanted to come inside.

Neither Ása nor Guðmundr ever spoke to anyone about what had been said between them. But over the remainder of the winter and in the early spring, it was clear to Ragnar and Hallgerður that something had changed. Ása and Guðmundr seemed much happier, almost as they had been in the first days of their life together. Guðmundr now spent more time with the farmhands as well, but he would often ask his father for advice. Even the children felt a difference in their parents.

Ragnar carefully avoided saying anything to Guðmundr for a long time, but one day, when they were both returning home from working on the farm, he touched his son's arm and said, "Things have changed. I am not asking what, but I want to tell you that I am glad to see it. You are my first-born and I want you and Ása to be as happy at Snæströnd as your mother and I have always been."

At first Guðmundr said nothing, instead thinking back to his talk with Ása. But he understood that his father's words, which once he might have resented, were important to him. He didn't quite know what to say, so in the end he simply answered, "Thank you Father", and embraced him.

When Ragnar later that evening told Hallgerður what they had said to each other, she thought for a while and then said, "Do you think he means it this time?"

"Yes", Ragnar replied. "I am his father. I know my son. This time he will not change."

"In that case, you did well", Hallgerður said.

*

As the year advanced, winter snows began to melt in the spring sunshine and Snæströnd slowly lost the cause for its name, becoming more green than white. The days became longer and the whole world began to come alive again. Neighbours were now visiting each other. One day, a messenger appeared at Snæströnd. When told that both Guðmundr and Ragnar were away from the house, he replied that he had come to speak with Ása.

She did not recognise the man but stepped outside to meet him. He seemed ill at ease and approached her closely so that only she could hear what he said.

"I bring word from someone who wishes to meet you", he all but whispered.

"If he wishes to see me, he can come here", Ása replied.

The man looked even more uncomfortable. "It is not a man", he finally said.

"Even so", Ása replied.

Now the man lowered his voice even more. "I was told that if you refused to come, I should tell you that the lady cannot come to Snæströnd for fear of her life."

At this Ása burst out laughing. "Tell your mistress – and I know now who she is – that her fears are exaggerated."

"I was also told to tell you that she needs to speak with you in secret but that what she has to say is of the greatest importance for you. It is for your ears only, and she bids you come alone. But time is short. She cannot wait for ever."

For a moment Ása was tempted to tell the man to go back to Jórunn – because it was obviously Jórunn who sent him – and tell her to crawl back to the pens of her father's farm. But curiosity won her over, and she told one of the farmhands to bring her a horse.

When they had reached the limits of Snæströnd, she was not surprised to find Jórunn standing next to her horse, which was tied to a tree. The messenger spurred his horse and rode up to Jórunn, but she waved him away.

Ása waited until he had ridden off and then rode up to Jórunn.

"Well", she said. "What is so important that you absolutely had to see me?"

*

That night, when they lay in bed, Ása told Guðmundr what had happened. When she said she had seen Jórunn, he stiffened. "What? Why? What did she want? What did she say?"

Ása laughed. "Don't worry. It was all very silly. She told me that she needed to tell me something. She had to tell me that you and she were lovers and had been meeting behind my back. But she was overcome with remorse and guilt, because I was her oldest friend and she could not continue to do this to me. It was all your fault, she claimed. She felt terrible at the way you were treating me – you, not she, of course – and finally decided that she had to let me know. She understood that I could not remain at Snæströnd or wedded to a man who dishonoured me like this."

"What did you say?"

"I fear that I disappointed her. I burst out laughing. She was quite put out. You see, when we were young, she was always the leader, the one who decided things and told me what to think. And I, I let her do it. I admired her. She was so beautiful, so self-assured. I think she assumed that I would be shocked and upset and would burst into tears."

"What did she say?"

"Not much, but that was not for want of trying. I just did not let her say anything. I told her that I knew everything about the two of you. That I had forgiven you. Oh, and I told her that I knew perfectly well that this was not all your doing. I was no longer her obedient little friend, and by now I could clearly see through her scheming.

"And then I turned the horse around and rode home."

Guðmundr said nothing. Instead he embraced Ása. But inside he thought two things. The first was that he had been right to tell Ása everything about himself and Jórunn. And the second was that choosing Ása over Jórunn was the best decision he had ever made.

They lay quiet for a while, then Ása said, "You know, I said I used to admire her. Well, now I only feel pity for her. She is all alone, sitting like a spider at her father's farm, trying to weave her webs to ensnare people. And one day, Einar will be the master there, and then nobody will care about her at all anymore."

"I don't pity her", Guðmundr said. "She has hurt too many people. But I thank all the gods that I am married to you."

*

When Jórunn returned to Gunnar's farm, she tried to go directly to her chamber, but her father spotted her and called her to him. He was sitting talking with Einar, but when she came into the room, he broke off what he was saying and looked at her. "You failed." It was a statement more than a question.

Jórunn began to say something, but Gunnar interrupted her. "I wish my children would stop treating me as if I were stupid", he said. "You are clever, Jórunn. Grant me the same recognition. If you had succeeded, you would have come here at once to tell me. You didn't, so therefore you failed."

She nodded.

"You might as well tell me everything so that we can plan something else."

Jórunn gathered her thoughts for a moment, then said, "As we had agreed, I sent a messenger to ask her to come to see me. She did, but when she came, she did not even dismount, so I had to look up at her. I told her about Guðmundr and me and how he had deceived her and treated her dishonourably. I said that, as her friend, I felt I could no longer carry on. I offered to help her get away from Snæströnd, either to come to us or to move back to her kinsfolk."

"She didn't believe you?" This was Einar who interjected.

"Worse than that. She laughed. The mouse laughed at me! Then she told me that she didn't believe me and that I was only jealous of her, because Guðmundr had chosen her instead of me. How dare she? After all I have done for her, she dismissed my pity, my offers of renewed friendship and help, and just laughed. I thought she would want to leave Guðmundr at once. Instead she swaggered back to Snæströnd without so much as a by your leave."

When she was finished, Gunnar shrugged and said, "It was worth a try. If it had worked, it would have been the ruin of Snæströnd – strife between Guðmundr and Ása's kin, and we would of course have helped poor Ása, so badly wronged by her husband. Never mind. We will have to think of something else. Now leave me, both of you, while I consider what to do."

Jórunn was pleased that her father had not been angrier. But Einar seethed inside. Once again, his father had favoured Jórunn and once again his oh so clever sister had failed. Well, this was the last time he would agree to one of her plans. It was time to take matters into his own hands. Now he would deal with Snæströnd himself, and he would do it in his own way. And when he had brought ruin upon Ragnar and Guðmundr, and Eirík goði lost their support, his father would finally have to acknowledge that he had been right all along.

*

Guðmundr and Ása did not know whether they should tell Ragnar and Hallgerður about Jórunn's visit. At first they thought it better to say nothing, since the older couple might otherwise ask more details than Ása was prepared to let them know. But Guðmundr said that he wanted to be open with his parents as well, and so a few days later they told them what had happened.

Ragnar felt that this was nothing to worry about, simply Jórunn up to her old tricks again. But Hallgerður was more concerned. "It is not Jórunn on her own that I am worried about", she said. "But I don't think that this is something that she would have done alone. I fear you may find that behind all this is her father's hand. And that means that it is not Ása or even Guðmundr that he is aiming at, but at Snæströnd itself."

Ragnar and Guðmundr tried to dismiss her fears, but she asked them both to be careful and suggested to Guðmundr that he should somehow make Eirík aware of what had happened, if it meant that Gunnar was planning some mischief for the Thórsnesthing.

Although Guðmundr felt his mother was worrying too much, he was in any case planning to visit Eirík. He said this was to talk about the Thórsnesthing, but he also realised that part of him wanted to let Eirík know how things had changed with him, and also to show how grateful he was for Eirík's support.

As the time for the Thing approached, therefore, Guðmundr rode off to Eirík's farm. It was not a long distance as things were in Iceland, but he still took his time. He had found that since he and Ása had reconciled, he liked doing some things in a more leisurely way. True, the spring sowing was on at Snæströnd, but he knew his father could deal with that without him, and he enjoyed the ride through the budding spring landscape.

When he arrived at Eirík's farm, he was pleased to find that Thór was also there, and for the same reason. The three men spent time discussing what might occur at the upcoming Thing. Both Eirík and Thór were pleased to see the change in Guðmundr. Eirík felt that he would once more be able to benefit from Guðmundr's advice, which he had missed; and both were glad to know that Snæströnd was again at peace. Guðmundr also noted a change in how the two goðar treated him. Previously, he had been a valued counsellor and, at least for Eirík, a friend. But this time, he felt that there was something more. Although he was not a goði, he sensed that they were treating him almost as an equal.

When Guðmundr told them about Jórunn's visit, Eirík scowled, but Thór laughed. "Her father thinks he is a skilful chess player, sending out pawns like Jórunn to do his bidding. But pawns are all he has, people like Leifur and Jórunn. Most of his supporters were attracted by his wealth and strength. Well, his wealth, I hear, is diminishing. And the three of us, united as we are and with Christ on our side, are more than a match for him. He should be careful so that his king is not slain."

Eirík was still worried. "He may not be as wealthy as men think, but he still has much support. And I hear it is increasing. Not here perhaps, but at the Althing he is well respected and has a growing following. I also hear that he is often meeting priests and king's men from Norway who fill his ears with much silly talk."

But Guðmundr and Thór both felt he was overly concerned and said so. Thór added that there was nothing wrong with a good Christian meeting a priest. Eirík agreed, but said he was concerned because these meetings took place in secret, and it was only by chance that he had found out.

As the evening wore on, there was much drinking of both ale and mead, and when Guðmundr began his ride home the next morning, although he felt much better inside than he had for a long time, he also had a headache.

He had not ridden far from Eirík's farm when he spotted another rider coming towards him over the heath. Neither he nor the other rider were moving very rapidly, so it took some time before they were close enough for him to see who it was. When he did, he groaned. The dark hair, the scowling face, the squat figure – it could only be Einar Gunnarsson. Was he now fated to encounter members of this cursed family wherever he went? He began to edge his horse away so that they would not meet directly.

Einar had ridden out without any specific aim in mind, simply to get away from the farm where his father and sister were once again drawing up complicated plans that would somehow weaken Eirík and possibly harm Guðmundr and Ása. He could not understand why they continued their careful and elaborate plotting when it had never worked and refused to listen to his ideas. It was so obvious that his more straightforward approach would work much better. If they had listened to him instead, the whole problem of Snæströnd, and by extension Eirík goði, would already have been solved.

When he saw a stranger riding towards him, he at first paid it little heed. But as they drew nearer and he recognised Guðmundr, he suddenly felt a savage joy. This only increased when he saw that the other man was clearly trying to avoid him. Instead of letting him ride away, he urged his horse to quicken its pace until it was clear that he would cross Guðmundr's path.

When Guðmundr saw that Einar was determined to approach him, he halted his horse and sat and waited. He wondered what this was about, but could not think of any reason why Einar would want to speak with him.

When they were within earshot, Einar called out, "You! Don't try to get away. I want to speak with you."

Guðmundr almost laughed but decided to remain calm. "I am not moving", he said. "I am waiting for you – as you can see."

The calm answer only seemed to anger Einar. "As well you should", he called.

When they were finally close to each other, Einar seemed so angry that he was lost for words. As for Guðmundr, he was still waiting to hear what the other man had to say. Finally Einar spoke up. "What are you doing here?"

The question surprised Guðmundr, but he was still trying to remain calm. "I do not know what concern this is of yours", he replied.

"I make it my concern if I choose to", Einar snapped back. "You are always skulking around where you are not wanted. The world would be far better off without you and the other scum from Snæströnd."

Now Guðmundr suddenly had enough of trying to be patient. What was this fool up to? Was he deliberately looking for a quarrel? If that was what he wanted, that was what he would get. "I think rather that the world would be far better off without you and your greedy father", he replied. "Now, is there anything else you wish to say to me? If so, do it quickly, because I have other things to do than bandy words with you."

"I do not take words from a man who betrays and dishonours his wife. You will stay as long as I wish you to stay!"

"Who are you to tell me what to do? You are nothing but a dog, who barks on your father's, or even your sister's, command. She should wear the man's clothes and you should wear her dresses." Guðmundr laughed.

Until then, Einar had not known exactly what he wanted with Guðmundr. But the mocking laughter and the insult, coupled with the praise of his sister, infuriated him. Everyone was always saying that Jórunn was so clever. Well, all of her vaunted plans for bringing down Eirík goði had turned to dust; and here was Guðmundr, a mere bóndi, insulting him and rubbing salt into the wound by praising his sister. With a wordless cry of rage he drew his sword and swung wildly at Guðmundr.

Guðmundr was taken aback. He knew that Einar was hot-headed (a hot-headed fool, he always thought), but he had not expected that the other man would go so far as to attack him in broad daylight and without provocation or warning. He pulled frantically at the reins of his horse to make it move and twisted his body away from the sword. He reached for his own sword, only to realise that he had ridden out without a weapon. The only thing he had to defend himself with was a knife. He switched his reins to his right hand and drew the knife with the left, still attempting to move away from his enraged opponent.

He was unable to move fast or far enough, though, and Einar's sword drew a long gash along his right arm, from which blood rapidly began to flow. He realised that he would not be able to avoid Einar for ever, and he could not know if his horse would be able to outrun the other man's mount. Without consciously thinking about it, he changed tactic, urging his horse forward so that it crashed into Einar's. The force of the collision was not strong enough to cause either the horse to tumble or Einar to fall off, but he was thrown off balance by the unexpected charge and flailed wildly about him with his sword.

Guðmundr was better prepared. When his horse struck Einar's, he twisted his body to the right and chopped down with the knife in his left hand. The sharp edge managed to strike Einar's wrist just as he was raising his hand, either to ward off the knife or to hack again at his opponent. When the knife hit, Guðmundr felt the jarring shock as his knife cut through skin and sinew and hit bone.

Einar cried out in pain as the sword dropped from his hand, which suddenly seemed to hang limp from the wrist. Guðmundr pulled his horse away and looked at his opponent. Should he kill him? That might be safest, but he did not know how badly hurt Einar was, so he was not certain that he could do it. Better to leave before Einar could pick up his sword and attack him again.

Before he had even finished thinking about this, he turned the horse around and urged it away. When he looked back, he saw Einar clutching his right hand in his left while trying to control his horse. Now Einar looked after him and screamed, "You will pay for this, Guðmundr!"

Guðmundr looked at him for a moment more and then called back, "You got what you deserve. Be glad it is not worse."

Then he felt the pain from his arm and urged his horse on faster. For a moment he wondered if he should ride home, but he quickly decided that the best thing to do would be to return to Eirík's farm. It would in any case be best to tell the goði what had happened.

Behind him, Einar managed to bring his horse to a halt, still clutching his wounded hand. He wanted to stop and pick up his sword but realised that if he dismounted, he might not be able to get back on his horse again. Cursing, he urged his horse around and began the ride back to Gunnar's farm, attempting to stop the flow of blood with his tunic.

Eirík was surprised to see Guðmundr again so soon, but when he saw the blood on his friend's arm, he quickly called for a servant to clean and bind the wound. Fortunately, although bleeding freely, it was just a shallow cut.

When this was done, the two men sat down and Eirík called for beer for both of them. While they drank, he bade Guðmundr to tell him everything he could recall of the attack, how it had happened and what each one had said. Then he thought for a while.

"It was good that you came directly back to me and told me the whole story. I do not know if this was planned by Gunnar, if it was Einar's own stupid plan or if it was just a chance meeting and he decided to grab the opportunity. But whatever the cause, I know this: next month's Thórsnesthing will be more lively than we thought it would be. I fear that Thór will be proven wrong, as Gunnar is certain to raise this and try to use it to his advantage. For whatever actually happened just now between the two of you, and whoever caused it, he cannot just let it pass."

"I think you are right", Guðmundr replied. "But I do not think this was Gunnar's idea. He is cleverer than that. This depended so much on chance. How could Einar know that he would meet me, or that I would be alone and unarmed? No, this was pure chance. But he attacked me and this cannot be allowed to pass either."

"It will not. But we need to think carefully about how we do this, because Gunnar will begin to gather his supporters as soon as his son comes home. And you have to ride home to Snæströnd and let your family know what has happened."

*

It took a long time for Einar to come home, because the loss of blood made him weak and his horse, sensing this, seized the opportunity to play up. The pain was worse than anything he had ever experienced, and his right hand seemed not to be functioning at all. While he rode, he cursed Guðmundr, but he also cursed his father and his sister. If Gunnar had not always favoured Jórunn, this would not have happened. He did not know who he blamed the most, his opponent or his father and sister. But whoever it was, he would get his revenge!

When he finally came home, he was so weak that he almost fell out of the saddle. Gunnar and Jórunn were not at the farm, but one of their thralls bandaged his hand for him, while he continued to swear at the pain.

When Gunnar and Jórunn returned, Einar was asleep, and the servants knew little except that he had come home wounded. The next morning, he said that he had been out riding when he had encountered Guðmundr. They had exchanged words, and Guðmundr had become enraged and attacked him without provocation. He had managed to wound his opponent, but even so, he had barely escaped the murderous attack with his life.

When Gunnar left, Jórunn remained behind. Her father had listened to Einar's story without saying much. But Jórunn was not convinced by it. When they were alone, she asked, "Is what you said really true? Guðmundr attacked you without any provocation? That does not sound like him."

Einar did not answer. Instead he looked away and said, "Do you not trust me? You may think this is unlike Guðmundr, but I see little good in him. It was a bad day when first you met him – nothing good has come of it for me." Then he turned and looked straight at her. "Let me ask you a question instead, sister", he said, "Do you want this man destroyed? Or do you love him? Tell me the truth!"

Now it was Jórunn's turn to avoid his gaze. In the end she said, "I do not know."

*

News of the fight between Einar and Guðmundr spread quickly. As a result, the Thórsnesthing was better attended than had been the case for some years.

Eirík and Thór had discussed the matter with Guðmundr and had suggested that they should wait for Gunnar and Einar to bring their case against Guðmundr. This worried Guðmundr, because he felt that the men at the Thing might think that he was the guilty party and that his guilt was clear from his reluctance to bring his own case against Einar. Thór had agreed that this was possible, but said that by letting Gunnar move first, they would find out what version of the fight he wanted the Thing to hear and thus would find it easier to rebut it with the truth. And that is what they agreed to do.

On the second day of the Thing, Gunnar rose to address the assembly. He said that by rights he should have let his son speak – "as befits a future goði" – but that Einar was still too weak from his wounds. However, Einar was present and was prepared to swear to the truth of his father's words. At that, Einar, sitting next to his father, nodded.

Gunnar told the story the way he had heard it from Einar. His son had been riding in the vicinity of Eirík goði's farm when he had spotted Guðmundr from afar. The other man had moved to intercept him, and they had exchanged words. Einar had upbraided Guðmundr for treating his wife badly – "as everyone here knows very well" – and urged him to mend his ways. Instead of listening to this well-meant advice, Guðmundr had drawn a sword and attacked. Einar had been badly wounded, and it was now clear that he would lose the use of his right hand. After the attack, Guðmundr had ridden off without waiting to see whether Einar was alive or dead. It was by pure luck and thanks to the grace of the White Christ (here Gunnar piously made the sign of the cross) that his son had survived. He urged the Thing to award Einar the largest possible damages.

When Gunnar had finished, Einar rose and in a weak voice said that he could attest that what his father had said was the truth and described exactly what had happened. Then he sat down again, while the assembled men murmured, although whether in approval or disapproval was not clear.

When the noise had died down, Guðmundr rose and addressed the Thing. He explained that he had been visiting Eirík goði – Eirík stood up and confirmed this – and was on his way home, when, in spite of trying to avoid him, he had been accosted by Einar. He admitted that they had spoken and that eventually angry words had been exchanged. Here one of the Thingmen asked what words, and Guðmundr repeated the conversation as best he could, including all the insults. When he said that he had suggested Einar should wear women's clothing a ripple of laughter ran through the assembly. Guðmundr continued, stressing that it was Einar who attacked him and that he had been lucky to strike a blow which enabled him to escape. He had at once ridden back to Eirík's farm and told him what had happened. Here Eirík rose again and affirmed that Guðmundr had spoken the truth.

He finished by saying that since he had been unjustly attacked, Einar and his father had no case against him and that if anyone should receive damages, it was him. However, since he had escaped the attack and Einar had paid for it by losing the use of his hand, he was prepared to accept smaller damages.

When Guðmundr was finished, the goðar and their advisors gathered to discuss the case. There was much argument back and forth, with some men supporting Einar and Gunnar, and others supporting Guðmundr, each side arguing that their man's version of what had happened had to be true for this or that reason. Towards the end of the day, it seemed that Gunnar had managed to sway enough men to gain slightly more support for his side than Eirík and Thór. At this stage, Eirík said that he wanted to ask Einar a question and that following the answer, he was prepared to let a judgement be made. This was agreed and Gunnar sent a man to fetch his son. When Einar joined them, Eirík said, "We just want to ask you one question. Your father has told us that you carried a sword, which you dropped when Guðmundr cut your hand. What weapon did Guðmundr have, that he managed to outfight you?"

Einar looked at his father, who nodded. "He too used a sword", Einar replied.

"You are absolutely certain of this?" Thór asked.

"Yes."

"That is strange", Eirík said mildly, "because when Guðmundr left my house, he was unarmed but for a knife. And the fight took place just outside the boundaries of my farm. Where did Guðmundr get his sword?"

Before anyone could say anything, Thór said, "I was there when Guðmundr Ragnarsson left Eirík's farm, and I affirm that Eirík has spoken the truth."

"So", Eirík continued, "we are to believe that Guðmundr, armed only with a knife, attacked you by surprise when you had already drawn your sword, since you told us you dropped it and therefore it was in your hand when he struck you."

At this, Gunnar looked furious and Einar left without saying another word. True to his word, Eirík suggested that they should now come to a verdict. As he had expected, this did not take long.

When the goðar emerged in front of the Thing assembly, Guðmundr looked expectantly at Eirík and Thór, but their faces showed nothing.

Now one of the other goðar stepped up and addressed the Thing. This was a strange case, he said, because the versions both men told were so different. Nevertheless, the goðar had agreed that some things were clear and that they could judge the case.

The first thing that was clear was that Einar Gunnarsson had attacked Guðmundr Ragnarsson. Whether this attack was provoked or unprovoked, they could not say, but it was also clear that Guðmundr's words had besmirched Einar's honour. Guðmundr had acted in self-defence. However, Einar was now permanently maimed and unable to use his sword-hand. For this Guðmundr would have to pay damages, but the damages would be diminished because of Einar's attack.

When the Thingmen heard the verdict, there was first some confusion. It seemed unclear to them who had lost and who had won. The partisans of Gunnar pointed to the damages awarded Einar, while Eirík's supporters spoke of the fact that the goðar had judged Einar the attacker and that Guðmundr had acted in self-defence.

Gunnar returned to his booth, where he found Einar nursing a beer. "You fool!" Gunnar snarled.

"Why? We won, didn't we?" Einar whined.

"We did not win. Oh yes, you were awarded damages. But they are insignificant. I wanted them to pay much more. This was our chance to ruin Guðmundr and his father. And we failed because you lied about the weapon. How could you be so stupid?"

"You nodded to me when they asked the question."

"I nodded to you to reply, not to lie."

"You were the one who told the Thing he had used a sword. I had to support you."

"You should have told me that he had used a knife!"

"I – I didn't remember."

"How could you not remember this? Once a fool, always a fool, it seems."

Einar said nothing. His father thought for a moment, then calmed down and said, "All is not lost. We are not going to be satisfied with this. I shall appeal to the Althing. And make sure you remember what happened this time."

His look was so harsh that Einar quailed. "Yes, Father", he replied.

Meanwhile, Guðmundr, Eirík and Thór had gone to Eirík's booth. As they sat down, Guðmundr looked at the others, but when neither of them said anything, he said "I was innocent. This is not to be borne."

"You were innocently attacked, this is true", Thór said. "But you did give him cause when you told him to wear a dress." He laughed. "Mind you, he should. Young fool. Thank God he was stupid enough to lie to us."

"In any case", Eirík said, "you are right to be disappointed. And we will not accept this. We shall appeal to the Althing."

*

When Guðmundr and Ása returned to Snæströnd and told Ragnar and Hallgerður what had happened at the Thing, Ragnar blamed himself. "I should have come with you", he said. "I still have some influence and some friends. I could have swayed them to support you." Guðmundr said that it was not his fault. It was after all true that he had insulted Einar, even if it was only after Einar had sought a quarrel with him. In any case, nothing was final yet as they had decided to appeal the case, and much could happen at the Althing.

Hallgerður and Ása both tried to calm Ragnar as well, but he refused to listen to them. Instead, he became ever more convinced that if he had only been at the Thórsnesthing, matters would have turned out differently. Guðmundr had often seen his father preoccupied with something or angry. But this was the first time he had seen Ragnar worried. He kept muttering, "This is the end of Snæströnd; they will ruin us", and he took to spending more time than he had recently done working in the fields.

One morning when Guðmundr woke up, he found Hallgerður already up and worrying because Ragnar was nowhere to be seen.

Guðmundr said that his father had probably just risen very early and gone out, but Hallgerður replied that he had been away all night. Now Guðmundr was also worried and left the house with two of the farmhands to look for him.

They did not have to go very far. When they came down to the beach that had once given the farm its name, they found Ragnar sitting, looking out at the sea. At first, Guðmundr thought that his father was looking for Kári's ship, which they all hoped would soon be coming back. But when he called out and Ragnar did not reply, he began to worry and ran up to his father. It was in this way that he found Ragnar dead. He was not wounded and they could see no cause for his death. But his body was cold, and he must have been dead for many hours when they found him.

Guðmundr told the farmhands to carry his father home, while he hurried ahead to prepare his mother. When he came home, he did not have to say anything. Hallgerður looked at him, and suddenly her eyes began to fill with tears. "Is he …?" she began. Guðmundr nodded. Suddenly he felt weary and sad. He wished he had spent more time with his father, but his years of unhappiness and his previous quarrels with Ragnar had made that difficult. At least they had reconciled in the last months, and he had begun to gain a deeper understanding of his father's strengths and motivation. And although he had tried to play down his father's concerns, he realised that he would have wanted Ragnar with him at the Althing.

Wordlessly he embraced his mother, and when Ása heard the commotion and saw what was happening, she joined them.

Eventually, Hallgerður stepped back. "Where was he?"

"By the beach", Guðmundr replied. "I think he may have been looking for the knarr."

"Perhaps", Hallgerður said. "I know he wished Kári would come back. He said we needed him here."

"I agree", Guðmundr said. It was true. Sometimes the brothers did not get along, and he had always felt that his father favoured Kári. But he still missed his brother, and now he missed him even more.

When Eirík heard that Ragnar was dead, he mounted his horse and rode over to Thór. Together the two goðar discussed what Ragnar's death meant for them all. Although it was good to have Guðmundr back advising them, Eirík said, Ragnar was still respected by many who clung to Iceland's traditional values and who still held the Law and its belief in personal freedom and individual responsibility in high esteem. Thór agreed, noting that Guðmundr was still not as well known or esteemed as his father. Both of them felt that this was bad for the Iceland they tried to uphold. In addition, Gunnar's case against Guðmundr worried them both. After all, they had lost at the Thórsnesthing, and they were concerned that the Althing, where Gunnar was still powerful, could end up imposing a crippling fine on Guðmundr and in addition show that Eirík and Thór and goðar of their ilk were powerless to protect their followers. If that happened, some people might well desert them and move to Gunnar's camp. Nor was Gunnar alone in his views. For this reason, it was important that they get the Althing to reverse the Thórsnesthing's decision. But how could they do this? The facts were already known, and there was little likelihood that anyone who knew them would change his mind. And they could be sure that Gunnar would already be busy trying to persuade those from other parts of Iceland to support him.

At this stage, the priest Willibald, who had been sitting nearby, reading his Bible, suddenly interrupted them. His understanding of the Norse tongue was much improved, and he could understand most of what was being said. He was also now increasingly confident in expressing himself. Now he approached the two goðar and said, "Are you saying that what you need is more support, in order to win the case for the young man Guðmundr?"

"Yes", Thór replied. "But it is likely to be difficult."

"Goði, I may have an idea", Willibald said. "Would you like me to see what I can do?"

Thór and Eirík looked at each other. Eirík shrugged his shoulders and Thór said, "What is your idea?"

"Goði, it is not yet a fully developed thought. It is just something I think might work. But I would prefer not to say anything until I have given it some more thought and perhaps spoken with one or two people to see what they think."

Once again Thór and Eirík paused for thought. Then Eirík said, "Why not? Who knows what may help?" Thór nodded assent.

"Thank you, goðar", Willibald said and returned to reading his Bible.

News of Ragnar's death spread quickly in the neighbourhood. When Gunnar heard about it, he was jubilant and called his children to him.

"This was one fear I had", he exulted. "That the old fool with his talk of 'freedom' and 'respect for the Law' and 'Iceland's past' would sway people at the Althing. Without him, Guðmundr is as good as lost, and Snæströnd will soon be no more than an annoying memory. This will turn out well for us, my daughter."

When Einar heard Gunnar's words, his face darkened. Once again it was Jórunn, Jórunn, Jórunn. "Father", he interrupted, "could I remind you that if we have a case against Guðmundr and we win it, it is thanks to me. Not thanks to Jórunn. And I also think it has come at a high price." He held up his arm with the now lame hand to emphasise his words.

Gunnar looked scornfully at him. "Great power and great victories always come at a cost. This is the price we have to pay."

"You have not paid any price; I have paid it", Einar interrupted again.

"Yes, yes. But stop thinking about your hand and think instead of the power that will be mine and one day yours, when Eirík goði is broken. At least your sister understands that."

Always the same, Einar thought. His father and his sister clearly thought of him only as a fool and a useful tool. He turned towards Jórunn and stared at her.

She looked back at him, and for a moment she was shaken by the hatred and loathing for her that was clearly visible in her brother's face.

Chapter 13

Spring – Summer 1067

Kári was glad to be back on the open sea, but strangely, he found that he already missed Lishbuna. Maebh came and stood next to him by the steering oar and he said, "I am happy we came to Lishbuna."

"So am I", she replied, looking at him.

Kári smiled at her, and said, "That is the main reason, of course. But I am also thinking of the trading. It is a good city to visit for trading. The courts are honest and so are most of the people. This will attract other traders. And I liked the warmth." He thought for a moment. "Mind you, I do not like what they do to their money."

"You can always come back", Maebh said. "I am sure your profits will be good. Although next time, I hope you do not find another woman to bring." Kári looked at her in astonishment. How could she even think this? But Maebh only laughed at his expression.

Sailing from Dyflin to Lishbuna had been straightforward. Aidan had told them the course to steer, and Kári had merely obeyed, although he had taken care to try to remember the landmarks and ask Aidan for as much information as he could about the return voyage.

Sailing back turned out to be a different matter. Almost as soon as they left Lishbuna and entered the open sea, the wind began to veer to the north. More often than not, they had to furl the sail and row. They passed the port of Vigo, which Aidan had pointed out to them on the way south, and there the wind swung round and helped them onwards. But once they reached the end of land, from where they had hoped to sail due north, straight towards Cork, the wind turned again. Now it blew them towards the east. Kári tried to remember exactly what Aidan had told him about the land and how far it stretched in that direction. Because Aidan had also warned him about winter storms, he finally decided that rather than sailing across the open sea, they would follow the wind and hug the coast, even though it would probably mean a longer journey. As it was, rowing from Lishbuna to the north coast had already taken them four days, almost as long as they had hoped the entire journey to Cork would take. Although sailing east was the wrong direction, at least they would move faster and, sooner or later, he was sure the coast would turn northwards and take them in the right direction again.

It took them another two days of steady sailing before the coast finally turned north. They continued along the coast for another few days, twice stopping at river mouths to take on fresh water. Meanwhile, the coast finally turned northwest, taking them towards Ireland.

Although the crew had not needed to do much rowing once Kári had decided to go with the wind, they were beginning to grumble. By now, they would have hoped to have reached Cork and then be on their way home to Iceland. They had enjoyed their time in Lishbuna, but they had been abroad for a year, on a voyage that should have taken no longer than a few months at most. Some of them had left sweethearts in Iceland, and the men from the neighbouring farms were eager to come home and show off their new-found wealth.

At last they reached the open sea and sailed across it for two days. Towards the evening, they spotted land ahead. Kári hoped that this would be Ireland, but as they approached, it became clear that this was only a group of small islands. Wherever it was, it was certainly not Ireland. Even so, he thought it might be a good idea to stop and take on more fresh water and perhaps find out where they were. At the same time, he was wary of entering any port with a small knarr loaded with wealth. In the end, by sailing slowly along the coast they came to a small brook that emptied into the sea, with a village next to it. There they steered in and landed on the beach. Kári dispatched four of the men to fill their casks from the brook, while the others armed themselves and waited by the knarr. They did not have to wait long before a group of men approached from the village. They were also armed, but with spears and hooks. Kári gave a sigh of relief. Whoever these men were, they were not soldiers, only farmers. He stuck his sword back in its scabbard and, holding up both hands to show that he had peaceful intentions, walked slowly towards them, with one of his crewmen following him.

When he was within earshot, he called out, "We come in peace. We only want water. Then we will leave."

The men stopped. One of them called something, but Kári did not understand him. Kári repeated what he had said. This time, the man seemed to understand, because he nodded. Then he slowly approached Kári in turn. When he was so close that he need not shout, he stopped, clearly unwilling to come any closer. Kári smiled. He did not blame him – he would have done the same if a band of armed men had appeared unbidden at Snæströnd.

The man spoke. His words sounded strange, Kári thought, as if he ought to understand them, but he didn't. He waited until the man was finished, then carefully and slowly replied, "Speak more slowly."

The man nodded and said, slowly and distinctly, "Take - water - go."

"Thank - you", Kári replied. Then a thought struck him. "Where?"

The man replied something, but Kári could not hear. "Again?"

"Syll-ing-ar", the man now enunciated. Then he continued, "Who? New - king's - men?"

Now Kári knew. Aidan had mentioned the Syllingar. They were a group of small islands southeast of Ireland. That was good news. But why did the man ask if they were King Harold's men? He shook his head.

Behind him, Hallvarðr now called to let him know that the four crewmen had returned with the refilled water casks. Kári turned again to the islander and said "Thank - you." Then he and his crewman returned to the knarr. When he cast a glance back towards the group of islanders, he noted that they were also moving away, although more slowly, which was probably because they were still not sure if the men from the sea were really leaving. A wise move, but their caution was not necessary.

Back at the knarr he saw that the water was already stowed and gave orders to leave. And now at least he knew in which direction to sail. They followed the coast of the small island until it turned north and then struck off towards the northwest, across the open sea.

The next evening, they saw a large bay with a narrow inlet opening in front of them and a landscape that shimmered in green in the setting sun.

"Ireland", Maebh said. "And that is the bay into which the An Laoi empties. Enter there and we find Cork."

The sail was furled, and with the crew rowing, Kári followed Maebh's instructions, steering through a strait and then through an even narrower one before turning west into the river that Maebh had called the An Laoi. The town was smaller than Dyflin, but there were still four churches. The harbour had two wooden piers stretching out into the river, and since there was space alongside one of them, Kári steered the knarr towards it.

It was with very mixed feelings that Kári felt the knarr settle into its berth. Until now, he had been able to avoid thinking about the future and simply live in the present with Maebh. But now they had finally reached her destination. This was where she had wanted to be taken from the start; this was where her family lived, and this was where she would be leaving him. Many times on the journey from Lishbuna he had wanted to ask her what would happen when they reached Cork, but each time he had held back, for fear of receiving a reply he did not like to hear. He justified this to himself by thinking that it would be unfair to ask her to choose between being a king's daughter in Ireland or a farmer's wife in Iceland, and in any case, he did not even know if she would want to stay with him.

Maebh looked out over Cork, thinking about how much she had changed since she had last seen it. It was little more than a year since she had been abducted. Before that, Cork had been a big city, the biggest she knew (and the secret target of her father's ambitions), and a wonder to visit on rare occasions. But now she had seen Lishbuna and Dyflin, both of which were larger, and Cork suddenly seemed rather smaller than she remembered. But the landscape was still as green, and much as she recalled. She wondered what would now happen to her. She had thought that she and Kári would talk about this during the voyage from Lishbuna, but he had not said anything to her, and she found this puzzling. Surely there was no question mark, either over what she felt for him or what he felt for her. Or was there? Anyway, first things first. She needed to get in touch with her father.

While Kári and his men performed their routine tasks, carefully going over the knarr to see what might need repairs in port and what supplies they needed to take on, Maebh left the harbour and went to the largest of the churches, the Church of St Sepulchre. She had known one or two of the priests there in the past, and they would know where her father was.

When she arrived at the church, she had the same feeling of memories playing her false that she had felt on seeing the town. It had always seemed so big, so impressive. But after Sancho's church in Lishbuna and some of the other temples there, it suddenly seemed much smaller. When she entered, it took her eyes a few moments to adjust to the gloom. The church was almost empty, but she did spot one priest and went up to him. He looked at her expectantly.

"Father, are either Father Domhnall or Father Cormac in the church?"

He looked strangely at her. "Father Cormac is dead. How come you do not know this?"

Maebh was taken aback. "I – I have been away", she stuttered. "And Father Domhnall?"

"Let me go and see. Who are you?"

"I am Maebh nic Cárthaigh. My father is Muirchertach mac Cárthaigh."

When she said this, the priest gave her an odd look and said, "Wait here", before striding off.

Maebh did not understand why he behaved so strangely. But she did not have to wait long. He soon came running back, with an elderly priest bringing up the rear. When he saw her, the older man exclaimed, "Maebh, my dear! We thought you were dead. Where have you – " Then he stopped and turned to the other priest. "Thank you, Father Finn. I will speak with the lady now."

The other priest took himself off. Meanwhile, the older man, whom Maebh recognised as Father Domhnall, led her to a bench. He gazed at her for a moment, and then said, "Your convent was attacked. We were certain you were dead or enslaved. What happened?"

"I was enslaved. But I met a man, a wonderful man, Father, and he saved me. He promised to take me back to Cork. It took longer than we thought, but now we are here."

"Yes. But you cannot stay here. You must leave at once."

"What? Why?"

"My dear, your father, King Muirchertach … your father – he is dead."

"How? And are you sure?"

"I am sure. I am sorry. I saw his body myself." He wanted to continue, but Maebh interrupted him.

"Where is my mother? I have to go to her. And is my brother Brian now king?"

Father Domhnall took her hands in his. "My dear girl, it is not just your father who is dead. They were attacked at a feast. The hall was set on fire. I fear – ". His voice broke. "All of them are dead. You are the only one left."

Maebh was horrified. All of her family killed? "Who did this? The Manxmen? The same who attacked my convent?"

"What? Oh no. No, it was not them. This was done by your father's enemies here in Ireland. It was known that he had planned to attack Cork. The men of Cork allied with some of the surrounding kings and struck first. And this is why you must leave at once. If you stay here, you will surely be killed."

"But nobody knows that I am here", she said weakly.

"That is not true", the priest replied. "I know. I would never give you away. But Father Finn also knows, and he is new here. I cannot vouch for him." He stopped talking, then resumed, "You said you met a man – a wonderful man, you said. Are you wed to him? Is he still here?"

"We are not wed – yet. But, yes, he is still here. His ship is in the harbour."

"Then go to him at once. And take me with you."

Maebh opened her mouth, but the priest said sharply, "No more interruption. We do not have time to waste. We must go at once." He seemed so frightened that Maebh stopped whatever she had intended to say and stood up. Together they left the church and hurried down to the harbour, the priest almost dragging the woman along.

When they reached the harbour, the priest looked around, then, spotting the foreign craft, pointed at it and said, "That one?" When Maebh nodded, he broke into another run.

They reached the knarr and Father Domhnall looked around, then asked, "Which one is the wonderful man?"

Kári had seen them coming and was already coming towards them. He heard the question and smiled, saying, "I don't know about wonderful, but you are probably looking for me."

Before the priest had time to say anything, Maebh exclaimed, "Kári, they are dead. All my family." Kári stared at her, at first not understanding what she said. Then, as the impact began to sink in, his smile was replaced by a horrified expression as he moved to embrace her.

As he was trying to think of something to say, Maebh broke free of his embrace and looked him straight in the face. "My family is dead", she repeated. "There is nothing left for me in Ireland." She seemed to be expecting an answer.

Kári felt confused. He had been upset at the thought of losing Maebh when they came to Cork, but he did not want her to think that he was merely taking her with him out of pity. Then he said, "There may be nothing left for you in Ireland. But there is a whole world waiting for you with me. Will you come with me to Iceland?"

"What took you so long to ask?" she said, and as she did she gave him a weak smile. Then she embraced him again.

Father Domhnall had been watching them, but now he interrupted. "This is good. But you must leave. You cannot stay here. And there is another thing."

Reluctantly, Kári turned to the priest. "Why do we have to leave at once? In any case, we cannot leave at once. I have men ashore that I will not leave. We need supplies, and also, the tide is coming in. We can leave tomorrow morning at dawn, I think. And what is the other thing?"

"But – you must leave as soon as you can. Maebh is not safe here. The people who killed her father and brothers will want to kill her." This shook Kári, who until now had not thought of why Maebh's family was dead. The priest continued, "Also, the Lady Maebh is a high-born maiden." Behind the priest's back, Maebh looked at Kári and raised an eyebrow. "She cannot travel alone on a ship full of men."

Kári began to smile, but, with some difficulty, suppressed the urge. Then he said, "Thank you, Father, for this warning. We will leave as soon as possible. As for travelling alone on a ship full of men, I am afraid that it is too late."

The priest straightened. "In that case, I insist that you wed the lady. Her honour must be protected." His face was red with indignation.

"But you have not asked the lady if she wants to be wed. Nor have you asked me, for that matter."

"In this matter, the lady's honour takes precedence", Father Domhnall replied.

During this conversation, the crew had stopped even pretending to work and were all listening intently, mainly with broad grins on their faces. Behind the priest, Maebh's face was showing a variety of emotions. At the moment, she was sticking her tongue out at Kári, who decided that, much as he enjoyed teasing the priest, they really did not have time for this. Moreover, it was clear that Father Domhnall was serious in his concern, both for Maebh's life and for her honour.

He composed his face and said, "Father, you are absolutely right. But I cannot force a high-born woman like the Lady Maebh against her will. So, if she is willing to wed me, would you marry us?"

The priest turned to look at Maebh, who quickly stopped smiling and became serious. Then she said, "Father, I say to you, and I say in front of everyone here, that I wish to have this man as my husband, and I would ask you to marry us as soon as you can." And she flashed a huge smile to Kári, a real smile this time, and her eyes were sparkling with joy.

And so, in the dusk of a Cork spring evening, Kári and Maebh were wed. Although both of them had wanted this to happen, neither had imagined that it would happen in this way, on Kári's boat and pushed into it by a well-meaning priest. But, as Maebh later said to Kári, this certainly fitted well with the whole pattern of how they had met and become lovers.

The rest of Kári's crew returned to the knarr before dark. The inbound tide was still too strong for them to think of leaving, but after Father Domhnall had gone ashore, embraced by Maebh and thanked by both of them, Kári took the knarr out into the river and anchored it there. Then he told the crew to arm themselves and arranged for three watches. Four men would stand watch in the first two, and then he and the two remaining crewmen would take the last watch. He was grateful for the nearly full moon. Though it meant that anyone coming for them could easily see the knarr, at least they would not be fighting in complete darkness.

Kári had difficulty falling asleep that night. He would have preferred to stay awake and on guard all night, but he knew that if he tried, he would sooner or later fall asleep, and that would be worse. Also, he wanted to be alert later in the night and ready to leave as soon as the tide enabled them to.

He had barely fallen asleep, he thought, before he felt somebody shaking his shoulder, with a hand on his mouth. When he opened his eyes, he saw that it was Hallvarðr, who was commanding the second watch. The other man motioned at him to be quiet. Kári nodded and then whispered, "Is it time?" Hallvarðr shook his head and bending close to Kári's ear, whispered, "Men are coming."

Kári suddenly felt fully awake. He was going to ask Hallvarðr to wake the rest of the crew, but the other man put one finger on his mouth and then signalled to him to look around. All around the knarr, Kári saw, sleeping men were quietly being woken up by their comrades.

Now he could hear the splashing of oars and muttered conversation across the water. The approaching men were not even very quiet. They were either not used to warfare, Kári thought, or assumed that the knarr would be an easy prey. He smiled grimly. Maybe it would have been, a year earlier. But not now, as the attackers would soon find out.

The crew crept towards the side of the boat, careful to ensure that they were not spotted, and waited.

They did not have to wait long. The splashing noises came nearer, and then three grapples were thrown across the railings and pulled tight. Then something bumped against the knarr, and there was a muffled curse. Kári almost laughed. How did these men think they could make a surprise attack if this is how they behaved?

He signalled to his men to wait. Now the ropes were tightening and swaying, and there were noises of something rubbing against the ship's side. A few moments later, three heads showed up over the side, followed by shoulders. Then, as the men reached over the board to haul themselves onto the deck, Kári yelled, "Now!" and sprang against the nearest man, hacking downwards with his sword. Next to him, the rest of the crew followed suit, screaming in rage. One of the attackers was so surprised that he lost his grip and fell back into the river with a loud splash. Of the two others, the one Kári had attacked screamed in pain and started to slither back over the side, but one of the crewmen managed to pin him to the rail with a spear that had gone through the man's tunic without touching his body. The last man managed to get on board but was attacked by three crewmen at once. One chopped at his legs and he jumped up to avoid the cut, but as he did, another hit his head with a club and he fell like an ox. They could hear the sound of boats quickly attempting to row away from the knarr.

The whole attack had only taken a few moments. Kári helped one of the crewmen haul the wounded attacker on board, then stole a quick glance towards the piers and saw two boats, lit by the moonlight, moving rapidly away through the dark. Then he turned to the two prisoners. Both of them seemed to have lost all desire to fight. One of them muttered, "Nobody said there'd be any fighting."

"Really?" Kári replied. "Just a nice quiet little killing, then?" Then he turned to Hallvarðr. "Take their weapons and then throw the men overboard."

One of the prisoners said, "I can't swim", but Kári was in no mood for clemency. These men had just tried to kill his wife.

"You should have thought of that before attacking us", he snapped.

Despite his harsh words, Kári was relieved to see both men managing to paddle towards the shore. Then Hallvarðr beckoned to him. "Look", he said. "The tide has turned. We can leave."

"Good idea", Kári replied. "Let's get away before they think of attacking us with fire arrows."

It took them some time and some careful rowing to leave Cork, but this time Kári was more worried about navigation than about pursuit. He remembered the narrow inlet to the river and feared that passing this in the dark would be hazardous, even with the bright moon. But they were fortunate. By the time they reached this passage, dawn was breaking and they had more than enough light to see what they were doing. Soon enough they were through the first passage and then the second and were out in the open sea, where they turned east and then followed the coast to the north.

In contrast with the voyage from Lishbuna, this time the wind was in their favour the whole time. They made good time passing Dyflin. Kári had wondered if they should perhaps make landfall for supplies since they had not managed to get much in Cork. But after speaking with Hallvarðr, it was agreed that they could manage to get to Kirkjuvágr if they used water and food sparingly. When Kári told the crew, instead of grumblings about less food and water, there was cheering. Kirkjuvágr was almost home. Once they got there, it was only a two- or at most three-day journey to Iceland.

When Kári mentioned his surprise at the cheering to Maebh, she smiled and said, "Your men trust you. This you know. But they also respect and like you. This is more rare. And together it means they will follow wherever you lead. Too many men think the way to get people to follow and obey them is to make them fear their leader. That may work, for a time at least. But your way is stronger."

She stopped and then went on, "And also, I have learnt one more thing from you, Kári. You told me that these are free men. To command the allegiance of free men is more than to wield the stick. Do you think they would continue to follow you if they did not also benefit from being with you? They know that you do not only think of yourself but that you care about them and that they owe you a great deal. Of course they are happy – they are going home. But they are happier for the fact that it is you leading them home."

When they reached Kirkjuvágr, Kári too felt excitement and eagerness growing in his breast. If they had only had more supplies on board, they could have sailed directly home, but now they had to take on at least some water. However, he promised the men they would only stay one night, and pointed out that this meant they would come home with more silver than if they had stayed longer in the port. At this, the men laughed.

As he always did in Kirkjuvágr, Kári went to Harald's inn. This time he brought Maebh with him. The little man brightened to see him. "Kári, my boy. I feared you were lost at Jórvik. How are you? And who is the lady?"

"Well, for one thing, she saved my life at Jórvik", Kári replied with a smile. "Now she is my wife. Maebh, this is Harald, owner of the best inn to be found in Kirkjuvágr. As for what happened, Harald, I will tell you everything, if you have time for a beer with us?"

"With you? Always. And some salt fish?"

Kári laughed. "Of course."

While they were drinking – and eating – Kári told Harald what had happened to him. The Dane was particularly interested in the stories of Lishbuna, sighing that when he was young, he would have loved to travel to faraway places and that somewhere warm was exactly what he needed now.

But it was Harald's news that astonished Kári and Maebh. Kári had asked if it was true that King Harald had died at Jórvik.

"Oh yes", Harald replied. "He died early on in the battle, and most of his men with him. Tostig too, although I doubt if anyone missed him. His son survived, though, and returned to Norway, where I hear he is now king. But that is not the biggest news."

Kári and Maebh looked at him. "Well", the Dane said, lifting his mug and draining it to draw out the excitement, "while King Harold and the main English host were up in Jórvik dealing with the Norwegians, would you believe that Duke William of Normandy landed in the south. So Harold got his army going immediately after the victory and marched them back down again. There was a big battle in the south somewhere … I forget the name." He paused to fill up his mug with more beer.

Finally Maebh said, "Are you going to tell us what happened or not?"

The Dane did not seem put out, particularly as Maebh's words were accompanied by a smile. "Oh I'll tell you all right. It's quickly done. Harold got himself killed, his brothers too. And Duke William is now King William of England, no less."

"Oh", Kári said. "Now I understand." Maebh and Harald looked at him. "When we stopped in the Syllingar, the man asked if we were the new king's men. I thought he meant Harold and couldn't understand why he even asked. But now I realise he meant William. That makes more sense."

*

The next day, the knarr set sail for Iceland. Once again, the winds were with them and it took barely three days for them to reach Snæströnd. As they rounded Snæfellsnes, Maebh stood next to

Kári at the stern as he pointed out landmarks to her. She looked at his eager face. "You really love this land, don't you?"

"Yes I do. And I hope you will love it as well."

"I am sure I will. But my greater feeling right now is rather different. Always in my life, I have been somebody else's to command. First my father; then the nuns in the convent and any priest who came there; and finally the men who captured me. Now I am not, not since I met you. And I can feel it. I feel free, freer than ever before. Free like those birds", and she pointed to a flight of seabirds who were passing them along the shore. "And I think I understand what you mean by freedom. From now on, I can be whoever I want to be!"

Kári put his arm around her shoulder. "And who is it you want to be?" he asked. But Maebh merely hugged him and made no reply.

By late afternoon, they finally reached Snæströnd. As they steered in towards the shore, Kári could see that they had been sighted, and someone was running up to the farm to give them the news. By the time they reached the shore, a small crowd had gathered to welcome them. Kári saw Ása and his mother but looked in vain for Ragnar. In front of them all, though, stood Guðmundr. Finally the knarr was beached and the men began to come ashore. Kári helped Maebh down and walked hand in hand with her towards his waiting brother.

When they reached him, Guðmundr said, "You took your time."

"True", Kári replied. "But now I am – we are – home."

Chapter 14

Summer 1067

Guðmundr looked at Maebh and at his sunburnt brother. Kári seemed to have changed, and it was not just the presence of a woman. Nor was it that he had matured. It was something more than that, almost as if he had gone away as a younger brother but returned as an equal.

"I can see that we have much to talk about", he said.

"More than you think", Kári replied. "But first, where is Father? I do not see him. Is he well?"

Guðmundr hesitated. "Father died a few months ago. I think he died waiting for you, because he often came here and spent his time looking out to sea. Indeed this is where we found him."

Kári blinked and thought for a moment. He had always known that one day his parents would die. He had just not expected it to happen so soon, even though he knew Ragnar had aged. Suddenly he felt a rush of things that he wished he could have told his father; now Ragnar would never hear of his voyage, his success and above all of Maebh. Finally he said, "I am sorry. I would have liked to see him again." He thought for another moment, and continued,

> Home is the Helmsman
> with heartfelt longing
> Father and family
> will feast on his tale

> Sorrow at Snæströnd
> stands there awaiting
> Grief as the Greybeard
> has gone from his hall
>
> Heavy the heart
> as I hear of his ending
> Silenced the Steersman
> So ends my rejoicing

Then he turned back to Guðmundr. "I must deal with my men and the load. After that, we will speak."

With the help of some farmhands from Snæströnd, Kári and the crew unloaded the knarr. Then the ship was carried back to the naust where it would be sheltered until they needed it again. By the time the knarr was safe the sun was already slowly sinking, although there were still several hours of light left in the long Icelandic summer day. Kári and his men went back to the farmhouse and there he gathered the crew around him.

"This has been our longest voyage together", he began. "We have lived through some dangers we did not expect, and we have seen people and places we did not even know existed. Yet we have all come back alive, and we have brought back more wealth than from any previous voyage."

"You certainly brought back something valuable", someone called out laughing. The rest of the crew joined in and, after a moment, so did Kári.

"You can now choose", he continued, once the laughter had died down. "You can wait until all the silk is sold, and then you will get your share in silver. This may take some time. Or else you can take your share in silk and sell it yourselves. You do not need to let me know right away. In any case, as you go to your homes, from my share I am giving you each a bolt of silk. I am sure you will find someone at home who will know what you should do with it."

This time the men's laughter was mixed with cheers for Kári and his generosity.

When Kári handed out the bolts, he noticed Hallvarðr and the other two Snæströnd farmhands hanging back. After the other crew members had received their silk and were making to leave for their homes, Kári came up to them and asked if they did not want their silk. At this, the other two looked at Hallvarðr, who said, "We were not sure that we were included in your offer."

Kári was surprised. "We have sailed together for many years and yet you still need to ask this? We have all shared in everything equally. Little do you know me if you think I would not treat you like the others." And with that he gave each of the men a bolt of silk as well.

Guðmundr had been outside and observed all this. Now he realised that whatever had happened to Kári while he was away had returned him a leader of men. For a brief moment he felt a sting of jealousy, but then he let it go. He had no reason to feel jealous and many reasons to be glad that his brother was doing well. Instead he clapped Kári on the shoulder and said, "We should go in. Although from what I saw earlier I doubt if we will get much chance to say anything." When Kári looked puzzled, Guðmundr just laughed and said, "You will see."

When they entered the farmhouse, Kári understood at once what Guðmundr had meant. At the large table, Ása and Maebh were sitting close together, surrounded by servants, with Maebh in the midst of talking, presumably, Kári thought, about how they had met, but constantly being interrupted by Ása's questions, while the servants were looking admiringly at a bolt of shiny blue silk that was spread on the table. Only Hallgerður seemed not to be part of the animated scene, sitting somewhat apart and studying her two daughters-in-law with a wary expression on her face.

"Let them talk", Guðmundr said. "I too wish to hear how you met, and also why you were away so long. In the meantime, you should know that much has happened here too, and we need to take counsel about that. But I think we should speak about that tomorrow. Today is your day – and Maebh's."

Guðmundr was right, Kári thought. Of course, he had already heard about Ragnar's death. But there had to be more. When he left Snæströnd, he knew that his brother's marriage was troubled, yet now he could see that this was no longer the case. Was that what Guðmundr wanted to tell him? Kári decided that he was not going to ask. If his brother wanted to tell him, well and good. And if he didn't, then it was enough to see that there was peace between him and Ása. With a shock, Kári also realised that the two young children close to his brother's wife were not a servant's children but Guðrún and Eirík, his niece and nephew. Seeing how much they had grown made him realise how long he had been away.

Now his thoughts were interrupted. "Kári", Maebh called. "I need your help. Your lady mother does not think that she should wear silk. Yet this colour is the same as her eyes. And as the mother of two such men, and the Mistress of Snæströnd, should she not dress as well as the highest in the land?"

Hallgerður gave a wry smile. "I am no longer the Mistress of Snæströnd", she said. "That title belongs to Ása. And who would care how I dress?"

"We care", Maebh and Ása said together. But try as they might to convince her otherwise, Hallgerður refused to have anything to do with the silk. Instead, she turned to Kári and said, "Your wife has told us how you met, in Orkney and later outside Jórvik. But I don't understand what you were doing in the Norwegian fleet. Sit and tell us."

'Your wife', Kári noted, not 'Maebh'. So his mother wasn't really rejecting the silk at all; she was unwilling to accept the strange woman in her household – for in many ways, and in spite of what she had said, Snæströnd was still her household as well as Ása's. Kári sighed. He did not want his mother and his wife on bad terms.

He sat down and said, "That is a story long in the happening, though I shall make it short in the telling. But let me first ask you this: did Maebh tell you that she saved my life?"

At this Hallgerður looked surprised. "No", she said. "Just that you saw her tied up like a dog and then saved her from a Manxman."

"This part of the tale was not for me to say", Maebh interjected.

"If Maebh had not healed me when I was wounded in battle,

you would not have your son with you today", Kári said. "And she saved me a second time, when we were in Lishbuna and a treacherous Swede tried to cheat me and have me condemned to slavery or worse."

When he said this, there was an outbreak of comments.

Guðrún asked "Is Lishbuna Swedish?"

Her father said "Wait, you were in the King's fleet and then you were cheated by someone?"

Kári held up his hand for quiet.

When all were silent, he drew breath to speak, but before he had a chance to do so, Hallgerður asked Maebh, "Is this true?"

Maebh looked her in the eyes and replied, "I did what every woman in love would do. But I do not wish to lie. I could not have done it without Kári himself and without the help of a priest of the White Christ. And you must also know that Kári saved my life once again, in Cork."

At this there were further exclamations, until Guðmundr called out "Quiet!" in a loud voice. Then he said, "Now we know that everyone saved everyone else's life many times. This is wonderful and I am pleased to hear it. But I think there is more to this tale than that, and if everybody is quiet, perhaps my brother will be able to tell us this in a way that makes sense. And perhaps we can also get some food and above all some beer. Because I already think this will be a story that makes the teller of it thirsty."

Once the servants had brought in food and drink and the entire household had joined them, Kári was finally able to tell the story from the beginning. When he reached the part concerning Odd going on pilgrimage to Rome, Guðmundr interrupted. "I wanted to ask why Odd was not with you. Will he be back?"

Kári thought for a moment before replying. "I think so. But it is a long way to Rome, and I think we will be fortunate if we see him before next year. They say Rome has many churches, and it sounded from what Hákon was saying that he intended to visit every single one of them."

Kári continued with his story, telling them about the storm and about his encounter with King Harald. At this, Guðrún wanted to know if he really had met a king. "Yes I did", Kári replied. "But he was not a nice man. He stole things from me and said that he was going to bring his fleet to Iceland one day."

Kári only intended to say this to stop the girl from asking more questions, but when he mentioned King Harald's plans for Iceland, Guðmundr suddenly leaned forward and asked, "What do you mean?"

"I am not sure", Kári replied. "I am not even sure that he knew what he meant. But he did hint that once he had conquered England, he felt that Iceland should also be part of his realm. Why do you ask?"

"Because there are strange things happening here", Guðmundr answered, "and what you say could well be part of them. But we will speak about this tomorrow. For tonight, you should continue your tale."

Kári then spoke about the voyage back across the North Sea and how he had first seen Maebh in Kirkjuvágr. He told them about how they sailed to England and the battle outside Jórvik where he was wounded, and how Maebh had healed him. The tale then continued with how they left the Norwegian fleet when King Harald was dead, and sailed to Dyflin. He spoke of the decision to sail to Lishbuna and what had happened there, including the trial and his decision to be baptised. Finally, he told them about their time in Cork and how they had been wed, and lastly the attack on the knarr.

When he had finished, everyone was silent. Then Hallgerður looked at Maebh. "Thank you", she said. Kári noted it but said nothing. Maebh just bowed her head. But Ása said that this was a good tale and that it was clear that God had intended Kári and Maebh for each other, and Guðmundr agreed.

The next day Guðmundr had much to do at the farm, and Kári spent much of the day with Maebh going through once again what silk they had, sorting through what was his and what belonged to his men and was to be sold on their account. It was therefore only at the evening meal that Guðmundr was able to tell them what had taken place in Iceland while they were gone. He did not speak of his reconciliation with Ása, but he did tell them of Jórunn's visit, saying that she had come to sow strife between the two of them.

While Kári listened he found himself getting angrier and angrier at the actions of Gunnar and his children. When he heard of Einar's attack on Guðmundr, he finally could not keep still. "How dare he?" he exclaimed, red in the face. "Give me one reason not to attack Gunnar's farm with my crew and kill them all?"

Guðmundr and Hallgerður said nothing, but Ása was visibly surprised at Kári's reaction. She had never seen him angry like this before. It was Maebh, though, who moved first, putting a hand on his arm and saying, "Kári, this will not help your brother. He is still here and unharmed. Wait until you have heard the whole tale. You are the one who is always speaking of the Law and how people in Iceland respect it and how important it is. Is this how you show that respect? What is then the difference between Iceland and Ireland if your first thought is of violence?"

Kári shook off her hand and was about to say something in reply when Hallgerður, who had been observing the scene, spoke. "Listen to Maebh. She is right. And what is more, you know that she is right."

Even in his anger, Kári registered that his mother had for the first time spoken Maebh's name. That made him hesitate and even as he did so, he knew that he would not act on his impulse.

Once Guðmundr saw Kári hesitate, he knew that his brother's anger was passing. He said, "There are many reasons why you should not do that. At least not now. The first is that both Maebh and Hallgerður are right. The second reason is that you gain little honour from killing a cripple."

"A cripple?"

"You should have waited to hear what happened. Einar attacked me, but the Norns spun a different thread to the one he had hoped for. He can no longer use his hand."

"That is good news and serves him right."

"It does, but there is worse news. Gunnar and Einar brought a case at the Thórsnesthing, accusing me of assault against Einar. Wait", he said, holding up his hand, as Kári opened his mouth to say something. "The Thing found against him but also against me for insulting and maiming him, and they have awarded Einar compensation. We have appealed to the Althing and so have they. And that is the third reason why you should not ride off at once and burn Gunnar's farm."

Kári drew a deep breath and said, "You might as well finish your tale."

When Guðmundr finished the story, Kári sat silently for a moment. Then he said, "I wish we still had Father with us."

"So do I", Guðmundr said. "His help at the Althing will be sorely missed. But I am glad that you are back. That will be useful too."

Kári smiled. "I will do what I can. But tell me this: why is it that I cannot leave you without you getting into trouble?"

"It is not as if you managed to avoid trouble yourself, it seems", Guðmundr replied.

*

A few days later, as life was beginning to return to normal at Snæströnd, Eirík goði and Thór goði arrived with their wives and some of their followers, and Thór also brought the priest Willibald. They were warmly greeted by Guðmundr and Kári. When Guðmundr asked what had brought them, Eirík replied that they had heard of Kári's adventures and wished to hear more of them. But Thór admitted that their wives had also heard of the silk that Kári had brought with him and wished to see this for themselves – and also meet his new wife.

Since the time of the Althing was approaching, this was also a good time for them to take counsel about what to do and how to deal with Gunnar's case against Guðmundr.

That evening, all of them gathered around the table. Before discussing the case, Eirík and Thór asked to hear some of Kári's story. When the two goðar heard King Harald's remark about perhaps becoming King of Iceland after he had conquered England, their faces darkened and Eirík drew breath sharply. Kári was surprised by their reaction and said, "It is not going to happen – he died at Jórvik."

But Eirík shook his head and Thór replied, "One king has died, true, but the dreams of kings do not die. Norway still has a king."

Willibald found the tale of what had happened in Lishbuna of greater interest. When he heard how Sancho had ensured justice by claiming that Kári was a Christian and that Kári had agreed to be baptised, he exclaimed, "Praise be to God and His Son Christ. This is a miracle."

"Perhaps", Kári replied. "But don't you think that it was rather a good man doing the right thing and helping the innocent?"

"Yes, yes", Willibald replied. "But surely you can see that it was a miracle that he was there for you. Just like God enabled you to return safely to Snæströnd after such a long and perilous journey. This is another miracle, another sign of God's grace towards you, Kári. God and His Son have great plans for you, this is now clear. That is why you have been preserved and been allowed to return to Iceland at just this time. You will soon know, yes, very soon." He fell silent.

Kári was puzzled by the priest's reaction. Maebh looked carefully at Willibald and seemed to want to ask something, but before she could say anything, Thór asked about what had occurred in Cork, some of which they had apparently heard from others.

When Kári had finished his story with the return to Snæströnd, there was another moment of silence. Then Eirík sighed and said, "Thank you. Were I younger, I might even be quite envious of your adventures! But we should now talk about the Althing. We all know what has happened –" here he looked at Kári, who nodded "– and the question is then, what can we do? Guðmundr and Gunnar are both unhappy with the verdict of the Thórsnesthing. For Guðmundr, the reason is clear: because he was the innocent victim of an unprovoked attack. I am not entirely sure of the basis for Gunnar's appeal, since Einar was awarded damages, but I think that what he really wants is nothing less than the ruin of Snæströnd."

He paused to let the words sink in, then continued, "Thór and I have discussed this, not only among ourselves but also with our friends in the other three quarters of the land." Here Thór nodded.

"I must tell you", Eirík went on, "that we bring only little hope. We will of course declare again that Guðmundr is the victim of a deliberate and unprovoked attack, and we will certainly have some support at the Althing, but Gunnar has strong support of his own, and it is difficult to judge the balance. Many goðar may agree with us but still say that the earlier decision should stand. Unfortunately though, we have not yet been able to think of any better plan. Guðmundr, have you and Kári any thoughts?"

"We have talked about this, but we have not had much time to plan", Guðmundr replied. "We were hoping that you and Thór would have better news for us."

"What is the worst outcome?" Maebh now asked.

"It depends", Thór replied. "In all likelihood, if the Althing believes Gunnar, just a fine, though probably larger than the earlier award and perhaps large enough to make paupers of Guðmundr and Kári. After all, Einar has lost the use of his hand and had his honour besmirched. But it may also be the case that Guðmundr is condemned to outlawry, although I think this much less likely."

"I am not so certain", Eirík added. "Gunnar has hated the people of Snæströnd for many years, probably even before Ragnar changed his allegiance to me. He may push for outlawry from the start."

"I will not leave Snæströnd" Guðmundr said. "If they make me an outlaw, they will have to come here and kill me." Ása put her hand on his arm but looked equally determined.

"And me", Kári added, "and this may not be as easy as they think."

"That may well be true", Eirík said. "But you would still lose the case. And Thór and I must also think of what this means for us, for those who live in the nearby farms who might be drawn into this feud, and for those of us who still uphold the Law and believe in the ancient freedoms of all Icelanders."

At this point, the priest Willibald cleared his throat. When everyone turned to look at him, he said diffidently, "Forgive me for intruding. But I once said to Thór goði that I might have an idea how to solve this. I have given this some further thought and I have spoken to people, and it may be that this is possible after all."

"Praise God!" Thór exclaimed. "Let us hear what you have to say."

"It seems to me", Willibald began, "that the question is how we can convince enough of the other goðar to support our case. Is this correct?"

The others nodded.

"It may be possible – I stress *may* be – that God will help us. The Holy Church has many loyal and faithful sons here. If we can show them that supporting Guðmundr also means supporting the Church, that may sway enough to ensure that we win the case."

When he heard this, Thór beamed as if it had been his own idea. "Well thought of, Priest. I knew that bringing a clever priest to my church was better than just appointing some useless relative." Eirík also looked pleased.

But Guðmundr seemed dubious. "I understand what you are saying, Priest, but how can you say that supporting me means supporting the Church?"

"More to the point", Maebh said, "what does the Church want in return?"

When he heard her comment, Willibald shot an angry glance at Maebh. Then he said, "I did not say that your case today is that of the Holy Church", he replied, looking at Guðmundr. "But it could be."

Kári looked at Maebh and then at the priest. "Speak", he said.

Willibald nodded. "Iceland has now been Christian for a long time. I have heard how the Althing decided almost seventy years ago that the country should worship God. But I also know that in many ways Iceland still remains outside the embrace of the Holy Church. For instance, even though the country is Christian, there are still men who worship the old gods and who even sacrifice to them."

"This was agreed at the time", Eirík said. "As long as they kept their faith to themselves, the men of Iceland were free to worship who they wanted. Later it was decided that everyone should be a Christian. But it is not so easy to change what people think, and we have found it better not to cause strife by prying."

"Yes, I know. But this is not good. It is an abomination. Their very presence pollutes the land. And it is not just that. If we knew who these men were, we could make sure that no Christian risks his immortal soul by consorting with them. But we do not know."

"Three times or more on my journey people asked me if I was a Christian", Kári said. "Each time I replied that this is not a question we ask in Iceland and that this serves us well. Would you have us change this?"

"I would. Not for my sake, but for yours", Willibald replied. "And for theirs. You confirmed your faith with baptism, Kári. Don't you think it is important that we save the souls of other Icelanders as well?"

"I think this is a choice that each man must make for himself", Kári said. "But above all, I do not see how this makes my brother's case the Church's case."

"It does not in itself", Willibald admitted. "What I hope is that this Althing will make the decision to have Iceland fully and properly join the community of the Holy Mother Church; and that you, sitting here, will help them reach that decision."

At this Eirík looked up. "What exactly does 'fully and properly join the community of the Holy Mother Church' mean, Priest?"

"In all of Christendom", Willibald said, "Christians help the Church. Of course, they do this by their example, by praying and by helping to spread the gospel of our Lord Jesus Christ. But they also do it in other ways. They pay a tithe to support the Church in their country, and they also pay Peter's Pence, a penny from every homestead for the Mother Church in Rome and the Holy Father, the Pope, the successor of Saint Peter himself. And the Church also helps by advising worldly rulers through its bishops and archbishops. But in Iceland, the Bishop does not even have a guaranteed seat in the Lögrétta. I am sure that if you convinced the Althing to agree to these changes, the Church would ask its friends to support Guðmundr."

When Willibald fell silent, Thór said, "I had not heard this plan before. But it seems to me that it is a good plan. Still, I would ask this: how certain are you that the Church will indeed support us? What does Bishop Ísleifur at Skálholt say?"

"I have spoken with many people", Willibald said. "Including with the Bishop, of course. I would not propose all this unless I felt certain that he would understand."

"That is as may be", Kári interjected. "Now Thór goði says this seems to him to be a good plan. I am not so sure. Above all, I do not understand why this is good, either for us or for Iceland."

"But surely you understood what I said about saving men's souls?"

"I heard what you said, and you should have listened to what I said. But even if this is good, it seems to me that what you are also asking us to do is to pay taxes to the Church. And not just here, but to the Church in Rome as well. Why should we do that? We have little enough say in what the Church does here and none at all in Rome. Yet you would have us give up our silver. For what?"

"The Church prays for all of you, Kári. Need I remind you of that? And as for the tithes, they are not very onerous. Did not people in Iceland use to pay a tax to the pagan temples? And even our Lord paid the Temple tax in Jerusalem, as the Holy Book says. This is no different. Remember, this is what every Christian already does in other countries. Surely you don't want Iceland to stand alone? Iceland should stand joyfully together with our fellow Christians in the Church."

Guðmundr had so far said little, but now he spoke. "Our ancestors came here to get away from kings and rulers. It sounds to me as if you wish to reimpose them on us, Priest. In Iceland we know that if you give power to a man, then it can be taken away if he uses it unwisely. But if we give power to a king or to the Church, by having the Bishop sit in the Lögrétta, then we cannot take it back."

Before Willibald could reply, Maebh spoke up. "Kári, do not agree to this. You can hear what is happening. The priest would impose the power of the Church on Iceland. But power is always dangerous. Some men, Christian and otherwise, are good, some are evil; but power is always dangerous because it attracts evil men more than good, and it enables them to do more harm. Also, you do not need this. In Ireland, we have a good Church. They pray for our souls and they do many good things. But there are no bishops, and the Church has no power. If you wish to maintain Iceland's freedoms, which you say you love so much, you should not give in to this." While she spoke, she became more agitated and had stood up, her face flushed. Kári looked at her, thinking that beautiful as she was, she was even more beautiful now, with the shadows from the log fire playing over her angry face.

Willibald had been taken aback when Maebh spoke. Now he turned to Kári. "Why is your woman speaking when there are men present?" he demanded. "By rights, she should not even be here when serious matters are discussed. Why have you not taught her this?"

When they heard the priest's words, Ása and Hallgerður both stood up and moved to support Maebh, all of them speaking at once. Kári didn't stand but his voice cut through the noise like a sword. "Priest Willibald, you have been helpful in the past, not least when you saved my brother, and for this we are grateful. But do not presume on this. In Iceland, women are listened to and you would do well to learn this."

"I do not know what the peasants of Iceland think, but I know what the Blessed Saint Paul wrote in his letter to the Corinthians: 'As in all the congregations of the Lord's people. Women should remain silent in the Churches. They are not allowed to speak, but must be in submission, as the law says. If they want to inquire about something, they should ask their own husbands at home; for it is disgraceful for a woman to speak in the Church.' This is true here as well."

"Be careful, Priest", Ása said. "You are our guest, but do not wear out your welcome."

"In any case", Kári added, "my brother is wronged, and we will make the Althing see this."

Willibald looked around at the now visibly angry family from Snæströnd. "I am disappointed by the lack of Christian spirit in what I thought was a welcoming household. Kári, my son, you are misguided. But fear not, I shall still pray for you – and even for your wife – in the hope that you will see the light."

And with that, Willibald stalked out into the night. Behind him, Thór shook his head. "This is a bad business", he said.

Eirík said nothing, but he was worried by what had happened. Willibald's plans had not come as a complete surprise to him. He had heard rumours of this kind of thinking from other Christians and feared that the old ways of Iceland were coming under increasing attack. Willibald had not said outright that Bishop Ísleifur supported his thoughts, but even if he did not, sooner or later some other bishop would.

He stood up. "I agree", he said. "This is a bad business. I do not approve of Willibald's proposals; they carry danger, and I fear there are others behind him who would take advantage. Yet by rejecting them we have lost one way forward. Now we have to think of something else. But time is getting short. And now, I think there is nothing more to be said tonight."

That night, Ása and Guðmundr lay awake and spoke of what had occurred. Ása said, "I was angry with the priest for what he said. But I worry that Kári rejected his offer too quickly. This man can create trouble for us."

"I am not so sure", Guðmundr replied. "The priest thought that he had us at his mercy and said too much of what he thinks. In any case, I trust my brother. Kári will not let me down. He will think of a way to help me."

"But how?"

"I do not know. But I am sure he will." And with that he embraced his wife.

The next morning, Thór and Eirík took their farewells of Guðmundr and Kári. Before they left, Thór said to Guðmundr, "I think you and your brother were too hasty yesterday with Willibald. After all, he meant well. I will speak with him again. But I also want to reassure you that I still stand by you against Gunnar and Einar."

"That is good to hear", Guðmundr replied. "And I appreciate the priest's efforts, if not his words."

But as Thór slowly rode home, he was still worried. He knew that neither the men of Snæströnd nor Eirík were as firm in the faith as he was. Although he felt that his priest had perhaps overreached himself, there was some sense in what he had suggested. Above all, it would have ensured that Guðmundr won his case. Now this was less certain. He would still support Guðmundr, for the sake of their friendship and because he felt the man was in the right, but also because he had made his support public and could not now withdraw it. Also, the alternative – supporting Gunnar – was unthinkable. But he felt uncomfortable about confronting his priest. He had not realised how much Willibald had changed from the quiet priest he was when he arrived into a more strident and outspoken cleric.

Later that day, Kári was walking with Maebh around parts of Snæströnd that she had not yet seen. During the walk, Kári asked if Maebh also felt that he had been too harsh with Willibald.

Maebh laughed. "You are asking the wrong person", she said. "Did you not hear what I said to him? And what he said to me? I think you were far too kind to him."

"It is not that", Kári said. "I worry that I may have condemned my brother."

"I cannot speak about that", Maebh said. "But I know this: if the Church sets itself up to tax people and to regulate how they live, how long will it be before they decide that they need the support of a king to help them? And where then are the freedoms of Iceland?"

"Still, I would not see my brother ruined or outlawed. After all, I owe him a life."

"Do you? How?"

Then Kári told Maebh the tale of the walrus hunt and how Guðmundr had saved him and how he had promised one day to repay this debt. When he had finished, she looked at him and said, "I understand. And you are right. You have to save him. But I think that you can trust the people at the Althing to do the right thing."

"I hope so", Kári said. And then nothing more was said between them about this.

*

The days passed quickly, and soon it was time for the Althing to meet. Kári and Guðmundr had not seen anything more of Eirík or Thór, but this did not worry them since the goðar would be busy with their own farms.

When the brothers and their wives, accompanied by Hallvarðr and three more farmhands, set out on the ride to Thingvellir, they were joined a day's ride from Snæströnd by Kári's crew. The men were all mounted and dressed in bright cloaks made of silk. When Kári saw them fall in beside him, he asked if they were not riding with their own families.

"Our families are ahead of us, with our fathers", one of the men said. "But we are your men, Kári. We ride with you. Also, we have heard of your brother's case, and we want everyone to know that we are supporting you. And so are our families."

Kári was surprised to hear this, but also proud of his men and thanked them. "This will not be forgotten", he said. Meanwhile, Guðmundr and Ása recognised afresh that Kári really had become a chief among men during his year away. As for Maebh, she rode along the line with Kári and thanked the men as well, speaking and joking with each one.

Maebh had asked Kári about the Althing, but he had on purpose told her very little about the actual place for it. When they suddenly came upon the Thingvellir and she saw the clear blue waters of Thingvallavatn and the morning sun sparkling on the water, she gasped. "This is beautiful! Far more beautiful than anything I have seen in Ireland!" she exclaimed.

"I am glad you like it", Kári smiled. "But wait until you get to the Althing itself. We have to go down a steep gorge – the Almannagjá – and then there is an open plain where we all meet. You will not believe the number of people that you will see there!"

There were already some booths set up when they approached, and more people were coming in from every side.

From the shadows of one of the nearby booths, a pair of eyes watched Kári and Guðmundr ride by. Then the watcher turned round and entered the booth.

"They are here", he said.

"What did you expect?" Gunnar replied. "That they would skulk at home, waiting for us to have the Althing condemn them? No, they were bound to come."

"They were not alone", Einar said truculently. "There was a whole group following them. I recognised some of them; they are from Snæfellsnes, from our neighbourhood. They are probably Guðmundr's friends."

"More likely Kári's crew. Guðmundr doesn't have many friends, I think."

"Even so, they could be troublesome."

"You worry too much. Everything is in hand, and this time we are not going to rely on you or even on your sister. Where is she anyway? Go and find her and bring her to me. I have a plan."

Chapter 15

Summer 1067

When Guðmundr and Kári had set up their booth, Ása asked one of the farmhands to accompany her as she showed Maebh the market that always took place at the Althing. There was much to see, and various people came up to Ása to greet her and ask who her new companion was. Maebh was surprised to see so many people and so much activity; truth to tell, her first reaction when she had arrived at Snæströnd was that it was very quiet and rather backward. Kári's family had of course been wonderfully welcoming – even Hallgerður had become much more friendly after her initial hesitation – but it was no wonder that Kári had been so excited by their time in Lishbuna if this was what he was used to. So she was glad to see the lively market and so many people clearly enjoying themselves.

Meanwhile, Kári took his crew to buy them ale to celebrate their reunion and to thank them again for joining the Snæströnd party. While they were drinking, some men who knew Kári came to greet him. Most were surprised to see him; he seldom came to the Althing as he was usually sailing abroad in high summer. Kári explained what had happened to him over the past year and said that this was why he was here this time; indeed, he was not planning to go away again until next spring. As for the Althing, Kári said that of course he would be there to support his brother. At this, there was much discussion of the case, with most of Kári's acquaintances agreeing that Guðmundr was blameless, but fearing that this would count for little against the support that

Gunnar could muster. Some of the men also said that Einar had only received what he deserved, but they still shook their heads at Guðmundr's chances.

Many also commented on the silk cloaks worn by Kári's men. To everyone, Kári explained that this was what he had brought back to Iceland and that he had brought more to the Althing market.

Over the next few days before the Althing began, a succession of people, many of whom were known to Kári and Guðmundr but also a good number who were not, came to the booth, both to express their sadness at Ragnar's death and, perhaps primarily, to look at the silk. Often they brought their women who would sigh at the beautiful colours and look admiringly and with longing at the silk dresses now worn by Ása and Maebh. Very soon Kári realised that the profits from this one voyage to Lishbuna were going to be much greater than he had thought, and he realised that there would be much wisdom, and profit, in a return to the city on his next voyage. And, of course, the warmth of the Lishbuna sun and the memory of the food there were also powerful reasons to return. True, it would mean one long journey in the year instead of two short ones. But it was certainly something to think about before he made any decision on next year's trading. He started wondering if his crew would be prepared to follow him back, although judging by the pride they took in their adventures, it was very likely that they would wish to come.

But this assumed that there would be a next voyage. Because what also became clear was that for every person who told him that they felt Guðmundr to be in the right and that the Thórsnesthing verdict was wrong and should be overturned, there was another who feared that, even though Einar had attacked Guðmundr, the goðar would probably say that he had been badly dealt with and, if anything, deserved even greater damages. Not least because Guðmundr had badly insulted him and therefore most likely provoked the attack. In the evenings, Kári would speak with Guðmundr and also with Eirík and Thór, who had both arrived at Thingvellir. All of them said the same thing, that it was not possible to judge how Guðmundr would fare when the case was brought.

And if Gunnar won and really did manage to ruin Snæströnd, it might well be that the knarr would be lost as well. Inwardly Kári cursed the day that his father had first decided to take Gunnar as his goði. True, Gunnar had promised his support in the case against Leifur all those years ago. But he had never honoured that promise – if indeed he had ever intended to in the first place – and the man and his family had since only sought to do them harm.

Hearing all of this, Kári once again wondered if he should perhaps not have been so quick to reject Willibald's suggestions. But whenever he thought this, he also reflected on what the priest's proposals would inevitably lead to, and realised that he could not have agreed to them. Even if it meant Guðmundr winning his case, the damage to Iceland, and above all to the freedoms that their father had taught them to care for, would be so great that he could not stomach the thought. Even Guðmundr had said to him on the way to Thingvellir that he did not wish to be remembered as the man who enslaved Icelanders in order to avoid paying a fine.

The one who said least was Thór. When Eirík had asked where Willibald was, he had only said that the priest had not come along. This did not concern him overmuch, because Willibald had rarely come to the Althing with him. But when he had spoken with the priest after their return from Snæströnd and tried to explain Kári's opposition, Willibald had merely said that he understood and that it was of little importance. Thór continued to worry about this; like Willibald, he was pained by the thought that there were still some men in Iceland who clung to the old gods. But while he understood why they did so, and even that it was impossible to stop them holding to their old beliefs, he still worried about their souls. And this was also the first time that he would be taking a stand against the wishes of the Church. He hoped that Willibald had taken note of the objections, not only Kári's but also Eirík's and indeed his own. It did not make them any less good Christians, he had pointed out. It was just that Iceland was a place where people did not try to force their neighbours to behave in one way or other. Whenever that was tried, the end result was usually bloodshed, and that, surely, it was better to avoid, even in a good cause such as the Church's.

But Willibald had once again dismissed his concerns, saying that the future of the Church was not in doubt, because it was all part of God's plan. His own efforts were surely unworthy, and if he did not succeed, then others would at the appropriate time. God would provide for His Church; He always had and always would. Meanwhile, he would indeed pray for Kári and Eirík and the others in the hope that they would see the light.

The last evening before the Althing began, Maebh mentioned to Kári that Jórunn was also at Thingvellir. She had seen her. She and Ása had been walking by the shores of the lake when Ása had suddenly stopped. When Maebh tried to see why, Ása had pointed out another woman who had been heading in their direction, but who had clearly also stopped when she saw them. The woman was beautiful, Maebh said. But when she and Ása saw each other, it was clear that theirs was not a friendship, and when they turned and walked in another direction, Ása had told her that this was Jórunn. Maebh had already heard enough about Gunnar's daughter to be glad that she now knew what she looked like and need not encounter her by chance.

And then the Althing began. Normally, Guðmundr would have joined Eirík in the Lögrétta as one of his two advisors. But Eirík had wanted Kári to be with him at the discussions, both because Guðmundr had a case to be judged and because it would look bad if both his advisors came from one farm, Eirík had asked him to give up his place in favour of his brother. Guðmundr had agreed willingly; indeed he was pleasantly surprised that he no longer felt any envy of or rivalry with Kári.

For Kári, this was a new experience. Although many of the cases were minor and did not need to be judged by all the goðar, there were still some that were debated in front of the whole Lögrétta and where the goðar were expected to carefully weigh the evidence and deliver a verdict that everyone would consider fair and just. He listened intently and tried to think how he would have judged the cases and if his verdict would have differed from the ones announced.

Meanwhile, nothing was heard of Gunnar's case against Guðmundr. On the third day, however, a goði from the Southern

Quarter had stood up and asked to be heard. He began by saying that it was now a long time since Iceland had turned Christian. Anyone alive at that time would by now be a very old man indeed, and those who had been present at the Althing would by now have been succeeded not only by their children but even by their grandchildren. As everyone knew, originally those who wished to continue to worship the old gods had been allowed to do so. But that had changed long since. It was also ten years since Iceland had received its first bishop. Yet in many ways, Iceland and its people remained outside the community of the Church. Was this not the time to change this?

When Thór heard this, he was both surprised and yet not. He was not surprised to hear similar thoughts to those expressed by Willibald. Indeed, these were views that he and other Christian goðar had often shared. But it was a surprising coincidence to hear it at this Althing. Still, he nodded his approval at what he heard and continued to listen as a number of goðar whom he knew to be strong in the faith and friends of the Church stood up to support the first speaker. At first, he did not listen very carefully. Many of the speeches, while similar in tone, were quite vague and talked more of how the Church was suffering and not being properly respected, but with few if any suggestions of what should be done about this. But as one goði after another began to sound like the previous speaker, Thór felt that this could no longer be a coincidence. Clearly, the Church had been active, speaking to its supporters. This would perhaps explain Willibald's ideas at Snæströnd. It seemed that other priests had been pressing the Church's case with their goðar, and this would explain why they now all said more or less the same thing.

For the moment, no one had said anything to oppose the speakers. A few goðar raised some objections, but no one argued very strongly against what had been said. Even so, Thór could see that a number of goðar, even men who he knew were firm Christians and whom he counted as his friends and supporters, were beginning to be restless and more vocal in their concerns. As for himself, he was getting tired more than anything else.

Another speaker finally came to the end of his talk and sat down. But it seemed that they were now all waiting for something to happen. And then Thór suddenly sat up and all desire for a rest disappeared at once. Next to him, Eirík also straightened up. On the opposite side of the Lögrétta, Gunnar goði stood up, greeted by an expectant murmur.

For a moment, Gunnar stood silent, looking around. Then he began to speak.

"Men of the Althing, worthy goðar. As I am sure many of you well know, I have a case to bring to the Althing. This is about Guðmundr Ragnarsson's cowardly attack on my son Einar. But that is a personal matter. Here at the Althing, we are called upon to rise above personal slights and think about what is important for Iceland. And it is about this that I would now speak.

"We have heard much today from other goðar about how the Holy Mother Church is still held back in Iceland. I agree with this. Now, I understand why this is so. There were good reasons to act in this way when Iceland became Christian. But the old ways, however well they once served us – and they did! – are no longer sufficient. The world is changing, and Iceland too must change. Of course, the most important issue for us is to help the Holy Church save men's souls." Here he crossed himself.

"But the Church can only do so much on its own. The Church helps all of us. It should therefore only be just for us to help the Church as well. Those of you who have travelled to other countries know that this is what they do there. In Norway, in England, all good Christians pay a tithe to support the Church. And they do so willingly, because what is good for the Holy Church is good for them as well. Not only do they do that, but they all know that the Church is what binds all of us Christians – Norwegians, Danes, Icelanders, yes, even Swedes –" here there was some laughter "– yes, even Swedes, together. Because the Church is everywhere. And so everyone, every household, also pays a small coin for the Mother Church in Rome and the Holy Father, the Pope. Only in Iceland do we not do this. But what is a small silver coin for any one of us? Surely we can afford this, to show that the people of Iceland are as good Christians as Norwegians or Englishmen?" Here Gunnar paused again, looking around to see how his words had been received. Then he continued.

"I think these are modest suggestions, and it would do little harm and bring us much honour if we agree to them. But I would also ask more of you. The Bishop, our own Bishop Ísleifur, who does so much for us in the eyes of God, is it not time that he also joined us here? Should the Bishop not sit in the Lögrétta? After all, this would help to ensure that we do not fall into sinful ways and also that our decisions are favoured by God. Sometimes – rarely, I know, but sometimes – men complain that the verdict of the Althing is unjust. Surely, if those verdicts were agreed with the Bishop and with God's blessing, that could no longer be said? This would also increase our honour in the eyes of other peoples. We are not alone, we trade with others. And I here would add one final thing. Surely we all agree that the Law, our Law, Iceland's Law is one of the most important things we have and that we have to safeguard it. But what is the Law if there is only weakness behind it? Only this year we heard how one of our number, Kári Ragnarsson from Snæströnd, was forced to join the fleet of the King of Norway. This could only happen because the King knew that Iceland is weak, that there was no power in our land to stop him. What I say to you is that not only do we need the Law, we also need order. We need to be strong and to be respected. And this we can do together with the Church, and maybe also by making a league with strong rulers who will protect us."

Here Gunnar stopped speaking and sat down. Even as he sat down, there was a murmur of approval from the goðar who had already spoken, as well as their advisors, but also from some others.

But Thór did not notice. He had been listening to Gunnar's speech with mounting horror. The previous speakers had only lamented what they felt was wrong with Iceland and the Church. But Gunnar had been much clearer in what he aimed at. And when he mentioned the tax for the Church in Rome, and even more the need for the Church to have a seat in the Lögrétta, in both cases using exactly the same words as Willibald had when outlining his plan at Snæströnd, Thór realised three things. First, that this was what the whole debate had been about. Second, that his own priest, the man he had brought to Iceland, had betrayed him and his trust by going to Gunnar with the same proposal that he had made at Snæströnd – the sentiments, even the words, were too similar and also too clever for Gunnar to have thought of on his own. And third, that this meant that when Gunnar's case against Guðmundr came up, the Church's supporters would all be supporting Gunnar.

He turned around and looked at Eirík. The other man's face was white with anger. When he noticed Thór looking at him, he nodded. "I know", he said. "It was clear almost as soon as Gunnar opened his mouth. This is now a very bad business. But everything is not yet lost."

So far, the direction of the speeches had all been in the same way. But once Gunnar had finished, other voices began to be heard. Thór recognised goðar from other parts of Iceland, men who he knew were also good Christians, who warned against moving too quickly to change things. Some asked why there was suddenly a need to rush through so many changes. Others wondered why it was suddenly seen as necessary for Iceland to follow what other countries were doing, as if that was a good reason in itself. And one or two spoke about the need to safeguard Iceland's old freedoms.

But although much of what was said was met with murmurs of approval from many of the goðar who had not yet spoken, it was clear to both Eirík and Thór that none of the speakers had managed to make the same impression as Gunnar. Indeed, some who objected to what he had said had still praised him for how he had said it and seemed unwilling to oppose him directly. The only clear rejections came from a group of goðar from the Eastern Quarter who had already experienced the Church's idea of justice and were adamant that to give the Church and its supporters even more power would be very dangerous. They spoke well, and persuasively, but even Thór could see that there were not enough of them and that they were not convincing many of the undecided.

While one of these goðar was still speaking, Eirík leaned over to Thór and asked him something. Thór thought about it, then nodded and returned his attention to the speaker. Eirík beckoned to Kári to come closer and spoke with him. As he did, Kári listened intently, then also nodded and began to make some comments of his own. Eirík looked at him and finally grasped his arm in a gesture of approval and gratitude.

Once the current speaker had sat down, Eirík rose. Since it was widely known that Eirík and Gunnar were vying for the leadership of the Western Quarter, many men looked at him and wondered if he was going to answer Gunnar directly.

"Men of the Althing. Many people have spoken today. Some have spoken at greater length than others. We have heard many arguments. But one of the arguments that Gunnar goði used was that Iceland is different from other places. We do not do what they do, he says, but we should. Yet few of us will understand exactly what that means. And so it seems to me that perhaps we should listen to someone who has recently travelled widely and who has seen for himself how others really behave. I would ask you to listen to one of my trusted advisors, Kári Ragnarsson, from Snæströnd."

As Eirík sat down, Kári stood up. He knew that as Eirík's advisor he had the right to speak at the Lögrétta, but it was still polite for Eirík to ask the others to listen, and he waited a moment to see if anyone would object.

As Kári moved forward so that he could be seen and heard better, men craned their necks to get a better view of him. Some of them had by now heard about his long voyage, while others had been told about the silk he had brought back from Lishbuna; for many, though, the first time they had heard his name was when Gunnar had mentioned him in his speech. Many who saw him felt that he looked like a chief of men, wearing a linen tunic, over that a cape of red silk with silver embroideries and a golden ring on his left arm.

"Worthy goðar, men of the Althing. Thank you for allowing me to speak. As Eirík goði said, I have travelled widely over the last year. Although as Gunnar goði noted, not all of that was of my own free will." Here some of the listeners laughed. "But it is perhaps precisely for that reason that I feel that we should think very carefully about what has been proposed today. Gunnar says that our old laws and customs served us well in the past, but that they no longer do so. I disagree." Here he stopped and looked at the audience.

"Now, Gunnar said many things. It would be easy for me to try to answer each and every point he raised. In fact, I am sure this is what he would want me to do. Because if I do that, then each point can be discussed on its own. But if we do this, I fear we will fail to see what it is that Gunnar – and maybe others who have spoken today as well – are really trying to make us do. Therefore, I would like to talk about something he did not say, at least not openly." Here Kári stopped again. He could see on the faces of some of the goðar sitting nearby that he had caught their interest.

"I have seen countries with one king, with two kings and with many. Are any of those better than Iceland? No, they are not. Certainly, having kings does not make them better. What it does do, though, is to make so much dependent on one man. Maybe he is a good king, a king who upholds the law and maintains peace and trade. But if he is a bad man, a bad king, then he will think only of his own glory. He will destroy trade by imposing arbitrary taxes and duties whenever he needs money. He will go to war against his neighbours. He will ignore the law when it suits him, because he will consider himself above it. And his subjects cannot prevent this, cannot stop him. Because the king holds all the power.

"In Iceland, what a man owns is his, and we respect that. This is not what kings do. The king I met, the King of Norway, took my property. He took grain that I had bought for Iceland. He did not care about Iceland or that the grain was mine. He needed it. He wanted it. He took it.

"In Iceland, we have our Law and our freedoms. Sometimes we quarrel – but when we do, we let the Thing decide. Here, no one tells us to go and fight and die in a cause that is not our own, simply because as king he can force us to do so. This is why our forefathers left Norway. Yet now, it seems to me that Gunnar goði wants us to submit to a king. Did he not say that we should make a league with strong rulers who can protect us? What does that mean? What can we offer such strong rulers in exchange? Our service? Our loyalty? Our freedom? Does Gunnar aim to become the king's jarl in Iceland? Certainly, I heard King Harald of Norway talk about how he felt that Iceland would one day be part of his kingdom and that he would need good men here. Is Gunnar goði planning to be one of them?"

He paused for a moment to let the words sink in, then continued:

"Gunnar also says that Iceland must be more like other countries. Really? In Lishbuna, I saw rulers making coins of any metal, and forcing their people to accept them as if they were of gold or silver. I even saw people spit at coins they had to take. Is that what we want? Someone who cheats in his payments?

"There I also saw women who were only allowed to walk around heavily cloaked and guarded. Even here, in Iceland, at my brother's farm, I heard a priest saying that women should not be allowed to speak when there were men present. Who of you sitting here would be prepared to tell your wives or mothers that they are not allowed to speak and that they have nothing to say worth listening to?" At this, there was more laughter, stronger than before.

"What does all this have to do with the Church? Gunnar, and many others like him, as we have heard today, want us to pay taxes to the Church and to let the Bishop sit in the Lögrétta. Again we are told that this is what everyone else does. But this is not true. Many of you here have travelled to Ireland. My wife is Irish. In Ireland, she tells me, there is nether tithe nor Peter's Pence. In fact, there are not even any bishops. Does this make the people of Ireland less Christian?

"Why should we pay taxes to Rome? Rome, I am told, is a big and rich city. I am glad for their sake. But then, why do they need money from Iceland?

"As for paying a tithe here, what is the Church spending money on that it needs more from us? If it is for our sake, as so many have suggested, is it not better to let us keep our money, little as it is?

"And as for letting the Bishop sit in the Lögrétta, this is of course up to this council to decide. It is not for me to offer you my thoughts on this.

"Members of the Lögrétta, I have spoken at length, and you have all already heard many other speakers before me. I thank you for your patience. You have heard talk of saving men's souls, of joining with our fellow Christians in other lands under the Church, of taxes for the Church here in Iceland and of payments to the Church in Rome. All of this is important, perhaps even praiseworthy. But they are not the main issue. We are not discussing whether we can afford to pay or not, or if we are stronger or weaker if we come more closely under the Church's rule. This is about much more; about Iceland, about why our ancestors came here, about our Law and our freedom. We are asked by Gunnar to hand ourselves over to the Church and to its appointed overlords. But remember this: if you give power to a man, you can take it away again if he abuses it. If you give power to the Church – or to a king – you cannot."

With that, Kári stepped back to his seat behind Eirík. As he did so, Eirík stood up and said "Worthy goðar, thank you for allowing Kári Ragnarsson to speak. As I knew they would and I am sure all here will recognise, his words carry much sense and wisdom."

While Kári spoke, Thór had listened carefully. He still felt that he did not oppose everything Gunnar had said. But he now realised that strengthening the Church would also mean strengthening Gunnar. And that would certainly be bad for anyone who had ever crossed or opposed him, even more so if the Church were to support him in the future. When Kári finished, he was tempted to speak, but finally decided not to. Instead, he resolved that he would speak against Gunnar's proposals when the goðar discussed among themselves.

After Eirík's words, the Lawspeaker decided that enough men had spoken that day. It was already getting late. The advisers were dismissed and the goðar gathered to consider what had been said.

The next morning, Kári had barely woken up when he was told that Eirík and Thór wished to see him. Kári felt that he had barely slept, but one look at the two goðar showed him that they had probably not slept at all. Eirík said, "We wanted to come and thank you. I think your words swayed enough of the undecided."

"So it is decided?"

"Yes. The Church lost", Eirík said. "And I think they also lost because it was clear that this was not just about the Church, but also about power, and more importantly power unconstrained by Law."

"I agree", Thór said. "That is why I decided to oppose Gunnar."

"I know", Eirík said. "And I know that you would have supported some of the Church's proposals otherwise, and I am grateful that you did not."

"It was necessary", Thór replied. "Neither of us can afford to let Gunnar become the Church's favourite. Then there would be no defence against his greed, and we would all suffer."

"True", Eirík said. "And now, I think that I would like to have a rest."

"So would I", Thór added.

*

When Gunnar returned to his booth that morning, his mood was dark. A number of goðar whose support he had counted on had told him, some sadly but others with barely disguised pleasure, that they feared they could not support him in his case the next day and that they were keen to find an agreed solution. After the defeat of his proposal on behalf of the Church – for however many other goðar had also spoken, everyone recognised that he had been the driving force behind it – he was not surprised, and he knew he had no other option. He reflected bitterly that once again, as had happened so often recently it seemed, his plans had been foiled – and once again by one of Ragnar's sons, too. He should have had Kári whipped all those years ago, maybe that would have taught him some respect.

His mood was not improved when he found Willibald waiting for him inside the booth. When he saw him, Gunnar ordered everyone to leave them alone, then turned to the priest. "Yes?" he said.

"I came to you in good faith", the priest said, "because I was certain that you could be relied upon to do God's work. Yet look at what happened. Now the cause of the Church has been set back, maybe for a long time."

"You have only yourself to blame", Gunnar snapped. "If you had not saved Guðmundr Ragnarsson so long ago, none of this would have happened."

"Perhaps", Willibald replied. "Only God knows. But I know this: the Church will certainly not support your case against that young man, and nor will its faithful champions." Then he turned and left.

Gunnar sat quietly for a moment. Then he went to the door and called one of his servants. "Find my children", he commanded, "and bring them to me."

When Jórunn and Einar arrived shortly afterwards, Gunnar was sitting deep in thought. At first they thought that he had not noticed them, but when Einar finally said, "Father? What happened?" he looked up.

"What happened?" Gunnar repeated. "What happened was that once again I have lost. That was bad enough. But what is worse is that we now stand to lose the case against Guðmundr as well."

"Are you sure?" Jórunn asked.

"Of course I'm sure", said Gunnar irritably. "And at the very least, Guðmundr would then be awarded damages for Einar's attack on him. I cannot afford to pay those damages. And that is the best case. In the worst case, Einar will be condemned to outlawry. That has to be avoided. Somehow, I must convince Eirík to make Guðmundr drop the case."

When they heard this, Einar and Jórunn were both surprised. Einar asked, "What about my lamed hand?" and Jórunn said, "Are we going to let Ragnar's sons trample all over us once again then? Is that what you would do?"

At this, Gunnar lost his temper. "What have I done to be saddled with two such stupid children? Einar, you are and always were a fool, and you will remain one until the day you die. Jórunn, I thought you were clever, but all your plans have been useless. Once again I have to try to salvage whatever can be saved from your disasters. Hopefully not all of my bændr and Thingmen will abandon me."

"Always our fault", Jórunn spat. "What about your actions? You have never let either of us live our lives as we wish. I would gladly have taken Guðmundr for my husband, but you would never have let me do it. I could have been Mistress of Snæströnd if it were not for you!"

"You don't understand, silly girl. I could not let you stand in Einar's way. He is my son and will one day take over the goðorð. But with you at Snæströnd, along with Guðmundr's luck and Kári's cunning, men would have flocked to them. That would swell Eirík's support and your brother's authority would be diminished.

"If that is what you feel, perhaps I should leave you and Einar", Jórunn exploded.

"Yes, I think you should", Einar said nastily. "You and your dalliances with that man have done enough to ruin our family. Now leave and take your scheming with you!"

For a moment, Jórunn was taken aback. She had not really meant what she said. But now she realised that she had to leave. Gunnar could still live for some years, but he would no longer indulge her, and it was useless now to expect him to arrange a good marriage for her; the result of her father's defeat meant that he was reduced and less attractive as an ally for an ambitious suitor. And she already knew that Einar hated her; once her father was dead, her life if she still lived at home would become insufferable. She turned and walked out, wondering what she would now do. Then she remembered something she had heard at the Althing. Maybe there was still one choice open to her.

That afternoon, Gunnar made his way to the booth of Thór. The other goði was surprised to see him, but invited him inside. For a moment, both men sat looking at each other, neither saying anything. Then Gunnar sighed and said, "This is a sad day for our Mother Church. I did my best for the White Christ, but the Norns spun it another way."

Thór said nothing, waiting to hear what Gunnar really wanted to say. The other man continued, "I do not wish there to be enmity between us. I would like there to be peace in our Quarter of Iceland. And so I have come to say this: I think that we should put an end to Einar's quarrel with Guðmundr. I suggest that both sides withdraw their appeals to the Althing."

Thór looked at him, thinking how this had suddenly become Einar's case against Guðmundr, as if Gunnar was simply a concerned father. But the fact that Gunnar was willing to withdraw his appeal if Guðmundr did the same, meant that he knew he would lose, and that was good news. The Church might have lost, but Gunnar had clearly lost more. Then he said, "If both sides withdraw their appeals, then the verdict of the Thórsnesthing stands. That will not please Eirík and Guðmundr, who feel it was unjust."

Gunnar tried to keep his face impassive, but inwardly he raged. Still, he knew when he was beaten. He spread his arms and made the final, humiliating concession. "If Guðmundr withdraws his appeal, Einar will waive the damages awarded by the Thórsnesthing."

"This is a wise course", Thór replied, "and I am sure I can convince Eirík and Guðmundr to do so."

After the Althing was concluded, Kári, Guðmundr and their party slowly rode back towards Snæströnd. There was no hurry, and many people wanted to stop Kári along the way and talk with him about taking their sons as crewmen on his next trip or arranging to buy more silk if he was going back to Lishbuna. Kári promised each one that he would think about it. But his next trading voyage would probably be a short one to Scotland to buy grain, which was sorely needed before the winter.

Maebh asked if they could be certain that Gunnar and Einar would not try to harm them again. Ása replied that, on the contrary, they would almost certainly try, but Gunnar's power was now so diminished that he would have to be more careful in case any new attempt further added to his disgrace. Guðmundr thought that they no longer had anything to fear from Gunnar.

"I hope you are right", Kári said with a smile. "Because, after all, now I have kept my promise to you, so next time you may be on your own."

Guðmundr looked at him with surprise. "What promise?"

Now Kári was surprised in turn. "Don't you remember? After the walrus hunt? When you saved my life on the ice floe, I promised I would one day save yours. Now perhaps I have."

Guðmundr laughed. "You know, I had forgotten it, but now I remember. Yes, you did promise. I suppose that in the future I have to be more careful then."

"That would be good", said Kári, laughing as well.

When they approached the borders of Snæströnd, they suddenly spotted someone waiting for them. As they came closer, they saw that it was a woman, and a short while later it was clear that it was Jórunn. When Guðmundr recognised her, he said angrily, "What is that witch doing here? Hold here and I will chase her off."

But as he began to urge his horse forward, Jórunn called out, "I wish to speak with Kári."

When he heard this, Kári rode up to Guðmundr and put his hand on his arm. "Let me speak with her and hear what she wants. Then we can decide what to do."

Guðmundr seemed unwilling to agree, but eventually nodded.

Kári slowly approached Jórunn. When he was close enough, he dismounted and looked at her without saying anything.

Jórunn seemed nervous, twisting her hands over and over again. Finally she said, "I have heard that you are sailing abroad again?"

"What is that to you?"

"Take me with you."

Kári was astonished. This was the last thing he had expected.

"Why should I do that? Have you not caused my family enough harm as it is? You have tried to come between one brother and his woman; do you now think you can do so with the other?"

Jórunn looked sad. "Kári, that is not my intention. Whatever you think, I am not evil. I am no witch. All I ever wanted in life was the same as you – freedom and independence, to live my life as I wanted. We are kindred spirits, you and I. Otherwise I would not ask this of you."

"You are wrong", Kári replied. "We are not kindred spirits. If we were, you would know that freedom also means respecting the wishes and interests of others. This is something you have never done."

"But there is nothing for me here any more. My brother hates me, and my father despises me. I cannot stay."

Kári nodded. "That you have to leave, I can see. But I will not take you. Your part in our family's life has ended."

Jórunn looked at him again. So like his brother in some ways, but so unlike him in others, stern and unbending, and implacably opposed to her. She realised that there was nothing she could say that would sway him. So she nodded disconsolately, turned and walked away towards her horse. Then she mounted and rode off without looking back.

Kári watched her go, and then returned to the others. As he said nothing, Ása asked, "What did she want?"

"She wanted to leave Iceland and for me to take her. Leave she will, but not with me. We have seen the last of her, and now you are free of her for ever."

When she heard this, Ása took hold of Guðmundr's arm and squeezed it. He looked at her and at Kári and nodded.

As they rode up to the farmhouse at Snæströnd, Hallgerður came out to greet them. She looked at their faces and then, satisfied, said "You won."

"Yes", Guðmundr replied, "the farm is safe, and we have nothing more to fear from that family."

But Kári said, "We won this time. But the Church will come back and try again. And although we have made new friends, I fear that we have made some powerful enemies as well."

And as he spoke, he looked out towards the sea. But instead of seeing the waves with their crests whitened by the brisk wind, he thought about the future and wondered what it would bring to Snæströnd, what it held for Iceland.

Printed in Great Britain
by Amazon